W9-CUN-072

"AYE, YOU ARE AS STRONG AND VALIANT A WOMAN AS I HAVE EVER KNOWN. YOU ARE ALSO THE MOST HARDHEADED. ADMIT THAT YOU ARE MORE COMFORTABLE HERE THAN ON THAT PILE OF STRAW," BORGIA CHIDED.

"Nay, 'tis a miserable bed with you in it," LeClaire murmured.

"That is your fault, damoiselle. 'Twould be most comfortable if you could relax, share it the way 'twas meant to be shared by a man and a woman."

"Aye, shared in marriage," she reproved.

"Do you beg a betrothal?" he asked, and she could hear the wicked teasing in his voice.

"I would as soon marry your horse."

"Ah, bratling, poor Ares could not do for you in this bed what I could." LeClaire blushed furiously, and turned her face away. Borgia's fingers traced the edges of her hairline down to her jaw. His thumb brushed her lips, parting them, then tipped her face back and up to his. "Need I tell you the way of things so you are not afraid, tell you what pleasure—"

"'Tis not for me to know," she said quickly, inexplicably shivery under his fingers. "'Tis not . . ." Her words faded with his touch, her lids fluttering closed as his knuckles slid down her neck.

"Then how can you naysay me? You should know what you refuse," Borgia said, and pulled her close.

"Then tell me!" she gasped, for even intimate words were much safer than the intimacy of his body pressed to hers.

"'Tis better to show you. . . ."

High praise for Libby Sydes and her novels:

THE LION'S ANGEL

"*The Lion's Angel* is a treasure rich with the flavor of the times, a story that is pure reading delight. Ms. Sydes' characters sparkle with life. She has written a book that goes beyond ordinary, one that is sure to make an impression upon readers of historical romance."

—Elaine Coffman

"A principled woman . . . a determined conqueror . . . an engrossing, sensual tale filled with all the romance a reader could want." —Anita Mills

BAYOU DREAMS

"A wonderful love story filled with adventure, humor and poignancy. An irresistible heroine and a hero you won't forget." —Patricia Potter

"Libby Sydes hits me with the three W's: she's warm, wonderful, and witty." —Linda Howard

"A refreshing new voice! Libby Sydes writes with verve and passion. Don't miss her debut novel."

—Myra Rowe

"A valiant first book." —*Heartland Critiques*

"Powerful historical set in Louisiana during the early 1800's, depicting the pride, passion, and honor of the Cajun people. Great reading!" —*Rendezvous*

"A strong debut novel. Ms. Sydes re-creates the aura of Louisiana with vivid descriptions of the land and people . . . historical details . . . mounting sexual tension . . . surprising plot twists and engaging characters make a winning tale." —*Romantic Times*

Also by Libby Sydes from Dell:

BAYOU DREAMS

LIBBY SYDES
THE LION'S ANGEL

A DELL BOOK

Published by
Dell Publishing
a division of
Bantam Doubleday Dell Publishing Group, Inc.
666 Fifth Avenue
New York, New York 10103

If you purchased this book without a cover you should be aware that this book is stolen property. It was reported as "unsold and destroyed" to the publisher and neither the author nor the publisher has received any payment for this "stripped book."

Copyright © 1992 by Libby Sydes

All rights reserved. No part of this book may be reproduced or transmitted in any form or by any means, electronic or mechanical, including photocopying, recording, or by any information storage and retrieval system, without the written permission of the Publisher, except where permitted by law.

The trademark Dell® is registered in the U.S. Patent and Trademark Office.

ISBN: 0-440-20575-1

Printed in the United States of America

Published simultaneously in Canada

August 1992

10 9 8 7 6 5 4 3 2 1

RAD

To my sisters, Jane and Jennifer.
Through every wonderful, funny and crazy phase of our lives, you have always been there for me, remaining loyal, loving, forgiving, understanding and generous. There is no finer testament or proof of the power of love. This story about the joys and trials of sisterhood is for you.

Acknowledgment

I would like to extend a special thank-you to my editor, Tina Moskow, who had enough faith in my writing to buy my first book and has been completely supportive since. I hope I never give you a reason to regret your decision.

I
THE
PROPHECY

"The German dragon shall hardly get to his holes . . . for a people in wood and in iron coats shall come and revenge upon him his wickedness. They shall restore the ancient inhabitants to their dwellings, and there shall be an open destruction of foreigners . . . After this shall succeed two dragons, whereof one shall be killed by the arrow of envy, but the other shall return under the shadow of a name. Then shall succeed the Lion of Justice, at whose roar the Gallican towers and the island dragons shall tremble."

—Geoffrey of Monmouth, Prophecies of Merlin

Prologue

Weary. LeClaire of Ravenwood's tawny lashes lay like iron weights against her cheeks, too heavy to keep aloft in the somnolent whisper of a spring breeze. Rough bark scraped against her back where she leaned against the base of a hawthorn, but she noticed little save the scent of new flowers budding and the fading chatter of her younger sisters as they toiled. Though her rest was well deserved, she felt guilty for indulging when there was work yet to be done, but her arms and legs felt as weighty as her drooping eyelids. She would pause only a second to gather energy, just the briefest moment . . .

The fulfillment of the prophecy began in time immemorial, too long past to be identified with history or tradition, but came to fruition during January in the year of our Lord 1066 with the death of England's King, Edward the Confessor.

One of the ever-abiding messengers of Fate, who exist among the heavens in perpetual readiness, awaited command from the Hierarchy to descend and change forever the course of one soul's destiny. On this morning in April, the order came.

The Guardian hovered nearby, his wings spread in an arc of glorious light that shone about the four maidens. Their clothing was threadbare, their eyes dull as they struggled in the fertile garden trying to coax life from the ground. But one of the maidens saw him, only one, whose heart was as pure as her mind. It was that purity and clarity of purpose, that unfailing and unquestionable love for their Maker, which allowed communication between the two.

Eyes the brilliant blue of the heavens blinked, then lifted to question the messenger's presence, but the maiden stood steadfast and unafraid. "Art Gabriel?" LeClaire of Ravenwood asked.

"Nay," he answered, his voice but a whisper of wind to the others. "I am the Guardian, a warrior of the Realm who brings you tidings from the One you serve."

It was not the first time in her seven and ten years LeClaire had sensed the presence of the celestial being, for he had ever walked with her, representing the sustaining force in her troubled life, but it was the first time she had seen him so clearly. She was given to wonder at his magnificence, the manly and mortal features that bespoke strength and power. As if chiseled from stone, he stood tall and strong before her, finely hewn and masculine, exuding greatness and dominion in an aura of pure silver light. And she wondered if it was within her own mortality that she viewed him thus, for she knew God's angels were spirit not flesh and blood as he appeared to her now.

The Guardian spoke again, his voice deep and resonant, bringing a peace that mirrored the uncompromising faith within LeClaire's heart. "There is a restlessness in the land; it grows turbulent and will affect you all. But you have naught to fear. These things were ordained ere you were a seedling in your mother's womb. Stand firm, child of God, steadfast in your faith, and know ye that in all things, He is with you."

LeClaire nodded and let the warmth of his peace cloak her within the security of its radiant folds to ward off the tremor of dread following his message. She knew of that which he spoke. England was ripe with dissension. Men's loyalties swayed, erratic as the ever-changing winds with the threat of attack from several factions. King Edward

was dead, and the reign of his successor Harold Godwine,
king elect of the Witan, had been essentially a time of prep-
aration for war.

Harold was making ready to face invasion, either by his
brother Tostig from Flanders, Hardrada from Norway or
William from Normandy. The question uppermost in all of
England was which enemy would strike first. Her hands,
small and overworked for one so young, went to her heart.

"I will keep your words here, brave warrior. I will re-
member and heed the promise. I am His servant in all
things."

"Nay, not His servant," the Guardian said, a look of
compassion for the things to come in the glittering depths
of his eyes, "but one who serves Him well. Hold fast to His
teachings, child, and His grace and mercy will follow you
all the days of your life." He bowed as if paying homage,
then rose in a shimmer of silver and firelight and dissolved
into the incandescent rays of sunset.

LeClaire awoke with a start and blinked to clear the
sleep from her eyes. She sat against the base of the hawthorn, remembering she'd only meant to rest there a second when the world had faded from sight and the dream
had appeared—the dream or the vision. She could not
say which, save that it was real to her, as real as her own
sisters now hurrying away from the central wellhead
with their heavy buckets. She curled her knees tightly to
her chest and made herself as small as possible so as not
to catch their attention and waited in the still aftermath
of their departure for a time, wondering why the illusion
had come upon her every day for almost a sennight when
it had never done so before.

Ah, well, it was of no import she supposed when there
were more pressing matters at hand. Nightfall was upon
her, and the darkness offered no comfort, so she rose
from her spot beneath the tree and walked slowly toward
the hall.

She spoke not then nor later of the things she saw and

heard that last week of April, for who would have believed her? But she kept the vigil, as did all of England, their eyes turned heavenward in awe and fear. For that entire week, the night was split by a star with a long fiery tail that blazed in the northwestern sky. Most shivered at the strange sight, some crossed themselves and hurried to their dwellings lest it mark them or their unborn, a few recorded it for posterity. All, save LeClaire, were glad when it was gone, for with its passing the dream did not come again.

In the months that followed, the gales of war erupted, scorching the land in the fierce heat of battle as kin met kin without regard for the blood that bound them, only that which was let. By summer's end the King of England's levies marched north under the banner of the Golden Dragon of Wessex, the "German dragon," to defeat both Tostig and Hardrada at Stanford Bridge in a victory gained and cheered throughout the land. Truly Edward the Confessor had been right in naming Harold his successor, for the King's military prowess had proved worthy.

But by September, the last threat, the one that would prove fatal, had transferred his invasion force to St. Valéry at the mouth of the Somme. And it was only a matter of time before William the Bastard, Duke of Normandy, would sail for England with a fleet of ships numbering in the thousands.

And at his side would be a man equaled only in legend by William himself. Borgia de St. Brieuc. The Silver Lion.

II
THE
ATTAINMENT

Behold, I set before you this day a blessing and a curse.

Deut. 11:26

1

England—The year of our Lord 1067

The early morning mist crept along the sodden marshes, lending an eerie quality to the silence that hung heavy in the still air outside Ravenwood. The feeling of impending doom was an almost tangible thing, hovering over the young woman like a decaying shroud, permeating the very air with its foulness until LeClaire's breathing was nothing more than a shallow rasp. She was of small build and had seen no more than eight and ten summers, but she was strong. Aye, she'd had to be.

"Let not the fear overtake you!" she whispered with a fierceness that crawled in echo along the cold stone walls, then felt more the fool for having spoken to herself aloud.

She gathered her knees to her chest and huddled by the stone hearth, losing herself in the crackle and hiss of the leaping flames to ward off the madness threatening to seize her, while she wrung her hands demurely as befitted a lady of her station. A nervous sigh escaped her pale lips as she slung a heavy lock of hair, the brilliant color of firelight, over her slender shoulder and listened to the commotion below.

Agonized moans and blasphemous curses drifted up the bleak stone corridor, and she could picture the soldiers as she had left them, clutching their bellies, writhing on the rush-strewn floor or dashing for the garderobe. Contrary to what the men thought, they were not within the lurches of death—only wishing they could die. The drug she had put in their wine was not poisonous but merely a purging mixture of fleawyrt and senna. A bit too much of both, she admitted with neither rancor nor guilt, for the men below were but outriders, men-at-arms sent to do their lord's bidding.

They had caught her unaware, riding up so bold and fearless. A hundredfold or more they had come, and LeClaire had reacted with unaccustomed haste and foolishness out of fear they would slaughter the serfs and raze the keep. Desperation had consumed her, and so unlike her usual calm self, she had acted desperately. It had been imperative to incapacitate them while she thought of what she must do, searched her mind for options, if in truth there were any. Never before in her life had she acted so impetuously, without a thought for the consequences, and given where that had led her, she probably would not live to do so again.

LeClaire wrapped her knees tighter to her stomach and rocked slowly back and forth as she sought to regain her composure and equilibrium. King Harold had been defeated by William, Duke of Normandy, and the men below had been sent by his vassal, Borgia de St. Brieuc, a most infamous and ruthless knight it was rumored, to seize her holdings. Wretched though they were with no possession but a crumbling keep, barren fields and aging serfs, they were her lands! The only possession left to her with which to provide sustenance and dowry for her three younger sisters. She had no fight with this new King or his knight; she had not the men nor arms to stand against his Norman invasion, and would not have done so anyway, for she favored William as well as any on England's throne. But her uncle had sworn fealty to Edward the Confessor, thereby owing allegiance to his successor Harold, and now Duke William would claim his due.

The thought of losing her land could not be borne, and LeClaire vowed that, though all of England lay in waste and brave Saxon warriors lay dead or scattered hither and yon, she would not be defeated meekly—even by a knight whose reputation for terror had preceded him.

For two years she had struggled to make Ravenwood, the dilapidated estate inherited from her uncle, worthy to be called home—two long, lonely years fraught with uncertainty and strife. Having been raised far to the north on an isolated farmstead boasting naught more than marshy ground and a simple wattle-and-daub hut, she had not been trained to manage a large estate, especially a failing one, but she had persevered after the death of her parents and subsequent demise of her uncle, and the lands were finally beginning to show a little prosperity. Given a few more years Ravenwood would be a thriving, self-supporting system.

Given a few more years. Despair wrapped its heinous tendrils around LeClaire's heart, choking her. Alas, it appeared now she did not have a few more years, and all her labors had been for naught. She had stalled the men-at-arms, but the man himself would come, and there would be no stopping this one. His legend was well known. He was said to be no more than a score and seven years, but the name St. Brieuc was spoken throughout the land even before William had come and conquered. It was a name synonymous with power and wealth and the ruthless pursuit of both. Since the conquering it was a name known to cause Saxon women to shiver in the night and their men to lay down their arms without so much as a scuffle. The name conjured up atrocities—part rumor, part fact—committed at William's side that made the bravest forsake his honor in exchange for his life.

Hearing the distant clatter of hoofbeats, LeClaire

lunged to her feet and raced to the window. A cloud of dust arose in the distance and drew closer, the thunder of horses loud and foreboding. The fog was heavy and hung about the land as it mingled with the dust, impairing her vision, permitting only an occasional flutter of something blood red to appear. Her heart slamming against her ribs, she slipped from her room and crept down a set of seldom used stairs until she reached a storage room. Carefully concealed from the men-at-arms in the main hall, she peered from a window at ground level.

LeClaire's heart gave a sickening lurch to the pit of her belly, and her knees threatened to buckle. The hour of reckoning was at hand. Hiding behind the scraped hide, she saw more men, an entire army, and knew by their standards they traveled with him. St. Brieuc. He had come at last, just as she had feared.

Out of the mist they came, a thousand strong, eerie specters in the fog that swirled around them, then seemed to drift away as if their mighty presence overwhelmed it. Onward they rode, their banners waving victoriously, pressing ever closer until they reached the entrance to the keep and someone trumpeted a halt. The ranks dismounted, archers and crossbowmen first, infantry and pikemen next, then finally the cavalry knights. In the foreground one stood apart, resplendent in his armor and his bearing, and LeClaire knew it was he. The Silver Lion. He had gained the title for his cunning nature and devouring of his enemies and was the man to whom her lands had been awarded.

He stood only a moment, gazing negligently around him, before his lengthy, powerful strides brought him to the entrance of the hall. In his coat of mail, he was as menacing and foreboding-looking as any man LeClaire had yet to encounter, and his presence, so near now she could see every detail of his shield, sent a faint trembling along her limbs. Done in *argent* and *gules*, the lions rampant represented with the richness of silver and crimson seemed to be a reflection of the man. He towered over the companions beside him, not in size but in dominance, his air of authority an awesome thing to behold. LeClaire felt her composure waver then shatter miserably when the brute doffed his helm to scrutinize the land, then pushed the coif to his mail-clad shoulders.

A sudden and startling cry of alarm burst from her lips, and she jerked away from the window and staggered back against the wall, rendered speechless by the sight of something more frightening than his arrival.

"God in heaven!" she cried, stricken by the sight of him. Her fist pressed against her knotted stomach, as if that piddling action would hold her together, then rose to cover her trembling lips. "Nay, 'tis not possible," she whispered and forced herself to turn back, to face that which was surely an illusion, a trick of the light or her anguished mind. Inch by agonizing inch, she crept back to the window, blinking away tears of panic and confusion to clear her vision.

He stood there still, his likeness undeniable, damning in its clarity. His nose was fine and straight, his jaw firm and unyielding, his lips thin and well formed. And her heart wept with the bitterness of so profound a betrayal, and her mind cried out a denial still.

His head covering slipped back to reveal a mass of charcoal hair, worn long in the style of the English rather than the shorn or plucked of the Normans. His windswept locks were neither black nor gray but a darkened ash that fell in thick waves away from his sun-bronzed face and glinted almost silver in the sunlight.

Almost detached now from the horror before her, LeClaire watched as he surveyed the bailey, if the grounds surrounding the keep could be called such, for there was no palisade or fortress to protect her meager holdings, no moat nor drawbridge. In truth, the ramparts meant for defense were nothing but piles of turf and rotting timber. His huge destrier shifted impatiently, and he reached out absently to still the movement. A rich cloth draped the war horse, done in midnight blue with a slash of deep red and a band of silver stitching. A broadsword hung there in a like casing, but at his side was strapped a thinner, longer sword, a masterpiece of Moorish artistry. Its jeweled hilt winked in the feeble sunlight like the steady gleam from the eye of a serpent—deceptive, deadly—just like the glint of pure silver in the knight's eyes. Like a shaft of icy moonlight his gaze swept all surrounding him. Naught in his stance showed either interest or revulsion or any other emotion, yet LeClaire sensed he saw everything, missed nothing.

One of his soldiers staggered from the hall and fell prostrate before his lord. LeClaire heard not his muffled words, but there was a look of guarded calculation in the Norman lord's eyes, and his pause was so brief it could have been nonexistent. Then with disconcerting and alarming casualness, he moved with fluid grace, his casual strides taking him from her view and into the hall. With an aching void in the region of her heart, LeClaire knew he had just discovered the condition of his men.

She flung herself away from the window, darted out of the closet and raced back up the stairs until she was once again in her chamber. Merciful Father, she had not thought he would arrive so soon, had made no provision to hold this threat at bay. Forsooth, had no forethought at all beyond drugging the men when she had. In all the terror and confusion it had seemed necessary at the time; it seemed deadly foolish now.

Time hung suspended, measured only by LeClaire's erratic heartbeats and tattered breaths, and her ears strained to catch any sound from below. Naught but silence and the occasional whisper of wind through hide-covered windows greeted her ears. Even the groaning of the drugged soldiers seemed muted now in the aftermath of his coming. She felt her spine dissolve and had to sit down to quell her trembling limbs. And she waited, her breathing arrested, until she finally heard the ominous rattle and clank of armor. Sweat beaded her palms, she could scarce draw air, eyes stark and dilated stared with morbid fascination at the door, and she fought the urge to run and hide and the added, unbearable need to see him. To see that face.

The sound grew louder with heavy footsteps, too many of them, trespassing up the stairs. Her pulse quickened, pounded in her ears, beating a frantic rhythm with the footfalls that brought them closer and closer still.

Stand firm, child of God, steadfast in your faith.

"Aye," LeClaire whispered, her words but a tremble of breathless air past her lips, but she wondered if faith would be enough to stand against a fallen angel. For surely the man below was just that, fallen from grace, a perfect counterfeit of the Guardian she had seen and trusted.

Borgia de St. Brieuc's face was a mask of cold purpose and quiet, while dark violence lay just beneath the surface. He had not thought to find resistance here.

Ravenwood was rumored to be a weak fortress, not fit for habitation since well before its old lord's death, but the rumors were wrong. His men, brave and fearless on the battlefield, lay moaning and wailing that a fierce and cunning witch had cast a wicked spell on them with seductive words of welcome and offers of meat and wine, then had poisoned them unto death.

Borgia doubted death lurked any nearer than the garderobe they were all seeking. Their symptoms had all the markings of a strong and powerful herb, harmless in small dosage. Some, more embarrassed than harmed, were already recovering. In a word, his men had been skillfully duped.

" 'Tis an outrage," gasped FitzRalph, the young squire beside Borgia. He was scarce four and ten, but he was strong of heart, ambitious and loyal. When he continued to voice his shock at such a coward's trick—and a female at that!—his liege lord silenced him with a cold gray look of scornful amusement.

"A fool indeed," Borgia said, his voice silken and implacable. "The bitch should have used hemlock, not some kitchen herb."

Borgia ignored his suffering men for the moment as his eyes assessed the hall. For all its decay, the keep was clean and well kept as the grounds outside had been. The disgraceful condition of the main room had been disguised with magnificently painted murals on two walls. The campaigns of Charlemagne covered one, while a gathering of saints lent beauty to another. The use of pale tincture for the backgrounds added light and openness to an otherwise dank and dreary habitat.

On yet another wall hung a tapestry, intricately stitched by a talented hand, depicting man's unending quest for the Holy Grail. It began with Joseph of Arimathea holding the cup of Christ to the cross, then spanned years of legend and folklore to end with a nun, the sister of one of the knights of King Arthur's Round Table, holding it just out of reach of Sir Galahad, Sir Perceval and Sir Gawain. At the bottom, almost unreadable from this distance, was inscribed in Latin, "Only the pure of heart."

The reports Borgia had received of this place were sorely lacking, it seemed. Impoverished, yes, but some attempt obviously had been made to restore Ravenwood. Despite rumors of irreparable decay, he had wanted this land grant above all others, for it was the estate of an individual lord, a rare occurrence in the south. A detailed and cautious man, he had learned as much as he could about Ravenwood before sending his men, but there was little to be gleaned from the conflicting reports, except that this establishment had once been part of the holdings of the powerful Godwine family of which the deceased King Harold was kin.

William had claimed it, as he had all Saxon holdings from the nobility to the humblest peasant, and Borgia found it odd that part of a former King's domain had been so slovenly attended. The situation was puzzling, and a memory stirred in the back of his mind, something from many years past when Edward the Confessor had been on the throne and one of his principal supporters, the Godwines, had fallen from favor and their holdings confiscated.

The memory was vague, for Borgia had been just a boy of eleven years in 1051, but he knew the Godwines had managed to wheedle their way back into the King's good graces and their land had been returned. Except Ravenwood. He knew not why for certain, but suspected it was because Ravenwood had been in such a deplorable state it would have proved a heavy stone about any lord's neck, a drain on his coffer, and no one had wanted the responsibility of it.

So be it, Borgia thought with satisfaction. For his own purpose, he had petitioned William for Ravenwood, knowing the restoration would be a tremendous undertaking, but he would be a man unto himself. Answerable to no one, his only obligation would be to provide William with knight service when military force was necessary.

Borgia's icy gaze traveled over his ailing men, then lifted to the second floor. To the young soldier still standing anxiously beside him he said, "Tell Sir Roger to have the men outside secure the grounds and make camp. It will take no more than a handful to secure the keep." His eyes never left the dark corridor above as he signaled his four personal guards. "To me," he said. "To St. Brieuc." Then he proceeded up the stairs.

2

All was suddenly silent.

LeClaire shivered when it descended like a death knell. No more tramping feet, no clink of armor, no muted voices. Just shrill silence. It beat with the pulse in her ears. Her imagination, usually so restrained and grounded in practicality, now scurried at random like pestilent rats, scratching and gnawing at the frayed edges of her sanity. Madness and mayhem flitted through her mind. Had they slaughtered her people? Set fire to her keep? Did she sit here now in passivity awaiting her own execution and that of her sisters?

She tucked her feet beneath her on the bench and tried to stop her mind from spinning, but serenity remained just out of her grasp as heinous images overwhelmed the calm disposition to which she was accustomed. Her heart clamored for ease, and her spirit sent forth a thousand prayers until suddenly her efforts came crashing to a halt at the creak of rusty hinges. Her eyes widened and her cheeks went ashen when her bedchamber door came open slowly, slowly, grating upon her heightened senses.

Four armed men, cautious but aggressive, rushed in with their swords held before them but drew up sharply when they saw nothing more daunting than a delicate child in ill-fitting rags curled upon a window seat.

"B'God!" one of them shouted, his accented English making LeClaire want to shout *traitor* at him, but she merely sat in mute acceptance, small and wide-eyed in the fiery gold drape of her hair, holding onto her unraveling composure with every last ounce of strength within her.

After a quick and thorough perusal they ignored her and turned their attention to the sparsely furnished room for others who might be hidden. When assured there was no treachery afoot, as a body they parted, and LeClaire felt the cold intrusion of immense power long before she saw its origin as Borgia de St. Brieuc strolled into the room. With naught more than a nod from their lord, the men hastened back out into the corridor.

Borgia's eyes swept the chamber casually. The room was lit by three windows with arched tops cut from the stone and overlooked the courtyard. A small table, much scarred, holding a board of jet chessmen, stood by the hearth. A few backless stools were scattered about, as if there were several who gathered here regularly. A ponderous wardrobe and several iron-bound chests were the only clothing accommodations save the various hooks and racks on the wall. A large carved bedstead sat majestically in the center, and near one of the windows was a small, empty shelf meant to hold a reliquary to display holy relics.

Borgia missed nothing—neither the lack of ornamentation, nor the cleanliness, nor the terrified little girl huddled on the long narrow window bench. Her hair held the warmth and color of flame, her eyes were a deep clear blue. Enlarged in her pale face, they gave off an air of innocence but were much too wise for her apparent youth.

"I suppose 'twas fleawyrt?" he said, as if he inquired about nothing more pressing than the weather, his voice all the more threatening for its deadly quiet.

LeClaire could only stare mesmerized at the man, her throat locked on a strangled gasp, her fears crashing down around her as the hideous truth was revealed. He had the face of a demon—or an angel. His features were strong and sharp, finely etched with an air of omnipotence that said he was accustomed to commanding hordes of men with nothing more than a look from his steel gray eyes—*eyes she recognized!*

"Nay," she cried in a broken whisper as her world threatened to topple. "Merciful Father, nay!" She would not accept what stood before her, this offensive apparition with the power to desecrate her beliefs and destroy her faith. He was no angel but a man. No Guardian, but conqueror. A man whose very likeness was a mockery of all she held dear. His eyes glinted silver as he stared at her, diabolically magnificent, for they could have been the eyes of a saint had they not been so thoroughly cold and filled with darkness. And she knew in that instant that Satan was a master of disguise.

"Nay? Mayhaps senna then?" Borgia inquired easily.

Though his tone was calm, soft even, LeClaire sensed the hiemal violence that for now lay dormant, controlled by his will. It was evident in his eyes and stance, as if he but waited upon his own choice of moments to unleash the fury within him. In the flesh, he was more frightening than his legend, for she had never credited gossip with fact. Yet, as he faced her—tall, cold, ruthless savagery etched into the powerful lines of his body—she no longer doubted the rumors and knew it was time to confront him.

LeClaire rose from her seat with the grace of a princess and a poise that belied her fear, and Borgia could see she was no child but a young woman—a comely serf mayhaps with her unbound flaming hair spilling over rough woolen garments. The fact that she had not cringed nor gone into a screaming frenzy when his men burst into the room intrigued him, set him to wondering if she was slow-witted or merely uncaring that the lands she was bound to had just fallen to him. He decided on the latter, for although there was a calmness about her that could bespeak the former, there was also a keen look in her clear blue eyes that said she certainly had all her faculties.

LeClaire faced the man without flinching and spoke with a serenity that had gentled many a recalcitrant serf in the past. It was a serenity hard fought for. "Your men have not been harmed. 'Twas merely a medicinal herb. I fear they've had a trifle much."

Her voice was song, the lilt of a finely strummed lute that danced along the edges of Borgia's mind, then faded abruptly away. Fueled by the deception Fate had played upon her, heat fanned rosy across her cheeks and the melody was replaced by a hint of outrage she could control no longer.

"The fault is their own for coming here unbidden and assuming they could overindulge at *my* table."

His silver eyes narrowed, and his smile flicked her like the sting of a lash, biting, threatening in its contempt and arrogance. "You?" he said smoothly, insolently inspecting her meager frame. "*You* did this to my men?"

"Aye," LeClaire said softly, unable to say more.

"Indeed." The dark knight showed no surprise; if anything her challenge seemed only to have entertained him to some extent. It was a struggle of mighty proportions for LeClaire to hold onto her sensibility, her shock at his appearance rapidly giving way to an astonishing anger.

He moved to circle her, and LeClaire's spine tingled in apprehension at his cold eyes upon her. He took her measure front and back from the tiny leather slippers, up the shapeless peasant's garb, which whetted his curiosity as to what lay beneath, to the crown of fiery curls that hardly reached the neck of his hauberk. His eyes settled boldly upon the alabaster perfection of a face that bespoke noble breeding despite her impoverished clothing, and he wondered at her connection to Ravenwood. This was no serf or by-blow of the old lord's. No matter her commoner's gown, no peasant would be so collected nor have taken it upon herself to do what this girl had done. A smile, cynical and devoid of tenderness, quirked the corners of his strong mouth.

"Christ's blood," he drawled. "Aren't you the little bratling."

"Nay, my lord," LeClaire said, lifting crystalline blue eyes so full of piety and righteous assurance they would have forced a weaker man to his knees. "I am LeClaire of Ravenwood, lady of this hall."

His stormy eyes gleamed as he absorbed her words, and for the briefest moment he lauded her daring. But the mocking smile vanished; the silver gray eyes grew intense and watchful. "You are wrong, damoiselle," he said coldly. "I am lord of this domain now, and I have no lady. You are a mere slave, a fairly worthless one given your propensity to cause trouble. You will be dealt with in time, as will all who had a hand in tricking my men, but for now know you this: I am the lord of Ravenwood."

Her composure never wavered. In truth, Borgia doubted she even blinked those enormous blue eyes. But her hands clasped and unclasped a thousand times within the ragged folds of her kirtle. Cloaked with nothing more protective than quiet dignity, LeClaire lifted her piquant but stubborn chin and said with unswerving faith, "I will not give it up."

"Ah, but you will." He grinned, then bowed in a mock display of gallantry. "One way or another, damoiselle, you will give all."

Intimidation crawled up LeClaire's spine and she longed to lash out at him with a vehemence alien to herself but managed to restrain her temper. He was danger personified in his coat of mail, his eyes a dagger-sharp reflection of the metal links. The padded garment worn under his hauberk to prevent chafing only increased the width of shoulders already broad and unyielding.

"I will swear my fealty to William," LeClaire boasted with a confidence present only in the tone of her voice.

" 'Tis too late for that," Borgia said languidly. "But have no fear, damoiselle, you will indeed give your loyalty to the new King . . . and your servitude to me."

"Never," LeClaire whispered without forethought, then spun to face the window. She stiffened her shoulders against the expected blow, for one did not speak to a man so, especially the enemy. This man was well known for his cruelty to those who stood against him. His name was whispered far and wide, invoking reverence in those who called him friend and fear in those who did not. It was rumored the ladies of William's court flocked to his side, and he played heavy upon their hearts and free with their bodies.

Having been sheltered and isolated her entire life until her parents' death, LeClaire knew naught of court, the richness and grandeur, nor of men and women and their ways, but she did know that had her mother spoken to her father so, he would have sent her reeling across the room with his blunt fist as he often had done. Naught but silence met her vulnerable back, and she was given to wonder if the man was tolerant, which she doubted, or was merely shocked by her outburst and had not yet acted upon it.

Borgia was neither. Never had he struck a female unless attacked; he'd never had to. His mere presence—and some would whisper his wealth and handsomeness—was enough to cower the boldest wench into subservience. Though this slight girl deserved his fury and would surely see it before long, he found for the briefest moment she amused him standing there so regal and proud in her beggar's cloth. That he should be amused in the least by an ill-kempt, childlike female had not occurred in more years than he could number, and Borgia found himself waiting to dole out punishment just to see what she would dare next.

Her back rigid, LeClaire stared out her chamber window and gazed at the men below—strong men, armed, as accustomed to their profession as she was to poverty. She could not fathom why they would want her meager holdings when surely there were greater, more prosperous lands to be had. Even with her back to him, her words rang clearly in the large room.

"These lands are mine by right of birth. My uncle died without issue, and I am his next of kin. By what right do you claim them?"

"By right of conquest," came the cool response. He hadn't known of an heir, but all Saxons were subject to William now. "They were given to me by the King for services rendered."

LeClaire could well imagine the "services." Death, destruction, the desecration of a people. She took a deep breath and fought for control, for the ever-present calm and rationale that had always been a part of her. She turned back to face the man, but caution fled in light of the injustice being served.

"I do not recognize your right. There was no contest here. We have not taken up arms against your King." Her small hand swept the room. "I have no army, no retainers. We struggle for our mere existence here. There is naught you could want from such a pitiful estate. Take your men and go!" she pleaded, demanded, hoping from the boundless depths of her soul to appeal to some gentler side of this dark knight. "Conquer someone else's land, but leave me and my people in peace!"

How becoming your spirit, damoiselle. How useless. With no more forewarning than a slight lift of his brow, Borgia raised his sword in one effortless motion and sliced it through a heavy chunk of wood by the hearth. LeClaire cried out and hastily stepped back as he brought it back up and raised it to her. His eyes were as cold and emotionless as the honed blade and as piercing.

"You are the conquered one," he said in a low voice and with the frightening implacability of one who would not be swayed. "This keep, these lands and its serfs are now mine. Pitiful, yea, but of all the lands awarded me, these are privately owned, and I have need of them. Your pleas move me not, for I have heard their like aplenty this campaign." The threat of death lingered above her. "You cry that you have not brought arms against the King, but the condition of my men below belies that fact. I give you a choice. Take your belongings and leave in peace, or stay and serve me. But be warned, bratling, death awaits you should you cross me or mine again."

Punishment . . . slavery . . . death . . . cast out? What choices those? Something vital inside LeClaire died a little as her life, which had been no life at all until she inherited Ravenwood, flashed before her. All that might have been shriveled to dust like seedlings in a rainless garden, and the barrenness that now lay before her was a hopeless thing. Her forlorn sigh echoed in the still room as her fingers clenched in her kirtle, and she was unaware of the knight carefully watching her expressive face until she lifted her eyes to meet his.

"I have nowhere else to go," she said simply.

"Swear your loyalty, and you may remain as slave."

LeClaire lifted her chin with a stubbornness that would bring a glimmer to the war-hardened knight's eyes in the days to come. "I prefer death, my lord."

Well done, damoiselle. Borgia stared at the slight girl in cold amusement mingled with approval. Her radiant face showed no fear, and he would allow her courage. Many a warrior had not shown such valor in the face of death. Had his own lands been threatened, he too would seek death before servitude. But not before he took his enemy with him. Death was always a foe to be faced head on and conquered. This little waif had no soldier's training, yet she faced him with logic and courage as any seasoned warrior would. Had all the Saxons stood before him so proud, so composed, mayhaps he would not have been so heartless with them.

"Methinks, damoiselle," he said, a cynical twist to his

lips, " 'twould be a sore waste of young womanhood to offer you to my eager sword."

LeClaire's face may have looked composed, but her mind screamed with terror. So frightened was she that had she not been frozen with the horror of her situation, she would have been trembling from head to toe. Yet, her fear was not for herself. She would almost welcome death as an easy escape from all the pressures thrown cruelly upon her two years ago. Being lady of the estate had been no easy task for the untrained young woman, but to suffer slavery at the hands of this frightening man seemed a fate worse than death.

Nay, not for herself but for her sisters did she fear. For the youngest, Kyra, who at ten and two had not yet reached womanhood. Her stable and steady countenance, her patient understanding of her duties, had been a godsend to LeClaire over the past years. And for Maire, whose quick temper often caused her tongue to outdistance her reasoning. But most of all it was for her sister Aurel that LeClaire found cause to be afraid—sweet, silent Aurel.

If LeClaire were slain, who would look after gentle Aurel? Would the boisterous Maire? Nay, more like she would have them all beheaded within a fortnight. And Kyra was simply too young. LeClaire sighed heavily, the weight of responsibility too mean a burden for her tender years. Oh, that she could seek death with its peaceful conclusion and end this torment.

Stand firm . . . stand firm . . . stand firm! The Guardian's words echoed through her mind but brought no ease when his mirror image, a dark forgery, stood before her in the flesh, sword raised.

"Have you naught to say, mite?" Borgia asked, sunlight glinting off the blade held in readiness to sever LeClaire from this world.

"Mere words escape me, sire," she laughed in soft reply, dangerously close to hysteria.

"You do not plead for your life, damoiselle. Do you not fear me?"

If possible her eyes grew even rounder. "Oh, aye, lord. I am much afeared. But not of yon blade, for surely 'twould do plenty to relieve me of the burdens of this life, and I am certain to find lesser troubles in the next. 'Tis for my kin that I find just cause to be afraid. My sisters will suffer greatly at the hands of you and your men have they no wish to join me in the afterlife."

Dark brows creased slightly, and LeClaire was frustrated in her attempt to penetrate that oh so urbane facade. He had shown no emotion other than boredom or cool patience, and those few intimates of his had they been present would agree that St. Brieuc was an infinitely patient man. Deadly infinite.

"Your sisters?" he said with mild contempt. "Serve me well and your fear is unfounded."

"Alas," LeClaire sighed, thinking mostly of Maire, "we are not an obedient lot."

"Best you hasten to become so," Borgia warned softly, piercing her with his steel gray eyes more effectively than any sword could. "Your bravery is misplaced here. 'Twill better serve you to admit defeat and accept your fate."

Fate? Merciful Father! It was not God's will surely that had brought this man here, but the Devil's own design. LeClaire's anger rose and threatened to choke her with its intensity. How dare this arrogant swain think to take what was hers as if it were naught more to him than a handful of grain to be held, doled out or sifted through the fingers in neglect. Ravenwood was bequeathed to her, gained at the expense of her uncle's death. LeClaire had guarded it carefully, planting each kernel, tending and nurturing every facet of the keep and lands until they were beginning to blossom under her ardent care. It was she and her sisters who should reap the harvest of their labor, not a host of crass warriors who cared nothing of their toil.

A deep and abiding sorrow burned within her, born of fear, frustration and righteous indignation, and was reflected in LeClaire's eyes as they rose to face him. Her countenance shone with an inner light and purity, both forged like steel in the fires of adversity until well honed and strong, the essence of her. Her chin lifted as her eyes swept the man before her, his image staggering her with its wrongness. He was bold and handsome, a wealthy nobleman whose holdings were renowned. Even his soldiers' trappings were richer than anything she possessed. He had no need, as did she, of her pitiful estate, and it rankled her sorely that he would claim it all.

Christ in heaven, nay! she decreed silently, 'twould not be so. She would not accept defeat at the hands of this cold, heartless man who had the face of an angel and the black soul of a demon. Having fought various forms of evil her entire life, she would not give up all now just because it appeared with the countenance of a saint. Come what may she would hold her inheritance with every last ounce of strength, courage and cunning she possessed.

Thin lips crooked in a slight smile, Borgia lowered his sword and watched as a melee of emotions crossed the young woman's face—bravery, fear, confusion—then settled on one. Determination. Yes, he admired her courage, misplaced as it was, and he waited, much as a wolf stalking its prey, for her next move. Though all the variables of feminine nature had their place within the elastic boundaries of civility and seduction, he abhorred a woman's flitting about in indecision, pleading favors or flooding a man's world with tears, and wondered which of these little bagatelles she would employ. *Ah, tears.*

True to his expectation, LeClaire's eyes began to fill with clear, shimmering droplets, but contrary to Borgia's impression of feminine frailty, she neither let them fall nor begged his leniency. She simply lifted her chin higher and stared at him with those vibrant blue eyes.

"If you are of a mind to slay me, my lord, then be done with it quickly, for I shall never give up my place as lady of Ravenwood and serve you as slave."

Borgia may not have been impressed with her tears, but he was intrigued by her rebellion. The gauntlet had been cast, not in anger but in righteous valor, and he knew she would not be easily cowed. Her eyes were luminous in her pale face, her composure stalwart. Small and slim she dared to stand before him like a sentinel, proclaiming she would not surrender when a third of the Saxon lords whose keeps he had razed had cried peace without drawing a sword.

Oh, fearless and foolish maiden, do you know what you are about? Grieving widows begged the King to be given in marriage to his Norman knights so that they might keep their lands, yet LeClaire of Ravenwood, this noble peasant, thought to stand against him with words and tainted wine. One powerful arm lashed out, caught the delicate girl by the neck of her tunic and with graceful certainty wrenched her completely off the floor. Gray eyes met and clashed with frightened, defiant blue ones, not a hand's breath apart, as he held her dangling before him.

LeClaire strangled on a cry as she was brought eye to eye with her enemy. She stared into the endless charcoal depths, feeling as though she had just been hurled into the deepest, darkest chasm where light was only a misguided hope and her salvation lay only in the iron grip against her breastbone, which meant there was no salvation at all. She sought to collect herself, to not be devoured by the darkness, but his next words sent all chance of redemption skittering from her mind.

"I'm of a mind to have you stripped to the waist before yon household and flogged until your bones show," Borgia said with cruel nonchalance.

LeClaire swallowed convulsively; a shudder racked her body, but her eyes never once wavered from his. "In truth, sire, 'twould be a wretched way to die. I prefer the sword."

Something powerful and undefinable kindled within him interest, understanding and more. She was bold and quick with her words but frightened half out of her wits if her trembling body was any indication. A traitorous spark of humor rumbled through him. Even suspended helplessly before him, clothed in the poorest garments, she held herself with a dignity as commendable as it was ridiculous. Aye, by God, she did amuse him with her bedraggled appearance, brilliant blue eyes and irreverent defiance so swelled up with futile bravery. His mirth increased until it erupted in a brilliantly cold smile and brief chuckle.

Something inside LeClaire snapped at the sound of his contemptuous humor when all her world lay in shambles. She squirmed within his grasp, helpless against his strength, and seethed with the shame of being ridiculed in her own house. She lost all coherent thought and began to flail her arms about wildly in an attempt to free herself.

"Put me down, you beast!" she raged with no more aplomb than a fishwife as she swung her fist at his face. She would smite him where he stood, aye, and be glad of it! It didn't enter her enraged mind at this moment that he outweighed her by at least ten stone, and his men waited outside.

She felled a blow to his cheek and felt as if it splintered the tiny bones of her hand. Borgia's laughter only deepened, and he dragged her closer still, capturing her arms in a crushing embrace. Her hands useless now, she tried freeing herself with her dangling feet, but they were as ineffectual as her fists had been. She felt like a stringed puppet, dancing to the master's whims, her will stolen by strength greater than her own.

Amid her cries and fruitless struggling, Borgia surveyed the chamber once again to assess its worth with an indifference that further outraged LeClaire. She might as well have been nonexistent, no more bother than a fly upon a horse's rump, for all the attention he paid her—and her struggling for her very life against a man who seemed to be cut from granite! The indignity and injustice of it could not be borne, and LeClaire twisted and turned anew, determined to show her mettle. She was no weakling lamb to give up what was hers without a fight.

Her writhing served to rattle his chain mail with every twitch and sway but little else. The links bit through the thin cloth of her tunic, and she seemed to be the only one suffering from her exertions. The blows she sent his way merely glanced off his steel frame, and pain from her grazed knuckles began to penetrate her anger. Her breath purled out in thinner and thinner gasps as his hold increased.

Borgia's humor faded, and the coldness returned to his eyes as they searched the girl's flushed face. She was small as a sprite, had less strength than an elf, but her courage was a shining testament to her will. Who was the old lord of Ravenwood that he would let fall to neglect a once rich estate and leave no issue save impoverished nieces? One brazen and foolish niece in particular. He squeezed the bit of fire in his arms until LeClaire's breathing stalled and she went quiet for fear she would suffocate. He loosened his hold, sliding her slowly down his body until her feet touched the floor but kept her within arm's reach.

"Who has begun replenishing these lands?" he asked.

LeClaire, stunned but not undone, merely stared at him for a rebellious moment before she noticed the blood upon his face. Stricken by the effects of her rage, her hand reached out and touched his cheek.

Borgia eyed her narrowly and pulled his head back,

even as his hands clamped down upon her upper arms. "Who?" he asked again.

LeClaire stared at the blood on her fingers, realizing it was her own. Her eyes grew belligerent but her tone was breathless and wary. "My sisters and I."

His hold was like iron, imprisoning her with a soundness she had little seen in a man and had never felt. To be on the receiving end of that power was daunting indeed and caused her defenses to rise full force, all out of proportion for the normally cautious and reserved young woman.

Hooded gray eyes swept her slowly. "How?"

"With hard work," came a curt reply, her voice rising to match her anger.

"Have you a father, brother or uncle here?"

"Nay," LeClaire groaned, at the end of her tether. "Do you confess to a hearing problem? 'Tis just my sisters and I."

His reports had been partially correct and intolerably inadequate. His eyes wandered over her frayed woolen kirtle. "Then how came you by the resources to convert these ruins into a livable estate? Have you more wealth than your mean clothing would suggest?"

LeClaire dropped her eyes from his penetrating gaze, longing to call the man dense for such a ridiculous question.

"I would have an answer," he said dangerously, his breath fanning her smooth cheek.

Her head snapped up. "I have given you one," she replied. "Hard work." Though she strove for her habitual equanimity, the rage of panic and unfairness roiled within her, gaining in intensity, frightening her with its uncontrollable force, which demanded to be released. Hitherto even-tempered and collected in her judgments, she was so unaccustomed to the emotions that she did not think to deny them but merely acted upon them. "If 'tis a problem with thine hearing, my lord, mayhaps I can find a soothing balm that will clean out the blockage and allow you to better understand me when I say you have no claim here. *Be gone!*"

"Have a care," Borgia drawled with the low and lethal quality of one in command. His silver gaze darkened to molten gray slits as he pressed his point. "You are defeated, bratling. Although your courage is great for one so small, it moves me not. 'Tis foolishness. As for the renovation of this estate—if you had a hand in it, as you say—the effort was, albeit, a valiant one, a waste of your talents. You have merely lessened my load. For that I offer you my thanks but naught more. You will stay and serve me as slave or pack yourself and your sisters away from here."

Color flooded LeClaire's pale face. Was she to be grateful that he did not slay her where she stood? That he was giving her an option? Damn him to perdition, she would be grateful for none of this. She could not give up everything she had worked for, nor would she be a slave to this heartless beast. Despite the hard, lonely years, despite the unending, backbreaking work, the truth of her situation could be borne out in one undeniable fact: she had nowhere else to go.

It would be blasphemy to meekly hand over God's blessing as if His provision meant naught against troubling times. She could not do it, had not the right to profane such goodness out of fear, when she knew He was mightier than any mortal creation. It was His strength that she would call upon, His mercy and faithfulness that she would rely upon, not her visible circumstances.

In her mind and heart, she was resolved, but it was not her mind and heart to which this dark lord laid siege, but her lands. In faith she would stand against him, but in the flesh she knew not how it was possible when there were unalterable facts to consider. She had no army, no weapons, no wherewithal to hire mercenaries, and there were none who would dare stand against this man and his King.

Other than Ravenwood, the only possession left to her was a slip of parchment and a message her mother had imparted before her death. LeClaire stifled a gasp at the memory. Therein lay her deliverance. But that information she would keep locked safely away for the present. In a time when might transcended the law and murder for gain was common, it would behoove her to stay quiet. The secret might easily hasten her death at the hands of this cruel man instead of forestalling it. Yet, given at the right moment, the secret just might gain her back Ravenwood. Thus would she wait, carefully guard the knowledge and see if the reign of this new King would prove friend or foe.

"Sire," she began calmly. She must needs present her case with sound logic, but her heart thrummed nervously in her breast and logic flew swiftly off to the hinterlands. "I live in constant fear that the deafness which has afflicted you since your arrival is growing worse. Let me repeat. I will not leave this keep, nor will I be your slave. As I have not the strength to oust you and your men, and it appears you are not gentle-natured enough to take leave on your own, it seems we must find a more workable solution." She waited, chin tilted, eyes widened, a guileless picture of patience and expectation for his response to her more than reasonable request.

"Have you a solution?" Borgia queried softly, and LeClaire had the sudden and sinking impression that she had just been patronized in the lowest way. It was not a soothing impression.

"Nay," she muttered, and dropped down to a nearby bench. She had used all her strength to stand before him and was now so mentally and physically fatigued she did not think her legs would hold her. She had no other choice but to try and compromise until her secret was revealed. "I have no answer to this problem, lest we set upon a plan to rule this small demesne together."

With the arch of an eyebrow, his expression was no longer one of subtle condescension but of grating attentiveness, and she felt like a helpless mouse being toyed with by the cat before the kill.

"Aye, it seems an impossible feat, my lord, but can we not ponder this dilemma?" she asked, frustrated and wary of the ease with which he listened to her when she expected him to rant and rave his superiority. But of course he had no need of such tactics when his army encircled her land and one blow from his fist would send her to eternal rest. In truth, she could hardly comprehend why he had not done so already, but hope was vital to LeClaire and she clung to the inner assurance that she was protected. At least for now.

Borgia could feel her tiredness as if it transmitted itself to seep into the very bones and muscles of his warrior's body, but he was not moved. "I see no need for further discussion. I will be lord here. You will serve me well or be gone."

LeClaire's shoulders slumped, and her gaze dropped from his as her mind searched for options where there were none.

"I hear you not, bratling," he said with deceptive casualness.

Utterly provoked by this man beyond her usual good sense, she made a choice, and will her nill her she would see it out. LeClaire lifted bright blue eyes and faced Borgia squarely. "Aye, my lord, I have made a decision. I will remain here as lady of Ravenwood and tolerate you the best I am able." With that she rose from her seat and spun on her heel to leave.

A booted foot stamped down on the tail of her gown, and LeClaire lurched back in fright. But before Borgia could utter a scathing retort, a girl—of lesser age than the one before him who was a mere hair's width away

from being slain where she stood—marched into the
room, accompanied by one of his men. The girl's hair
was a rich sable, her eyes just as dark, yet there was a
familiarity about the two that bespoke kinship.

"LeClaire!" the girl began, snatching her arm free of
the guard's hold. She drew up sharply when she noticed
another stranger. Her eyes surveyed his handsome, mail-
clad figure insultingly and her chin lifted a notch. "God's
teeth!" she huffed, hands thrown to her hips in a gesture
of defiance that LeClaire was certain would soon see
Maire flat on her back in the rushes. She recalled not her
own defiance, for it had come from the heart and had not
been visible to her eyes as was her sister's.

"I see, sister mine, you have also missed one of yours."
Maire sniffed indignantly and sent a pointed glance at
the guard next to her. "I swear by all the saints, I
drugged each of the men assigned to me, then this one
appears from nowhere! Mayhaps Kyra has been lax in
her duties, but 'twas not I." Her eyes and nose crinkled
up mischievously and a saucy grin flitted across her lips.
"Ah, 'twas a good plan, was it not? But all has gone
awry, I fear. There is yet an army of men below still on
their feet." She shook her head sadly. "Somehow methinks we missed a few."

"Maire!" LeClaire whispered frantically to silence her
sister. Her face was drained of color, and her eyes darted
to the man who had stepped away and was watching the
sisters intently. She was wholly certain she did not like
the glint in his cold gray eyes. " 'Twas all for naught. This
knight comes claiming to be the new lord."

"How can that be?" Maire asked with a sassy toss of
her near-ebon locks. "Have you married without my
knowledge?"

"Cease, I pray you," LeClaire warned. " 'Tis no game
now, Maire. He means to put us out."

Maire, not known for weighing the consequences of

her actions, spun to confront the knight head on. "Over my death, you Norman pig!"

"Borgia de St. Brieuc," he introduced himself in a soft and insolent tone that gave no indication of his thoughts. Sunlight streamed in through the window and reflected a silver aura off his chain mail, and LeClaire was stricken anew by his likeness to the Guardian. He propped the menacing sword casually against his shoulder and smiled most pleasantly to the dark-haired girl. "Your death can be arranged with all expediency, damoiselle."

"St. Brieuc? The Silver Lion?" Maire squeaked. Her horrified gaze sliced to LeClaire, then to the man, then back to her sister again. "Trouble," she breathed.

"Aye," LeClaire agreed.

3

In the next instant a commotion was heard from without the door. Borgia's seneschal, his most trusted companion in arms, Roger de Amiens, came stomping into the room with a girl slung over his shoulder. Her clothing was as ragged as the others', but unlike the flame-haired LeClaire or the one called Maire, whose locks held the dark mysteries of a night sky, this one's hair shone like the fine gold of sunlight as it swung to and fro in her struggles. Viking ancestry was evident in her coloring and her long, lithe body. Though she made not a sound in protest, the wench was kicking for all she was worth, and Borgia surmised that this was yet another sister.

The girl twisted and writhed to the extreme that Roger, who was almost as big as he was tall, staggered as he came into the room and had to cinch his arms tighter until she hung limply in his powerful hold. When she ceased fighting, Roger thought the contest met and breathed a grunt of relief, but suddenly he was attacked by two other girls who were so vicious with their fists and feet he had to beseech help from his lord.

"By all that is holy!" Roger bellowed as Borgia pulled LeClaire free and started for Maire. "What manner of elfin army is this that a man cannot enter a room peacefully without being accosted by prankish sprites?"

"What indeed?" Borgia smiled wryly, struggling with

the two sisters so that Roger might put the third one down. "Cease the battle, maidens. Let Amiens speak."

Roger was the son of a lesser noble lord whose family was well acquainted with the St. Brieucs. He had been fostered at the age of seven as had Borgia to Walter de St. Brieuc, Borgia's uncle, and the two boys had grown up together, trained together, fought together. They had earned their spurs of knighthood in the same season, and much as Borgia would trust another, lest it be William the Conqueror, he was a friend to Roger. The two were well suited in their companionship, their ideals and ambitions much alike. Borgia's dark, cold countenance contrasted sharply with Roger's blond, towering strength, and they were known to cause quite a stir in William's court.

LeClaire and Maire went still as soon as Aurel's feet touched the floor, and Borgia deemed it safe to release them. "Have you a problem, Amiens?" he asked silkily, his eyes glinting with dark humor. He had never seen such a bewildered expression on his friend's face.

"Aye, this one"—Roger gave Aurel's arm a shake—"tried to poison me. Almost forced the tainted wine down my throat ere I learned her game. Then she had the insanity to attempt to slay me with this!" Roger held out a small dagger. "I swear this little stick wouldn't do a flea harm, but the bitch was going for my eyes!"

LeClaire exchanged awed glances with Maire that their sister, their meek and timid Aurel, had been so bold. In the next heartbeat, LeClaire peered anxiously at the Norman lord standing with deceptive leisure by her side—deceptive for she was horribly aware of his dark, unsettling presence, of his strength and of the danger behind his unfathomable hooded eyes.

Borgia smiled mirthlessly as his gaze swept Aurel and took in the girl's size. She was tall for a female, aye, but he doubted she could reach Amien's eyes without standing on a bench. "Art certain, Roger, she meant to do you harm?"

Roger glanced ruefully at the girl. Her beauty was striking, pure and flawless, radiant as an angel's, and he was galled that he had almost been swayed by her mystical lure. "When accused, she refused to deny the charges," he growled. "Aye, she meant to do me injury. Since your orders were that no harm should befall the people, I have brought her here for you to mete out punishment."

"Nay! Nay!" LeClaire gasped, as she rushed over and dared to pull frantically on Borgia's arm when she saw his eyes harden. "Do naught, I beg you! I—"

Borgia's eyes cut to the small fingers tugging his mail, and LeClaire snatched her hand back. Ignoring her, he turned to Aurel. Her face held the freshness of youth, and a beauty stunning in its simplicity. In streaks of blinding sunlight her hair hung straight to her flanks, while her wide, frightened eyes swam with the changeable colors of a moody sea. A goddess mayhaps, or a woodland nymph, he thought, for surely no earthbound creature was capable of possessing such perfection.

"Did you so blind my poor Roger with your charms, maiden, that you thought he would drink your brew?" Roger snorted in mixed disgust and embarrassment at his lord's perceptive claim while his captive shrank from all the attention directed her way. "How are you called?" Borgia asked, the glint in his eyes more threatening than his words.

LeClaire could feel the pressure of fear and anxiety building within her as she stared at the two men, one so dark and forbidding, the other fair of face but just as deadly. She tried to answer for her sister, but one quick rise of Borgia's hand silenced her. Two of the three girls flinched and covered their heads; only Maire did not instinctively cower from his raised hand but lifted her chin even higher. When a blow did not befall them, the other two cautiously lowered their arms.

Borgia eyed them speculatively, his gaze sharp yet unreadable, then turned his attention back to the golden-haired one. Aurel's eyes were dilated with fear as she sent a pleading look at LeClaire, but she spoke not a word. With alarming patience, Borgia posed his question again, but silence reigned omnipotent in the chamber, broken only by the nervous shuffle of leather-slippered feet and the rattle of readjusted armor.

Finally, Borgia rent the stillness, his voice a low and heartless thing to hear. He did not shout, he had no need of it, for his was a dark, cold force that cleaved and broke all before him. "She shall be locked away until such time as she agrees to answer the accusations against her."

At once, LeClaire and Maire rushed to their sister, snatched her from Roger's grasp and shielded her with their bodies. Terror shone from their eyes but they stood firm against the towering Normans.

"Sire—" LeClaire began.

"What is this?" Roger barked. "Think you that you can protect her from my lord's wrath? His word is law. The girl sealed her fate by her actions and her refusal to answer the charges. Lord Borgia is a fair man, but he will not tolerate resistance."

At Roger's signal, two of Borgia's guards walked into the room, one with his sword drawn, the other carrying ropes. LeClaire's eyes took on a feral gleam, and she spread her arms wide as if that feeble gesture would protect her sister.

"Nay!" she rasped. "You will not do this! Listen—"

"Your pleas move me not," Borgia stated with bored forbearance. "The girl had her chance." He nodded to his guard. "Take her."

Panicked now that no one would harken to her words, LeClaire rushed forward and rammed her shoulder into the guard's midsection. She so startled him that he stumbled back a step and she was able to wrest the sword from his hand. She staggered back, faltering under its mighty weight, and wobbled like a drunkard while trying to right herself. She almost had the blade raised when Borgia lashed out and smote her wrist. The stinging blow numbed her hand, and the sword clattered uselessly to the floor.

She stared at it dumbly for a second, hurt and confused, as if the weapon had betrayed her, then gasped when a large, slender hand suddenly cupped the back of her head.

Borgia's fingers tangled in the lush fire-gold tresses, tightening just enough to urge her head back and up to his inexorable and powerful face. Her elegant throat, smooth and pale as ivory velvet, was bare and vulnerable to his silvered gaze. Her eyes, bleak with despair, collided with his bold stare and her skin burned with the knowledge of her helplessness. Fiery curls tumbled in red-gold disarray about his fingers to spill over her heaving shoulders as she fought for calm.

"My lord," she implored softly, fighting hysteria and a dread more chilling than any she had ever known. "My lord, please! She is our sister Aurel. She meant no harm, I swear it." His hand slowly twined about her curls, imprisoning her, and LeClaire thought wildly that she would have preferred to have been seized by the guards. She swallowed back her fear but managed only a reedy whisper. "She would never hurt another. 'Tis not in her nature to do so."

His fingers splayed wide, drifted through her curls, then released them, but his eyes held her captive as easily as his hand had. LeClaire took a dazed and trembling step back and clutched Aurel's shivering arm.

"Why does she not speak up in her defense?" Borgia asked softly, coldly. It was a deceitful net these girls wove with their pure eyes and unearthly beauty, perfectly formed traps to snare the unwary.

"She does not speak," LeClaire answered.

Looking at their guileless faces, he could almost believe they meant no treachery, but he had twenty-seven years to his credit—almost three decades to learn that betrayal knew no age, no gender—and he could not be taken in by youthful innocence as his men below had. "The girl is a mute?"

"Nay." LeClaire shook her head, sending a cascade of shiny curls across her shoulders. "She is not mute, but she does not speak."

Borgia said nothing, just pinned her with his predatory gaze. And waited.

"Almost never," LeClaire corrected, her voice sounding as defeated as she felt. "Not much since she was a child." Her eyes searched Borgia's for some hint of compassion, but there was none to be found, only a coldness that sent a sickening into her belly. "Do not do this thing, I pray you. Aurel is terrified of strangers. She only followed my orders with the wine, and—"

"With the dagger," he offered.

LeClaire shrugged sheepishly and looked askance at Aurel, who ducked her head in embarrassment. God's truth, LeClaire didn't even know where her sister had gotten the sharp blade, much less what Aurel's intent had been. But she was certain it was naught more than panic that had driven her sister to raise the dagger. Aurel was too gentle-natured to carry through with any meanness. LeClaire took a deep breath and decided to regroup and forge ahead.

"As I have said, my lord, Aurel was only following my orders with the wine, and she meant no disrespect with her silence. If one must be punished, then take me, sire, for I gave the command."

"Aye, and me," Maire said, her eyes bright with challenge as she stepped to LeClaire's side. Even Aurel lifted her tremulous chin to stand with her sisters.

Borgia arched a sardonic brow at this display of unity, and LeClaire quickly grabbed onto Maire, who took instant umbrage at his display of arrogance. "Ere I make a decision as to what I'll do with the lot of you, is there another waif like to come barging through yon door?"

The girls eyed each other in wary eloquence, before the door swung open, and a child was shoved gracelessly inside by a guard. "Oh, Kyra," LeClaire whispered.

Roger snorted in disgust at the appearance of yet another brat. "Welcome," Borgia commented with a grim smile, taking in the girl's soft brown hair, hazel eyes and coltish adolescence.

"M'lord," Kyra answered, appropriately polite. Her eyes sought the oldest sister with scholarly reserve. "I presume we have failed in our endeavor then?"

LeClaire fought the urge to groan and grabbed her sister's hand and tugged her over to stand with Aurel and Maire, then turned to Borgia. "She is not apt to give you trouble, my lord," she hastened to explain. "Kyra is patient and steady in her emotions, and she has a quick mind. She will not fight your rule as we have, but will serve you to the best of her abilities if allowed to do so."

"And how might that be?" he asked.

LeClaire did not miss the sweet skepticism and boredom in his tone, and her mind raced madly over her youngest sister's good qualities, searching for the one most like to satisfy this warlord and do no harm. "Kyra's intelligence is superior, and she is good with calculations."

"This girl can cipher numbers?"

"Yea, lord." LeClaire nodded, unsure by his tone that she had made the right choice. "She can read and write and figure numbers. She keeps the accounts for me."

Roger rolled his eyes at the very idea of such and looked to Borgia to see if his lord thought the girls as daft as he did. But after the bit of cunning he had faced so far from these maidens, he would reserve judgment as to the limits of their capabilities. Still, lest the unlikely girl was studying to be a prioress, the idea was ludicrous.

"Impossible," Roger scoffed. "A girl who has the training of a court male? No common knight can do this. If she is so learned, how did she come by this knowledge?"

"Our father despaired of ever having a son when Kyra was born," LeClaire quickly explained, her eyes darting from the severe and chilling look in the darker lord's eyes to the mistrust in the hulking blond man's. "The parish priest agreed to tutor her, though he felt it beneath him. Our mother was accomplished in these things, as well, and helped to teach her."

"Do you all have this knowledge?" Borgia asked.

"Nay," LeClaire admitted as if it embarrassed her to do so. "We all have a smattering of erudition in letters and numbers, but we were not diligent pupils like Kyra. Therefore, our mother trained us in those things which interested each of us most." Heartened that he seemed obliged to listen for the moment, her voice lightened and she pointed to her sisters as she spoke. "Aurel is accomplished with the needle. She has an eye for cloth and can weave and make beautiful tapestries. She also makes our clothing."

At the last remark, the two knights took in the girls' coarse woolen tunics. Seamless and bound at the waist with either twisted lengths of crude leather or hemp, they covered even thinner shifts beneath.

"Countless hours were spent at that task, no doubt," Borgia said dryly.

Aurel pursed her lips, and LeClaire, cheeks flushing, jumped to her defense. "My lord, we would not ruin fine cloth with scrubbing and gardening. 'Twould be a waste of dear Aurel's talents to misuse the rich garments so."

"As lady of this hall," Borgia said silkily, "you should have servants to do your bidding."

"Aye," LeClaire agreed soberly. "But we have only passed two winters here, and it has taken many hands to make this place livable. What kind of master would sit back and let his holdings ruin because he was not willing to labor alongside those who serve him?"

"What kind indeed?" Borgia mused, thinking of the many noble lords who would let their lands fall to neglect before dirtying their own hands. He was intrigued by the knowledge these girls claimed to possess. Such a thing was highly uncommon and commanded attention. "Well, what other talents are to be found here?"

"Maire has a fine voice and the ability to make music," LeClaire offered. "She has entertained us many a cold winter's night with her beautiful verses put to song."

"Not that you'll ever hear them, Norman—Ouch!" Maire cut LeClaire a reproachful glance at the pinch she received, then sullenly held her tongue. LeClaire felt not a whit of remorse; a sulking Maire was much less dangerous than a spouting one.

"And what of you, damsel?" Borgia said, once again turning his probing stare on LeClaire. Her guileless face was lifted to his, fresh, unmarred by the struggles she must have undergone in this hovel. "Where do your proficiencies lie? I already know you capable of wielding your tongue like a sword."

LeClaire sighed, then shrugged, uncomfortable with his nearness, the intensity of his gaze. She was not such a country miss that she did not know he mocked her, but to what purpose? "Alas, I can boast no special skill," she said.

Aurel and Kyra shook their heads adamantly, and Maire stepped forward in defense. "Not so, Your Worshipfulness."

Roger's eyes shot to Borgia at the disrespectful title, but Borgia merely shook his head once.

"My sister is expert in many areas," Maire continued with pert effrontery. "She has taken this pesthole she calls a keep and made it livable. She has seen to the planting and harvesting this past year so that we may not starve. What she does not know about healing, she strives to learn and sees to the sick." With a lofty flip of her hand, Maire concluded with exaggerated drama, "In truth, Your Greatness, without LeClaire's leadership and care of the ill we would all have perished."

"They are a loyal bunch," Roger chuckled.

"They are that." Borgia nodded, not bothering himself with Maire's embellishing of his title. The spirited lass would get her comeuppance when she pushed too far, as would they all, but it was something they would learn on their own. Lessons learned by hard experience were much more easily remembered. He crossed his arms over his chest negligently and perused each of the girls with a directness that brought a blush to all cheeks save LeClaire's, who had more to worry about than the meaning of such an offensive gesture.

"Now, what to do with them?" he said, and cast his cold stare on Aurel, Kyra and Maire. "Your sister says she will not be my slave. Are you in agreement with her?" The three nodded without hesitation. "Even with the penalty of death?" Though his tongue was glib, the hardened steel of his eyes assured them it was no flippant question. Aurel's and Kyra's eyes widened, and Maire gulped. The latter spoke.

"I've not been the most dutiful daughter in my lifetime, Your Excellency, and I've no wish to stay overlong in purgatory ere my ascension into heaven. A dreadful thing, you understand, with all that wailing and gnashing of teeth. I am quite certain I could not bear it. Will you provide us with a priest ere the evil deed is done? I've a need for confession."

LeClaire expelled a long sigh of exasperation and lifted her eyes heavenward. Her sister would surely be the death of them.

"Do not get priggish with me!" Maire exclaimed. "You

are as much in need of absolution as am I. You gave the order to drug the men."

"Do I take this to mean that you would rather stand with your sister in death than serve me in life?" Borgia asked, his civility and patience paradoxically grating against LeClaire's nerves.

Two nodded quickly, but Maire was skeptical. " 'Tis hard, Your Kingliness. How long a time will you grant us to think on this ere demanding an answer?"

Roger's eyes widened when Borgia answered earnestly, "And how much time do you need?"

"Years, I think," Maire said soberly. " 'Tis a weighty decision."

"Granted," Borgia said. The faces around him, even that of Roger, showed their surprise, but LeClaire trusted not his show of generosity. He was too controlled, too alert, sinister even in his humor, and the back of her neck tingled as she but waited for the ax to fall. "Methinks you will provide us with too much entertainment to do away with just yet." His voice lowered; his tone grew dark as a moonless midnight that they not mistake his meaning, and LeClaire could feel the ax cut deep and deeper. "But be warned, maidens, your days are few should you cross me or mine again."

"Aye," Roger agreed. "When brought to heel, the men will find such comely wenches most entertaining."

LeClaire understood not Roger's words nor the odd glance the two men exchanged. It troubled her, but she knew not why. Alas, it was of no consequence, she reasoned, when all of England was troubled now. She and her sisters had been granted a reprieve, if only temporary, and she wanted nothing to snap the tenuous hold she had on Ravenwood. Consulting the warlord never entered her mind as she turned to her sisters, and the expression on her face told them to tread gently.

"Go to your chambers," she requested. "Aurel, keep Kyra with you should you need to call for me."

Aurel nodded and took the youngest sister's hand, her eyes filled with pain and fear for LeClaire. Even Maire was subdued for the moment. They gave their sister a searching look, knowing there was naught they could do but willing to try. LeClaire nodded once, and they turned to leave. At a gesture from Borgia, Roger also quit the room.

Alone now with nothing but strained silence and the silver beast, LeClaire waited for him to speak, but he seemed content just to look at her out of those hooded eyes. It riddled her nerves to the snapping point; not once had he reacted as she would have thought. He did not shout or threaten by might, but watched and stalked and waited. She knew not what to make of his unpredictability, could not read him, could not assess exactly how much danger she was in.

"Is this the master chamber?" he asked.

LeClaire nodded.

" 'Tis mine now. Have your things moved out by eventide."

A shiver of fight moved within her and she struggled to suppress an angry retort. The man had shown a small portion of leniency thus far, and she must go lightly to ensure it. Though she was not foolish enough to feel safe in his presence, he had not yet beaten nor beheaded them, and she did not fear him as greatly as she once had. For all his great legend, he seemed normal, as any other man, but her experience with the opposite sex was sorely lacking, and she knew she must be cautious treading unfamiliar ground. She cleared her throat and spoke softly but firmly.

"Nay, 'tis mine. Find yourself another room."

The corners of Borgia's mouth lifted as did his eyebrows, but there was no warmth in the smile. "You wish to share this chamber with me?"

"Nay," LeClaire gasped. A slow flush crept up her cheeks, heightening her fairness. Crystalline blue eyes

darkened to azure and the sunset blaze of her hair fell
about her dusty brown tunic. The collage of colors created a rainbow of vibrant hues that most men would find
arresting.

Borgia was not most men. " 'Twould seem appropriate
that the lord and lady share the same room," he said
quite gravely.

LeClaire did not understand. "You jest," she said nervously. " 'Tis no solar here but merely a chamber. To
share it . . . 'tis not done outside of wedlock, I feel certain."

"You *feel* certain?" Borgia asked, a note of sardonic
wonder in his voice. *Just how innocent are you, damoiselle?* "Do you not know?"

Puzzlement crossed her face, and LeClaire felt intimidated by his question. She recalled the ruthless strength
that had held her only moments ago, and briefly she panicked. For a breath-stopping second she looked up into
his piercing eyes, and knew with frightening clarity that
he missed nothing, nothing at all. Alarm and confusion
tempered her words.

"My sisters and I were raised on a farmstead; we are
not accustomed to the ways of a great hall, but . . . aye,
I do know. 'Twould not be seemly for us to share this
room."

Borgia's expression darkened. He did not treasure the
idea of playing protector to a group of innocent females.
No matter their tender age, his men could only be
counted on to use as much discretion as the girls themselves used. Ones as puerile and ignorant as these in the
ways of men could easily be swayed by the seasoned warriors who had spent time in William's court. Games of
seduction were played with much finesse among the
knights and their ladies, and were not for young girls of
common upbringing. Their rare beauty and lack of experience would cause much trouble, he mused.

"I will take this chamber," he said. "I see your willfulness, and I warn you now, damoiselle, 'twill earn you the loss of your maidenhead should you press to keep this room. I have no wish to share my quarters, but the winter winds blow cold, and I will not put you out at risk to myself. Your beauty is uncommon and will serve me well until spring, I vow.''

Borgia paused to see if his threat had struck her as intended. Her expression was blank, but her eyes were stark with emotion, and he detected an inkling of rebellion lurking there. He pointed to the fern- and feather-filled mattress resting atop a carved wooden dais.

''Do you insist upon staying? The warmth I seek will be at your expense in yon bed.''

LeClaire's hands began working feverishly again in the folds of her kirtle, and her eyes widened to enlarged pools of bewilderment. Until this knight had come, she had never been overly emotional. In the past, she was never quick to anger nor to laughter as was Maire, but neither was she shy like Aurel. She had always worked from dawn till dark and beyond, scratching out a meager living for those under her care.

Living a solitary existence before coming to Ravenwood, she knew not how to manage this bold lord who claimed her beauty rare then threatened her with things of which she had no physical knowledge, nor did she know how to deal with the turbulent emotions he wrung from her. She had always done what she must to survive, and there had been little room for anything else—least of all learning to spar with arrogant, conquering men.

LeClaire forced her fingers to still lest she tear a hole in her threadbare gown, and peered up at the legendary lion from beneath thick, mahogany lashes. The Guardian had admonished her to stand firm, and she would, for his words and her own faith in them were the only strongholds in her life at this moment.

She glanced around the chamber that had been hers since arriving at Ravenwood. It was the largest room and served her needs well with a place for her herbs, a separate corner for the trunks filled with her mother's treasures and the small wooden kneeling bench where she said nightly prayers. The windows overlooked the courtyard, and she could watch her people at work or play. It was hers, and he should have no claim over it.

"I do not wish to leave this chamber," she said softly. "It has been mine since we arrived here. I do not think I should have to give it up."

Stubborn. The wench was as stubborn as a lazy team of oxen. "I do not *think*," Borgia drawled, "you have any choice . . . unless 'tis your want to share it."

LeClaire knew without a trace of doubt that she would rather choke on her own spittle. "Nay, I do not want to share it! I do not want to leave it! I do not *want* you to be here!"

Deep within she felt much as if she had gone mad, for there was a great urge to throw a fit, to smack his handsome face, to cosh him about his arrogant head. She took a deep breath to still the unreasonable impulses and wondered how he had done this to her. With naught but cold words and that superior smile he had caused her to lose her temper and, no doubt, her sanity, for she was certainly lackwit to speak to him so.

Borgia's slow grin reeked with irony. Christ's blood, the girl was obstinate, and she dared much with that wayward tongue. Yet, he would be no less stubborn in her place. Any other man of his acquaintance would have thrashed her soundly by now, but he had never found it necessary to use physical violence except on the battlefield. But this girl treaded crosswise on his patience, and he was not known for patience where women were concerned. He tolerated them, he ignored them, he used them—at times he even adored them when it served his purpose—but he was never patient with them. A heavy swat to her backside might do much to quell her tongue, but even that thought, tempting though it was,

was abhorrent to him given her small size. She could not withstand a blow from him unless administered with caution, and he was not feeling cautious at the moment. And, of course, there were other, much more effective and satisfying ways to tame a bratling.

"I've not the time to argue the point, damoiselle. Thanks to you, the men belowstairs are retching their lives away. If you have some potion to ease the havoc you have wrought, 'twould be to your advantage to fetch it now. I am past my limits, LeClaire the Conquered. Get thyself from this room or prepare to be my bedmate this night."

The way he said her name, as if it were a slur when she had not even given him leave to use it, made LeClaire's chin drop, and her forehead furrow in a frown.

"The potion will wear off soon enough," she murmured, looking rather lost. "I do not know how things could turn out so badly!" Borgia only stared at her young, delicate features, thinking things had turned out tolerably well. LeClaire lifted her head with a return of blatant but controlled defiance. "The only other chamber in suitable repair is the one adjoining this one. 'Tis only an antechamber, in truth, but larger than some others. If I choose it, will you oust me again in favor of one of your men?"

"Nay, the men will guard the hall and use the sleeping platforms. If there is another room to be readied for Roger, you may keep the one of which you speak."

LeClaire nodded, too dispirited to argue further, and she dare not push him. The road she now traveled was too narrow, too full of pitfalls. It was too easy to lose everything she had worked for with the slip of the tongue. In part, she would never conform and accept him as lord, but on another more basic and immediate level she was grateful she and her sisters had not been cast out. She must needs do all in her power to ensure their continued safety.

She glanced around her, despondent but accepting for the present. She had always thought Ravenwood had the strangest arrangement with its small walled rooms, more like the sleeping quarters of a monastery, instead of a large solar where everyone of rank retired for the night. She was grateful now for the design. She and her sisters would not have to share a chamber with their enemy or take their pallets to the common room.

With great reluctance she transferred her things over the threshold to the adjoining room. The grand knight had won this battle, but LeClaire remembered well the biblical story of Goliath. Just as David, so full of faith and purpose, had gained victory, she too was determined to win the war.

Chaos ruled the main hall when Borgia descended the stairs. Although his men were slowly recovering, they were sore ashamed of being caught in such an unmanly situation by their liege lord. Ravenwood's serfs felt disloyal taking orders from anyone except LeClaire and continued to scurry around in a frenzy of fear and confusion, catching a cuff to the head or a boot to the rump when they were not quick enough to sidestep the ailing men. When Borgia began to give orders in the precise, direct manner that said he was accustomed to being obeyed, they stopped dead still to stare at him as if he were a demon up from hell come to fetch them.

Unnatural and eerie silence descended upon the hall, enveloping all who waited there. Heartbeats quickened; limbs quivered; ruddy cheeks paled. A sudden gust of winter wind moaned through the cracks of the heavy oaken doors and shattered the stillness, providing the impetus for what happened next. En masse, the serfs turned to look at one another, then suddenly roused and fled the hall in terror.

A dangerous and deadly smile crossed Borgia's face as he looked around the hall, which was deserted now save for his weakened men, who could do little more than stare back at him in bleak-eyed apology. Some of the stronger ones rallied and staggered after the fleeing serfs, while others held their stomachs and groaned in misery at the price they would pay for being deceived.

The narrowing of Borgia's silver eyes caused all who knew him to quake inwardly. The reckoning would come, and none wanted to be near when it did.

4

Dusk gathered quickly. Naked tree limbs stood black and lifeless against the gray winter sky, mirroring the bleakness in LeClaire's heart as she turned from the antechamber window. She expected any moment to hear a summons from belowstairs, but none came. When it did, she would ignore it. Let the beast rage; she could not find it within herself to answer his demanding call and was too tired and heartsore to fear his wrath at this moment. She should be about her duties, but her arms and legs were as heavy-laden as her heart from the day's anguish and the future's uncertainty.

Alas, there were those who would go hungry if she did not see to the evening meal, and that, mayhaps more than aught else, caused a vicious wrench in her gut. Never had she failed those under her care; never had she neglected to provide that which was needed most, whether it be food, clothing or reassurance. Guilt was a cruel enemy to the spirit-crushed young woman, but it stiffened her backbone and dried the hot rush of tears to her eyes.

Self-pity was a mewling thing that could sap what strength was left to her quicker than the hardest day's work, and LeClaire knew she would need every ounce of strength she could conjure to get through the days, weeks and months ahead.

Her fingers trembled on the sheet of parchment in her

hand—her only hope, her physical salvation. If the information proved to be worth no more than the foolscap upon which it was written, what was to become of her and her sisters? She had told the warlord she would not be a slave, but it was not true. Though she had meant no deception at the time, she would do whatever she must to survive, to keep starvation far back in the hinterlands where it was ever ready to snare them, to keep a roof above their heads whether it be the grand manor she had envisioned or a simple hut.

The chamber door creaked open behind her, the sound eerie when followed by nothing but tense silence. Le-Claire braced herself against the unwelcome intrusion into what should have been her private domain and refused to acknowledge the man she knew was standing there.

But she could feel him, could feel the prickle of raised flesh along her skin as his eyes roamed idly over her. He had not afforded her the courtesy of knocking or allowed her the luxury of bidding him enter. Power gave him privilege; she could not deny it. But his supremacy did not extend to her innermost self, could not touch the deepest heart of her, and it was within herself that she would wage war against him. She knew not how she would go about it, nor where her determination might lead, but Ravenwood would forever be hers, if not in truth then in spirit.

She curled her fingers tightly for a moment to stop their trembling, then finished sifting through the odd bits of parchment and slipped them back into a plain wooden box. Written on the prepared goatskins were various scriptures her mother had translated from the Latin Vulgate by St. Jerome to the French language LeClaire could read and understand.

She desperately needed God's covenant now and His wisdom in dealing with the Norman enemy. Quietly, discreetly, she closed the wooden lid. Also hidden among the sheets was a chart, painstakingly drawn, that outlined her lineage.

"Your serfs are as loyal as your sisters, it seems," Borgia commented casually. Too casually. A darker meaning lay beneath his tone, something dismal and threatening. "Know you they thought to hide in the woods and swamps? That they ran like good little cowards . . . right into the arms of my men?"

LeClaire's head snapped up at his implication, and her heart began a slow, painful thudding in her breast. She could not help but feel heartened that her people had not flung themselves at the feet of the Norman foe, but her care-worn eyes held untold misery for their plight. When she spoke her voice was light and airy as birdsong, but the underlying bitterness held a waspish sting.

"What shall I do, my lord? Command them obey my enemy?"

"Nay, lady," Borgia said softly, so easily ominous she rued the folly of her words. He stood with lazy indolence inside the door frame, piercing the very soul of her with his wintry eyes. "They will obey me whether you say yea or not. If they have to be continually beaten into submission, so be it."

Aghast, LeClaire slumped back against the table so that it might bear her weight, for her legs had gone all aquiver. " 'Tis commendable they are loyal to me!"

" 'Tis foolish," Borgia corrected. He took a step into the room to tower over her, his sovereignty screaming at her from every line of his powerful body. The very air seemed to take on an urgency, the palpable hint of danger, as he pointed at the window and drawled, "Look to your people, damoiselle, if you dare."

LeClaire scrambled to the small embrasure and pulled back the hide to see several captured servants herded together like oxen in the courtyard. They were stripped to the waist and chained to a post for public flogging. The youngest, no older than Kyra, was straining against his bonds and crying piteously next to his mother. Le-Claire's heart splintered asunder, stabbing like sharp fragments of glass in her chest, and the emotion manifest itself in a hurtful cry as she whirled back around.

"Have mercy, I pray you! They are good people, hard-working and honest! They are noble to stand with me just as your men do you."

"They are in defiance," Borgia said with a cold-blooded lack of compassion.

"Then take me," LeClaire grated out over the harsh and relentless pounding of her heart. "Lash me to the post! Fault them not for their loyalty; they have little enough in their lives that's admirable."

Borgia's sharp gaze flared briefly with some indefinable emotion as it traveled over her slight form. "You would stand in their place?"

"I would die for them," she whispered.

How noble, damoiselle. How absurd. "You cannot stop what has begun," he said, "but you can spare them further whippings. I give you that choice."

"Please," she moaned, all the agony in the universe shining from the depths of her crystalline eyes. "Ceodrid is just a child. How can you—"

"The choice is yours."

Trapped in the small room with the devil incarnate, LeClaire could not retreat, had not the wherewithal to flee nor the strength of arms to fight. She cursed the tremble in her voice, the stricken look on her face that told him he had won. "Art a cruel, despicable man," she choked out. "I will not have them suffer because of me. Tell me what you would have them do, and I will order it done. Or take me in their stead. That is the choice I give you!"

Ah, maiden, beware. You cannot win with courage. "They will obey me, and not through you," Borgia warned. "If you wish to spare them, tell them that."

"As you wish," LeClaire said, but there was blazing

fury in her eyes and a rigid set to her shoulders that told Borgia it was not only the servants who needed to be beaten into submission.

A strange certainty in his eyes, he tossed her a silk embossed cloth, and LeClaire supposed it was his standard for it bore a silver lion rampant stitched on either side of a shield against a field of crimson. She could not make herself touch it and allowed the cloth to flutter to the floor, fighting the urge to crush it beneath her heel.

"Take it with you," Borgia ordered, "if you have a care for your health."

LeClaire let her eyes fall to the banner, such a simple thing really to be the deadly symbol of her defeat. "I cannot move about my own lands unmolested?" she queried, teeth gritted against the pain and loathing within her.

"They are no longer your lands."

His words held the impact of a mace against her skull, staggering, bludgeoning to death all hope within her. But as with the cyclic nature of things, rebirth follows death, and hope was born anew. Though fledgling and feeble it sprang from the depths of her soul, and with it rose her determination. The emotions burned brightly in her eyes as, suddenly and without forethought, a decision was made. She snatched up the banner, darted past Borgia and raced for the courtyard.

Before she had even crossed the main hall she was assailed with the cries of a villein as the lash struck and struck again. Feeling as if her heart had collapsed in her breast, she burst through the heavy oak door, waving the flag wildly, and flung herself into the din of strident voices, both soldiers and servants.

Milderd, a stream of blood trickling down her back, choked on a sob at the sight of her lady and slumped against the post. Tobias, the first to receive punishment, fell to his knees, his back mutilated from the lash as were his wrists from fighting his bonds. Ceodrid sniffled next to his mother, his eyes nearly swollen shut from crying, his chest heaving from suppressed sobs as he tried to stand before them bravely, as a man, when he was but a child.

LeClaire felt the bile rise to her throat and swallowed back her panic. "Cease!" she called, shaking the banner for all to see. "He has ordered you to cease!" She delivered the lie easily while staring straight into the stunned soldiers' faces, confident in her objective, if not in her plan. LeClaire watched as the wicked lash paused then, dangled from a meaty fist, curling insidiously toward the dust like a serpent. "See, I carry his symbol! You must needs obey quickly ere his wrath falls upon you!"

All eyes turned her way, some in painful gratitude, others in stunned disbelief. And one pair—icy cold and hard —stared from a second-story window.

Ah, bratling, how ingenious, how bold . . . how very, very foolish. A devilish laugh whispered through the window hide as he turned to depart the room.

There was a weary drag to LeClaire's steps when she returned to the hall. She assumed she had forfeited her life with her rash actions yet had seen no other path open to her. She did not want to face what lay ahead, but knew she must. She would not change what she had done, but a deep and abiding sorrow for all that would never be weighted her steps like iron shackles. She had made her peace with the people and prayed she'd be given time to make it with her sisters. She turned and stole one last, yearning look at the small borough in the distance.

The village was small, mayhaps a hundred dwellers all told, and isolated from the outside world for its poverty, shunned by most but the traveling draymen peddling their wares. It did not even have a priest, nor would it until LeClaire found one who cared more for God's work than riches. It housed mostly serfs who were slaves, churls who were freemen with little possessions and thegns of disgraced circumstance, men of some affluence who had fallen from favor or were once retainers of defeated Saxon lords. The wealthier merchants and cottagfers, had there ever been any, had left for more prosperous boroughs long before LeClaire arrived at Ravenwood.

Borgia's army was camped as far as the eye could see on her land from the keep to the village, and she'd had to endure much whistling and risqué language, most of which she didn't even understand, on her walk thither and from. But the banner clutched in her tiny fist proved its worth, for she had gone unharmed, and she knew the Lion's authority was absolute, her ill-fated destiny in his hands.

She had spoken to her people, offering comfort where she could, reassurance where needed. She had no answer for their many questions, and would not lie. Those captured had been released on her fraudulent promise, and darkness had sent them shuffling to their huts without a word of comfort for their anguished lady. Daylight would come much too quickly for their tired, worried bodies, and naught else could be done but rest and speculate as to what this new lord's rule would mean in their lives.

Bound to the soil, it should not matter which lord Ravenwood's villeins served but, with the exception of a few who felt it beneath them to serve a lady with no husband, most all had grown fond of LeClaire.

Unbeknown to the thin, overworked young woman who turned back to Ravenwood's main hall, her kind and gentle leadership, her firm but fair nature in dealing with disputes, had gained her the people's respect, trust and unfailing loyalty. From town smith to tanner, shepherd to swineherd, their hearts always, and the toil of their bodies when possible, would forever belong to LeClaire—no matter who called himself master.

She took a deep breath as she pushed open the door, a calmness settling about her. She had thought to be taken by now, lashed to the post or even slain. She knew her actions would not go unattended, but fretting about it had gained her naught,' so she left her future in God's hands, as she had done her entire life. She would face the Lion's wrath now with dignity, not as a martyr given upon the altar in sacrifice, but with the assurance that above all God's will would be done. If her time was near, then so be it. But with the acceptance came a saddening, for she did not think her life's work done.

She braced herself as she entered the hall and her wary gaze swept the common-room, expecting the soldiers to rise up and seize her. Their conversation lagged momentarily, but after little more than a cursory glance they returned to their individual pursuits. Le-Claire took a fortifying breath and stepped farther into the room.

The drone of masculine voices rang discordantly in her ears, troubling to her spirit. Common sights, sounds and smells of a hall that at day's end had been her haven were replaced with cloying variants that smothered her like musty woolen. The French and English with which she was familiar mingled in disharmony with the languages of other foreign mercenaries whose loyalty was paid for not freely given. A menagerie of faces, forms and dress assailed her from every direction, upsetting her well-ordered balance with its strangeness, its erroneous claim on her life.

Other than furtive glances at her, the men carried on as before, and she wondered what insidious game was being played out here. If they thought to act as if naught had occurred, so would she . . . and took another tentative step.

She spied the huge communal pot hung in the hearth. The aroma of rabbit and winter greens filled the air to tantalize her hungry senses. "Bless Aurel," she whispered with a pang, adding the prayer to the many she had already voiced this day. Despite the command for Aurel to stay in her chamber, her sister must have sneaked down to the kitchen and urged Hannah to prepare the evening meal. Maire would have starved unto death before giving aid to the Normans, but it was not within Aurel to deny others. And LeClaire knew it was for her own benefit that Aurel had braved coming in contact with the men to see to the meal.

Her heart thumping uneasily, she braced herself and eased over to the pot. Taking a trencher, she ladled out a small portion of the stew while keeping a cautious eye on the men surrounding her. There were at least twenty soldiers staying inside the hall, and every last one of them stopped and stared back at her, stiff-backed and silent, as if awaiting some profound occurrence. LeClaire swallowed back her fear, then leaned against the wall to support her tired body, for she would not sit among them, and took a bite of the meal.

A great sigh arose from the crowd of men, and they rudely elbowed each other aside as they scrambled from the benches and pressed their way to the cooking pot. Certain they were at last coming for her, LeClaire squeaked a protest and skittered away from the crush of straining bodies, only to find herself ignored. Confused and heedful, she sought safe haven and crept over to a darkened corner well away from the madness and watched as the soldiers descended upon the cooking pot like a cawing flock of blackbirds.

She nearly jumped from her skin when Borgia's low, cynical laughter sounded close to her ear. "They feared the stew poisoned."

She suppressed the bubble of satisfaction rising to her lips. There was little gratification to be had when the moment she had dreaded had arrived. She was not content to stay in Borgia's presence, awaiting her own sentencing, and would have hied herself off to her chamber, but his command for her to stay quelled any retreat she entertained. Her heart plunged to her toes and her eyes darted anxiously in his direction.

Whatever horror she had anticipated did not occur. He merely stared back at her, an unidentifiable look in his frosty eyes. He had changed from his soldier's garb into soft woolen chausses and linen *sherte*. His knee-length velvet tunic was embroidered at the border and neckline with fine golden threads and fairly proclaimed his noble breeding.

LeClaire longed to reach out and touch the fabric, for she had never owned such. How truly grand to feel that softness against the skin, perhaps like rubbing her cheek on the fluff atop a wee babe's head. She feared for her sanity when she suddenly realized she waxed fanciful over a simple length of cloth, but still her eyes traveled over it again and the man beneath it.

Tall and well muscled, lithe and graceful, he made a striking figure—so out of place in her humble abode. His features were finely molded and strong, the ageless beauty of archangels or pagan demigods that an artisan seeks to reproduce in stone or paint. He did not belong here among the rubble and decay, yet looked as if he had dominated it forever. His darkling presence sent a quiver of apprehension through her, and she wondered what brand of changeling was he that he appeared the gallant lord one moment, his mortal beauty rivaling the more ethereal splendor of the Guardian; and other times the ruthless conqueror whose evilness could only have been spawned of the Devil.

Her mind grew restless with the conflicting images and she craved the peace that now seemed but a long ago memory. She could no longer bear the uncertainty of her future and lifted her eyes to his with more valor than caution.

"What is to be done with me?" she asked bluntly.

"Have you committed crimes of which I am uninformed?" he returned, the coolly amused glint in his eyes rasping along her strained nerves.

Not for one second was she fooled by his ease. He toyed with her, drawing out her agony with utmost care so as to inflict the most pain. She would not give into the impulse to rail at him or beg his mercy. She had not the energy nor inclination. "What is to be done?" she repeated.

He leaned against the wall in careless refinement, his thick charcoal lashes half-lowered as he studied her out of cowled eyes. "Did Tobias receive ten lashes?" he asked with grating nonchalance. "Milderd one, and Ceodrid none? Did the rest, Hannah and Athelstan and Hadrian, look upon them in horror and fear should they be next?" LeClaire gave a brittle nod, startled that he knew the servants' names. " 'Tis all that was ordered," Borgia finished.

LeClaire's face blanched in shock. The heat of shame and remorse rose to stain her pale cheeks, and she cast her eyes to the rushes. Her rebellion had gained her naught but his displeasure. She had saved none of them, had profited nothing by her actions except to sow further discord between them and make an idiot of herself.

Merciful Father, he had known! Had known when he handed her the banner that she would do something rash, and he had stood at the chamber window watching her play the fool. He was not a god, neither all-knowing nor all-seeing, but he was perceptive, more perceptive than any person she had ever encountered. And thereby much more dangerous.

Her head lifted slowly and she stared at him, wondering at the ruthless complexities, the lack of compunction that moved him to use painful force to bring the villeins under his rule instead of placing before them their options as he had her. And yet, he had not whipped them soundly as any other lord would have but used only what force was necessary to make his point, wasting neither time nor effort. The lesson was not lost on LeClaire. She would never underestimate him again.

Feeling the pains of defeat keenly, she dropped her eyes from his lazy scrutiny and made quick work of her meal, not daintily as a lady should, but with a thoroughness that vanquished the stew down to the old bread on which it was ladled.

"Do you save nothing for the poor?" Borgia asked, eyeing her empty trencher. The sodden crusts of bread were usually saved for the less fortunate.

"We are all poor," LeClaire answered, uneasy and unwilling to match wits with him in her exhausted state. "No one goes hungry at Ravenwood unless he will not work." She pointed to the huge pot. "All are welcome to sup there if they have done a day's toil and find nothing at their own hearth. There are no beggars here, my lord."

The starkness of her words struck him, for he had not thought the Saxon wench so hard. He wondered if eyes that held the warmth of a summer's sky also hid a cold and wretched heart, wondered if she stood by the villagers in voice only, while abusing those of fallen circumstance?

"What of the lame or blind?" Borgia asked. "What of those hurt in battle, who served well then were maimed for their effort?"

LeClaire tilted her head to look up at him. "They are not turned away," she said, perceiving a hardening but uncertain at its cause. "But neither is their usefulness ended on the battlefield. There are many things to be done here and many hands needed, even those crippled by valor. They can teach the children whilst mothers tend the fields. They can entertain us with stories of their travels, showing us by their words other places few of us have seen."

Frustration knitted her brow as she sought to make him understand those things that should be commonplace. "A man's worth does not decline with age or the loss of strength. His wisdom is as valuable as his able limbs once were. Only bitterness or laziness can rob a man of his true merit, and both those weaknesses can be defeated if the man is willing."

There was a wealth of compassion in her clear blue eyes and deep understanding in her voice. Red-gold curls framed a soft oval face in pleasing disarray, causing a halo effect in the shadows cast by the firelight. She was young, he surmised, too young to attract his interest, but there was a serenity about her as soothing as a lullaby and a world-weary maturity that belied her youthful looks though it could not taint her innocence.

That calm, placid demeanor seemed as much a part of her as her stunning hair and eyes, and Borgia suspected that this, the patient and sure mistress, was the girl the people cherished. But he knew there was more to Le-Claire of Ravenwood than the villeins saw, for he had experienced it firsthand—a defiant nature even the girl herself hitherto had not known she possessed, and a purity of spirit rarely seen even in those ordained to the Church. The last he had no use for, but the other would cause him as much trouble as entertainment, he mused.

She intrigued him, a combination of virtue and passion, brightness and determination. He was given to wonder how she had gained so much insight in her short, impoverished life. He thought hardship would have stolen such kind consideration for those helpless and hopeless beings whom most viewed as a burden and plague on their conscience. Yet, he felt the need to ask one last question, perhaps to measure the total depth of her reasoning.

"And what of the very old, damoiselle? What of the sick or bedridden who can no longer teach or speak or even rise from their pallets?"

LeClaire's eyes dropped to her hands, and Borgia thought she must be seeing those of whom he spoke in her mind's eye, for her look was troubled. "When one has walked this life in vigor and given all he has," she began softly, " 'tis time we minister to his needs. The pot still hangs there, my lord. His family, his friends, those he has served well his life long can prove their worthiness by fetching his meal and tending his cot. He has earned his rest and the right to be treated with dignity."

LeClaire glanced up to see Borgia watching her with an unsettling intensity, as if he would strip away her mantle of truth to find fault beneath. His eyes were charcoal gray in the darkened room, his thoughts unfathomable. The hint of a smile clung to his strong lips, but it was wry and did little to soften his harsh features. Her breath snared in her throat when his hand reached out to lift a curl of firelight from her shoulder and rub the silken strands between his fingers absently, his eyes never leaving hers.

Skittish at his nearness and probing gaze, LeClaire pulled back. Her hand rose to retrieve the length of hair, but he wound it around his wrist until it tugged gently against her scalp. She was helpless to understand his actions, and waited for . . . she knew not for what she waited, and cautioned herself to tread lightly until she did. She shivered from the contact but continued to stare up at him, wondering from the rumors she had heard what Norman women saw in him that made them give up their hearts and souls into his reckless keeping.

He was handsome in a bold way, his face fine and strong, his presence commanding attention. Mayhaps that's what drew them, the power, the sovereignty, the nimbus of dominion he exuded, but it frightened LeClaire. Her hard but uncluttered life had been shattered by his coming, and his presence here was nothing less than the destruction of her future.

Her eyes dropped to his hand. His jeweled cuff sparkled in the firelight against his bronzed skin, too rich and finely made to cover such merciless strength. Her gaze lifted over the soft velvet past wide shoulders to his mouth, and she thought of Tobias's mutilated back. One word from those firm lips had brought irrevocable scars to a strong, honorable man. She sickened at the thought and her eyes lifted farther to clash with his.

Gray eyes, frosty as winter gloaming, stared back at her with a chilling and penetrating insight. She sensed that escape was impossible, mayhaps even foolish, but she longed to move away from him without impunity, to stand before him with the strength of her emotions and condemn him to his face.

The conflict roiled within her as his fingers flexed in her hair then went quiet. He made no threat, yet his very stillness was a threat unto itself. And LeClaire knew not why his silence suddenly made her want to protect herself as his ultimatums had not.

"Why are you here?" she asked, the words coming desperate and raspy from a dry throat. "Why is Ravenwood so necessary to you? Haven't you enough without taking all I own?"

Borgia merely stared at her for the space of two heartbeats. Born to wealth but not as a titled eldest son, he had made his own way by his wits and the sword, fighting beside William as one of the Conqueror's most trusted companions. But he was done fighting, had reached a time in his life when he was weary of his wandering and warring way and ready to carve a future out of all his strength had wrought.

"Aye, I've gained much finer lands," he said, "but none are privately owned. Some men are well content to rule in their father's shadow or pay knight service to a liege lord. I am not. With these lands I serve only the King. So, you see, damoiselle, Ravenwood is more necessary to me than all the rest combined."

LeClaire wanted to bury her face in her hands and weep like a babe at the utter finality of his words, but she only stared back at him, hurting soul-deep yet determined he would never bear witness to such weakness.

He tugged once on her hair, then released it, going still when LeClaire winced. " 'Tis time to retire," he said curtly and took a step back from the fire of her hair, the gentle perfection of her skin, the damnable compassion in her voice that called softly to a bone-tired warrior until he was caught, until he ached with the need to rest his head upon her breast and let her words give him ease. *Careful, St. Brieuc, you grow boringly poetic over the chit.*

His eyes narrowed as he swept her length with the thoroughness of a buyer inspecting livestock for purchase, but for all her shabbiness he did not find her lacking. She was his for the taking—by right of conquest, by right of lordship—and no one would take issue with those rights save the girl herself, who had no voice in the matter. But he did not take innocent children—even if that child proved to be an appealing young woman.

" 'Tis time to retire," he said again, and touched her shoulder possessively as if to usher her along.

LeClaire shied away from his hand and wondered horribly if she would ever come to terms with this man who was one moment cold and implacable, the next all courtesy and sophistication. He seemed to see things, know things outside the realm of her experience, yet there was a dearth of common emotion there with which to gauge his temperament. And there was not an ounce of purity inside him.

His hand rose again, and she took another step back, knowing not if he meant to escort her or force her to achieve his goal. "The hall needs cleaning," she said.

His lean fingers encircled her upper arm. "There are others to do slaves' work."

LeClaire went still as stone beneath his touch, unwilling to test the extent of his equanimity. "I am but little else," she said without self-pity, "when there are so few who abide here."

Borgia sent her a droll frown. "Why have you not gathered more women from the village to see to the needs here?"

"There is naught more than aging men and women and young babes. The hardier men went to fight with Harold; their widows have their own troubles keeping the land tended and their wee ones fed. I would not ask more than they can give."

"Foolish maid," he said with lazy contempt for her reasoning. "If you fiercely cling to your right as lady of Ravenwood, then you must set yourself above them. 'Tis not your place to toil as one of their rank."

"Then whose?" LeClaire asked softly. Though his words might well have angered her, they did not. No one but her mother had ever worried over the long, arduous hours she and her sisters labored. That this cold knight would show the slightest bit of concern, even steeped in ridicule, sent unaccustomed warmth through her—she who had been the one her family and people turned to, she who'd had to be strong and unfailing, having to hide her fears lest they all be overwhelmed by them.

But she would do well not to let it go to her head. To live the easy, unfettered life of the nobility was something far outside her grasp. Now more so than ever.

"Do you profess to make a slave of me, my lord, then scorn me for doing that which must be done?" she asked.

Borgia laughed lightly. "Nay, bratling, but I would be remiss in my duties as lord if I worked you unto death. What good would you be to me then?"

Oh! his words rankled, as he knew they would. The composure which had been so much a part of her life seemed to have vanished since his coming, and LeClaire felt again the prostrating anger so foreign to her. Coupled with despair she found it nearly impossible to contain. Unfair that he who lacked for nothing should take everything! Her fists tightened at her sides, and she snatched her arm from his grasp as her mouth opened to decry his mastery.

As if divining her intention, Borgia pressed a calloused finger to her lips, and the feel of him, strong yet deceptively gentle, strangled the words in her throat.

"Never gainsay your lord, damoiselle," he warned. "Thy thoughts will earn you a flogging if spoken aloud."

His fingers splayed across her cheek to curl under and cup her chin firmly as his thumb lightly traced her full lower lip. LeClaire gasped and jerked her head back, but his hold was unbreakable. His touch was warm and strong against her flesh and, like the man, it was too unmanageable and unpredictable for her inexperienced mind. She knew not what he would do or why, and her heart raced with a dreadful uncertainty that threatened to turn to high panic. In a self-protective gesture, she swung her head sharply to the side to escape his hold, but his fingers only tightened.

Like a wisp of fog upon the night-darkened moor, her bravery evaporated, leaving naught to stand in her stead save the empty chilled air. Never had she felt so alone when the keep housed thrice times the number of people customary, thrice times the danger. She stared up at him, her throat tight, and waited.

With a slow, caressing flex of his fingers and an inscrutable expression on his face, Borgia released her. LeClaire took a hasty step back and offered him a stiff smile followed by a graceful curtsy, which held little courtesy and less respect.

"Truly thy wisdom is great, my lord. As you have commanded, I will take leave of you . . . and yon mess."

She spun on her heel and had departed the hall before Borgia realized the subtle bite of her words. The discarded remains of the evening meal littered the room; smoldering remnants of stew clung to the sides of the heavy pot; drinking horns and chalices lay overturned. And his men, damn their worthless souls, snored drunkenly from their pallets. And in all of Christendom, Borgia was certain, there was not a serving maid to be found.

5

The air held a biting crispness that stung LeClaire's cheeks and caused her to wrap her arms more securely about herself as she returned from the village. The empty herb basket hooked on her arm bumped rhythmically against her hip with each hurried step she took on her errand to replenish it.

There had been a warm breeze earlier in the week, and she had set the villeins to preparing the land for sowing barley, oats and beans. The change in weather had also brought with it many illnesses of the lungs, and her limited knowledge of the healing arts was much in demand. But, perfidious as a testy old matron, the weather had turned cranky once again, spewing out arctic blasts of swollen, wet air.

She searched for the tender green buds that would herald spring, but there was no hint today as her feet crunched across the frost-spangled ground that the winter months were bending to the passing of time. Dark clouds hung low, ready to drop their freezing contents on a land already numbed by cold. LeClaire thought it fitting that the day was as bleak as her thoughts and believed her entire world reflected the dreariness that had befallen her since Borgia's coming.

He and his men had inhabited Ravenwood for a fortnight, a mere fourteen days that felt more like a lifetime to the girl who had found it a constant battle to mediate between her people and the Normans. Confusion had beset the hall in those first few days whenever LeClaire was away, so she had attempted to stay within the walls of the keep as much as possible, soothing and consoling and trying to keep the peace among her loyal servants and the demanding knights. But, more like than not, her duties took her to the village much of the time.

There was always so much to do, so much to oversee. Grievances listened to, ills tended, cleaning done and meals prepared, the making of candles, soap and linen. Serfs had to be sent to the wasteland to gather litter for animals and thatch for roofing, furze and turf for fuel and tree toppings as winter browse for livestock. Others were sent to the woodland for timber and to gather acorns or beechnuts as food for the pigs, which, in turn, provided food for the people. Those few knowledgeable in healing were sent to the marshes to gather wild herbs for medicine, or if need be she went herself.

The first few days had been the worst—desperate days full of violence, saturated with the blood and cries of her people. Confused and frightened, the servants had been sluggish about following Borgia's orders, stalling for time until they could obtain LeClaire's direction. They had done it out of a sense of affinity for their lady and no small amount of rebellion, but Borgia's wrath had fallen heavily upon them, and all quickly learned how ruthless he could be when faced with disobedience.

No one was immune, neither man nor woman nor youngest child. Unable to endure their pain, LeClaire had begged the villagers to keep safe by obeying the new lord.

It had been so difficult for them, for she had never used force when she sat in judgment. In some ways her manner was more direct. If accused and brought before her, the guilty would pay recompense or be banned from Ravenwood to take his laziness or sorrow to some other township. She had little use for troublemakers or those who could not work in harmony with others. If her numbers were not great, the villeins were at least hardworking and honest. There was little crime and disruption in her well-ordered world, naught more than petty squabbles. The people were unused to harsh punishment, and it had taken days for them to realize there would be no open rebellion here. The end had come quickly, and it had not been LeClaire's words of caution but Borgia's wrath that had bought their subservience.

If LeClaire had little use for troublemakers, Borgia de St. Brieuc had even less. He needed every man to achieve the potential he saw in Ravenwood, and he would see them crushed or prospered but naught else.

Though a silent rebellion prevailed, a semblance of peace settled about Ravenwood by the end of the second week. LeClaire learned to anticipate the added needs of supporting so many, and in turn, Borgia recognized the benefit of her presence in the hall. Tasks were performed without issue and the atmosphere was much calmer, but her self-assigned duties of seeing to the sick, overseeing the clearing and planting and every other facet of life at Ravenwood still took her off to the village, and he had begun to command her to let others perform those chores he considered menial or better suited to another.

She tried to obey his orders, but her innate sense of responsibility would not allow her to sit back idly and leave to chance the things that needed to be done. When she had arrived at Ravenwood, she found what little land used had been planted by individuals as garden plots. Since none had been left to lie fallow, the nutrients were slowly being sapped, the yield poor, the villeins starving.

Her uncle, what little she knew of him from childhood stories, had been a quiet man, given to deep thought and eccentricity. Although a great lover of the science of horticulture, he had not been a farmer. LeClaire had arrived at Ravenwood to find that other than the lavish garden cloister he had begun in monastic style, he had been mismanaging the land as a whole in the style of the Roman Britons whose high material civilization had little use for crop development. In essence, he had purchased everything he needed.

LeClaire had no more coin for buying goods than the impoverished villagers, and set about immediately to change things. By her direction, tracts of land were assigned to the people for cultivation. They were divided into strips, the size determined by what a peasant could plow in one day, usually two parallel furrows. Assessing the needs of all, she told them what to plant and where, when to harvest, what to store, then took a share to support Ravenwood keep. It had become the pattern of her days, the security of sameness, accomplishment the reward.

It was the same with the livestock, the mill, the tannery and other areas of Ravenwood. Without money, bartering was the only means she had of purchasing salt for seasoning and preserving from Cheshire, and iron for tools from Kent. It had seemed to LeClaire a workable solution and had proved somewhat prosperous, but Borgia had taken issue with her involvement and his words of a sennight ago still rang clearly in her ears.

"You make idiots of the people by not allowing them to think or make decisions for themselves," he had said. "And you make them lazy because they see no need to do more than you request."

LeClaire had been dumbfounded and hurt. It had ever been her nature to delegate authority to no one else, and though she continued to see to the needs of her people with unfailing devotion, his words weighed heavy on her mind and heart.

When she had come to Ravenwood, so young and afraid and alone, the task before her had been overwhelming. But survival had risen strong within her, as had the need to overcome and rise above her lot in life. She had used what knowledge she possessed, then expanded upon it, learning everything she could in an effort to make life better for her sisters and the villagers. The people had been confused since the old lord's death and seemed eager enough to let LeClaire take control.

And now St. Brieuc claimed she was doing too much. LeClaire paused and glanced at the churning sky. Mayhaps he was right, for she was exhausted by the end of each day and fairly crawled to her room after the evening meal to say nightly prayers before collapsing on her cot. Many a night she had awakened in the early haze just before dawn still on her knees, her head slumped upon her pallet. But how did one change lifelong habits, the labor of love for those who depended on her? Borgia argued she did too much, but as LeClaire crossed the fields of Ravenwood daily, saw the neglect and poverty, she knew it had never been enough.

Though the threat of freezing rain hovered near, this day was no different. She had settled numerous disputes in the hall, for the villagers were afraid to bring their woes to the new lord. When Borgia had gone out early to dispense justice, he found naught but peace in the land, no brawling villeins to be clapped in the stocks until sundown, no lads in the corn bin, and he had moved on to survey the noisy falcon house before returning to other matters. And LeClaire had breathed a sigh of relief; there would be no violence done this day.

She quickened her stride to escape the cold and hurried toward the walled garden, one of the few places of sanctuary to be found now at Ravenwood where she could turn her back on the hostile, barbaric world. Borgia stood with his men at the quintain, the area he had set aside for military exercise, and watched as she approached.

He thought she looked weary though the day was young. There were dark circles under her eyes and a hollow look in their blue depths. She assumed he knew nothing of the villeins' troubles, when in truth there was naught that escaped him. Let them ply their woes to the lady—their foolish, headstrong lady—she would learn. If the lesson be painful or gentle, it would be her own choosing, but she would learn.

Her cheeks were wan, her walk brisk as she crossed the brittle ground. Only the flaming color of LeClaire's hair gave life to her pale face. Huddled in her thin cloak, her shoulders hunched against the frigid winds, she looked like an urchin in need of shelter. The wind caught a lock of her hair and tossed it into the air. Like a suspended ribbon of fire, it swirled on the playful breeze, then dipped and finally came to rest on her breast, a vivid contrast to the dull brown of her cloak.

Roger paused mid-sentence to note Borgia's unusual reaction to the fiery dance of a single lock of hair and sent his lord an inquiring look. Borgia's icy gray eyes seared across his face, cauterizing off any question Amiens might have asked. Roger's mouth snapped shut but he continued his bemused expression as the lord of Ravenwood left the quintain without orders or explanation and headed in the girl's direction.

"Damoiselle."

LeClaire paused, then quickened her pace as if she had not heard the call, increasingly amazed by the dangerous spark of revolt within her whenever she encountered him. It was disconcerting when she had always been so serene, even in adverse circumstances, and she wondered what other hidden natures would be called forth before this intolerable situation with the Normans was resolved. Hoping Borgia would not be inclined to follow her, she slipped through a gate set between hedges of thorn, sweetbrier and yew, gaining entrance into her garden where she could seek its replenishing powers.

For two years now, it was here that she sought refuge and strength, here that the enormous responsibilities of being Ravenwood's mistress were allowed to fade so that she might gain perspective and renew her spirit.

The walled meadow was large and well shadowed with budding trees that pledged blossy green boughs soon. Portable wattle fences protected tender young plants from foraging animals and inconsiderate footsteps. The barriers constructed of vines woven between stakes were not particularly durable, but they were easily built and inexpensive. In the center, like a gracious old queen residing over her court, sat a well from which to drink, a cistern for watering or bathing and a tub for holding fish during the Lenten season.

Vaguely patterned after the Monastery of St. Gall, the kitchen portion for vegetables and herbs had been added off to the side by LeClaire in an effort to make Ravenwood self-sufficient and existed in an orderly fashion like soldiers lined up for duty. Beds of lentil, cabbage, onion, turnip, garlic and shallot ran side by side with parsley, chervil, savory, parsnip, leeks and coriander. In the third row grew the dill, poppy, carrot, beet, celery, and radish.

But there the appearance of organization ended, for in the middle around the central wellhead was the large pleasure garden where fruit and nut trees flourished seemingly at random.

LeClaire slowed her steps, for one could not walk here in haste, not among such soothing splendor. Woodbine ran along the hedges while quinces, pears, plums, hazelnuts and almonds stood their gracefully majestic places among the other fruit and nut trees. All were necessary for physical nourishment, but for the nourishment of the senses were the strawberries, roses, lilies, columbines and daisies.

Off to the other side, well away from the kitchen plants that they not be mistaken and picked as such, was the physic garden of herbs used for medicinal purposes. Peppermint, rosemary, sage, pennyroyal, fennel, tansy and cumin were only a few of the healing plants in abundance. LeClaire suspected her uncle had spent much time in this vast cloister, for it was the only spot at Ra-

venwood that had shown the care of a loving hand when
she arrived. And it did not lack for attention now.

It was mayhaps one of the few things in her life that
LeClaire was selfish about. Like her hour in the crumbling stone chapel where she said morning prayers, she
also gave time to this garden, time that might have been
spent elsewhere attending to the never-ending tasks.
Here she found asylum, much needed peace and beauty
even in the winter months when the walled yard was
only a promise of what it would become in the spring. Its
worth to her was as immeasurable now as it had been
two years ago.

Always she was brought back to the simple sentiment
penned by Abbot Walafrid Strabo, of Ruchenau Abbey, in
the ninth century. His words, though plain, had a rhythm
and stark gracefulness that spoke eloquently of his love
and devotion to the necessity of such a haven. He frankly
urged one to get a garden, what kind mattered not, proclaiming the various joys and the worthwhile endeavor
of gaining practical knowledge of nature's domain. Le-
Claire had harkened to his words, finding the garden
useful for her inquisitive and practical mind, while it
also supplied her need for peace and serenity.

"Damoiselle, I require a moment of your time."

LeClaire flinched when she heard the voice—too
strong, too commanding—and fought the urge to dash
into hiding like an errant child. As if the clouds had become rulers of the sky, her world darkened and she
paused, wishing the sun were not such a fickle thing to
play hide-and-seek when physically and emotionally she
needed its restorative warmth.

She refused to face the intruder, offended by his presence in her place of retreat. Among the apples, figs and
medlars, she needed not to hear another complaint this
morn. Not from him, and not here where the beauty of
iris and hollyhocks would grow with special care in a
raised bed, where imported carnations, citrus fruits, tu-

lips and spices from the Holy Land had been brought as gifts to her uncle at great personal expense by Crusaders.

She stirred the ground with the toe of her serviceable leather slipper, mentally tired of confrontation and physically exhausted from lack of sleep. To have to deal with the new lord of Ravenwood placed another pall upon an already gloomy day, and there was so much yet to be done before she could seek her rest.

The empty herb basket snagged on a thread of her kirtle, reminding her that Ruth was aggravated as usual with stiff joints and phantom head pains and Thomas must needs have his boils lanced again. She'd also found no time of late to visit Oswulf, a landless old Saxon knight nearly blind now in his dotage, and listen to his many stories as if she had not heard them a thousand times.

Time permitting she would seek out Oswulf, Ruth, Thomas and many others this day—time permitting. LeClaire glanced again at the boiling sky. Time permitting, weather permitting, strength permitting. Nay, she needed not to hear another complaint from Borgia de St. Brieuc this morn.

She stiffened when she felt his strong hand upon her shoulder and turned slowly to face him, feeling the faint tremors of dread that always accompanied his presence. How much longer would he allow her and her sisters a place in the hall? How soon before he turned them out or reduced them to the lowest level of humanity—slaves with no rights, no choices.

The wind whispered its ageless song through the naked trees, and LeClaire went still as sudden affirmation bathed her atmosphere. *Goodness and mercy will follow you all the days of your life.*

Aye, she agreed silently out of firm commitment when deep within she could no longer feel any optimism. Her gaze lifted to the lowering, bloated clouds and she knew that beyond what her vision allowed, beyond what her mortal eyes could see, there was a bright and vast blue sky, open and brilliant and infinite. Her eyes drifted closed for the barest second, and she let the warmth of the words flood her, knowing there was no goodness or mercy in becoming a slave, hence no reason to believe it was her fate.

Her eyes opened again to see Borgia staring at her, his outward appearance so like the Guardian she was almost moved to approach him, yet his inward self so opposite she was repelled back a step. The cords of conflict and confusion tugged at her, pulling her mind in too many directions to condense her thoughts into anything rational. Though she tried to stop the faithless fear, denounce it as groundless when she had her faith to cling to, she still found her thoughts a fretful traitor to her beliefs. How long would her usefulness serve the Lion, and would it be long enough for her mother's secret to be revealed? Oh, aye, it must be.

"Good morrow, damoiselle," Borgia said, all polite civility.

"There is sickness in the village," LeClaire explained, inching away with the hope he would not detain her.

"But I require a moment of your time."

She knew the request for what it was—a demand that she best not disobey. He had been as ruthless with his tongue as with the lash over the past two weeks, his stinging reprimands delivered as easily as he did all else, swift and decisive. He never raised his voice and was all the more dangerous for his subtlety. Cunning and brilliant in everything he did, he made commands that sounded like requests, lulling one to think there was room for discussion when, in truth, he expected complete loyalty and compliance. There was no space for argument.

But LeClaire had tried on many occasions to disagree with him. He always listened attentively, his gray eyes alert and compassionate as if her opinion was of utmost importance, then had gone about his original plans, leaving her thwarted, confused and angry.

She knew she trod dangerous ground by gainsaying him on this command or any other. In his eyes and the eyes of all, she was no longer lady of Ravenwood, but in her heart and soul where her devotion still shone brightly despite her circumstance, she remembered the Scriptures. *Faith is the substance of things hoped for, the evidence of things not seen.* She could see with her eyes that he held Ravenwood, but her hopes stayed firmly rooted in her faith and, God willing, she would one day see it restored to her.

Thus she faced him, resigned to the fact that, for the moment at least, there was no other option available to her. "I am at your disposal, my lord."

"Really?" he asked. "But to what extent?"

LeClaire did not deign to answer a comment she could not unravel for its hidden meaning, though she sensed there was one. A gust of icy wind sent her cloak flapping open, causing her to shiver, and she hurried to pull it together. Borgia eyed her briefly, a nondescript look on his face, then, in one lithe movement, removed the thick dark blue mantle from his shoulders and draped it over hers. Though the rich garment just reached his knees, it trailed nearly to LeClaire's ankles. Well made and heavy, it smelled faintly of the man. And without a doubt, it was the warmest thing she had ever known.

Like the dawning of a forgotten memory, her senses awakened to the outdoors scent of earth and wind, the manly tang of wool and leather—common smells that caused an uncommon restlessness within her. Startled, she almost flung it from her shoulders, but paused, her mind awash with turmoil, trepidation . . . and wonder. Why had he done such a thing? She lifted her eyes hesitantly to question him.

Ah, bratling, take care. Every emotion shows on your face. Is there no coyness, no subtlety in aught that you do?

Have you no ageless feminine instincts with which to sur-vive this world?

Borgia's eyes harbored a cold and hard silver glint as he stood over her. "I have seen the falconer," he said, though her thoughts on the subject were of no real concern to him. He merely wanted to inform her of his actions so there would be no question later. More like than not his words would cause another rift between them as she sought to defend one of her people. At times he enjoyed sparring with her over some small matter, for she was a formidable little opponent with her logical allegations, untutored bravery and abject loyalty. This morn, however, he was in no mood to listen to her claims. "I've replaced the fowl keeper with one of my own men."

"I see . . ." LeClaire took a deep, stabilizing breath, her slender shoulders lifting and falling beneath the heavy mantle. There had been so many changes since his coming, so many worthy ones, she admitted, though it pained her to do so. A portion of his army had been sent on to his other lands, but those retainers who remained were building cottages in the village and opening shops of trade.

Already the paltry, scum-coated drainage ditch around Ravenwood was being enlarged and would eventually become a protective moat. The ramparts were being repaired and added to, stones piled for a wall to eventually separate an inner and outer courtyard, an armory established in the keep.

Soldiers had been provided to help the villagers repair their impoverished cottages with Borgia bearing the cost of materials. Pasture land had been set aside for the enormous destriers, and more livestock added to the wasteland, which provided brushwood for rough grazing. Hills unsuitable for cultivating were turned over to the sheep, which had been grazing in the village common meadow, and though she knew not what he had in mind now for the meadowland, she was certain it would prove, like all else, worthwhile.

LeClaire suppressed a disgruntled sigh, and fought to keep the bitter envy from destroying what little peace remained in her tattered life. She had never been selfish, knew the changes benefited all, but it was hard to look upon them—the reflection of her own inadequacies. She sighed again, a sadness unlike any she had ever felt creeping in to cloud the wondrous changes Borgia's lordship had wrought. She had not been able to do in two years what he had begun in only two weeks. That she had never had the wherewithal to pay and feed enough men to begin the improvements seemed insignificant at the moment, and she felt peevish for begrudging the people their newfound prosperity.

And now the falconer. Another worthy change, a welcome one. She felt galled and embarrassed by her impotency in yet another important concern. The falcons, with their strong curved beaks and long sickle-shaped claws, were birds of prey. Allied to the hawk, they were bred and trained for hunting wild fowl and were necessary in helping to provide Ravenwood with meat.

"My thanks," she said stiffly. "The man, Alberic he is called, has been a thorn in my side since I arrived here. I knew the poor birds were ill-cared for, but I had no one to replace him. He has been warned time and again, my lord, but I had little recourse in the matter."

"Ah," Borgia purred, with the barest hint of a smile, "you are offering me your gratitude?"

LeClaire instantly bristled at the suggestion, then realized it would profit her naught and forced herself to calm. But she had little to be grateful for with his forceful presence controlling every corner of her life. She was losing the villagers to his generosity and prosperity, but could fault them not for accepting and flourishing with the very things she had wished to give them. Swallowing

her inadequacies was a bitter draft, but she did it for
their sake.

"Alberic has a child I worry over, but as far as the
birds are concerned, I am grateful."

Borgia's lips lifted in a cynical smile. That she did not
sound it in the least was not lost on him, but that she
accepted the value of his action was clearly defined in
her silence. She would have argued with him had it been
otherwise. She would not have swayed his decision once
made, but she would have tried. Her gentle stubbornness
awarded her a measure of esteem in his eyes, even as he
knew it would eventually be her downfall.

This marked the first time they had agreed openly on
any issue, though Borgia found her most proficient in
running Ravenwood. He'd had to make few enough
changes due to her penchant for cleanliness, organization and dedication to hard work. Without the strength of
coin or laborers, she had done well, and he had concen-
trated mainly on those things she had been incapable of
doing. And in truth he enjoyed watching her curiosity
expand with each new improvement, her insatiable thirst
for knowledge as she asked a thousand questions concerning each endeavor. She never asked him directly,
but spent hours drilling his men on the what and where-
fore of each modification.

"It seems we have been at cross purposes much of the
time, bratling," Borgia said. "Though our goals are the
same, I think."

"Mayhaps," LeClaire murmured reluctantly, "but 'tis
hard for me to admit it." If there was one thing she
clearly disliked, it was to hear him calling her "bratling"
as if she were a child, and she even more disliked the
way he said it, possessively, as if his ownership of her
were stamped on parchment. The idea brought to mind
another document, her mother's legacy, and LeClaire
smiled softly, hopefully.

The wistful gesture lightened her countenance,

changed her somber features and erased the signs of fatigue Borgia had noticed of late. Until now, she had never turned that arresting smile on him, though she was quick enough with it for her sisters and the village children.

And there was no artifice or womanly wile about it now, naught to encourage a man to look beyond what was offered. The girl knew nothing of flirtations and dalliances but was honest and virtuous to a fault. She was, he thought with sardonic wickedness, as unspoiled as a newling lamb. But for all that it was nothing but a simple smile, as sweet and radiant as a child's, it suddenly held the force of an alluring and accomplished courtesan.

Borgia's eyes narrowed intriguingly upon her. *What have we here? Lust for a babe? Careful, St. Brieuc, you grow intolerable.*

His gaze wandered over the slight form swallowed up in his cloak, and he made no excuse for his momentary lapse in concentration. But he would not forget. Nay, he would never forget that for the first time in his life he had been caught unguarded by something so inconsequential.

He inclined his head to her. "It occurs to me that we did not have one disagreement yesterday."

"Aye." LeClaire shrugged. "Miracles are well known in these parts."

Her dry wit brought an odd glint to his eyes and wrung a slight chuckle from him. LeClaire thought the sound, full and rich, a competent reflection of the man. Even in laughter, his strength was pronounced, and there was no denying the power and authority he wielded over all their lives.

The eyes that lazily studied her were like polished granite now, unlike their usual storm gray. Mayhaps she was too used to the seriousness of life, or merely tired of the battle between them, but for whatever reason, Le-

Claire found his easy mirth appealing. He did not look so fierce, so threatening, when he smiled. He did not—

Her thoughts came to a staggering halt and she shivered. He did not look so very different from the Guardian.

The light in her eyes dimmed; a dull pain settled in her heart and a mournful sigh escaped her. Yes, he was different. No angel of light but a dark parody—a counterforce of all that was good and trustworthy.

As her smile faded, Borgia grew watchful and intense, assuming exhaustion once again claimed her. There was no sympathy in him for her plight. She brought much misery upon herself with her constant lordship over people who should know their duties by now. Soon, soon she would learn.

"If this peace continues, methinks we should have a spring festival," he tossed out carelessly to see if she could be enticed by the suggestion. Her sober countenance did not brighten, but it mattered little. A bit of frivolity was good for the morale of his men after a hard winter. *And for you,* he added, wondering if she mourned a carefree childhood, or if her life had always been filled with toil. "Would you be opposed to such an idea?"

"Nay." LeClaire hesitated, her expression showing confusion. It was the first time he had asked her opinion, and she was at a loss to give it when she knew nothing about such things. "What is this festival of which you speak?"

Borgia's voice grew mildly reproachful. "Have you never been to a celebration? A village fair?"

His tone vaguely implied ignorance or falsehood on her part, and LeClaire felt her lack of experience drag heavy as a millstone about her neck. She watched his dark mantle sway as she stirred her toe in the dirt, feeling the need to explain, repelled by that same need. There was no shame in not having worldly knowledge, but still she felt the weight of it.

"We lived in the Northumberland ere coming to Ravenwood. 'Twas little more than forest, marsh and wild moorland. Traveling to the isolated outpost of the old Anglian settlement was too long a trip to make often. My father usually went alone." She lifted her eyes to his with a stubbornness that denied his right to either pity or ridicule. "Tell me what preparations are needed and I will see to them."

"Nay," Borgia said with a hint of sarcasm. "You labor too hard. 'Tis not my want to overtax you, bratling. The servants can prepare the feast. 'Twill be a time of rest and enjoyment for your sisters and my men."

Rest and enjoyment. She had never known such and could not credit it now, but she nodded to sustain the false peace and made to remove his mantle so that she might continue on with her chores. Borgia reached out to stay her, and LeClaire gasped and stumbled back a step, then seemed to rigidly collect herself.

"Who has ill-used you so?" he asked in a quiet voice, but his eyes were narrowed and hard as his hand purposefully rose then slowly lowered to encircle her upper arm.

LeClaire had learned from an early age to be beware of a man's raised hand. Though her father had never struck her or Aurel or Krya, she and her sisters had seen their mother and Maire bear enough of his brute inequity to make them ever cautious.

But she did not tell Borgia this; she could not. His touch rooted her to the ground. Not because it was harsh, though it was undeniably restraining, but because it comprised a greater portion of gentleness, as if he had her most tender concerns at heart. There was a terrible calling in naught but the circle of his fingers, and she felt a quiver beset her at so profound a reaction at such a simple gesture. Confused, she attempted to pull away, but his hand only tightened.

Her heartbeat stumbled and she froze, not knowing

what she should do. She cared not for contact with this man; it made her feel inexplicably edgy even when lightly applied. She knew his gentleness was a lie, a hideous contradiction meant to unbalance her, for she had seen his brutal force applied to her people. Above all she must remember what he was capable of.

Her eyes wandered down to the fingers gripping her arm. It was a large hand, strong, capable of such destruction. His fingers were long and slender, the nails well kept, also capable of camaraderie when he saluted his men or clapped one of them on the back for a job well done. Unbidden came the memory of those fingers tangled in her hair, his palm cupping her chin, his thumb grazing her lips. She felt the quiver intensify until it shimmied down her arms and backbone.

And she realized that freely given his strength could offer protection, as easily as it promised defeat. The thought bewildered her and caused her mood to go melancholy. Blue eyes, cloudy with question, lifted to meet the steel gray of his.

"Keep the mantle," Borgia said darkly, then released her. The arm beneath his fingers had been thin and firm, like a servant's, not soft and fleshy as the ladies of court. Still, the feel of her, fragile yet strong, compelled him, lingered on in his mind like the cry of a haunting melody one cannot dispel. Sunlight bathed her trim features in muted golden tones, softening and filling the hollows in her cheeks, reflecting the radiance of a deeper, inner peace in her outwardly troubled eyes.

His hand rose slowly to her face, cautious, as one would approach a wary animal, and he watched as she struggled to stand her ground. His knuckles glided down her cheek and neck until she blushed and turned her face away with a small sound.

"Ah, so much discomfort, damoiselle, when I intend no misdeed." Nay, when he planned a seduction the maid knew it well enough and there was no need for missish coloring or maidenly stammers. He let his hand continue to drift lower until it came to rest on the jeweled clasp of his mantle above her breasts.

LeClaire felt the air rush into her lungs as his fingers worked the fastener, and her cheeks heated again at the intimacy of having the service performed for her. Once done he did not remove his hand but fingered the gems one by one, his eyes inscrutable as they gazed into hers.

Uncertainty kicked soundly in her belly, giving rise to the alarm that fluttered with her pulse. She tore her gaze from his and stepped back, anxious to be gone from his presence, but his words again forced her to pause.

"The child, Kyra, is indeed well learned," he said. "I have not fully researched all the accounts yet but all seems in order. I do not like to burden one so young with the chore, but I hesitate to replace her at this time with one of my men when their talents are better used elsewhere."

LeClaire stared at him as if he had gone mad, when in truth it was her own thoughts swirling like airborne leaves in a storm. No man had ever touched her so strangely, but he seemed unaware of the gesture as anything more than commonplace. He did but make idle conversation now, but why he did so was beyond her when he never had before. She nodded like a dullwit for him to continue.

"Maire is a constant source of dissension with her unruly tongue, but I find that she is agreeable to take as much ribbing as she gives. Her lively retorts sharpen the men's wits as they are forced to reply, lest they appear outdone. As long as she does not overstep her bounds, I will not take her to task."

Borgia did not mention the many men who entertained thoughts of lifting the lively vixen's skirts. Much to their displeasure, he had commanded his men to take their leisure on the village women and leave the sisters alone for now. He did not need the aggravation of whining women crying misuse in his household when there were others far more accommodating with the enticement of coin and camp followers aplenty to see to the men's needs.

Borgia pushed the thoughts aside. He was not father nor brother to these girls, but looking at LeClaire's delicate features, alive and compelling with naught but a frigid winter day for diversion, he wondered without any emotion or hesitation if they would be his responsibility soon enough. There were long-range plans to consider, aims and goals to accomplish, and the sisters' continued position as neither slave nor free was untenable. They would eventually have to be reduced to serf or offered protection under his guardianship. He would make no decision hastily, but a decision would have to be made.

His eyes idly traveled the length of LeClaire as if he could see past ragged woolen and thin linen. The sack-like garment bespoke a lack of vanity even more than a lack of coin, hiding whatever feminine delights lay beneath. Even female serfs, gowned no better, postured within their rags to best advantage, cinching their girdles tight, allowing their bodices to dip low. But this one seemed content to be just as she was, and he wondered what a length of velvet or silk stitched properly to fit her would reveal.

LeClaire shifted nervously beside him, wary and uncertain under his regard, and he brought his eyes back to her face. He would not alarm her, and surely his thoughts concerning her at this moment would do so if spoken aloud. Instead he smiled coolly and returned to their conversation.

" 'Tis the lady Aurel," he said. "She is not about the hall much. Has she taken ill?"

A look of deep sadness flitted across LeClaire's face, then was quickly covered. She needed not his concern, certainly not his pity. "Nay, lord, not ill. Aurel is not comfortable with strangers. Because she does not oft speak, people assume she cannot hear . . . or that her mind is weak. She has been subjected to much ugly teasing."

Borgia's expression never wavered but his voice was stern. "If any of my men—"

"Nay." LeClaire stopped his words by placing her small hand on his chest. The gesture was impulsive, given without forethought, but at the feel of unyielding strength, she jerked the hand away and clasped it with her other. He was solid as a stone fortress beneath his leather tunic and just as formidable. His bronze face suddenly grew closed and tight, and LeClaire felt her nerves twist at the hard look in his eyes. Self-conscious, she tried to avoid those eyes, her fingers twining about themselves absently as she stammered, "Y . . . your guards have been naught but considerate, though Aurel steers clear of all men when she can. 'Twas the soldiers sent on to your other lands who caused her most recent grief."

She shook her head when his expression grew colder and, as was her nature, reached out a consoling hand though she did not dare touch him again. "Nay, my lord. Do not concern yourself over this. Aurel would not want so much attention directed her way. This kind of treatment is not new to her. In truth, methinks it hurts me and her other sisters more than it does Aurel." Her voice grew soft with an understanding and acceptance gleaned from years of dealing with the injustices of life, and her eyes begged him to heed her plea. " 'Tis best to leave it be. One would not think it, my lord, but Aurel can be most put out when aggrieved. We will handle this ourselves."

Borgia had the disgusting urge to snort at her naïveté. Handle it themselves? She and the others would have been flat on their backs beneath his men many times over by now were they not protected by his orders. How much she needed to learn, how much she needed to realize that the world she viewed behind an immaculate veil of innocence was in reality a many colored pool of vagary and caprice that ran both hot and cold, predictable only in its unreliability.

There were no delusions in Borgia's own life, no room for them. He knew well the pettiness of men, as well as their vindictiveness. Because of the wealth and nobility of the St. Brieuc name, then his own strength as he grew to manhood, none had ever dared ridicule him. But these maidens had no such defense against common cruelty. Men were slaves to their urges, contained only by respect or fear. And LeClaire, with her soothing smile and the jeweled brilliance of her hair and eyes, held their regard with neither.

Oh, they desired her. Some wistfully contemplated wooing her when she'd turn those enormous blue eyes their way in some soft witticism or compliment. Others were moved more by base instincts and would have tumbled her against a floor or wall without remembering her name once done. But all left her alone by command, not by the trust she had placed in them. She feared the men's presence at Ravenwood, but she knew not to fear the men themselves.

"I hear your words, mite," Borgia said, "but if Aurel is unduly set upon by the inconsiderate louts, I will take matters into my own hands. Is that understood?"

"Aye," she said softly. Though his tone was firm with the order, something behind the command soothed the unhappiness within LeClaire, made her feel safe and strangely warm in a way she had never known. Ever the provider, the protector, she was unused to having another come to her sister's defense. It felt . . . odd, as if someone had heaved a sack of grain from her shoulders instead of making her carry it.

Her heart quavered and a tingle along her limbs gave rise to gooseflesh. She would have liked to hold the feeling close, to keep it locked away as if it were a rare and precious treasure to be taken out and gazed upon from time to time.

With the swiftness of a dove in flight, a melody of old suddenly tinkled through the budding trees, a reminder, a keepsake, as the sun battled the clouds to bathe the garden spot in warming rays. LeClaire lifted her face heavenward to catch the warmth and listened, a dreamy contented smile touching her lips.

"Do you hear it?" she whispered in awe, absorbing the sun and the song. " 'Tis the aria of angels."

Borgia eyed her askance, noting the undiluted joy of a smile unearthly in its radiance. His own smile was derisive. " 'Tis but the wind, bratling. Do you grow fanciful?"

LeClaire's face fell as the clouds rushed in to steal the light and a chill swept through her. The seraph's descant faded, leaving an emptiness within her. Nay, she could not afford to be fanciful at this point. Things had not changed. If the new lord had lifted the weight of Aurel's troubles for a moment, there were still many more burdens to carry, and she was not truly safe as long as Borgia de St. Brieuc laid claim to her holdings.

"There is much to do," she said and stepped away, uncertain how to proceed with him. "I have tarried too long. Good day, my lord."

Borgia watched as she walked quickly toward the physic garden, his cloak billowing out around her like a great winged beast, as if it would devour her. An odd and strained restlessness suddenly moved throughout his body with startling force and potency, then went ominously still to settle dark and humorless within him.

6

The great, neglected hall of Ravenwood was undergoing tremendous changes. LeClaire had ever been fastidious in keeping it clean and free from fleas and lice, but she had not been able to accomplish even a portion of the renovations now being done with all haste. The cracks were being filled, the rotted wood replaced, more sleeping rooms repaired.

Yet, for all the wondrous transformations, LeClaire was appalled. She had not known when Borgia spoke so glibly of a festival the amount of food-stock necessary to accommodate such a feast. Already distressed by the extra provisions needed to feed the increased number of men at Ravenwood, she now knew a fear as deep and unsettling as any since Borgia's coming. Her storehouses would be depleted rapidly if his plans were to be carried out as ordered, and by spring's end they would all be starving.

Much as Borgia warned her against interfering LeClaire could not help but involve herself in the preparations. She fussed and fretted without ceasing over the long days, at last becoming a pleading little tyrant as more and more of her stored goods were requested for dishes so elaborate she'd never even heard of them. But she could not stand back and allow everything she and the villagers had toiled for to be squandered on one day's pleasure.

Borgia followed LeClaire's interference with cool amusement that was quickly turning to dark cynicism. He and his men would continue to hunt game through the winter, and whatever else was needed he would purchase to increase the larder. He was not without coin as was LeClaire, but saw no need to explain himself when his word should be followed without question.

Yet, she would not be stilled, and those closest to the new lord of Ravenwood were not deceived by his indulgence. They knew a confrontation was in the offing. Like storm clouds gathering in the distance, the time was ripening when she would push too far, and they all watched as their lord waited, much as a predator watching his prey, for the moment of reckoning.

"Enough," Borgia demanded softly, too softly for LeClaire to immediately recognize the inherent danger behind his words when she refused to hand over the key to the storage closet for the third time that day. His men stared in silence from the long-tables in the main hall, stunned that the girl would deny any request St. Brieuc made and uneasy because they knew well that shaded tone of voice. The Lion was done, and now she would pay. "You try my patience," he warned silkily as she shook her head. "Give Roger the key and get thyself from my sight."

"Nay," LeClaire said with a composure that was quickly fleeing her. She knew to the last morsel what was stored, but she knew of no way to replace what had already been used up. " 'Twill be a lean spring," she continued a bit stubbornly, a bit hysterically. "You mustn't take more for this one feast. 'Tis foolish to use up everything on one simple pleasure and starve for it later."

She stood her ground with staunch determination, a veritable fortress of righteous intentions as Borgia approached her, his eyes cold and intent on the fight. But when his hand lashed out to snatch the key from her clutched fingers, her good intentions fled as swiftly as a startled doe, and LeClaire panicked. Having no pocket or purse for safekeeping, she took a hurried step back and dropped the key down the front of her kirtle where it lodged between her breasts.

Borgia's eyes widened only briefly, then narrowed as a slow, devilish grin spread across his face. He began to chuckle—lowly, knowingly. "Think you, bratling, I won't go after yon key?" The dark light in his eyes sent a hot shiver through her, and she took another step back, trusting not his easy smile. It was far too calculating, far too intense. His eyes dropped slowly, leisurely, until focused on her breasts.

LeClaire blushed crimson, then began slowly, steadily, to back up. She had not thought of the backlash her hasty action might cause and knew it was foolhardy to have provoked him. But overriding all else was the vision running rampant through her mind of empty larders and starving villeins. She shook her head vigorously as Borgia took a step toward her. He continued with infuriating patience to bear down upon her, stalking her step for step, until LeClaire had the sinking feeling that he would not stop until his mission was complete.

She held her hands up as if to ward him off and pleaded, "The basil and thyme are gone!" And still he drew closer. "The meat is low." Closer yet. "We must needs be frugal—" Nary a foot now separated her from his outstretched palm. Her face paled as he took another step closer and all her pitiful defiance dissolved into a frightened squeal as she spun around and ran straight for the stairs. She stumbled once on the hem of her gown, then hiked her skirts up to her knees—which brought an appreciative leer from the surrounding knights—and navigated the steps as if the hounds of hell were after her.

A raucous cheer was raised when Borgia casually yet inexorably went after her, and Roger along with several other knights urged their lord on. With a smirk, he turned to the man seated beside him. "Think you, Sir Bryson, he will catch her?"

"Aye," Bryson chuckled. "But what will he do with her when he does?"

Roger swung his long legs over the bench, stretched back against the table and crossed his booted feet at the ankles. "The possibilities are endless."

The men raised their tankards in salute and began to wager the outcome. Loyal swains that they were, Borgia was favored by far over the wench, but no one knew exactly whether they were betting for or against him.

LeClaire slammed shut the door to her chamber, but shrieked when she realized there was no bolt to protect her from the evil without. Borgia came in upon her then, his every movement all the more terrifying for its inhuman speed and grace, and she fled through the connecting portal linking her room to his. There was no time to slam that door before he appeared behind her, and she darted to the center of the room. With slow deliberation Borgia closed and locked the door himself, then dared her with a mocking smile to try for the other door leading into the hallway.

Slowly, purposefully, he began to advance with a look of savage determination that chilled her blood. His face was set, his eyes shrewd as he drew closer, and the scent of her own fear was odorous in her flared nostrils.

Merciful Father, she had never seen such an expression in a person's eyes. She suspected men had overthrown kingdoms with less dark ambition. God help her, she had done it, had pushed too far and was trapped, caught fast in a web of her own making. And imprisoned with her was a silver lion.

Her eyes, enlarged in her wan and distraught face, never left his as she backed up steadily until she slammed into the wall. Her hands flew instinctively to cover her chest, and she could feel her heart pounding in wild, frightened beats against her clenched fists.

Borgia stopped dead still a few feet from her, the distance meager comfort when she expected him to pounce and strike any second. Instead he crossed his arms over his chest and cruelly let her wallow in her own fear. His gaze swept her with lazy thoroughness from her scuffed leather slippers to her disgraceful peasant apparel. Dressed in that manner she made a mockery of the title she would claim, of the authority she strove to hold on to. Yet, for all her beggarly appearance her face and demeanor shouted her worth. Her hair was a tangled mass of sunlight and cinnamon falling past her hips, tempting a man to stroke it back away from her small face, to gather it up and let it flow like a fiery waterfall through his fingers.

Borgia's hand flexed then opened. If he did not cast her out upon her stubborn little rump for her defiance, he might just be tempted to do that at some future date. He lowered his eyes coldly upon the girl and held his palm out while holding her impaled with his icy stare, daring her to defy him, provoking her to try. And a part of him wanted, expected her to do so with a need beyond reason, for this reckoning was long overdue.

LeClaire stood frozen beneath that gaze and could do naught but stare back at him, feeling his eyes scorch her so that she was alternately hot then cold, light-headed then heavy. And in that instance she saw him as few would live to know, as she wished she had not—hell-fire and ice, night without day. Darkness without light.

The silver of his eyes glimmered as if to deny her, but she could feel it, sense it, taste the profound and bitter emptiness of it. And her heart sank when she realized suddenly why his reflection so perfectly imitated the Guardian's—he was the complete and total reversal. The agony of despair cried out within her for the bleakness of his lost soul, the blackness of his heart.

His hand lay outstretched, waiting, but she could not have approached someone so unreachable, so outside the realm of her thinking if her life depended upon it. And she sensed that to do so, to cast herself upon his mercy, would be to throw herself into the darkness of his lost world. It was then that he moved, lightning quick and noiseless. With the graceful and lethal silence of the cat going in for the kill, he closed in on LeClaire in two lengthy strides, lifted her and shook her until her teeth rattled in her head.

"You dare defy me?" he drawled with velvet sarcasm. "If the key falls not free of your scrawny frame, I'll go after it."

LeClaire may have looked small in her ill-fitting rags, but the young woman's figure beneath the woolen tunic and linen kirtle was lush enough to hold the key in place —much to her overwhelming despair. With mixed outrage and mortification she glowered at him, unknowingly and enticingly defiant. Borgia accepted her challenge with a slow grin as he lowered her feet to the rushes, then pried her fingers apart and plunged his hand down the front of her gown.

Shock, absolute and complete, froze them both when he found the key imbedded between two creamy mounds of flesh—full-grown, womanly mounds. LeClaire was paralyzed by the invasion; no man had ever touched her so, had ever tried. Her heartbeat grew quick and shallow, drumming against her burning skin. Slate gray eyes locked with blazing blue ones as his fingers spread wide and cupped her tender skin.

Flung from her paralysis, LeClaire let out a squeal of protest, then twisted in a gale of fury and acute embarrassment. One shoulder blade dug into the wall as she turned, then the other as she swung back, but her movement served only to shift his hand from one ripe swell to the other, the friction causing her to gasp and Borgia's eyes to darken at the hot blaze of awareness that knifed through him. His fingers splayed, encompassing all of

her, his taut body leaned into hers to pinion her against
the wall, and he began slowly, thoroughly, to caress her.

LeClaire faded back into the stones as if she would
become one with them, but the chamber walls had with-
stood generations of assault from mankind and nature
alike and rejected the flight of a mere frightened girl.
Harsh and cold it stood against her back, while Borgia
pressed in upon her from the front. She was small and
firm in his palm, her flesh like warmed silk, and he
kneaded her breast gently, surely, testing the realness of
his discovery until the peak stood firm against his hand.

"Nay!" LeClaire cried out shrilly in fear and confusion. Never had her modesty been so evilly trampled,
never had she seen such dark heat and hunger in a man's
eyes. And never, in all her eight and ten years, had she
felt such ice and fire warring for dominance in her veins.
The emotions were worlds apart, yet frighteningly alike,
and although her mind froze, her cheeks flushed as did
the rest of her body. The hand that touched her was calloused and strong, adept at inflicting pain . . . capable
of caressing without it. Her breathing grew fluttery as a
bird's wing, her mind fretful as her hands scraped the
relentless barrier of stone, then rose to fight the relentless barrier of man. Both were immovable.

Desperate and shaken by the turbulent feelings, she
pushed against him. Again. Then again and again and
again, using all her strength until a breathless, agonized
cry was wrenched from her throat. Her strength was
naught compared to his, and her struggles only caused
her breast to rub more firmly against his hand, her soft
feminine body to graze maddeningly against his hard
male form from chest to thigh.

Deep within Borgia rose a groan—intrigue, satisfaction, need—and with the groan rose his other hand,
which tangled in LeClaire's hair, tilting her head back.
In horrified fascination, she watched as his eyelids low-

ered slightly, his head descended and his mouth drew
closer until it hovered just above hers.

"How old are you, bratling?" he whispered darkly.

"I . . . I have known eight and ten summers," she
breathed. "P . . . please, do not—"

The hand on her breast moved again, a forceful grip
that caused no pain but mindless agony and was quite
effective in cutting off her breath and strangling her
words. A roaring rushed in her head and with a small
sob she grabbed his wrist and tugged, but his hand was
precise and possessive in its endeavor, ruthless in its
constancy. Her fingers barely encircled his wrist, but still
her nails dug into his skin as she fought to pull his hand
away from its sinful intrusion.

"Eight and ten," he echoed in approval. "You have
hidden this woman's body well."

"C . . . cease!" she cried out. She had not deliberately concealed anything from him, save her mother's
secret. She had not realized herself until now how much
her body had changed over the past few years, had never
been around men who would take notice.

"Eight and ten," he confirmed again, nothing in his
voice to hint at his thoughts, but LeClaire sensed her
admission would not be to her good.

"Please," she begged, but her words faded into the silence that swelled, then lengthened, drawn out by the
charged moment, labored under the heavy nuance of desire and fear, fire and ice.

Borgia's lips lowered further until they pressed once
against LeClaire's, a confirmation of things to come,
while his eyes delved into the deep blue recesses of hers
as if to tap her soul. She cried out deep in her throat, the
sound garbled and mewling, then clamped her teeth together and tried again to pull away. Icy fingers of fear
clawed their way through her as his eyes, cold and gray
as winter rain, held her prisoner even more forcefully
than his hands did.

His fingers curled beneath her breast, flicking the key against her skin. And like a beautiful, wicked beast from a child's fable, he smiled before he sprang. His mouth lowered again and captured hers with smothering impact. His lips parted and moved over hers with deliberate calm and purpose. The heat of shame rose within LeClaire to dispel the chill of fear, unlocking the door to her anger. She jerked her head to the side to escape his lips, but his hand was in her hair still, and he easily turned her back.

"Ah, the child is not child." He grinned in predatory awareness. "But a woman fully grown. The question, LeClaire of Ravenwood, is are you fully known?" He caught her bottom lip between his teeth before she could answer, his eyes never leaving hers. But she could not have answered anyway with the tactile awareness of his lips and teeth imprisoning her. His body swayed heavily into her, rocking her back against the wall, and his fingers began to play languidly through her locks. Hair of fire, eyes of ice, skin like both beneath the hands that stroked her. His height and weight and overwhelming presence drowned LeClaire until she gasped for air.

With consummate awareness, Borgia took the advantage of her parted lips to more firmly press his suit. His mouth opened over hers, and he moved with quiet control from one delicate corner to the other, mindful of his intent and so subtle in his ruthlessness. With the experience of a master he enjoyed the feel of her, round and firm beneath his hand, warm and shivering against his body, and he used his knowledge against her to elicit a response. But the only response forthcoming was the tightening of her body beneath his agile hands and the anxious tossing of her head as she tried to free her lips.

The turmoil of emotions inside LeClaire threatened to rob her of sanity. The press of his lips coupled with the weight of his body swamped her with feelings hitherto unknown. She felt helpless, violated, enslaved in the

Devil's embrace. A dreadful weakness assaulted her
limbs until she felt fainthearted and light-headed. She
moaned, sad and frantic, beneath his lips at her puny
strength, felt his mouth capture the sound and absorb it,
felt the slick glide of his lips over hers, experienced the
moist warmth of all he was doing invade the hidden
reaches of her body.

His fingers combed through her gilded hair, lulling,
almost soothing, before he paused and drew his head
back the slightest inch. His eyes glittered with unholy
brilliance into hers as his thumb flicked once, aware and
intentional, over her nipple. Air crashed into her lungs as
she sucked in a breath, and she cried out as her knees
buckled. Her body curled limp between the wall and the
man, and she would have crumpled to the floor had his
body not supported hers.

Merciful Father, this was no mere act, no stolen kiss of
an eager young man and a maid behind the buttery that
she had once been embarrassed to come upon. This was
nothing so safe or so simple.

Without warning, his hand slid to her shoulder and he
lifted her upright, then moved back the smallest space,
his gray eyes lingering on her rosy, swollen mouth as he
asked silkily, "Art fully known?" Though his tone demanded an answer, LeClaire could do naught but gaze
up at him in wide-eyed confusion and repulsion. "Others
think you a skinny mite beneath this beggar's cloth," he
continued with a cynical smile. "I would see what else
you would have hidden from me."

It took several moments for his words to penetrate Le-
Claire's befuddled mind, but when they did the fury and
panic rose within her like a wild thing, renewing her
strength while devouring every bit of reason, fear and
caution. She squirmed against him, unwittingly aiding
his quest with the furious twisting and turning of her
body. Borgia's fingers tightened in her hair and held her
fast; his hand, which with one fatal swoop of his sword

could slay a man, moved with fluid grace over her bare flesh from shoulder to breastbone, then lower. And his strength and gentleness were a terrible thing.

She cried out again in helpless frustration and struggled even more, seeking escape from the hot and powerful press of his body, from the knowing experience of his fingers, from the glittering gray eyes that now roamed her figure as if the clothing were stripped from her.

"Nay," she moaned weakly, embarrassed, flustered past caring that his hand was caressing her boldly, for it was his eyes that she feared most—silver-ringed, knowing eyes that promised in the same heated gaze they threatened. And she understood not the promise nor the threat.

"Be easy," Borgia soothed with the same terrible tenderness in his voice as in his touch. LeClaire nearly sobbed aloud her fright and revulsion. He was a wicked, evil man to so seductively cajole while trespassing upon her chastity. "Come, maiden, be not shy. Let me see if the rest of you is as well formed and sweet as this part." His fingers flexed then squeezed her breast, taking the whole of it to cradle its weight.

LeClaire flinched and shrunk farther against the wall, the stones digging into her back. Her head swam with a maelstrom of emotions, and humiliation flamed within her until her cheeks burned a rosy hue.

"Nay!" she cried again. "Leave me be!"

His voice came like an insidious dark breeze against her ear. "Not until I have seen the rest of you. Be not afraid, LeClaire. Feel me." Dark lights danced in his eyes with the words, fascinating, compelling, too dangerous for a young woman who had never come against such. "See how your flesh welcomes my touch." His fingers brushed across the tight aureole of her breast, and LeClaire gasped and stiffened, then began to swat fretfully at the offensive hand.

Shaken by his tempter's words, her mind screamed,

Liar! Blasphemer! Despite his claim, there was no welcome within her for his evil ways. "You shame me, my lord!" she cried out in fury. "How dare you think to put your hands on me and spew such words? You have taken all I own then shame me too. Have you no conscience, no guilt?"

LeClaire's voice quivered off into silence as her knees went watery, and she pressed farther against the wall as if she could burrow into it. The expression in Borgia's eyes changed, his hand flexed once then slid slowly from her, yet strangely the heat within her did not ebb.

"I do as I dare in my own demesne," he assured her with a heartless lack of concern. "I place my hands where I will with neither conscience nor guilt to gainsay me." The richness of his voice dared her to do so. "You would do well, damoiselle, to learn that."

She grabbed the neck of her gown, bunching the fabric at her throat as her breaths skipped and staggered like a drunkard. He brushed her fumbling fingers aside and pulled together the folds of her kirtle with a brisk efficiency that intensified LeClaire's anger and embarrassment at how controlled he was, how unconcerned, as if her first kiss had been naught more to him than a mere trifling.

He finished straighting her laces, then regarded her with chilling amusement. "My men would be hardpressed to keep their distance if they could see what I just felt."

Mortified by such bold words, LeClaire felt the hot rush of color to her cheeks and the salty sting of tears in her eyes. "They will never—" she began, then clamped her mouth shut at the horrible intimacy of such a discussion. She wanted to scream and rail at him for his boldness, but she was not that brave when he stood so close, so hard and threatening before her. She gathered her faulty composure and merely stared back at him with the depth of her anger and hurt shining from her brilliant blue eyes.

"Nay," he said slowly, smiling. "Be assured, they never will."

He stepped back and once again put his hand out. "The key, damoiselle," he said with a wry smile, his wintry eyes taunting her with the certain results of further defiance.

LeClaire turned her back on him and grappled for the offensive scrap of metal. Finding it, she spun around and slapped it into his palm. The price was too high; they could all starve to death in the coming months for all she cared at this moment and prayed to God this beast would be the first to feel the pangs of hunger she had known a goodly portion of her life. Cheeks flushed, shoulders braced, she swung away and marched from the room with as much dignity as she could muster.

Borgia did not watch her depart, rather his attention was centered on the small scrap of iron in his hand, still warm from her body. His jaw tightened but there was an odd gleam in his cold eyes as his fingers slowly closed over the key.

7

Borgia de St. Brieuc descended the stairs in a dark temper, though only Roger who'd received a blistering sarcasm moments ago could attest to his friend's mood. The lord was dressed to meet the day in tan woolen chausses, heavy linen *sherte* and a knee-length tunic of leaf brown belted with a simple girdle and attached short sword. A thick woolen mantle hung in careless negligence over one shoulder, but his boots were a rich leather polished to a high gloss that bespoke meticulous care. Each leisurely step he took radiated grace, sophistication and the confidence with which he had conquered Ravenwood. It was that indelible authority that sent all who labored within the hall scurrying to their duties.

His dress was both as elegant and serviceable as the day required, and the manly way he wore it nearly caused the new maid, Agnes, to swoon when he appeared. If the lord would but glance her way with anything more than cool regard, she would better serve him in ways other than dishing up the morning meal. Agnes had taken heart when he fetched her from the village two days past, but since then he had done naught but ignore her. With a flutter of pale lashes and a pose that nearly put a hitch in her back, she pushed her ample bosom tight against her simple bodice and flashed him a coy smile. Agnes's shoulders slumped back down in pique

when she received naught for her effort save the ever-
present boredom on his handsome face.

Borgia scarcely noticed the comely maidservant as he
crossed to the trestle tables that had been set up to feed
his men. He was too busy contemplating a flame-haired
vixen with crystalline blue eyes. LeClaire, late of Ravenwood and soon to be doomed to hell if she continued on
her present path, continued to defy his orders. Though
she was more cautious now and like to do it in his absence, she seemed bent on hoarding over the foodstock
like a squawking mother hen.

Those of Ravenwood would vehemently deny that
charge; their lady's voice held a musical quality that en-
couraged their flagging spirits, soothed their battered
souls, and her eyes were ever upon them in concern and
sympathy. She asked after each of their families, calling
the members by name, and was forever sending an herb
or cure for their ailments.

Borgia gave no thought to the villeins' devotion, for his
mind was steady on the girl. She looked no different
from before in her sacklike clothing as she moved quietly
about the keep issuing orders contrary to the ones he had
already given concerning the feast, but he'd had a taste
of what lay beneath the cloth. And the memory of it now,
a sennight past the occurrence, was sharp as he watched
her sweetly admonish the cooks under his command that
surely they need not require that much dill for seasoning.

Roger, attuned to his lord's black humor over the long
week, had suggested that Borgia take one of the serving
girls, mayhaps that blond wench so recently summoned
to help with meals. For his efforts Roger had received a
scathing retort as to precisely what he could do with the
maidservant himself, which at first sent heat to even his
veteran warrior's face, then a burst of laughter as he
contemplated the possibilities.

But Roger knew Borgia was not one to frolic with a
servant of his household or to test an unwilling maid. He

had better use for his time and intellect. An intensely private man, whatever carnal pastimes were enjoyed by St. Brieuc were known only to him. There were those Roger suspected, of course, a brief affair with his distant cousin Eleanor, and a lengthy one with Anne of Mortain. And speculation was rife as to whether that last liaison had been put to rest since Anne's recent marriage. Nay, Borgia had spent his years since manhood in fighting not wenching, giving little thought to wooing and gallantry. Smooth words and false declarations were for besotted young knights, and Roger knew of no lady who could truly claim deception from St. Brieuc, though there were those who had tried.

And yet, Roger thought as he watched Borgia's eyes travel the length of the main hall, there was a look about St. Brieuc these days, a darkly controlled restlessness eclipsed by his damnable constancy—constantly in command, dangerously unpredictable. Roger's hand tightened on his goblet as a shadow of foreboding passed through him. He had seen the look before, the planning, the patience, the strategy, often spanning years as Borgia waited to bring an enemy down. The Lion always succeeded. Always.

A trickle of anticipation and dread slithered down Roger's spine. The look was there; the enemy, no doubt, Saxon. But the ironic twist this time was that the enemy was also female. And no threat at all.

He made an innocent comment about the weather to further test his lord's mood but received naught but a bland stare for his foolery.

Borgia sat down at the table and went back to studying LeClaire. The idea of having the girl had taken root days ago; the fact that he had not yet acted upon it was credited to her inexperience. Satisfaction was greatly limited in virginal resistance, and he had not been so much as tempted by one of that species since his youth. Had he not been so intrigued by LeClaire since the incident with the key, he would have let the matter drop. But his memory of firm soft breasts and slender hips was clear and, in this case, relentless. It was so utterly fascinating to him that he did not scorn such a thing, he was forced to consider it.

The object of his thoughts walked past him with quick, hurried steps, her chin tilted in a defiant angle. LeClaire bore her threadbare clothing with a dignity that would have done a queen proud, and just as regally she refused to glance his way. She had, in fact, deigned to ignore him this week past. Every time their eyes met she blushed a becoming apricot, which earned her a smooth grin that only made her redden more and increased Borgia's amusement. She would stiffen her shoulders and send him a burning look of condemnation from beneath her meekly lowered lashes before scampering away.

A brilliant strategist in the art of warfare, he knew his effect on the virtuous maiden and played well upon it. With no more than a look he unnerved her, sent her calm fleeing, and it was just a matter of time before the unrest caused her surrender.

Ah, but there was the crux. A peaceful surrender meant waiting out the siege. But Borgia was an infinitely patient man.

No one knew the reason for the lord's hard temper, and most gave it no more than a passing thought, for he had ever been an enigma even to his own men. He possessed the grace and bearing of the nobility, but his superior knowledge and cunning on the battlefield made him a cold and deadly enemy when crossed. If any of his men thought to question his dark humor, they dared not out of fear of his wickedly cutting tongue or the respect and loyalty he had earned.

But Roger was a different mien, one of the few men besides William whom Borgia truly called friend, and he was immune to the full wrath of his lord's displeasure. He had seen the guarded looks passed between St.

Brieuc and LeClaire, had seen Borgia use more energy in vexing the miss than ever he had used in courting one. Intrigued past caution he baited his lord from time to time but usually gained little more than Borgia's cynical wit and none of his intentions toward the girl.

"Poor mite," Roger observed with dramatic sympathy, his eyes following the sway of LeClaire's hips. "Is aught amiss with the lass? She seems to be avoiding you of late."

" 'Tis to her credit," Borgia said but added naught else and allowed Amiens his game.

"Aye," Roger agreed. "She knows her place well. She is diligent in running this hall and serving you in all things, meek and biddable, I vow. Aye, the picture of obedience that one. She did return the key, did she not?" Roger paused at the strangely sardonic look on Borgia's face as the girl crossed the hall, and the sudden flush of anger on LeClaire's as she caught his stare.

"She did," Borgia said with a slow smile. "With gentle persuasion, she put it right in my hand."

Roger choked on his food at the comment and felt a shiver of doom raise the hairs on his neck along with the first real pangs of true sympathy for the defenseless girl. The Lion was not known for his gentleness with women lest it pleased him to be so, a fault often whispered among the ladies of William's castle. He drove them to the brink of distraction with his unconcern, and never did a soft word of affection or pleasure pass from his tongue. He was equally cursed and sought after by the fickle ladies, each thinking, hoping, she could garner more from him than her competition.

But Roger could not comment upon any of this, for he was caught amid a fit of coughing at Borgia's bland statement. He finally grabbed a tankard of ale to wash his food down, then cast his lord a jaundiced stare. "Christ, man! If you're about murder this day, do so with yon sword. 'Tis quicker and less painful than drowning me in my food!"

"But not nearly as satisfying," Borgia said. His dark and mirthless laughter rang out in the hall, causing all who labored there to pause in their work, cross themselves and watch him suspiciously.

All save LeClaire, who endeavored not to look at him at all. She found his humor not amusing in the least, grating on her already frayed nerves. The Lion had taken so little interest in her before the incident abovestairs that the attack upon her person had come quite unexpectedly. It had left her irritable, jumpy and cautious. And she understood not the reasons for what he had done, the madness that had seized him.

She had known a portion of fear all her life but never anything that had felt like that, all fiery heat and burning humiliation and an icy dread more chilling than deepest winter. Most, at least those of Norman persuasion, would declare she had given Borgia reason to beat her for her defiance, but his hands had not been heavy upon her in that way. Nary a drop of her blood had he let with his strong but gentle hands. Nay, his punishment had been more subtle, and infinitely more devastating.

A spiral of conflicting emotions, a whirlwind of fire and ice had been her penance. And she knew not how a touch could cause such things, nor incite the fear that had accompanied it. Nor could she comprehend why his eyes were always upon her these days, so fiercely cold and piercing, so penetrating they left her bare and shivering from the impact. Embarrassment rode her hard every time he glanced her way, and she was compelled to stay out of his path lest she be forced to suffer another debasing attack. It was frightful to be caged with the evil knight, no succor in sight, and she bade her time in nerve-riddled anxiety, clinging to her mother's secret as if it were a sturdy branch in a raging storm, for there was naught else to cling to. And she hoped in time it would be enough.

Borgia climbed the stairs slowly to his chamber, past exhaustion from a day spent in excessive military exercise, and every muscle and tendon in him protested the effort it took to gain his room. There were rumors of Saxon uprisings, isolated incidences thus far, but he and his men must stay ever on guard. He propped his sword near the bed as he entered and tossed a gauntlet onto the trunk. It landed on his dark blue mantle, which had been neatly folded and placed there a sennight ago.

Ah, the stubborn wench. She would not accept his charity, but neither did she openly reject the gesture— she would have to approach him for that. She had merely returned the mantle in his absence and gone about her days as before, a far cry from the ladies at court who strutted about in their jeweled gifts like the mindless peacocks they were.

Borgia tossed his other gauntlet down and cursed his errant thoughts. It was an unfair comparison, for there were many intelligent women who graced William's Norman castle, at times his own mother and sisters, but he was not in the mood to be charitable to the gentler sex at the moment. He was annoyed that the flames leaping in the hearth reminded him of hair that color, just as the cloudless sky by day's end had reminded him of eyes with the same deep blue clarity.

Borgia removed his leather tunic, wincing slightly at a bruised shoulder muscle that had taken the brunt of Roger's lance. Favoring the nuisance, he bent to test the waters of his bath. He paused when the soft trill of feminine chatter drifted from the antechamber. It proved a gentle balm to his masculine ears and reminded him of evenings spent in his father's house when his sisters would gather to exchange pleasantries and gossip. Talk of court, new gowns and knights were ever on their lips, and their mother stood near to chide her daughters and steer their thoughts in a more ladylike direction.

Borgia eased the door open and leaned against the frame to study the four maidens while they spoke among themselves. It was not his desire to eavesdrop, though he would be wise to make certain they made no plot against him. In truth, he merely wanted to watch the sisters at their leisure when the day's toil was ended and no servant claimed their attention. But Borgia found that even nightfall had not brought them rest, and the frivolous chatter of young ladies when they gather was not universal, for it touched not these four of Ravenwood.

Young Kyra sat hunched over the accounts, entering the day's activity; Aurel plied her needle to a poor tunic that looked more ready for the rag pile than repair; and Maire, her voice lowered for once, canted a haunting melody while plucking the strings of a lute. LeClaire, her hair a shimmering cascade down her back, stood at the window staring pensively at the moon, looking for all the world as if a hundredweight sat upon her shoulders.

"He asked about the rents," Kyra said, a worried look on her young face.

LeClaire turned to the sister she would always think of as a child, though the passing seasons belied the notion. In another few years Kyra would be of an age to marry as the rest of them were now, and LeClaire wondered if Kyra's chances for happiness would look as bleak as theirs did. For herself, she had hoped to enter a convent and spend her days in service to the Lord, but that future had been taken from her with the death of her parents. Aurel, too, had hoped to spend her years cloistered in an abbey married to the Church, and mayhaps it was not too late for her, though LeClaire did not think Aurel would readily leave them in this time of upheaval.

Maire was different. An adventure awaiting happenstance, excitement and mischief bred into the very bones of her body, Maire would never be fit for a life of seclusion, but what future here? Marriage to one of the villagers when she deserved better than the hard life she had known thus far? LeClaire's thoughts sent a lonesome ache to her heart, and she looked back at Kyra with sympathy.

"Fret not, young one. I will meet the lord's questions. Let it not dismay you."

"He did naught but ask," Kyra hastened to reassure, lest she give her sister more to worry over. "I told him the truth—there are no rents collected here, but you wring a tithe from the villeins in goods, meat and the like."

"What say he?" LeClaire asked, a bit more anxious than she cared to be over the matter.

"That you would beggar us all."

LeClaire laughed softly and in her eyes shone the warm, protective glow of love for those surrounding her. It was an idyllic scene in the anteroom, one of peace and unity in stark contrast to the turmoil hidden in LeClaire's heart. "Aye, mayhaps he is right, but the people have little enough, and they do well to hoard what coin they hold for now. 'Twas my plan to ask for rents when Ravenwood began to prosper."

"Bah!" Maire said imperiously. "There is no chance of that now. Methinks we should have poisoned the wine with deadly nightshade instead of drugging it." Her head tilted back in ponderous thought. "Belladonna or wolfsbane . . . think you, sister mine, we could get our hands on some—"

LeClaire's soft laughter ended Maire's murderous contemplations. " 'Tis too late for all that now, and I would not have wanted to face the King's wrath had we done so before." Her voice dwindled a bit. " 'Tis said he is favored."

"*He* is a beast," Maire snapped. "And all who stand with him."

LeClaire's eyes went to her sister's dark beauty and

she wondered again what the future held for this precious wayward sister, so outwardly full of bluster, so inwardly full of compassion. "Do not let the hatred eat at you, Maire, 'twill spoil your sweet and loving disposition." The others giggled lightly at LeClaire's teasing and nodded their agreement. "We must all look to God's purpose and pray this Norman invasion is His will."

"The Devil's will more like," Maire said. "They are all demon spawn if you ask me, and a bolder group I have never met."

LeClaire's eyes widened. A faint blush stained her cheeks, for she knew only too well how bold they could be and feared her sister, too, had been wrongly set upon. "What say you, Maire?"

"The one called Bryson. Sir Bryson, for he boasts he was knighted this past year though he had yet to reach a score and one. Sir Imbecile would take liberties with me, but I set him back," Maire huffed. "The bloody wretch thought to put his paws on me, but I took care of him."

The color drained from LeClaire's face; a slight trembling seized her, and she had to swallow past the sudden tightening in her throat before she could speak. She could keep her sisters from starving, could keep them clothed against the cold, but this . . . how could she protect them from strength greater than her own?

"What did you?" she whispered.

"I kicked him smartly in his man's place," Maire said without one ounce of fear or regret, then burst into a trill of girlish laughter. "No doubt his baubles will be sore for a sennight; he walked with a funny enough gait afterward."

"Merciful Father," LeClaire groaned, and closed her eyes. She could not even take issue with Maire's vulgarity in light of the fear that beset her for her sister and the consequences of the well-deserved action. "Did he not strike you?"

"Nay." Maire shrugged as if it were of no concern, but

her eyes were bright with mischief. "He could not catch me."

Kyra began to giggle anew, and Aurel's shoulders quivered suspiciously as she hid her pinkened cheeks behind her sewing. LeClaire's expression was pained yet relieved, her voice most direct when she spoke.

"You stay clear of them, Maire. All of you take heed and listen to me." All eyes fastened on the eldest with a reverence that spoke their respect and trust. "I pray you, Maire, have a care. Mayhaps you will not get away so fast next time."

"And mayhaps he will have a care for his man parts when next he approaches me!" Maire countered. She saw the concern on her sister's face and softened her tone lest she cause LeClaire more grief. "I will take care, sister mine. I give you my oath."

LeClaire attempted a smile to lighten the reprimand. What was done was done and cautioning them in no way assured their safety, but it was the best she could do—all she could do. A weary sigh escaped her. It had ever been like this, doing what must be done only to find it not enough, never enough. The feelings of guilt and inadequacy festered within her like an open wound. Ravenwood had been a fine dream, a chance to escape the impoverished life they had led thus far, the opportunity to prosper. And like all dreams dashed it hovered ever near to taunt her with all they had lost before it was even gained.

LeClaire pushed the thoughts aside for they were fruitless and embittered her, and she must needs maintain her faith along with the calm and serenity that kept her life on an even keel and also kept her sisters from becoming fearful. She bent to pick up the stitchery Aurel had been working on for many months when time permitted. The head of the unicorn was finely stitched, its horn beautifully done in golden thread. The artistry was remarkable. So alive and authentic did the mythical creature appear, one almost expected him to rear his golden hooves and spring from the fabric.

" 'Tis wondrous, Aurel," she said. "We will hang it in the main hall with your other works. 'Twill be done soon?"

Aurel smiled and shrugged, then dropped her eyes to withdraw from attention and continued placidly on with her sewing. It saddened LeClaire to see her sister's talents go to waste on such mundane things as repairing clothing better suited for cleaning soot than covering their backs. But she had learned long ago there was no help for it. Each of them did what they must to carry on, and fanciful dreams were poor company for empty bellies and chilled bones.

Borgia watched on from his place against the door frame, intrigued by the conversation and the roles necessitated by life they seemed to have fallen into. For weeks he had observed them covertly, assessing their strengths and weaknesses for his own purposes in prospering Ravenwood, deciding whether to send them packing or leave them be. Each obeyed the eldest—the primary source of their needs, the protector, the soother—not out of fear but with a respect LeClaire had earned with fairness and intelligence. Borgia wondered if the leadership qualities she possessed had been inborn, learned or forced by trial. He suspected a bit of each.

The child, Kyra, struggled with a calculation, her brow knitted in concentration until she found the answer. This one they cosseted to the best their lives allowed, but he wondered if she ever romped and played as an ordinary girl her age should, as his own troublesome sisters had in their youth. She was fine-boned and fair of face, a simple combination of her other three sisters. A gangly, coltish child she would one day be as tall as Aurel, but her dark looks were patterned after Maire and promised beauty in time if toil did not rob her of it aforehand. She seemed to have no true identity of her own but was a sober and serious reflection of LeClaire. Though a child in age and looks, she was bookish in her mannerisms, a perfectionist at her work, and though Borgia could respect her intelligence, he found her diligence an unnatural waste of youth.

His gaze wandered to Aurel. Withdrawn, aloof, she seemed to exist in some other world as fleeting and untouchable as a wisp of cloud to be gazed on from afar but never reached. Borgia remembered another girl, one of like beauty whose sunlight hair had caught his eye over a decade ago, and who like Aurel had been as compelling to a young knight and just as untouchable. Though, in truth, he had touched her many times and in many ways, he had never been able to reach the woman in her, for she had been just a girl, a child-bride, timid and frail and unwilling. It was repulsive to think on her now, and his eyes released Aurel's ethereal beauty to seek out Maire.

Her olive skin and sable hair lent her an exotic look so different from Aurel's fairness, just as their temperaments were so vastly different. Maire was a wild thing, a capricious wind that set everything askew when she blew in. One moment she was a hostile and defiant troublemaker, the next a humorous and prankish court jester as seemed to befit her mood. Borgia wondered from where her rebellious nature had sprung. She used neither wisdom nor caution in her exploits, and he feared she would be her own destruction. He understood well why Bryson had approached her. Her eyes sparkled with unholy delight, promised a man an easy, unbridled romp if he could but get close enough to enjoy her favors. And Borgia wondered which of his men would be the first to step beyond Maire's teasing come-hither glances to taste the earthy delights she offered as naturally and as innocently as she breathed.

Her fingers stilled on the lute when Maire glanced up and caught Borgia staring at her from the doorway. Her mouth opened, then closed suddenly as a sly look crossed her face. Eyes narrowed shrewdly, she turned to LeClaire.

"Think you he is handsome?"

"Sir Bryson?" LeClaire asked in concern. "You have forsworn you would stay away—"

"Nay," Maire interrupted. "The Lion. What think you of his manly face and form?"

LeClaire blushed faintly and would not meet Maire's eyes. "Do not ask foolish questions. He has stolen Ravenwood and made slaves of us. I have given no thought to his appearance, but what he represents. The annihilation of our future."

"Oh, aye." Maire nodded, but sweetly persisted. "But what if you had met him another time, under different circumstances? What would you think of him then?"

" 'Twould never have happened, so there is no need to think on it," LeClaire said, and her glare warned Maire their conversation was ended.

But Maire was dogged in her teasing and determined the sneaky lord in yon doorway would know the full extent of loathing LeClaire, with her kind nature, would probably never reveal to him. "But just pretend this had all been different," she continued. "We were called to court to represent our uncle and—"

"Where is Father," LeClaire interrupted, "that we should be called instead?"

"Dead and rotted," Maire snapped without remorse. " 'Tis a pretty game, do not spoil it." LeClaire rolled her eyes and let Maire play on, imagining the things of which she had little knowledge—gowns and jewels, gallant knights and ladies in waiting, feasting and dancing and the frivolous pursuits of the gentry. Moonlight twined coppery highlights through her hair as she turned back to the window and stared into the night, listening to the sounds below rather than Maire's racing imagery. ". . . and then the King presents the Silver Lion as one of your suitors."

"Which King?" LeClaire asked in an effort to distract Maire's inane enthusiasm.

"It matters not," Maire said, peevish and frustrated. "What think you of the Lion as he gives you a courtly bow and raises your hand to his lip—"

"Cease!" LeClaire spun back around, done with this play but well aware of Maire's grinding tenacity. There were already too many pictures in her mind of Borgia touching her; she needed not for Maire to conjure up more. A hint of panic shadowed her words. "I would no doubt swoon over his handsomeness and attention and beg the King—whoever that might be—to allow the Lion to pay me court, then no doubt offer him my heart. There. Does that satisfy your fanciful mind?"

"Aye," Maire said, sullen and thwarted. She sent Borgia a disdainful glance and turned back to her sister. " 'Twas just a game."

"One I have no wish to play," LeClaire returned softly, feeling a world gone all akilter slowly balance back on its axis. "Forgive me, Maire. I meant no harshness." At her sister's nod, she turned back to the window, her hair once again reflecting burnished ribbons of candlelight and moonlight where it swirled about her shoulders and tumbled in reckless coils to her hips.

Borgia's reaction was swift and sure, a honing of the senses combined with a keening of the blood, and with it came anger and derision that she had such an undeniable effect upon him. It was a testament to the power she unknowingly wielded over people—her sisters, the villeins, even his own men were drawn to her by some unseen force that commanded they listen when she speak and treat her with respect. It was also that same compelling draw that sealed her fate.

What a consummate little martyr she would make. Yet, he sought not to break her but only to bend her will to his, to tap the passion she showed for her people. Borgia pushed away from the door frame and stepped into the antechamber, his sudden presence causing a hush to fall.

All eyes darted his way—Aurel's in fear, Maire's in challenge, Kyra's with acceptance. Only LeClaire's were unreadable. They were wary yet controlled, troubled and evasive. Too many emotions warred for a place in the glittering blue depths to give credit to just one.

LeClaire continued to stare placidly at him, but Borgia's sudden appearance had shattered her peace, sent remembrance crashing through her quietude to unsettle her, and she wondered how much of the silly chatter he had heard. His stance was relaxed but his narrowed eyes were sharp and swept her with a silvery gaze as forceful as if he had put his hands on her. Unconsciously her hand went to her throat and she shied away from the unspoken threat in those eyes and sought protection in busying herself with tidying up the room. Her sisters rose to escape the thick tension and made ready to depart.

"Must you leave?" LeClaire asked anxiously.

"They must," Borgia said. Only Maire was brave enough to gainsay him or mayhaps foolish enough to remain in his presence as Aurel and Kyra hurried from the room. "Damoiselle Maire," he said softly, so deceptively calm that it took her a moment to credit his tone with the deadly gleam in his eyes. "Your presence here is unwelcome. Good eventide."

Despite her defiant stare, Maire swallowed hard and cast her stubborn eyes to LeClaire. "Sister mine, do you wish me to leave?"

"Nay, I—"

The words were barely past her lips before Borgia's hand rose for silence. LeClaire cringed but Maire stayed belligerently firm. And Borgia frowned at their reaction, wondering again whose heavy fist had been raised to them before that they would be moved to cower or fight back. In a motion as quick and silent as a stalking lion, he took Maire's arm and ushered her from the room. Though she protested vociferously, the door was slammed in her face and Maire found herself in the hall staring at the impregnable barrier of wood and iron. Enraged, she pounded on the door until her fist ached then went numb, and she knew her efforts were futile. She could summon help, but the people of Ravenwood belonged to Borgia now and there was nowhere to turn for aid.

"Knave! Norman pig!" she yelled to no avail. The door stayed barred as Maire strolled back and forth a short distance then decided to change tactics. "Your Holiness, a word please." Silence met her sugared plea, and she was called back to her original inclination. "Beast! Oaf! Grant entrance, you coward, and face me if you dare!"

Maire heaved a disgruntled breath and slammed her fist against the door one last time. LeClaire had always been the strong one, the protector, and Maire would have to leave her sister to her own devices. Her heart heavy with feelings of inadequacy and betrayal, and a defeated droop to her shoulders, she shuffled off to her room to curse one man, all men who stood with him and life in general.

Borgia stood braced against the door, for there was no bolt, and his eyes swept LeClaire when the pounding and name-slaying ceased. She stood skittish before him, ready to dart for cover, though she must know there was no place for her to hide. He was lord here; the villeins might give her shelter, but unless she managed to leave Ravenwood altogether, there was nowhere she could escape for long. Shapeless and trim in her peasant's garb, she posed no outward temptation to a man's desire beyond her face and hair, hardly enough to entice one. She was hardworking and responsible, but the vexation she caused him far outweighed her worth in that area. He would soon hire a castellan who would be as efficient in running Ravenwood and not cause him grief at every command.

LeClaire felt his eyes upon her as tangible as a touch, and she shivered from the impact. She knew not why he was here nor why he had ordered the others from the room when he had never done so before. And she was suddenly and inexplicably frightened. Frightened of his cold, moody stare and the way his eyes stroked over her leaving no place sacred. The tension built as the silence was drawn out, hummed like a current of lightning striking a darkened sky, and she found herself awaiting the crash of thunder that would shatter this suspended agony.

"Would you really swoon?" he asked.

Color flooded LeClaire's cheeks. "Eavesdropper," she accused.

"And beg the King—"

"Oh, cease!" LeClaire pleaded. " 'Twas only Maire's silly game. I spake those things to hush her."

Borgia's hand went to his heart. "You wound me, bratling."

LeClaire ducked her head to hide a treasonous smile. She could not be further baited and they both fell silent. But a storm grew within the small space that separated them, until the tingle along her nerve endings could not be borne, and she sucked in a gulp of air to steady herself as she lifted her head. "Why are you here? Why did you send the others away?"

He said nothing, but moved toward her, his steps long and predatory, quickly closing the gap between them. LeClaire braced herself to face him. There was nowhere to go, nowhere to hide in the sparse room to escape his dark presence. His hand reached out and she flinched, but he only lifted a lock of hair from her shoulder as he had before and rubbed the silken strands through his fingers. He spoke not a word, but his eyes questioned, commanded, bore into hers with a look as terrifying as it was incomprehensible.

"I have need of you," he said.

Mere words, surely harmless. But they sent icy shivers clawing up LeClaire's spine and caused her heart to race in a frenzied beat as if it would escape her breast. She shook her head dumbly, at a loss to answer him when there had been no question, knowing yet not knowing what it was he wanted of her. Whatever his intent, it was made from evil. That much she recognized from the coldness in his eyes and the taut, leashed power in his body as he loomed over her.

"I have need of you, LeClaire." The words were grainy, more forceful this time, though his voice had not risen at all.

"Nay," she whispered, and knew not what she refused, just that she must. "The day is done; night has fallen. If you have need of me, the morrow is soon enough—"

"Now." His hand tightened in her hair until she was forced to tilt her head up or endure pain. "I have need of you now."

Before she realized his purpose, both his hands were on her shoulders, drawing her close until her slight body was pressed to his, and she was captured. His hands slid around her until his arms imprisoned her with the strength of iron, and in his eyes was a dark glint of something immeasurable. His fingers splayed wide over her slender back, pulling her closer into his body.

"My lord, nay!" she cried, and struggled against him, her threadbare clothing offering scant protection as her body twisted against the rich fine cloth of his garment. Fear gave her strength, but confusion sapped it, and there was nothing but a tangle of linen and wool, of a woman's softness and a man's hard intent, of ineffectual twisting and squirming as he held her effortlessly in a grip more powerful, more threatening than any she had encountered.

"Why?" she cried out in painful confusion.

"Hush, bratling," he said, his deep voice almost soothing as his fingers began an endless play along her spine,
holding her firmly but caressing and massaging the tense
muscles as if he would gentle her. Patient and steady he
continued, and even time bent to his will to stand still
and motionless. The air hung thick and hot about them,
as did the shadows and smoke from the resinous torches
on the wall.

LeClaire's frantic eyes searched his, sought out a reason for his actions, but he only stared back at her, his
thoughts hooded, his gaze icy hot. It seemed no threat
was pending, for he did nothing more . . . or less than
the soothing circular kneading and plying with his
strong fingers. She was lulled by the tireless minutes of
continuous motion and felt herself weaken beneath his
hands as he eased her weary body into complacency.

Her mind drifted with the onslaught of his meticulous
care and her lids grew slumberous as her body searched
out a nesting spot against his virile, hard form. She could
not remember being coddled or held as a child, and this
warmth and stroking were as foreign and enticing to the
young woman as it was devastating. Her limbs were not
her own but cumbersome weights, too burdensome to
hold aloft and she let her arms go slack, her head leaned
to one side and her fingers floated down the soft linen of
his *sherte*.

Unwittingly her nails raked across the fabric covering
his abdomen, and suddenly, without preliminary or
warning there was a violent shift in the air, an eruption
of tension that radiated outward, stretching and swirling
until it encircled them. His hands slid down to the small
of LeClaire's back where his fingers dug into the soft
flesh and pulled her hard against his coiled length. His
eyes grew sharp and hungry as they narrowed on her,
and awareness stabbed at LeClaire's limp body. She stiffened immediately at the sudden change in him and was

brutally conscious of the heat and force of his fingers biting into the rounded curve of her buttocks, the hard overwhelming length of finely hewed muscles pressing against her from knees to breasts.

Her body, seduced to a dangerous peace, was slow to react, and her mind did not seem connected to her will-less limbs. Fear replaced languor and she tried to pull away, but he held her firm and swayed slowly, completely, against her in an exact rhythm, his eyes glinting with a strange, mysterious heat. Her skin grew tight and flushed every place he touched and her heart set up a rapid beating that shouted warning and implored her to flee, but she could not get away, could not escape his powerful hold. Her chin tilted up and her eyes blazed with the panicked fury of one trapped.

"Unhand me," she begged over the quick rise and fall of her chest. "There is naught that cannot wait until daybreak."

His eyes glowed with cool amusement and more, and his smile—if the fierce, calculating twist of his lips could be called such—was chilling. "This cannot wait." One hand released her and rose to stroke her cheek, caressing the smooth and flawless skin. LeClaire swung her face away, and his other hand rose with excruciating slowness to tangle in her hair, turning her head back so that he might pleasure himself further. His fingers, calloused and strong, traced her hairline from temple to jaw, his thumb brushing repeatedly across the heightened color on her cheeks. "Art lovely, damoiselle," he whispered, and lowered his head.

LeClaire cried out and fought to turn away, but his lips pressed down upon hers, and his hand tightened in her hair until she was forced to give up the struggle. How quickly things changed with her resistance, how aggressive he became when she no longer stood docile in his arms. He was no gentle man and tread not kindly upon her feelings and fears but forced his intent upon her unwilling lips.

Yet not with bruising pressure. That she expected and would have been able to combat, but with unparalleled expertise and devastating passion. His mouth grazed hers, subtly at first, gliding hither and fro until she struggled as much to keep from answering his unholy quest as she did to turn away. The scent of horseflesh, leather and hard work surrounded her, and it was not unpleasant. She knew each smell intimately and the value of a day's toil. The kiss deepened, became devouring, a live flame that seared an unwelcome path through her weakening body. She felt helpless, swamped by his size and strength, suffocated by the overpowering warmth that invaded her skin and caused her heartbeat to quicken, her breathing to accelerate until she gasped for air.

There was naught of their first kiss in this one, nothing of that petty occurrence that had so rattled her at the time. She wished she could call it back, chance its emotionless rhetoric in place of this more destructive assault, this consumptive force that drew her tightly into its web of fatal longing.

She made a strangled cry for leniency, but he gave no quarter and played heavily upon her anguish by threading his fingers through her hair, then running his knuckles lightly down her neck to her shoulder. His lips moved along her cheek to her ear, and he murmured something softly there, his breath a warm breeze that sent ripples along her spine, before he caught the delicate lobe in his teeth and tugged.

Something startling shot through her and she moaned a protest, but it was weak, disembodied. Her fingers curled clawlike into his *sherte* as she struggled to maintain her grip on reality. But there was madness upon her now, its tempest swirling through her mind to cloud her reasoning and she knew that she must get away, must flee this insanity. She pushed urgently with her fisted hands trapped between them.

The muscles of his abdomen bunched against her fingers, there was a quick intake of breath that seemed far away and she found herself wedged even tighter against his lean stomach. Shock waves rolled through her body as a new force was introduced, a solid thigh pressed close, then between her own and she was brought against his loins. With a horrified gasp she withdrew her hands and shoved against his shoulders, but he took her wrists and placed her hands back to their resting place, while his grin flashed white in a slow, triumphant smile.

LeClaire stared back at his smile, his eyes, with morbid fascination as his mouth once again lowered to hers. Her feverish head swam and she could feel herself slipping . . . slipping . . . lost in a sea of wintry gray where ice was fire and understanding tangled with the incomprehensible until the two meshed and she could not tell real from imagined, hot from cold, fear from desire. She felt weightless yet heavy and knew not how she managed to remain on her feet save for the strong hands that seemed to be all places and none. And she sensed that if she relaxed one inch of her fading strength, she would crumble in a boneless heap about his feet and all would be irreversible.

Borgia's hands lingered only moments on her wrists, then rose to seek out greater treasure. They captured her cheeks, his fingers warm and firm at her temples, his thumbs grazing so lightly over her jaw and down her neck that every inch he touched tingled. He found her skin fine as a babe's, her scent a heady thing that glided across his senses like a gentle caress. There was no perfume to mask an unwashed body, merely the fresh smell of cleanliness that was more potent than anything he had encountered. He inhaled deeply to capture her essence as his mouth moved to her neck, and he nipped at the strained tendons there, ever careful to keep a firm grip on her lest she flee his hold and the struggle begin again.

She shuddered beneath his hands and lips but could no longer be made to relax and kept her body tight and rigid against him, her hands fisted at his middle, inadvertently seductive even in resistance. Borgia swept up along her neck to recapture her mouth.

"Yield, damoiselle," he whispered against her lips, the deep timbre of his voice making her quiver anew. They were alluring words, soothing, arousing, with a hint of promise she could not define. His knee lifted slightly as if to emphasize his words and bits of LeClaire shattered around him as she cried out.

"Nay," she begged, her heart pulsing madly, her cheeks burning with embarrassment at the disgraceful position and her own awful heated reaction to it. "Why do you do this?"

"I've need of you." A few simple words that seemed to mean infinitely more.

"Merciful Father, why?" she cried out again, unable to discern the meaning though she sensed the underlying danger.

"Why?" Borgia pulled back slightly, his eyes glittering shards of silver ice. "To ease this agony," he said, and pushed her hands lower on his body.

LeClaire's eyes widened and fell to his lower parts, then rose back quickly when she realized what she had done. Crimson blazed across her cheeks, and the heat of righteous indignation sparked in her azure eyes.

"Mother of God!" she gasped, more embarrassed and incensed than she had ever been in her too innocent life. "Art the crudest man I have ever known! If you've a need to relieve yourself, seek out the garderobe! Lest you fancy yourself a babe in training, you hardly need me for such!"

Borgia reared his head back slowly and pinned her with a dark narrow-eyed gaze. LeClaire pushed against him and stumbled back a step, her breath ragged and drawn from the outrage, but he only waited, his eyes cold, his slight smile demonic. She struggled to gather the shredded threads of her composure, to make some right of so wrongful a situation, but could grasp no meaning behind all the turmoil and confusion. Her eyes rose to his as if the answer might be hidden in the icy depths there.

As if a candle had been lit to dispel the darkness, his meaning, his unholy intentions, began to dawn in her befuddled brain. "Lord God," she said in a vaporous whisper, and her trembling fingers rose to cover her lips. Her hand curled into a fist and dropped to press against the wildly throbbing pulse at the base of her throat. "You . . . you wish to bed with me?" The words were out before she could call them back and she cursed her scattered wits. "You cannot . . . cannot mean . . . cannot want . . ."

"Want?" he said with a cryptic lift of his brow. "Aye, LeClaire, I want."

"Please," she whispered, and took a step back. The bounds of his wickedness knew no limits. If she had not been completely convinced of it before, she was now. By his own words he would do what he dared, take what he wanted, as he had all else at Ravenwood. Her mind raced over alternatives, solutions, bargains, as was her nature—healer, problem solver, pacifier.

"If—" She cleared her throat with a little cough. "If you are in need of a soothing ointment . . ." *Fool! Fool!* She could not fathom the liniment used for sore muscles doing him any grand service there. More like it would set him afire.

Borgia took a step toward her, the contempt on his face so pronounced LeClaire found herself quickly backing up. "Be not ashamed," she said sincerely, her hands held before her in supplication, her voice a mere puff of wind because she herself was so embarrassed by this conversation she did not think she could bear it.

"I do not need the garderobe," Borgia said in scornful humor. "I do not need an ointment. I need you." He reached out and cupped her chin, pulling her face closer to meet his. "You wear your innocence like a mantle, cloaking yourself in ignorance when the need arises and casting it off when stupidity does not serve your purpose." His fingers bit into the tender skin of her face, not brutal but more . . . branding, like the lion upon his standard, and LeClaire wondered miserably if she would wear his mark for days hence.

"Ah, but you are not stupid, bratling," he said lowly. "You had begun restoring Ravenwood too well for that. You merely see what you want to see and disregard the rest." His fingers loosened on her chin and drifted down to the slender column of her throat. "Your kind is a bane to man's existence. Untouched and unwilling, you flitter about, tempting a man until he would try you despite your inexperience. Then you cry rogue and scoundrel at him for doing that which he was driven to do."

His eyes seared her with a hint of self-derision for allowing even a measure of his lingering hunger to rule his words. There was infinitely more pleasure in seduction than in force. "Withhold your favors then this night, damoiselle innocent, as if 'tis a precious thing. Soon enough, I vow, you'll think it a curse." His hand tightened lightly on her throat. "There will be other nights."

His words were so completely foreign to her that LeClaire could only stare at him in wide-eyed confusion. It almost seemed as if he spoke to someone else. That he threatened her was evident, just what that threat encompassed was unclear. Her tongue darted out to wet her lips, but she found that she could not speak beyond the dryness in her throat. His eyes were upon her cruelly, and her heart fluttered against her ribs as she but waited for some horror to befall her at his hands.

Her fear and confusion did not go unheeded, and Borgia stepped back apace. The heat in him had waned, cooled by her virtue. But she would not stay in innocent slumber forever, and he would be near for her awakening. In truth, would hasten it along. His eyes moved slowly over her as he absently rubbed the muscles of his bruised shoulder. Nay, she would not service him in that way this night, but she could serve him in others.

"Make ready to attend my bath," he ordered cordially, then turned and strode from the room.

8

LeClaire stared blindly after him, frozen where she stood until he disappeared behind the connecting door. Relief washed over her in slow tides, a rippling effect dissolving the tension in each of her strained muscles, but leaving her limbs atremble. There was a newer and greater danger now, one she had not anticipated since Ravenwood was first taken. When a warlord lay siege to another's holdings his soldiers often raped and pillaged entire villages with his blessing. But it had not been that way here. Borgia's reign had brought prosperity in its wake, not degradation of that type. Her fingers fidgeted nervously with her gown at the shadowy threat emerging before her. She wanted not to see the full possibilities of this new terror, knew not how she could stand against him and defend herself should his will demand her compliance. He had left her merely shaken and confused this night, with her virtue intact, but what of other nights?

Ah, God help her, he had said there would be other nights.

"Stand firm," she whispered in a feeble voice, a wasted mimicry of the Guardian's full, rich command. A burning behind her eyelids caused her to lower them and her bottom lip trembled slightly. "I know not how!" she begged, but her words echoed back, taunting her, lacking the faith that had been the cornerstone of her existence. And she knew she mocked her Maker and His great power with her weak and will-less trust. "Aye, I will do it. I will stand firm!"

She felt buoyed by her resolve, though she knew not where it would lead her. Her knees stopped their trembling and she stood taller, braced to face the unknown trials to come. Weapons were useless in her hands, but she would arm herself with knowledge. There was much she must learn about men and their ways, their needs and wants, and how to counterbalance them.

But where to turn? Her maidservant, Hannah, was forward-speaking and had a husband and sons. She would ask Hannah about men's strange desires when she could amass enough courage to approach the delicate subject. Mayhaps she could learn of a potion or an ointment to ease Borgia's unwholesome condition and discreetly place it in his chamber so as not to cause either of them further discomfort.

LeClaire's lips pressed firmly together. She should do naught to offer him aid but should let him rot in his own misery. How easily he had come and conquered, taken her land, her home, made little more than slaves of her and her sisters and might yet cast them out. But, alas, she did not delude herself into thinking she could ignore the situation, and she was not one to withhold what little comfort she could give others.

But he had said he needed not an ointment. Well, he needed not *her* for his licentious notions either! What he needed was a wife if he could not control his wickedness, but she could think of no poor damsel she would wish that fate upon. Men often took a leman for their needs, married or not, but she did not look upon that as an honorable solution to suggest to him either.

God's own truth! It was not her place to pass judgment or worry over his black immortal soul. It was no sin of hers if he took a leman, as long as she was not the mistress taken. But something deep inside her cringed at the idea, though she could not say why. Mayhaps the wrongness of it or the fact that a woman favored by him would hold a place above her own at Ravenwood. That thought sent a panicky quickening to her heartbeat. To not hold Ravenwood as her own was tragic enough, but to have another . . . She could not finish the horrifying thought, would not even imagine that such a thing were possible. There was a way around this dilemma, there must be—

Attend his bath? LeClaire's head snapped up when she recalled the command, but her heart sunk to her toes. She had no experience with such things, though she knew it was commonplace for the ladies of a castle to attend those matters, usually for visiting guests. There had never been guests in her father's cottage, and her mother had seen to his needs herself. Nay, she could not, *would not* do it. She would ignore Borgia's command, aye, pay it no heed whatsoever. And mayhaps he would forget he had even given her an order.

And mayhaps warhorses could fly, she thought when her name sounded from his chamber.

"Nay!" she called back, then decided she best seek cover. She knew what it meant to defy him, knew a price would be forfeit for daring to, but still she spun around and scanned her room. But there was nowhere to hide in her tiny chamber and no time to search out a place when of a sudden her door swung open and she was snatched up from behind. A steely arm clamped around her waist, and her feet took leave of the floor. She grabbed the arm to free herself, and the palms of her hands met flesh—wet, muscular flesh.

The Lion was naked!

Or at least that portion of him squeezing the life out of her was unclad. She clenched her eyes shut, daring not to look to the rest of him for fear of what she would find. Merciful Father! Had a maiden ever encountered the troubles forced upon her?

"My lord," LeClaire said in breathless anxiety. "My

lord, I know not how to attend a man's bath. You must excuse me from this chore.''

No words answered her plea, and with a squeal of dismay, LeClaire found herself being propelled backward against his hip, hauled like a sack of greens under that wet, naked arm. She set up a disturbance when they passed through the doorway connecting her room with his, attaching herself like a leech to the door frame, but her kicking and clinging proved worthless given his size and strength. Her fingers were pried away, and she found herself in motion again, but she would not be defeated without a valiant effort on her part. With all the virulence of a crazed woman, she kicked and bucked and squirmed until Borgia'd had enough.

LeClaire suddenly found herself shifted over his other arm, further upended, and two heavy swats to her backside sufficiently quelled the fight in her. Her entire body went limp, and her eyes stayed closed but her buttocks tightened in anticipation of further thrashing. So, he would beat her now, and she would return bruised and bleeding to her room, but she would not have to attend his bath. She thought the trade worthy lest he rendered her unconscious or murdered her. It would be hard indeed to go about her duties in either of those conditions. She almost giggled aloud at the hysterical thoughts, certain now that insanity had finally overcome her and she would spend the rest of her days as a mindless old crone. It was nearly anticlimactic when naught else occurred, save she was moved farther into the room.

His room! ·

Her body was jostled; she heard the splash of water, then her abused rear scraped against the rim of a wooden tub. With one arm, Borgia spun her around and released her only long enough for his fingers to grab the front of her kirtle.

Yea, he was naked, all of him!

Or so she reasoned. In truth, LeClaire saw only a

broad, iron-thewed chest and the firm slope of his belly above the water before her eyes flew past his face to the ceiling. Holy Mary, he was trim to be so strong! And bronze! As if the sun had touched all of him. Nary a hint of anxiety or embarrassment tinted his sculptured cheekbones, and his eyes boldly stared at her, lightning-struck granite in their brilliance, his expression cynically amused. And he sat naked in a bath, completely at ease, his fingers clutched in her gown.

She could think of no way at all to escape without ripping the clothing she wore right from her body and fleeing—naked as he—back to her room. What would that avail her? He would only come after her, and they would both be bare as fresh-hatched babes. The thought of facing him in that manner was unthinkable, unbearable, and LeClaire knew sensible reason was her only hope now.

"My lord," she said calmly to the beams overhead as if her heart were not pounding furiously in her breast. "I . . . I am not trained in this duty. Mayhaps Hannah or—"

There was a pull against her breastbone, and the sound of popping threads and ripping linen rang like thunder in her ears. Her teeth snapped shut, and her breath lodged fatally somewhere between her chest and her throat. She blinked rapidly at the roof above and wondered wretchedly if her torn gown was about to fall around her ankles. She would die of the embarrassment, most assuredly, or swoon. Heaven help her, she had never swooned. The thought of doing so now—naked if he released her ripped gown, for his fingers were the only thing holding it together—almost caused it to happen.

Her head grew light, dizziness assailed her, the room spun. Only when she swayed drunkenly and air came whooshing out of her mouth did she realize the fault was her own for holding her breath. She took several deep gulps of air by way of recompense, and the room righted itself.

"Hold out your hand." It was a command, indisputable.

LeClaire's head jerked down before she thought, and her eyes met his. Vibrant blue and storm gray clashed and held, and LeClaire was swept away on a tide of fierce and instinctive need to protect herself.

He was . . . magnificent! Long and broad of limb and girth, sleek bronze skin stretched taut over bulging muscles, hair and eyes like thunderstone—he was the embodiment of all things of power and beauty, ancient and present. Beautiful and primitive with the trappings of civilization stripped away, virile and overwhelming, a pagan war god risen from stone. Thor or Adonis or . . . the Guardian. LeClaire cried out softly in repentance. It was little more than a sacrilege to view him thus, and blood red washed her cheeks as she made some garbled response before snatching her eyes back to the roof.

"Your hand, damoiselle."

Calm. She must needs calm herself and deal rationally with him. He was just a man, a mere mortal, with a sound mind and . . . Lord in heaven, a sound body. "Nay, I—"

Another tug, another rent. The gown went slack on her shoulders, reason fled as if it had never existed, and her hands flew up to claw at his, her nails biting into the iron strength gripping her kirtle. Her eyes never left the farthest corner of the room, but the struggle ensued forthwith until her fingers were pried away and a damp cloth pressed into her palm.

"Damn she-cat," Borgia said in wonder, for she had bloodied his hand. "I ought to have you beaten."

"You would have another do again what you have done already in yon doorway?" LeClaire said tremulously. "Have done then, so that I might retire!"

"Art an insolent wench," Borgia said dryly, "and

brave to the point of foolery with that errant tongue."
His eyes traveled over her in speculation, seeing the people's heroine wrapped up in a beggar's package. She would decry his mastery over her, but she had been a slave to her own sense of responsibility long before he had come and made her one to his will. There was more to LeClaire of Ravenwood beneath the common clothes the world did not see, would not see, for she was their champion and it would weaken her in their eyes if they knew how vulnerable she was.

But he sensed it and more. Aye, there was more than just the devotion, the honesty and virtue. There was anger, pain and loneliness. With three sisters and an entire village of people, there was abject loneliness. His fingers tightened and he gave her a little jerk.

"You call that little tap a beating, damoiselle? 'Twas merely a warning. When next I put my hand to your rump, you will know the difference."

He awaited a response, but she did nothing but hold her body rigid, as if surrounding herself with an unseen shield of protection, and stare upward. He folded her fingers around the cloth and held them there. "You serve the others of Ravenwood so well, bratling, 'tis time you serve me."

"I know not how," she cried, detesting the whine in her voice almost as much as she detested him. Why could she not stand courageously before him as Maire would, or with calm intellect as would Kyra? Instead she quivered like a pulled bowstring, uncertain and afraid, much like Aurel would, only not as gracefully silent.

" 'Tis the lady's duty to see to the lord's bath."

"I swear I know not how!" LeClaire exclaimed. "I have knowledge of the custom, but I've never been called upon to do it. There were no guests in my father's house."

"You clean soot from the hearth," came the silken

taunt. " 'Tis little enough for you to learn to scrub my back."

"*Art naked!*"

His soft laugh was an awful thing to her ears, mocking and insulting coupled with the sound of water sloshing the sides of the tub. They seemed to meld and flow in heathen rhythm with the flicker of shadows along the candlelit wall and the drum of LeClaire's frightened heartbeat. "Aye, bratling, 'tis most uncomfortable to bathe otherwise. Now, apply the cloth."

"I cannot look on you," she pleaded. "Let me fetch Hannah or someone else."

"Cease ere you insult me, damoiselle. A maid only tends a lesser noble. The lady sees to the lord and visiting royalty. You do proclaim yourself lady of Ravenwood, be about it. The cloth."

" 'Twould shame me! I pray you—"

"Be still," Borgia commanded. "I am not ashamed. Since I am the one naked, why should you suffer embarrassment?"

There was just the tiniest bit of logic in that statement, just enough to stall LeClaire's response. It took only a second, however, for her to mull it over and decide he toyed with her. "Art an evil, *evil* man, Borgia de St. Brieuc."

"Aye, and a dirty one. Come, maiden, attend me as you would the most noble visitor to grace this grand hall. You cannot mean to convince me that you have *never* seen a man unclad."

"I have not, and will not, no matter how noble the man be!" LeClaire's answer was delivered in defiance but it sprang from absolute truth. Hope that he would release her when he realized that truth grew all out of proportion for her dire situation if she had but realized it. But she thought only of giving her explanation rapidly, before her gown landed at her feet. "As I have said before, I was not raised in a great hall. I have never attended a man's bath, and would make a mess of the whole affair, thereby insulting you with my miserable efforts. I would beg leave to fetch someone well versed in such matters." She had no notion just whom that someone might be but was quite satisfied with her logic.

Having said that, she made to move away but found his fingers still clutched in her kirtle, and the step she took was modest compared to the one she made when jerked back. She stumbled against the side of the tub, the edge cutting into her hipbones as she almost toppled over it. Her hands flailed down to steady herself and met with naked knees, then slid over wet, hairy flesh to naked thighs.

"Merciful Father," she gasped, jerking her hands back too quickly to prevent the weight of her forward motion from propelling her right over the rim of the tub. A cry and a splash echoed in the chamber, and LeClaire found her feet dangling in mid-air, while her face and chest rested just beneath the surface of the water atop naked legs. *Merciful Father!* The water surrounding her face, filling her ears and nostrils, did naught to cool the fire in her cheeks. It was what hell was truly like, not the fire and brimstone of fleshly nightmares but emotional slaughter—slow burning humiliation, helplessness, fear.

Borgia tried to wrench her back up to keep her from drowning, but LeClaire thought a watery grave a much nicer alternative to sharing his bath. After a quick and slippery struggle, where his hands seemed to be everywhere at once, Borgia lifted her by the waist and swung her half-circle until she lay fully upon him, soaking wet, and thoroughly mortified. His fingers went down beneath her chin to force her head from the water, and LeClaire had no choice but to face him—eyes closed.

"Please," she whimpered. He was a solid mass of muscle and sinew beneath her and surrounding her. The tub was not quite large enough to accommodate his length, so his knees were drawn up, and she lay between them.

She could not think of the firm wall of his chest and flat stomach where her hands braced, his skin warm and water-slick beneath her palms, nor of the hard barrier of his thighs on either side of her waist and hips. Nor could she think of that which probed her belly, for it sent her heart skipping off on such a wild flight she feared it would desert her. The coolness of the water caused a ripple along her flesh, puckering it in places better left uncounted. Stinging awareness shot through her, knowing he could see everything through her thin wet gown.

But the heat and strength of him beneath her was even more damning, for her mind and imagination could see clearly what her closed eyes refused to—the power and beauty of his physical form fitted to her tiny frame in unbelievable harmony as if it were meant to be just so, the flimsy gown of linen scarce protection from her first feel of a man's nakedness.

A whisper of the forbidden tapped the young woman's secrets—dormant wonderings she had not known existed. Questions seeking answers. Curiosity came begging at the door of her sharp mind and quivering heart, imploring her to explore the new sensations swirling within her. Wondrous and wretched things called softly, shivering delight and astounding bewitchment, longing and needy fascination so profound she could not fathom them and wanted to curl up in Borgia's strong arms, to escape, to hide from herself in the power and warmth of him.

"Bratling," he drawled, his voice a dark caress over her wet cheeks. One hand rose to brush a lock of hair back from her pale face. Candlelight played in shimmering waves through her wild tresses, amber, topaz, ruby, gold. Jeweled droplets of water danced there like fairies at the witching hour, sparkling and swaying to the tune of an enchanted lute. One drop tumbled free and rolled down her cheek to her neck, then slipped into the valley of her breasts. Borgia's eyes followed its path until it was lost from sight. "You attend me quite well for one who claims no training."

"You play me for a foolish child," she said, feeling like a youth caught in mischief, the deed exposed for all to see.

His hands spanned her tiny waist, the thumbs circling her hipbones while his fingers spread across the small of her back. Petite in length and breadth, the weight of her was nothing on his warrior's body—nothing but tremendously disturbing. His body hardened in response, and he wondered had another ever enticed him just by being, merely by her existence, the way this one did.

"I would play you for a woman," he said, his voice grown husky. Her torn bodice gaped open, unwittingly abetted by her efforts to strain away from him, and revealed a smooth expanse of milk-white skin and softly rounded breasts. The tips were covered but teased the sodden fabric, as if they would tempt him with hidden delights. The lure was wanton, stretching out to ensnare him like a silken ribbon.

He shifted beneath her, the entire hard length of him rubbing against her like a fluid caress. With the water to aid his purpose, his movements were slow and controlled, designed to create the greatest pleasure but gave torment instead, and his voice was hypnotic in its urgency. "Aye, I would play you for a woman, but you cry foul. Play the game, LeClaire. Know that which other women know; you are not too young, just too inexperienced."

"Your words have no meaning to me," she said, eyes tightly closed, cheeks aflame. His masculine presence was devastating in its command of her senses. Her pulse hammered in her ears, the fresh smell of soap wafted up from the water and her limbs seemed as weightless as the dancing bright sparkles of color behind her clenched eyes. She was awash with sensations hitherto unknown, unfelt, and her mind cried out for release. Reason was elusive, calling to her from the outer realms to take hold so that her world might right itself and stop its infernal spinning. "I *am* a woman; I know plenty. 'Tis unfair! One who is ignorant is incapable of learning; I am not like that. I will—"

One hand released her waist to slide leisurely over her rib cage until his palm covered her mouth, his thumb stroked droplets of water from her cheek. "You see what you will, nothing more. 'Tis childish and ignorant. You are old enough to know a man, but you do not. Hear me, damoiselle." His hand left her mouth to thread through the glossy hair at her temples, tipping her face up to more fully enjoy her fair beauty. Her lashes were long and dark, fanning the apricot-tinted cheeks, her lids crinkled slightly from squeezing her eyes shut. Her lips were parted and a shade redder from the previous pressure of his hand. Desire came slowly, warmly, like the colors of LeClaire—peach and azure, the earth and the sky, nature as yet unspoiled by man. His deep voice was as smooth and potent as mulled wine. "Open your eyes, damoiselle, and look to me."

Fearful of what she would see, though she knew that was unreasonable, LeClaire kept her eyes closed. She was not superstitious, he was incapable of casting a spell upon her. But the feelings were much the same, as if he wielded some unnatural power over her mind and heart. His hand drifted down to stroke the top of her breasts, and her startled eyes snapped open, as was his intent.

"You want this," he whispered, his hand going back to her face. He held her motionless with eyes as still and cold as winter's frost. She shook her head dumbly, but could not answer, could not form the words to deny him. "Aye, you do. A woman's age, a woman's body. A child's mind?"

"Nay," she whimpered softly, and knew not why his words hurt her so.

"Show me," he said. "Touch me as I will touch you."

His words were a seductive caress, a luring challenge, touching every nerve in her body, plucking at the threads of her barely held composure until it was unraveling into bits. With a toss of her head, LeClaire tried to shrug his hands off, and again her eyes squeezed shut. She could not look into his silver eyes; they beckoned her, called forth truths she would deny. Her clothing was wet and clung to her, a scant barrier against his nakedness. She could feel him, feel every hard plane and angle of his powerful body. His fingers were strong on her face, the thumbs outlining her cheeks, and however gentle their touch, she knew the strength of him. It invaded the very pores of her skin to become a part of her, not one with her but overpowering her, replacing her inner control with his indomitable will.

Her back ached from arching away from him in the close confines of the tub, and her mind was a substance-less mass of confusion from his strange words. She felt the need to defend herself, but knew not against what. His accusation that she did not know a man? She knew little enough; that was true. Mayhaps she was as childish and ignorant as he accused, for she certainly seemed lacking in wits now.

But she had not thought it was so, had never thought she was so devoid of good sense. She knew she was not worldly, had not experienced those things of grace and grandeur her mother had often spoken of; she did not have Aurel's beauty or Maire's gift for song, and she would never be able to cipher numbers as quickly as Kyra. But she knew all manner of things about survival, and in the end, did it not all come down to that? It had always been sufficient; why did it seem so paltry now?

She awaited further argument, but the silence unfurled between them like a tightly wound ribbon released to writhe and curl and streamer down in suspended motion. Her head drooped forward as if in defeat, her red-gold tresses floating atop the water, and her sigh was loud in the still room.

"I would rise," she begged.

His hands slid from her face, glided down her neck, then lightly drifted across her breasts. She stiffened in response but could not seem to gather the wherewithal to flee or even deny him. A small sob shuddered through her, and her locked arms quivered.

"I would rise!" she pleaded again.

"One day," he said softly but without tenderness, "you will crave this."

Nay, nay! She would not! She would never—

His lips found hers, softly, so softly one would have thought him a man of great compassion and gentleness. But there was nothing at all of that in his kiss. It was a dark promise, a bottomless threat into which she was hurled, an undeniable assurance of what would be.

Her eyes flew open and she reared back until almost kneeling over him, uncaring that her sodden clothing revealed all. Her breathing was rapid and harsh as she pressed her knotted fists to her aching stomach. "You hurt me!" she accused, bewildered and panicked.

His eyes flickered, then a slow appreciative grin traced his mouth. "Nay, 'tis desire you feel, LeClaire." His hand fitted itself beneath hers and his fingers splayed wide over her lower stomach. " 'Tis pleasure I would give you to ease this pain."

"Nay," she whispered, shaking her head wildly. She gripped the edges of the tub, her arms trembling. "Nay!" she cried again when his hands went to her waist, but he merely picked her up and placed her over the side.

Bone-weary, his muscles bruised and sore from the day's exercise, Borgia needed the ease of his bath now more than aught else, even the girl. And she needed time to reconcile herself to the truth.

Ah, sweet innocence, it was a poison, but he had drunk its lethal dew before, the heady nectar that beckoned then turned rancid with the tasting. He wanted her without the fight and scratch of an offended kitten, wanted her with the soft and yielding passion of a woman. He watched as she blindly made her way from the room, not deigning to open her eyes, he was certain, until in her own chamber. But *his* eyes were open. Flintlike and smoldering they took note of the way her soaked clothing clung to her slender frame, of the way her hair when wet held the sheen of polished copper, of the abundant curves and swells on so tiny a figure.

He sighed deeply. He would crush her when he took her.

But he grieved not for that fact. Everyone lost their innocence; hers just was later in the coming, and he did not think she had ever been truly innocent. Physically, yea, but her mind was quick, her dedication absolute, and she had known toil most of her life. There was little innocence left in one who had viewed the world from the handle of scythe, from beneath the dirt of an herb garden, from the clutch of a scouring rag. He should have her before the work broke her and made her hard, while there was still a newness about her.

The honey beckoned and was sweet, too sweet to ignore. He would have the taste of it on his tongue, the scent of it in his nostrils, the creamy feel of it beneath his fingers until he had devoured every drop. Let the venom do its worst; he was not susceptible to its sting. He was not a callow youth but a man, jaded by almost a decade of fighting. She might prove . . . refreshing.

He gave her inexperience no more thought. It took only one stab of a man's desire to banish a woman's cursed and overrated chastity. But in some deep and blackened spot within him, he admitted the unchangeable truth. Her faith and virtue were a part of her, intrinsic, alive, not learned, or mimicked or memorized. They could not be banished as easily as her innocence.

Conscience tapped at the edges of his mind, but he

thrust the niggling guilt aside as insignificant. It mattered little whether or not she was willing. He would make her so.

Visions of another unwilling maiden intruded upon his thoughts. A shy and nervous child-bride who had seemed eager enough to become betrothed to the youngest St. Brieuc son. Knighted earlier than was customary for his superb military abilities, he had been a bold and arrogant lad of seven and ten years who thought himself a man. The wedding had been a grandiose affair, uniting two powerful families as marriages were meant to do, but the spoiled bride had gone horrified to the marriage bed and had loathed the groom's attentions every night henceforth, until death had released her from her vows. Borgia coldly tossed the sickening thoughts aside. There had been no spirit in his wife, a woman given to histrionics and pampering. He had grown bored of her in a sennight, her meekness and mediocrity stirring naught in him but cold indifference.

Hair of fire and eyes of blue ice replaced the memory and Borgia leaned back leisurely in the tub.

Ah, virgin, beware. Your days of innocence are numbered.

9

LeClaire stumbled to her room, shed her ruined clothing and, on knees that threatened to fold beneath her, crept to the security of her cot. She pressed her hands to her eyes as if the darkness were not enough to shield her vision and felt the heat of confusion and embarrassment yet burning on her cheeks. Deep within her was an ache, a low keening that hummed now in restless indecision as if it could not choose whether to scream or die. She could not put a word to the feelings, for she had never felt them, but the restive humors wept for ease.

Her mind tumbled over minutes past, cresting and crashing, eroding the edges of her calm as if it were a fine grain of sand to be swept out into bottomless depths. She sighed so deeply her chest hurt and would not allow her troubled thoughts free rein, for she could not abide them and sought safe passage in sleep. But sleep was an elusive thing, creeping near to beckon her then darting quickly away like an impish child. Visions of the Lion—his bronzed skin sleek and wet, the glittering gray of his eyes when he looked upon her, his movements beneath her—could not be put to rest but continued to invade her thoughts, causing her heart to thud uneasily. She pulled a fur hide up to her chin and huddled beneath it, curled into a tight protective ball.

Borgia de St. Brieuc, with his overwhelming stature,

overbearing personality and overweening pride, made her feel . . . defenseless.

Another sigh echoed in the small room, taunting her with its useless melody. On one level she had always felt this way, helpless, unable to accomplish those things she wanted most to achieve, lacking the courage or knowledge or wherewithal. But this was a different kind of inadequacy. This thing he wanted, she was incapable of giving but knew he was wholly capable of taking.

"Lord," LeClaire whispered desperately, "what am I to do?" But she knew the answer even before tolerance and patience and love flowed through her tarnished mind and troubled soul. She must stand firm.

The cottage was a crackling, hissing furnace of deadly heat and smoke when Borgia arrived in the village followed by the servant who had roused him from sleep. The sight was alarming yet competent. An organized line had been set up and villeins passed buckets of water to quench the fire while the hut nearest was being chopped to the ground to prevent the blaze from spreading. A woman wailed incoherently, her face ravaged by hysteria and a man covered in ash and soot held her crumpled body restrained in his arms.

Borgia stepped forward but drew up short when Le-Claire stumbled from the blazing hut, her face blackened from the smoke as was her shift. She dropped a squalling child at his feet, then attempted to run back in. Realizing her intent, he grabbed her arm and commenced dragging her away from the suffocating heat. With a fury he had never seen, she rounded on him with a shove that caught him off guard and sent him stumbling back a step. His hold slackened to catch his balance, and she wrenched free and raced back into the flames.

He took off after her, fighting the broiling death as flames leaped and boiled with the smoke pouring outward from the hut. He could see nothing as he pressed forward, his lungs seared, and the stench of his own charred hair burned his nostrils as he tried to enter the cottage. His cloak held before him, he found the threshold, but LeClaire was already on the way out, clutching a tiny bundle close to her breast. She stumbled past him, then fell to her knees with the baby, coughing and choking until she thought her lungs would collapse.

"Is there another?" Borgia shouted, beating at the flames licking their way up her shift.

"Nay," she rasped, her throat so raw and burning it was an effort just to breathe.

The babe was quickly gathered up into the arms of the man who had been holding the distraught woman, and his wife's screams echoed anew as the hut fell in upon itself in a heap of sparks and flying embers. Borgia dragged LeClaire away and doused her with a bucket of water before returning to oversee the scene.

The villagers and his men worked side by side, doing all possible, but after a time nothing more could be accomplished. The hut lay in a rubble of smoldering ash and charred wood, and the fire had been contained by destroying the second cottage. Borgia ordered the families who had lost their homes to be taken to the hall and cared for, then left some of his own men to stand guard should the flames erupt again.

His eyes strained through the darkness and smoke to find LeClaire. She sat crouched and coughing where he'd left her, a small crumpled sodden mass of femininity. Something shifted and settled within him at the sight of the great lady of Ravenwood, the noble peasant, defender of virtue, the people's champion . . . the lost little girl.

He moved to stand over her, his eyes as chilled as the winter moon, but there was another emotion, little seen by those who knew him, glowing from the silver orbs. He reached a hand down, but LeClaire winced in pain when he tried to help her to her feet. He could see welts of burned flesh beginning to fester on her exposed skin. Amid and despite her sudden cry of protest, he swung her up in his arms, slapped his hand over her mouth to ensure silence and proceeded to carry her. LeClaire, taking note of the fierce and severe look on his face, lay quiet in his arms, too tired and hurting to give further argument.

He slung her over his shoulder long enough to mount his charger, Ares, then again settled her before him, cradling her with one arm while his other took the reins. LeClaire leaned over his arm to stare a long, long way down to the ground below, then turned her gaze back up to Borgia's. He gave her a hard look, then put his palm to the side of her face. Pressing her head to his chest, he started for the hall. LeClaire sighed and rested there, her cheek bumping gently against him in rhythm with the horse's gait.

This day had been the longest of her life and filled with more mind-numbing turmoil than she had ever encountered. If she had wanted to protest Borgia's handling of her, she could not have, for she was completely drained of strength and so exhausted her eyelids would not stay open. The winter wind blew cold, and set her to shivering but there was naught she could do about it had she the energy. Borgia spoke not a word but pulled his mantle from his shoulders as he had once before and tucked it around her, enfolding her in warmth and security. And for the briefest span of time she reveled in it, snuggling her face deep into his chest to block out the wind and the world and the man . . . even as she took comfort from him.

Borgia felt her burrow against his breastbone, felt her slight body pressing against him from thighs to chest, felt the familiar kick in his gut that flooded lower, hot and swift. His body tensed and by sheer force of will he restrained it, made himself relax before he lost control and suffered damage to himself or her atop his mount.

But restraint was hard when he could still see her running from the blazing hut in a thin gown charred by the results of her stupid sense of responsibility. His hands tightened on the reins, but his desire was to pull her tighter against him, to wrap himself up in her warmth until the fire she faced was his own, until between them it flickered and flared and blazed out of control, until the mating of flesh against flesh seared everything in its path to finally burn itself out and there was naught left but smoldering ash, panting breaths and sated bodies.

With a soft curse, he kicked his destrier into a faster pace. LeClaire's chin tilted up, and for a moment she merely gazed upon the strength and beauty of his face. Cruel, ruthless, cold—Borgia de St. Brieuc was all of these. He should not be so beautiful.

"Art angry," she said.

"Aye." His eyes lowered to hers with the word, then lifted again to the hall ahead of them.

"Why?"

He ignored her as he reined his horse in, then dismounted with her in his arms. Hannah met them at the top of the stairs, startled by the sight of the lord carrying her grimy lady cradled like a child.

"Oooo, my lady," she crooned, wringing her hands in her apron. "Oooo, my poor sweet—"

Borgia leveled Hannah with a look that garbled the rest of the words in her throat, then ordered the maidservant to bring water and fresh linens as he kicked open LeClaire's door. He paused only briefly at her pitiful straw-filled pallet, then walked into his own room to place her on the high bed. LeClaire found her voice despite her parched throat, and started protesting. Borgia ignored her and began stripping away her blackened shift. She desperately tried to cover herself, moving her hands this way and that, clutching and grabbing at his unerring fingers.

"Cease," he commanded, and drew out a lethal-looking blade. LeClaire squealed and cringed back into the mattress, but he merely cut the fabric away from her shoulders so he would not have to wrest it from her singed arms, then made a quick slash down the side seam. Hannah rushed back in then and shrieked her own protest at finding her lady in such an improper situation. "Hold your tongue, woman," Borgia warned the servant.

" 'Tis not fitting, my lord!" Hannah wailed, then almost choked on her own impertinent tongue.

"Silence, I say." Borgia rounded on her with a stern look that nearly caused Hannah to faint dead away. "Can you not see the girl is burned? Help her or leave the rags and I'll bathe her myself."

A series of scandalized moans and hand-wringing greeted his icy words.

"Nay!" LeClaire cried, raising up on her elbows only to hurriedly drop back down as her shift fell away. She clutched what was left of it to her breasts. "Please," she begged, turning her eyes to Borgia, "Hannah will care for me."

"Then do so," he said to the servant, but made no move to leave the bedside. Hannah, trembling as if the earth quaked beneath her, covered her lady in a length of linen then removed the tattered gown. Borgia stared at the ruined scrap of cloth, then turned his cold glare back on LeClaire, and she thought she had never seen him quite so formidable. "Why?" he said slowly, his look most cruel. "Why did you do it?"

LeClaire shied away from the expression on his face and turned on her side as Hannah began bathing her face then arms. "I do not understand your words, my lord."

"Art daft?"

LeClaire sensed more than heard the underlying rage and fear put her on the defensive. "Nay, I am in pain. Leave me!"

Hannah's hands faltered and her quivering increased.

"Why did you go back into the hut after I forbade it?"

LeClaire sighed in exasperation mingled with exhaustion. Making certain she was covered she eased onto her back to face him calmly, hoping to banish beforehand any of the rash or disparaging remarks so quick to form on her lips these days.

"There was an innocent babe inside and no time to explain it to you. If I had not gone back, the infant would have died."

"*You* almost died," Borgia said with cool disdain. "How could you think to risk your life for the child of a villager?"

Stunned and shaken by his cruelty, LeClaire lifted her chin in hauteur, her eyes blazed with ridicule. She gave no thought now to tempering the words that burst from her. "What say you? The child of a commoner is of less worth than one born to a great hall? You despicable beast! Is one innocent babe more expendable than another by virtue of blood or lack thereof?"

Hannah was nearly swooning and was spilling more water than bathing LeClaire with it.

Borgia grinned, but his eyes were like ice. *Despicable beast?* God's wounds, she was the bravest bit of fluff he had ever encountered. He leaned low toward her angry little mouth and fought the urge to press his lips to hers to silence her. She was a sight with her delicate face all soot-blackened, her eyes snapping blue fury, her compassion for her people ringing from the depths of her soul. And he was moved as he had not been in years, shaken to the very center of his cold, jaded heart by her courage, her logic, her love.

"Nay, bratling," he said, a mere inch from her grim-set mouth. "Blood is blood. It spills red whether from nobleman or commoner. But why could someone else not go in after the child? 'Twas not your place."

"Then whose?" LeClaire sighed, somewhat drained of

her anger by his admission. "The family was distraught; the men were working to curtail the flames. No one else was available."

"Had there been another, you would not have sent him," he accused.

"Nay," LeClaire admitted softly. " 'Twas only on my mind to get the children out."

Borgia's voice deepened, his eyes flashing with something akin to ire. Yet, it was not anger but more, something LeClaire could not put a name to. " 'Twas foolish of you. Why did the parents not get their children out?"

LeClaire stared up into his forbidding countenance and thought she had never seen him so cold . . . nor so disquieted. It sent a measure of unrest fluttering through her, for even in anger he was always so controlled.

"If I have the right of it, the father saw a fire in the distance. He sent word to the main hall, then went to offer aid. When he arrived to see it was his own hut, he rushed in to pull his wife out, then roused the older children, but the blaze took hold then. The wife grew hysterical and would have killed herself getting to the younger ones, so he held her whilst I went inside. The fire did not seem so bad at first, but escalated when the thatch roof caught."

" 'Tis no explanation. Half the village was there. Even I could have gone in after the last child," Borgia said, as if it were a foregone conclusion and she witless for not seeing it.

LeClaire was too stunned to take offense; her world tilted crazily, toppling her reason end over end. Warmth moved through her, replacing the chill of the night's grueling activity, but still she shivered. Her fingers flexed and she almost reached to touch his strong jaw, so moved was she by his words, as if he might care that she almost came to harm. Her grip tightened again. Merciful Father, the smoke must have gone to her brain. There was no caring in this man, just a silvery hardness to his eyes that bespoke contempt. He was the ruthless beast, the legendary Lion, the conqueror of her holdings. If ever she saw tenderness there, she would think him ill.

"There was no time to explain," she sighed. "I knew exactly where the babe slept. 'Twould have taken precious time to tell someone else."

He continued to stare down at her with an unfathomable expression on his stern face. LeClaire felt weakened by his pensive side, the times like this when he studied her and, she assumed, found her lacking. She almost wished he would make further argument, for it was hard to reconcile the dictator of Ravenwood with this silent, probing man. It was not his face, which was firmly set, nor his cold eyes that made her uneasy, but something instinctive within herself that sensed he was more than bothered by her actions, that he was almost . . . concerned? For her? Nay, it was impossible and she could not think on it, for her mind was already such a twisted mess of confusion she would not heap more atop it. And she was tired, her forearms aching as were a few places on her legs. She flinched and had to bite her lip when Hannah started bandaging a particularly tender spot.

" 'Tis over now," LeClaire said serenely. "The children are safe and no one was injured."

Borgia cocked a wry smile. "No one but you."

"A few scrapes, my lord. 'Twill heal in no time."

He continued to stare at her, then drawled softly, "I suppose I should be thankful you do not whine and moan as other women."

"Truly?" LeClaire said, her eyes bright and questioning with honesty. "I have not known those who did."

"You have been isolated overmuch I fear. You lack womanly wiles, which is to your credit, but you also lack common sense in many ways." His voice lowered and his eyes penetrated the clear blue depths of hers. "Do you fear nothing, bratling?"

"Oh, aye," she said lightly, then winced again at Hannah's cleansing. "There is much I fear, and . . . mayhaps nothing at all. 'Tis hard to explain."

Indeed, hard even to understand. She had known fear all her life—fear of her father's wrath, his violent mercurial moods, fear of starvation, fear of her sisters catching the fever that had claimed her parents and knowing not how to treat them, the paralyzing fear of being alone. And in the presence of so lifelong a collection of fears, she had grown in many ways to fear naught.

" 'Tis foolish not to fear some things," Borgia said. His eyes took on a strange, almost amused light. "Methinks you fear me at times."

LeClaire smiled and shrugged. "Nay, my lord. Betimes I abhor you, but I cannot think of a single incident when I have feared you." It was a blatant lie, but she found the play eased her mind from the stinging abrasions on her body.

Borgia smiled but it was cynical as his gaze roamed her lightly veiled body. Naught but a thin sheet of linen covered her, revealing a provocative combination of crests and valleys that rose and fell faintly with the cadence of her heartbeat. "Even when I search for a key, damoiselle?"

LeClaire's eyes widened then squeezed shut as she felt the traitorous heat rise to her cheeks. "Nay, not even then."

"Or when I am in need of help with my bath?"

"Nay." Oh, the wretched, evil man!

Borgia bent lower still, his breath warm on her ear as he whispered, "When you are in my arms, atop me in that same bath?"

LeClaire's eyes flew back open, but any protest she intended was lost as Hannah took hold of one of her ankles and began to apply a salve to the burned calf. She lay still and cautious, knowing Borgia could see her exposed limb. Her skin grew flushed and expectant, as if all her nerves had risen to the surface.

"Skinny runt," he teased. "How do those sticks carry you about?" In reality, he found the slender legs shapely though small and too muscular for a lady. They were more like the sturdy limbs of a busy young squire. Borgia could appreciate athletic beauty, but he had never seen it on a woman of quality, and the sight brought home Le-Claire's lowly status and the extent of her toil.

Hannah tied off the bandage and straightened. "Are there any more places in need of tending, m'lady?"

"Nay," LeClaire answered too quickly. Whatever dignity she had managed to maintain throughout her eighteen years was in grave danger of being destroyed, and she was most heartily embarrassed by Borgia seeing her unclad legs. The only other injuries she could feel were in even more indecent places that would see her sitting tenderly for a few days, but she would suffer them festering before she would let him see them. When Borgia turned his mocking glance her way she hastened to explain. "I soaked my shift ere entering the hut."

He reached down to hook his finger in her discarded undergown and held it aloft. It was thin and worn, unsightly in its flimsy, charred state. "What were you doing in only this for protection? Do you oft chase trouble about nearly naked?"

"I did not take time to dress," she said sheepishly, a blush rising to her cheeks. She had taken her cloak but knew not what had become of it. She could hardly defend her actions when she only now realized what had occurred. Holy Mary, the entire village must have seen her half-undressed!

"And here I thought you a modest little virgin," Borgia drawled.

Her color flared higher The man was utterly depraved to speak to her so! LeClaire groaned and turned her face into the pillow. *His* pillow. She'd never felt the like. It was feather-filled, soft and luxurious, and held a clean masculine smell. It was nothing like hers, for her puny pillows were fern- or straw-filled and not nearly so wonderful. Her head rolled slowly to and fro to savor the exquisite comfort and she noted something more—beeswax candles. It was unheard of to own such! They were so rare, and she found them astonishing, for they did not give off the awful odor and smoke of the resinous torches. Truly his wealth must be great to have brought such things with him.

Borgia dropped her ruined shift and watched her struggle with embarrassment and some sort of odd fascination. She seemed for a moment to be in ecstasy as her face buried itself into his pillow, then childlike wonder as her eyes traveled across his chamber. His loins quickened at the sight of her momentary abandon in his bed, his muscles contracted and he steeled himself against the swift, unexpected arousal.

"You are not to be called first again when there is trouble," he said. "I will give the servants the order but 'tis up to you to obey. And you are ordered to rest. If you are seen belowstairs ere the sun is high, I will personally carry you back to this chamber and beat some sense into your burned backside. Is that understood?" At LeClaire's dazed nod, he continued, "And remember my words about the people. You will not be summoned first again."

"There was no disrespect intended," she said. " 'Tis only that the villagers are used to coming to me. It has been our way." She gave him a tremulous smile, hoping he was not bent on retribution. "You will not punish them?"

"A tongue lashing only," he admitted, tucking the cover around her. "You could have been injured far worse, and I would not have that on my conscience, LeClaire."

"I had not thought you had one," she whispered.

Neither had he.

* * *

Roger sat in the long hall enjoying a draft of mead when Borgia descended the stairs. Waving him over, Roger offered him a tankard and bade him sit. "Is the girl well?"

"Aye," Borgia responded absently, his eyes on the landing at the top of the stairs. He almost expected Le-Claire, in defiance of his orders, to come down those steps any moment to see to some common chore, cleaning the hall or sticking her bandaged arms in wash water. So help him, burned arse and all, he would beat obedience into her if she dared. "Minor burns and the like. 'Tis her stubbornness that most concerns me. She could have been hurt worse or killed."

Roger eyed Borgia with a curious grin. "Does it matter? She is but a slave?"

"Be not absurd." Borgia fixed his friend with an icy gray stare. "She is needed here. I have found no other capable of running Ravenwood as well, for she knows the needs here and sees to them with more concern for the people's well-being than for coin as a steward or bailiff would."

"You do not mean to let her continue doing the job you would assign a man?" Roger asked, stunned.

"Not likely," Borgia returned cynically. "I will hire both soon enough, but I can not overlook the girl's worth until I do."

"Then why, if I may be so simpleminded to ask, do you continue to beleaguer her efforts and take issue when she does as you wish?"

"Because, my halfwit friend, she does too much."

"Ah," Roger nodded. "That makes a multitude of sense."

"Know you what I am saying," Borgia grinned sardonically. "The people go to her for everything. They think I know not that they follow my commands to the best of *her* abilities. They bring her their woes and play upon her sympathies, hoping she will take the brunt of my anger if their efforts displease me. They seek her out for the simplest things, and she never denies them nor complains but goes about resolving the ills of her world. I vow, they could work her unto death and feel no remorse."

"Mayhaps," Roger said, serious now. "But methinks they love and respect her but have never been called upon to use their own judgment."

Borgia nodded. "Aye, I will not deny it, Roger, but the people are not as ignorant or helpless as they would have her believe. They've been indulged with her easy manner and diligent care. They take her too much for granted."

"Aye," Roger agreed. "Many a goodwife could mix her own cures, the farmers could prepare their own fields without direction and the livestock tenders need not come to her for every decision."

Borgia smiled coldly. "They do not wish to accept responsibility for their own decisions. If they fail, they can lay the blame at her door. I have put a stop to some of it."

"Think you she fears being cast out if she and her sisters do not prove their worth?"

"She would be wise to consider it," Borgia said, then smiled. "She does not accept defeat meekly."

"Aye," Roger chuckled. "She would be lady here and have everything go on as before, as if we'd risked our arse for naught on these shores. The lass is used to ruling her domain, but which is it? Does she relish the power or is it merely that she knows no other way?"

"Mayhaps a bit of both," Borgia murmured. They had both known too many women who enjoyed the rule of their house, the power they wielded over others and having subservient people at their command.

Roger knew Borgia's look, the silver gaze of introspection he had not seen in years. "She is not Margaret of Beaumont." At Borgia's slight frown he continued, "There is a bit of the conniving witch in all women. By the saints, do I not know it. The lot of them are thorny little rosebushes, are they not? Pluck the flower, get pricked!"

Borgia swung his long legs over the bench, leaned back against the table and raised his tankard. "One must know how to go about such things."

"You are the wisest of lords," Roger said, his smile ruining any attempt at seriousness.

"If you believe that, Amiens, you are the biggest of fools," Borgia said sardonically. "What wisdom have I shown here? I beat the people into a submission more surface than real and, in turn, am usurped by a child-woman. 'Tis enough to make a grown man crawl off with his tail tucked betwixt his legs."

Roger gave a hardy laugh. Such a thing would never happen, and it was merely a reflection of Borgia's true confidence that he could banter so lightly. "Well, there are solutions to every problem, my lord."

"Oh, aye," Borgia said with self-derision. "I could lock the girl in her chamber, then the servants would revolt and I'd have mutiny on my hands."

"You could beat her into compliance," Roger offered.

"Yea, and have one of her sisters murder me in my sleep."

"Aye, they are such fierce Amazons. Well . . ." Roger began slowly, a look of grave consideration on his face. "You could marry one of the maidens." At the dark and severe expression on Borgia's face, he hastened to continue, "Hear me out. If you wed one of the sisters, no serf could disclaim your absolute authority here. You would then be lord in the eyes of all."

"I am anyway," Borgia said calmly, but there was a shadow of controlled violence beneath the surface of his gray eyes. "You dare much with that suggestion, Amiens."

"Aye, aye," Roger said in a placating tone. "But think of the rewards. 'Tis time you took a wife to mate with, to warm your bed and bear you sons. What good all these plans you make if 'tis not for patrimony?''

"I have no wish to marry again," Borgia said softly. "You of all people know that. And I certainly need not a wife to beget heirs."

With a bastard King on England's throne, it was hard for Roger to belabor the point. "Surely you have not thought to *never* remarry," he said in genuine sincerity now. "Even for you the King will not go that far. 'Tis imperative to unite his kingdom with Saxon and Norman alliances. He turns the Saxon widows to his favor by allowing them to keep their lands if they but wed his Norman knights. When their only other choice is to lose everything, they are only too happy to comply. Know you this, Borgia, whether you will see it or not. And now that you are titled in your own right, not just the youngest son of a nobleman, there will be fathers aplenty who wish to make contracts with you for their daughters to increase their own wealth and knight service."

"As there have always been," Borgia said.

"Aye, but think on what you have here. Four comely maidens, already dear to the people of Ravenwood, with no nasty relations to drain every drop of your blood for their greedy needs. But, my lord St. Brieuc, which one?"

"Which one indeed?" Borgia said, feigning interest so that Roger might spill his guts and be done with it. "Assuming, of course, I am not like other men to seek a dowered bride who will bring me greater wealth, my choice would be Kyra. She is soft-spoken and obeys without issue. Alas, she is too young."

"Kyra is nigh ten and three," Roger mused; "many girls marry as early."

"Do you forget that I, in the eyes of the Church and in good conscience, could not bed her until she reaches fifteen?"

"You have no conscience and have never cared overmuch for Church rule. Do you claim a change of heart now?''

"Nay," Borgia chuckled. "But to marry one so young as Kyra is distasteful to me, though not as distasteful as the thought of marrying one of the others."

"What have you against the lady Maire? By God, she is spirited and most comely."

"That one?" Borgia asked as if horrified. "I would be moved to cut her tongue out if we did not kill each other within a fortnight. If you take stock in comeliness, the lady Aurel is the most beautiful." Roger's head snapped up, and Borgia continued with keen-eyed interest. "But she is afraid of men, and I would not have her quaking in fright in my bed each night. I had that aplenty with Margaret."

"What of LeClaire?" Roger queried.

There was a moment of silence while Borgia contemplated his goblet, then he said in a smooth, dark voice. "That wench fears nothing." He smiled faintly. "Well, almost nothing."

"So!" Roger blustered, slapping his hand down on the table with such force it rocked the flagon of mead. "There you have it. Take her to wife! She is the most likely choice since she is the eldest and already declares herself lady of Ravenwood."

"Nay," Borgia said soberly, picturing thin bandaged arms and the delicate turn of an ankle. "Nay, Roger, none of the girls are for me. But what of you? As my sworn vassal I could order you to marry one of the girls yourself, then take her off to the lands I have given you stewardship over. Christ's blood, I like that idea! Mayhaps you could marry all four, and I would be rid of them."

A shudder rippled through Roger's broad shoulders. "Do you entertain revenge, I cry peace!" he groaned. "I swear I'll turn to the priesthood ere I get tangled up with a wife and kin after being raised with seven sisters. 'Twas merely something for *you* to consider," Roger proclaimed, as if he had not just played the sorriest game possible with Borgia. The subject of marriage was a forbidden one since St. Brieuc's first disastrous contract with the insipid Margaret of Beaumont, and Roger did go bravely in mentioning that less than holy state at all.

"I tire of this prattle," Borgia said. "I hold cheap any such discussion. Let us speak of other things or naught at all."

Roger knew when to change course and did so now, unknowingly bringing the conversation full circle. "How are the plans for the festival coming along?"

" 'Twould be complete if LeClaire would stay out of it," Borgia said, a glimmer of amusement in his veiled eyes. "She covets the larder as if we will all perish this spring for lack of a few stored goods."

" 'Tis justified," Roger excused. "She knows not that you have money to replace what is taken unless you have told her."

Borgia shook his head. "It matters not. She has no right to question my actions even were they foolish. She must needs learn the way of things."

"Mayhaps," Roger agreed. "But the lass has a good head for organization and would see to the welfare of her people. 'Tis a virtue to be commended not reviled when we have seen too many wither under less circumstances."

"Do you champion her?" Borgia smiled, a cynical cut to his words. "As I have said, she works too hard for the ungrateful lot of them."

"I would not call them ungrateful when they serve her well."

"Yea, against me." Borgia laughed darkly. " 'Tis foolish, this erroneous fight for control, and I tire of it. I will resolve the problem in short order or send the whole of them packing."

Roger raised his tankard for a toast. "You are a born

leader, my lord Borgia!" he expostulated as only a true and confident friend would dare. But his voice lowered, lost all teasing and he faced his lord squarely. "But methinks you will not send the lady away or you would have done so by now. Methinks, perchance, you lust after the wench."

Borgia lifted his own tankard in salute, his expression closed. "Amiens, what a wretched friend you are," he said, for there was naught else to say.

10

LeClaire awoke to more warmth than she had ever known in the winters of her lifetime. A flurry of excitement tingled through her as she realized spring must have stolen in during the night to heal the land and begin rebirth. She stretched, lazy as a well-fed cat, then recoiled at the pain on various parts of her body. The night's activities came swiftly to mind and she opened her eyes with grudging reluctance to realize she was still in Borgia's bed and the warmth came from his wealth of covers not the weather.

Discontent, she turned on her side, then her stomach, then her back. It was impossible to lounge abed like a sloth as he had commanded, and first light saw her creeping from the comfort of his covers to dress and pace the chamber, feeling restless and confined and wondering where he had spent the night. The spacious room had once been hers, yet she felt like an outsider now, uneasy in this masculine domain. The accoutrements of war dominated the chamber like centurions standing guard.

In one corner stood a sword with jeweled pommel and tapering blade, the steel made of layered strips of iron laboriously forged and tempered and equally effective for cutting or thrusting. On the wall rested a steel-pointed spear, and alongside that was a battle-ax. And next to both was a shield marked with his bearings—the St. Brieuc lion rampant.

Symbols of death and dominance, all of them, and Le-Claire felt she must needs escape the dungeonlike gloom they represented in a room that had once been her haven. As she had every morn since coming to Ravenwood, she laced her simple garments, combed her hair, then went quietly to the decaying stone chapel.

Naught but a few scarred benches littered the room. There were no jeweled boxes to hold the sacraments, nor delicately stitched altar cloths to lend beauty, no altar, just a crude wooden cross attached to the stark, unadorned wall. LeClaire saw none of the decay, the barrenness, nor did she feel it an unworthy place. The chapel might be void of material finery, but it was filled with the richness of God's presence. She felt safe here as she did no other, shielded from Ravenwood's troubles. No one ventured near, for the villagers thought it haunted since the friar's unexplained death. Trying to convince them otherwise had been useless, so LeClaire had ceased the tiresome chore. It became her haven, a place all to her own where she could find peace in the predawn hours to sustain her throughout the day.

Borgia had spent an uncomfortable night on LeClaire's pallet and was not in a congenial mood when he returned to his own chamber to find LeClaire gone. Hannah, up before cock crow, was helping prepare the morning meal and directed him to her lady's usual whereabouts. Borgia entered the wreckage of the chapel, his eyes a dark, forbidding charcoal.

LeClaire was on her knees, her head bent in supplication as she whispered her litany of morning prayers. Almost by rote she asked God's forgiveness and blessing, pleaded for the peoples' protection and prosperity, begged wisdom and guidance, then thanked her Lord for His keeping. A cool breeze soughed through the tattered hides flapping at the windows and mingled with the drone of LeClaire's melodious voice. The effect was a plaintive song, a mournful sighing of bequests and thanksgiving. And Borgia wondered how the girl was driven to offer praise in this sorry excuse for a church.

"Do you defy me already?" came his deep voice.

Startled, LeClaire swung her head sharply to face the intruder. Upon seeing Borgia, she gathered the hem of her gown and rose slowly to her feet. She had thought she would have time for this daily ritual, but she must have tarried overlong for he was here, looking as if a storm gathered within his cold eyes. But surely even he would not take issue with her slipping down to say morning prayers.

"Nay, sire," she said in answer to his question. " 'Tis habit that woke me and sent me here, but I have done naught else and plan to return to my chamber when I am finished."

"Ah, then you are learning to obey," he said, his face impassive while his tone dripped sarcasm.

"Aye, but 'tis hard," she murmured.

"Verily, it must be, for here you are in defiance of my orders. Do you remember my promise should I find you belowstairs ere the sun was high up?"

LeClaire took a step back, unease shivering through her at his casual tone when his eyes were darkened ash and he loomed over her in all his physical magnificence like a wrathful demigod. "I . . . I have taken my rest, and feel quite refreshed. I saw no need—"

"To obey me."

"Nay, my lord," she said in a tone meant to soothe him. Her hands fidgeted at her sides and she clasped them together in an attempt to stabilize their fretful motion. Lies did not come easy to her lips but embellishing the truth seemed advantageous at this moment. "I meant not to disobey. I simply needed to be done with my morning prayers so that I might return and await your command."

Borgia's lips twitched momentarily and a low chuckle rumbled in his throat, yet it sounded oddly humorless to LeClaire. "Ah, bratling," he said, leveling a gaze on her that was as cold as his smile. "Do you think to worm your way out of punishment with false excuses?"

It appeared she was doomed. LeClaire shrugged, sighed, then looked up at him with a resigned smile. "Forsooth, I thought I might try."

Borgia shook his head while wry laughter tugged at his lips. God's own blood, she did amuse him even at this early hour with her honesty and misbegotten bravery. "I admire the effort, damoiselle, for what little good 'twill do you."

LeClaire's smile faded abruptly when he took a step toward her and extended his hand. It might have been a gallant offering or a gesture of peace from another. But not from St. Brieuc. She instinctively took another step back. Borgia took a lengthy step toward her, leisurely in stride, but his eyes were unforgiving. Without warning he struck, his fingers encircling her wrist below the bandages like shackles of iron, and he dragged her off balance until she plowed into his chest.

"Where shall it be done?" he asked, his head bent to accommodate her height. "Here in the chapel where your God might witness your chastisement and your screams awaken my men? Will either of them come to your aid, bratling? Were your prayers worth the risk when there is none to champion you?"

"You know your men will not," she said in a reasonable tone that belied the fury growing within her at his sacrilege. "But my God stands with me. Mayhaps He will strike you dead for desecrating His hall, but whether you succeed or fail, He is ever mindful of me and sees your cruel treatment."

"Do you threaten me?" Borgia said softly, his expression and tone horribly ominous. "When my hand falls heavily on your rump, I'd say your God hath forsaken you. He hath failed you."

"Nay, 'tis you who fail me," she said softly, "just as you fail Him with your blasphemous words."

Her utterance gave him pause, then seemed to ignite the darker side of him. Borgia embraced her, sliding his hand slowly down her back, inch by unsettling inch, until it rested firmly on her backside.

"Call down his wrath," he taunted, "or know punishment in full measure."

LeClaire needed not to hear his words, she was already praying for all she was worth. When he began flexing his fingers to scoot her gown up over her legs, she cried out in despair and twisted so violently she went tumbling to the floor. She rolled out of arms' reach and scrambled quickly to her feet, braced to fight or flee. Her hair tumbled in a wild blaze of golden fire about her head, her eyes a fierce and burning blue flame as she faced him.

Borgia walked toward her slowly, steadily, his full height causing her to tilt her chin up to meet his gaze with a defiance that was quickly beginning to look like foolishness to her mind.

"M . . . mercy," she cried, breathless. "I beg mercy."

"Nay," he answered, his voice as boundless as an empty well and just as dangerous. "You were warned."

The sudden herald of a trumpet, the clatter of hoofbeats and voices from the courtyard caught both their attentions, and LeClaire ran to the window to see what was amiss. Borgia moved more slowly, and it was not the window but the girl he walked toward. LeClaire darted a quick, fearful glance at his expressionless face and wondered if she might leap through the opening to escape him, but knew there was no time. She pressed back against the wall as he drew closer and her hands flew up for protection.

"Riders! They bear the colors of your King!" she said.

Borgia glanced out the arched embrasure to see William's standard-bearer riding forth with the papal banner, a red cross on white ground with a blue border, a proclamation to all that the Norman duke had the sanction of the Church. Following in dusty pageantry were soldiers bearing other Norman cognizances, both banners and shields, so that in battle the warriors might know one from another and not perish by the hand of their own countrymen.

They rode forth in groups under individual standards. The dragon, an English emblem that William had deliberately adopted as an expression of his claim to be their lawful King. The famous raven of the Norsemen, recalling the descent of the Normans from the fierce and adventurous Scandinavian people who harried the shores of England and established themselves in northern France after the fall of Charlemagne's empire. And two gold lions, the traditional arms of the Conqueror.

"Get to thy chamber," Borgia commanded, and turned to leave the chapel.

LeClaire's heart skipped in anticipation, and a sense of well-being flooded her. She had awaited this moment from the instant Borgia's men had invaded Ravenwood. " 'Tis the King?" she breathed.

Borgia eyed her glowing countenance. The cheeks that had been leeched of color were bathed in soft rose. The eyes so full of fear and mistrust now shone with anticipation. "Nay, messengers," he replied, intently watching her color fade. *What have we here, damoiselle. Secrets?* "They do not carry the banner with the gold cross, the flag which received the blessing of Pope Alexander." His gaze sharpened with his next words. "But I suspect William will follow."

LeClaire nodded, her spirits renewed, and her smile was as bright as the daylight now streaming through the windows. "My God hath delivered me," she whispered, grateful for the timely interruption.

Borgia's eyes flared then narrowed, and LeClaire knew the error of voicing her thoughts aloud. "Do not delude yourself into thinking this is finished," he said softly. " 'Tis merely postponed and will of a certain go worse for you later. Not only have you disobeyed me, but you have gained my supreme displeasure with that brazen tongue. Pray until your knees are raw if you must, damoiselle, but even your God will not be able to stay my hand when the time comes."

LeClaire stared back at him. God had delivered her. He had brought the Israelites out of Egypt, felled the walls of Jericho, delivered Daniel from the lion's den. A God so mighty would certainly have no trouble protecting her from this fierce and unpredictable warlord if He chose to do so again. And although her faith in His abiding protection was strong, LeClaire did have the presence of mind not to boast her assurance aloud this time.

Borgia returned to the main hall to find Hannah already serving refreshments to the King's men, and he approached the nearest knight of his acquaintance. "Sir Fulk, have you news?"

"My lord," Fulk greeted, and rose only to be waved back down. "Yea, the King sends his regards. He is traveling throughout the land to visit his subjects and will arrive here in a sennight. Many of us have traveled long and hard, we would take rest here if you bid us welcome."

"Certainly," Borgia nodded. "Refresh yourself then tell me news of court."

LeClaire slipped from the chapel to fetch Maire. She reasoned Hannah and Agnes would need extra help in the kitchen with more men to serve now. Aurel and Kyra were also summoned, but Aurel refused to come belowstairs. She had not yet gotten used to Borgia's men and could not bear to be around even more strange faces.

LeClaire understood but knew her sister would eventually have to come to terms with her shyness, for it looked as if the men would be among them awhile longer.

"Aurel," she entreated softly, almost sadly. Her sister would deny her nothing no matter how frightening or distasteful. "The King comes. I need your help."

Aurel nodded in pained dismay and followed LeClaire down.

By evening most of William's men were firmly ensconced at the long-tables, filling their bellies and imbibing enormous amounts of mead, wine and ale. The air was festive as friend greeted friend and news was exchanged. Raucous laughter shook the walls of Ravenwood, and LeClaire had sent Kyra to her room hours earlier to save her young ears from the men's bawdy language. As much as she was able, she stayed away from the gathering, for it was grossly disturbing to her peace. But she could not let the others carry the full load alone and helped tote platters of food and flagons of drink.

Borgia's eyes followed her with lazy indifference as she helped, but she was not fooled by his indulgence. He would yet seek her out for retribution. He but awaited his own pleasure in doing so. She was too much needed for him to ban her to her chamber now, LeClaire knew, but it gave her no reassurance that his mind was momentarily turned from the subject of her punishment. He might tolerate her presence belowstairs now, but later . . . ah, well, later would come when it would, and she could not spare the time to dwell upon it.

Glancing right and left, LeClaire edged her way between several knights to set another platter of fish alongside the meat, vegetables and bread she had already placed on the table. She was returning to the kitchen for more common wine when a meaty hand clamped down on her backside.

"Damme, Lord Borgia!" roared the drunken soldier. "You've more comely slaves than is any man's right."

LeClaire gasped and skittered away from the man's grasp, outrage and trepidation warring for the highest place among her tangled emotions. To be accosted in one's own house, in such a perverted manner, by such a sodden fool! It was insulting, frightening, quite without parallel in LeClaire's annals of the accumulated wrongs having been done her thus far. Even Borgia's mauling had not affected her sensibilities as did this brutish lout's.

The hand found her backside again, and LeClaire squealed as the soldier called out, "Do you share the wealth, my lord?"

"Nay," Borgia said, leaning back idly to study Le-Claire's simmering countenance. "This one is not slave."

Roger's cup paused halfway to his mouth and his eyes cut to Borgia's, but he said naught.

"A Norman wife?" the soldier asked, dismayed that he would not be allowed to tumble the wench if her husband stood close.

"Nay, she is Saxon," Borgia said, his eyes never leaving LeClaire.

"A freed Saxon?" the soldier spouted, licking his lips in wine-induced lust as he tried to slip his bulging arms around the struggling girl's waist. " 'Tis not wise to give these conquered too much choice."

LeClaire twisted and dodged, using her elbows to exact blows that fell on thick muscles about as effectively as a fly on an ox. The man roared with laughter at her futile attempts to subdue him and dragged her closer to press a slobbery, drunken kiss on her lips. His unwashed body reeked of sweat and travel dust, his clothing soured by food and drink. LeClaire gagged, but if the man noticed he gave no indication and continued to paw her most crudely. Her eyes flew to Borgia's, unconsciously pleading with him for she knew not where else to turn. He merely stared back at her with cold indifference, and she felt the sharp bite of betrayal more keenly than at any other time in her life.

God help her, he bore the mark of the Guardian so well, so perfectly formed in his physical likeness she had momentarily sought his protection. But God help *him* that his soul was so completely given over to the Devil.

"Black-hearted deceiver!" she spat at him, so near tears of helpless fury that his vision blurred before her.

"Cease, Sir Guy," Borgia said smoothly, his eyes boring into hers. "The lady grows enraged. Beware that she does not call down her God to smite you."

"Lady?" Guy choked on his laughter while gathering a fist full of LeClaire's tunic. " 'Tis not the fashion at court to go about clothed as a peasant. 'Twould have the ladies screeching the castle down atop William's head to suggest it."

Many joined in Guy's laughter and several, having indulged in enough strong drink to make them eager for female companionship, called out. "Do you share the wench, Lord Borgia? . . . I've a need for a lady serf . . . Aye, and me! . . . Mayhaps she can teach me her gentle Saxon ways, and I'll teach her what a Norman thinks of such."

"Nay, me!" another called. And on and on it went, each jest growing bawdier than the last, until LeClaire's ears were burning with mortification. It was all Maire, who had been having her own set of problems with the inebriated swains, could bear. When the last shout was made, "She can take pretty *lady*like stitches in a new gown whilst I stick her with my—" she promptly raised a platter of meat and sent it crashing down upon Guy's skull.

The soldier jiggled his head to stop the ringing in his ears, then sent his fist crashing into Maire, catching her across her breastbone. The force of the blow knocked the breath from her and sent her stumbling into two other soldiers who promptly set her back on her wobbly feet.

LeClaire cried out and pushed aside the dazed man to rush to her sister's aid. But alas, Maire, not to be undone, grabbed up a pitcher and raised it high. But it was Aurel, her eyes wide with panic, who brought another platter down atop Guy's head.

He rose to his feet, roaring like an enraged bull and came charging at the girls. Maire grabbed Aurel's arms and dropped to the floor. On hands and knees they scrambled beneath the table and huddled there like entrapped prey. Guy grabbed the bench to fling it aside, but was suddenly caught by the scruff of his neck and hauled back to his seat. He swung around quickly to meet his enemy but met instead Roger's furious countenance.

"Leave the maidens be," Amiens growled.

Guy looked to Borgia, disbelieving that the lord of Ravenwood would sanction such behavior from mere women. "My lord!" he blustered. "You see before you a knight of the crown! Will you allow no retaliation for what the bitches have done?"

"You heard Roger," Borgia said quietly.

"But, my lord! They hath clobbered me atop my skull!"

"Aye," Borgia nodded, his dark grin steaming Guy further. "And mayhaps knocked some knowledge loose that you can put to use someday soon."

Guy's face mottled with rage as the knights surrounding him began to laugh uproariously. He was no fool to challenge Borgia in his own house, but he seethed at the wrong done him. Such indignity could not be borne, and he would lay his plans carefully to avenge this humiliation. A false grin creased his battle-scarred face as he looked to the men around him. "What sport in fighting a girl anyway, eh? One blow from my fist would send her to her grave. I can think of better things to do with the fairer sex."

Nary a hint of laughter came from the surrounding men, though many commiserated with their friend. But Borgia's sharp gaze spitted the agreements in their

throats, while his leisurely pose gave none of his true
thoughts away. None dared second-guess him, having
seen firsthand his ruthlessness, but many wondered why
he had upheld Roger's command. Some coughed nervously, others mumbled beneath their breath, but none
came forward to question the Silver Lion. Borgia de St.
Brieuc was as unpredictable as he was merciless.

LeClaire bent to help her sisters from beneath the table, then shooed Aurel off quickly to her room. She
gripped Maire tighter as tension built in the room, expanding like a soap bubble until it finally burst. Drinking
horns were raised once again, subdued chatter resumed
and the charged atmosphere seemed to dissipate into uneasy calm. Breathing a deep sigh of relief, she gave
Maire a gentle push toward the stairs, then turned alone
to face Borgia. He had not defended her, but he had
allowed Roger's decree to stand. She was grateful yet
wary as she stared into his hooded eyes. Mayhaps he was
not as cold and cruel as she had thought, mayhaps there
was a spark of light in his black heart.

All her warm thoughts were snuffed brutally when
Borgia lifted his chalice to her. "A toast," he said. "To
the fair lady of Ravenwood. May she seek her bed with
all haste, and may one of us be lucky enough to join her
there."

Thunderous laughter rocked the hall, paling in comparison to the flags of color that stole across LeClaire's
cheeks. With commendable dignity she nodded to Borgia, turned slowly and walked toward the stairs. She was
met with many a ribald jest as she passed through the
crowd of merry-makers, but not one dared stop her passage. Her quiet grace began to seep through their barbaric exteriors, her shabby gentility to touch an inner
softness that each would have sworn he did not possess.
Midway up the stairs she stopped, turned and stared directly into Borgia's winter-gray eyes.

"I shall pray for the restoration of your soul this night," she said softly but clearly, "as I do every night."

All eyes darted swiftly to the lord of Ravenwood; some shifted nervously upon the benches, others upon the rushes. Most knew not whether to cringe or applaud the wench's foolish courage.

Borgia grinned slowly. "Of all amongst us, bratling, you should know that I have no soul."

"No man is without redemption, my lord," she said calmly. "Not even you."

"Save your prayers for the needy," Borgia said, his eyes gleaming silver in the firelight as they swept her length with lazy admiration, and only LeClaire saw the warning there. "Offer a few up for yourself. Methinks you will need them this night."

11

The night air murmured through the hides, carrying the whinny of horses, the call of the watchmen, a baying dog. And every soft, familiar sound made LeClaire jump, certain it was Borgia come for atonement. She tossed and turned on her lumpy pallet, remembering the exquisite comfort of his bed with its downy mattress. He had been almost kind the night before when he brought her from the village, almost solicitous in his care of her.

Contemptible deceiver! Most likely he tended her as he would his charger, so that whatever services she rendered would not be interrupted by ailment. He called his destrier Ares, the Greek god of war, and everything in Borgia's life seemed to reflect the same sentiment. She had little reason to believe that his concern had been anything more than protecting the spoils of conquest.

LeClaire punched her straw-filled clump. The morrow would ripen with extended chores due to his guests, and she was angry that she fretted with apprehension, that her skin crawled with each sound, that she could not calm herself enough to get the rest she so badly needed.

She had prayed until there were no appeals left in her and knew her prayers were naught but repetitions anyway. God had heard her plead for protection the first time; she need not reiterate it as if He were deaf, minute after slow agonizing minute.

She peeked through the darkness as if all-seeing, wondering if Borgia was asleep in his room. She had not heard him enter, but he could move as stealthily as the lion for which he was called. She thought the name appropriate, for he ruled with insouciant efficiency, watching, waiting, allowing others their head until displeased. Then he struck with lethal speed, slaughtering down to the marrow any opposing action . . . or offender.

She heard the creak of the stairs and flinched again, then berated herself for her fearful imagination. Fear was, indeed, the absence of faith, for it was hard these days to find her fidelity, to hold it close as a shield against the misdoubt. She found succor now in logic. The sounds were just the old hall settling on its foundations, as she should be settling down for the night.

But she could not rest, and as she tossed again she was poked in the side by a brittle stalk. "God rot him!" she snapped in an irritated whisper, then felt compelled to beg forgiveness for her crudity.

But she was not truly sorry for wishing Borgia harm and hoped God's leniency was as long-suffering as His patience. She rolled to her back in frustration, knowing she tortured herself by imagining what horrible punishment St. Brieuc planned for her and wondering when he would act upon it.

She thought of creeping to his door to see if he was abed but would not chance waking him if it were so. She thought of sneaking into one of her sisters' rooms to spend the rest of the gruesome night but knew he would snatch her from there as quickly as he would her own room and rouse the whole keep in the process.

The hinges on the hall door creaked, then groaned, as it began to open inch by minuscule inch. LeClaire pulled back deep into her pallet, almost shriveling in her skin. A shadowy form appeared and she gasped, then sighed with relief at the muffled patter of small feet. Maire eased the door shut and crept forward, her distressed face lit by the glow of a shielded candle flame.

"Are you mad?" the younger sister whispered, kneeling beside the pallet.

LeClaire sat up and drew her knees to her chest. "I pray not. Why are you here when you should be asleep?"

"You bait the Lion in his den," Maire accused. "You beg the rest of us to keep safe, then confront him with all his men present. Have you taken leave of your senses?"

"I know not," LeClaire sighed, a pained expression on her face for Maire's concern. "Do not worry yourself—"

"A fine thing for you to say!" Maire snapped, then lowered her voice as her sister's horrified gaze flew to the connecting door. "Nay, he is still with some of the King's men. I checked ere coming here."

LeClaire dropped her forehead to her arms and groaned in abject frustration. " 'Tis not I who have lost my wits. How could you chance going back down?"

Maire placed the candle in a holder and reached out to stroke the top of her sister's head. "I fear for you," she said in an aching whisper. "I heard what he proclaimed. Will he do what he pledged belowstairs? Will you be forced to share his bed?"

"Oh, Maire," LeClaire cried softly, her eyes dreary as she lifted her head. "You should not know of such things, nor speak of them."

"I suspect I know more than you, sister mine. 'Tis not pretty what he plans."

"Nay, but he will not do it," LeClaire said with a confidence that was flagging despite her steady voice.

"And how will you stop him?" Maire wailed. "How! Think you that your puny strength—"

"Shush," LeClaire soothed, needing Maire's calm to support her own. "I must needs only hold him off for a time, until the King arrives. Just that long, Maire. You have courage aplenty, you must keep faith with me."

"I have not your conviction in a God I cannot see, in One who would allow us to be overrun with Norman barbarians! How can you ask it of me?" Her voice broke on a fluttery sob, revealing the fear that was so often cloaked in bravado. LeClaire gathered her sister close into a tight hug and stroked the sable hair back from her precious face.

"Oh, Maire, you will see," she cooed softly, hurting soul-deep for the devastation in both body and spirit brought to each of her sisters. "Trust me in this, sweeting, but do not speak of it. Take heart, Maire. The King comes, and all will be put to right."

Maire lifted her head, scrubbing at her eyes like a child, and sniffed disdainfully. "You would seek council with William as if you had the rights of a loyal subject, which you do not, since His Most Wonderful Excellency will have told him about the wine ere the King steps his royal foot inside the door!"

" 'Tis not Borgia's way to tattle," LeClaire said with odd conviction.

"Oh, sister mine, you know not if the Norman will even allow you an audience with the King."

LeClaire's eyes narrowed, a look that on any other would have been calculating, but on her it was merely stalwart. "I will speak to William whether Borgia says yea or nay. I am confident in this."

Maire raked her fingers through her dark locks in aggravation. "But what good will it do? The Lion is his vassal, surely William will not listen to your claims when his soldiers were given the right to conquer. You will swear us loyal, and Borgia will swear us traitors."

LeClaire took her sister's face in her hands, her words full of hope and anticipation. "But I've Mother's secret, Maire. Remember the secret!"

"Oh, aye," Maire scoffed, taking no stock in what they both knew. "But you cannot know what the King will say or if 'twill even matter. What if he will not receive you?"

"Then I will force my way into his presence and make him hear me out."

Maire groaned and flopped back on LeClaire's miserable pallet. "You have gone daft! Force your way? Oh, sister mine, our lives are no doubt forfeit. Let us take a dagger to our breast and end it all now. Let us throw ourselves from the parapet—"

LeClaire laughed lightly and shook her head. "Nay, let us wait. If the King's visit proves opportune, 'twill be worth a little patience. If not, we are no worse off than now." She took her sister's hand and gave it a loving squeeze. "Go now, I pray you. Make haste to your room and sleep; daylight will be upon us soon."

Maire sat up but looked at her sister in apprehension. "What if he comes here this night?"

She need not verify the "he." "He will not," LeClaire said. "In this I have faith also. If naught else, he waits just to torture me with the uncertainty of it all."

Maire found justification to believe that reasoning. 'Twould be just like the wretched beast to wait and stalk, then leap when least expected. She gave LeClaire a brief hug, started to rise, then froze at the sudden sounds from the master chamber. "He has come!" she whispered fearfully.

"All is well," LeClaire said gently, but there was no easing the sudden and furious pounding of her heart. "Go, Maire. I will handle him in this as I have all else since his coming. If he does seek me out this night, I have no wish for you to witness whatever passes between us. All is well, I swear it."

Maire nodded but uncertainty shone dully in her troubled eyes. "Kick him in his man's place with all your might! 'Twill stop him cold," she said, then gave her sister a quick kiss and slipped out the hall door.

LeClaire grimaced, then lifted her eyes to the ceiling as if she could see straight through to heaven's gate. " 'Tis I, Lord," she whispered anxiously. "Come again to beg protection." The connecting door swung open, and her eyes flew to the portal to see Borgia standing there in all his regal indolence. "Quickly, Lord, amen!" She rose from her pallet, for she would not be caught at such a lowly disadvantage.

Borgia just stood there, eyeing her old kirtle with its rope belt. Long sleeves covered her bandages, but he knew they were there still by the bulk on her tiny wrists. The fact that she was fully clothed spoke eloquently of her fear and that she suspected he might come. He strode leisurely into the room, stopping when he was several feet from her, and his eyes raked her with the disturbing incongruence of hot ash and silver ice.

"You will gown yourself on the morrow as befits your station, not in these beggar's rags."

Of all the things he might have said, LeClaire had not anticipated this. She could claim no station, neither slave nor free, lady nor peasant, so what matter her dress? "I understand not—"

"Those men below would eat you for a morsel and your sisters with you. They are William's vassals and, as such, do not answer wholly to me. You are not to wander the fields or forest alone either. Now, do you understand?"

"Nay," she said, her eyes grown wide.

"Does your naïveté know no bounds?" he asked, each soft, silken word like an insulting slap. "Rape. Do you understand that?"

LeClaire felt the heat climb her cheeks. "Aye," she whispered, "I know the meaning of the word, just not the why. Why would draping myself like a lady make me safer than going about as a servant? What difference when the maid is unwilling?"

" 'Tis just the way of things," he said with infinite patience. "The men must be able to distinguish you and your sisters from the serfs. Have you gowns that will suffice?"

LeClaire thought of the beautiful bolts of fabric in her chest. Some had been her mother's, others her uncle's stock. "I have cloth but 'tis not done into kirtles or shifts."

"See that 'tis done with all haste. You will not be allowed belowstairs until you are rid of these disgraceful tatters." His eyes roamed her again, lazy yet penetrating, and his smile was chilling. "But that is not why I am here."

LeClaire'd had the sinking impression from the onset that he had not come to talk of clothing. She lifted her chin and steeled herself to face the punishment he had promised in the chapel or the worse threat he had declared when she ascended the stairs. Her heart thumped once, sluggish, and fear mounted with each step he took closer and closer to her. He was no more than inches away when he stopped, and she could feel the heat of him, the overwhelming power radiating toward her like hearth-flame.

His finger rose and traced the delicate outline of her lips, and his eyes seemed to hold her immobile with some unbreakable force. "Such a pretty little mouth," he said easily, "to harbor such a bold tongue." LeClaire quivered, poised for flight, but seemed horribly unable to move. Her throat went dry, and her heart seemed inclined to skid about in her chest. "I could offer apologies," she said in a strained rush.

"You would not mean them," he said, brushing her bottom lip, then taking her chin between his thumb and forefinger.

Nay, but she would do anything to hold him at bay until the King arrived. "Forsooth, I would mean them well enough if 'twould turn you from calling me to account over them."

Borgia smiled, but the gesture lacked warmth. "I am certain you would. But, alas, you are held accountable—for many things."

So, he would not harken to reason. Words of apology would be meaningless, so she would not bother with

them. Of the two possible evils, she took the less treach-
erous path. "If you have come to punish me, have done. I
know you have not come to bid me good eventide."

"Have I not?" he queried, his brow lifted frightfully
over his fathomless eyes. "You are wrong, damoiselle. I
have come to do just that. To bed, bratling."

LeClaire swallowed hard. She knew not what depraved trick he played, but inched slowly away from him
and eased down upon her pallet. It was in that instant
that the fatal ax fell.

"To *my* bed."

LeClaire shot back up to her feet and faced him as one
would an executioner—with dignity, fear and every petition for clemency in the world tumbling through her
mind. "My lord," she said tightly. "I offer you my apologies, not my body!"

"I will graciously accept the first in lieu of punishment," he said, "as I have no wish to lay harm to this
sweet form." LeClaire's heart skipped once with brightened expectation. "But I will also gladly take the second."

All hope crashed in upon itself, and from the dust rose
her ire. "Then you will have neither!" she snapped.
"God's own truth! I am threatened with rape should I
leave the keep unescorted, and I am threatened with it
here in my own chamber!" She clamped her mouth shut,
embarrassed over such bold language and subject matter
and the futility of arguing with him.

"Ah, damoiselle," he said, his deep voice a forbidden
lure that seemed to tempt her pulse beat to a faster
rhythm. " 'Tis not rape of which I speak."

"Where is the difference?" she began, then stopped,
too appalled and flustered to speak of such. Her mind
began spinning over compromises she might make, alternatives she might offer as her fingers dug into one
another where she clasped them together in a death grip.

"Do not seek to bargain," Borgia warned softly. "You would not wish to fall from favor."

LeClaire flung her arms wide and laughed bitterly. "I have ever been out of favor with you, my lord. Why seek to change that now?"

Borgia's smile was sterile as he ran his knuckles over her cool cheeks. "I favor you above all others."

"Oh!" LeClaire gasped, and angrily swatted his hand away. "You ply your words as lightly as a minstrel sings for coin—with no truth, no real meaning beyond personal gain, and without a care for the one who hears his song." Her fingers curled into a fist, and without any forethought at all she shook it beneath his nose. "Play your evil game on some other poor maiden!"

"But I wish to play with you," he said softly and, with a swiftness that startled her, grabbed her small hand and pulled her to him.

Pressed against his expansive chest, LeClaire had to tilt her head back to give him the full effect of her outrage. "I do not want your attentions! Hie yourself off to—"

Her words died a quick, painful death beneath his lips. His mouth pressed firmly to hers, his arms gathered her suffocatingly close into his long, solid length until LeClaire felt as though she'd been immersed in the black waters of his intrepid strength. Her muffled cry did little more than abet him as he took advantage of her parted lips to deepen the assault. Like a marauder he ravished her, holding her with iron strength, taking each of her garbled protests, each of her frantic breaths into his mouth as if he would absorb all of her. And he did it all with nothing more than devastating gentleness.

He held her as if she were precious, yet devoured her with no regard at all for her sense of modesty. His fingers curled in her poor garments, permeating layers of coarse wool and thin linen, effectively as a touch on bare flesh as he pulled her more tightly into his body. She could feel the dense power in his lean muscles against her pounding breast and trembling thighs, and every inch of her felt the vital concentration of his hale vigor and his invincible might.

Yet the intangible power of his lips upon hers seemed even more daunting than his physical potency. It tugged her away from reason, clouded her mind like mist upon the moors, until she felt as if she were groping for light. Her fingers dug into his arms for balance, but his mouth glided across hers, moist, demanding, tender, liquefying her deep within until she was dissolving and flowing into his hard body. Her lashes drifted closed, and her head tilted back fractionally.

Borgia's gaze roamed over her flushed cheeks. *What is this, damoiselle? Surely you do not weaken so soon.*

LeClaire arched on tiptoe to maintain her footing, but he drew her higher, tighter, into his commanding frame until she was dangling physically as well as emotionally. Deep within she struggled to collect strength from a hidden reserve, searched the corridors of sanity and reason, but found her resources woefully empty.

Like a frenzied dancer her emotions leaped and pirouetted in dizzying spirals, seeking to fill the vacant, hollow ache left in the wake of his ravishment. She cried out low in her throat, a moan, a plea, a supplication for freedom from his torment. His teeth bit lightly on her lower lip, denying her liberty, draining what was left of her strength until she felt like a newborn foal, all wobbly and quivering.

A sob broke from her tingling lips as his body moved with hers, an alluring call to dance to the ancient, seductive song. The plush velvet of his tunic whispered the enticing melody against her simple clothes, swaying across every nerve-riddled inch of her body until her pulse thrummed out the tempo of each pounding beat. Her breath skipped with the erratic pace of her heart, and he took each fluttery sob, each melancholic sigh into him as he supped at her lips.

Like a thief he robbed her of breath and will and logic, stealing reason and conviction, and like a bandit he stripped away layer upon layer of protective innocence, until she was unsheltered, emotionally bare, and left with naught but vulnerable, quivery feelings and an intense all-consuming yearning where naïveté had once resided in the safe and insulated harbor of youth.

With polished care and caution, his hand crept up her side, his fingers circling the indentation at her waist, stroking each rib, caressing with unscrupulous sensitivity, drawing nearer and nearer their destination until completely engaging her breast.

Heat swirled within LeClaire, harmless as a blush at first, but with one flick of his thumb over her nipple a beacon flared, surging, whirling in a conflagration that seemed to pull her toward its burning center into some dark and depthless vortex.

"Nay!" she cried out and strained away, her neck arched back to escape him, but his other hand splayed wide across her hips and pulled her deeper and deeper into the icy hot core.

His tongue flicked the edges of her lips as his thumb flicked her stinging breast, and LeClaire groaned in acute distress at the ever-widening gulf before her, struggled to keep from being sucked into its bridgeless chasm. Her breath grew shallow and fast, and she fought the staggering emotions with physical defiance. Tilting her head back, she pushed against his chest and arms and shoulders.

"You must not!" she cried against his lips, her panicked eyes blazing into his.

"But I must," he said in cool assurance.

"We cannot!"

"But we can."

"Oh, cease turning my words back on me!"

"Quit chirping like a magpie."

His mouth lowered again, and with a small cry Le-Claire turned quickly aside, straining in his grip as his lips grazed her neck, then nibbled the hollow of her throat. His hands made bold forays on her modesty until her skin was tingling in exacerbated longing and she was swimming helplessly in her own impure thoughts. She slumped against him, undone by the forces raiding her from within and without.

"Yield," he said, forceful, compelling, his fingers flexing on her breast until a blistering flush spread throughout her.

Merciful Father, it would be so easy to yield, to ignore a lifetime of beliefs and give in to his tormenting demands and at last find some measure of peace. But as LeClaire tilted her head back to stare into his bottomless smoky eyes, she knew that peace would be a lie, for she would be forsaking her soul for it.

"Nay," she whispered in excruciating wretchedness. She would never yield, could never chance being swallowed up by the darkness. "Cease, I pray you. Content yourself with some willing lass and leave me be."

She gasped at her own perfidy, for she would not foist him on another. Even if some poor misguided woman were disposed to such infamy, it would not make it right.

Borgia cupped her cheeks as he stared down, deep down, into her blue eyes, and the abyss loomed before her, dangerously deep, waiting to engulf her. "And if you could be made willing?"

LeClaire moaned in despair, truly affronted by the frightful suggestion and intimidated by the confidence with which he made it, as if he could reach beyond her will to steal her thoughts and desires and make them his. " 'Tis not possible," she cried defensively. "I could not . . . would not even if I was . . . could . . ."

"Art rambling."

" 'Tis your fault," she accused, her lips trembling. "You scatter my wits!"

She gave a great heaving sigh, and with all that was left of her feckless strength jerked back out of his hands and plopped down on her pallet. No matter that he towered over her, she did not care. She was every bit as defenseless when standing before him as she was upon her straw—more so. She drew her legs up to her chest and dropped her chin to her knees, pulling them tighter to her throbbing breasts, wondering why they hurt so, like the pain in her lower belly, like the aching hum that yet sang discordant notes throughout her body. Only her eyes lifted to regard Borgia.

"What do you want of me?"

"You do not know?" he drawled in careless cynicism.

"Nay, I do not," LeClaire answered weakly. "I know you threaten me with carnal things, but I know not why. Why would you want to disgrace yourself and me with sinful pastimes? 'Twould profit you naught in this life nor the next."

"Assuming there is a 'next'?"

" 'Tis blasphemy to assume otherwise when the writings proclaim it." Her eyes probed his and saw with painful clarity that even holy Scripture held no sway over him. A sudden and grave sadness tipped the corners of her delicate mouth and her entire being was flooded with incomparable remorse. To be so lost, so without hope, it was beyond her reasoning. "Art a heretic," she whispered in stunned regret.

Mayhaps she had known from the first that war had hardened him, privilege had spoiled him, but she had needed to believe that the man beneath the armor would emerge with a conscience to face the truths of right and wrong.

But now she faced the truth. He was a man unto himself, without regard for any reasoning but his own to temper his actions. Mayhaps he did not even believe in sin, for there seemed to be no conscience to gainsay him, no inner voice to stay immoral conduct. Naught to answer to for his corrupt actions but himself.

She looked past her fear and resentment of him and saw what others must. He had wealth and honor among men, was magnificent in his handsomeness and strength, a worthy component in might and friendship.

But beneath the glamour and glory of his bearing, his hands were stained with the blood of innocent men, his conscienceless mind undisturbed by the identity of war. He conquered by might and held by fear, the respect he earned tainted by the cries of the defeated.

And like all men of great power, he was basically friendless. With the exception of a few trustworthy souls, he was a man isolated unto himself, cut off from simple companionships by the very things that made him important. Greed and jealousy and covetousness would always follow in his wake.

A tear glistened on her lashes, and she saw him then as her Lord must: a man alone, wandering aimlessly in his darkness, surrounded by those things that make men great—things that passed earthly time but mean naught in the infinite. There was so much in his life to recommend him, if one looked merely by sight, but there was so much else to damn him. Worldly treasures could not be taken to the grave; might and honor among men would be little comfort once his lifeblood failed. How lonely such an existence must be without the comfort of family and friends. Luxury was a fine thing but naught when compared to the others.

LeClaire felt a sudden deep and abiding compassion for the utter worthlessness of his life, the loneliness of his existence, the hopelessness of his eternal future. The Scriptures he would blaspheme flooded her mind, and for the first time in her life she shied away from their reality. For in the knowing was an obligation to acknowledge. To acknowledge was a commitment to act.

"And now these three remain: faith, hope and love. But the greatest of these is love." Borgia de St. Brieuc was a man without love.

LeClaire's eyes widened, startled and panicked. *Oh, Lord, nay! I cannot love him! He represents everything evil in my life. How can you ask it of me!* But there were no words to answer her, no inspiration or revelation to release her from what she already knew—her Lord loved all men, regardless of their commitment to Him, and if she would follow that teaching she must love him also. She wanted to weep with the complete unfairness of it all. The faith, which her entire life had sustained her, now seemed to strangle her with its commitment.

She sighed, mournful, for herself and for the man who had all, yet in the end had nothing. "I pity you, my lord," she said softly, "and any man who has no hope beyond this world."

A sudden hardening glinted in his eyes, and for all their silver brilliance, they appeared black as pitch. "Save your pity for one who wants it," he said softly. "Think you that all are doomed to eternal damnation for sating the natural desires with which they are born? 'Twould seem you honor a very confused God."

LeClaire's heart squeezed in agonizing sorrow for his misguided reasoning, for the lack of knowledge in a mind of superior intelligence. Her expression softened, and the concern she had so often shown for her people now shone for him.

"I do not admit to knowing the precise way of things; 'tis not for a maiden to know. But this . . . thing that you would do in the bedchamber . . . 'twas created for marriage, for binding two people together in a way naught else can, a sacred covenant for those who have pledged their life and love to each other. There is no greater gift that a man and woman can bring to each other than themselves."

Borgia stiffened at the tender glow in her eyes mingled

with her prosaic, touching words, and he fought a sudden, discomforting warmth. His voice was laced with cynicism. "Marriages are made for wealth and power. You are more gullible than I thought to believe otherwise."

"Oh, my lord, 'twas not meant to be so," she said gently, but had little hope that a man of his loveless nature could understand such. Her head tilted in guileless solemnity, and her eyes were troubled. "Why do men hold themselves so cheap as to want to share intimacy with women they care nothing for? How can they debase themselves so easily and have no regret for their loss of dignity? Does it not feel . . . embarrassing and impure to them?"

"You have never shared passion, bratling," Borgia said, but naught else. He too was rapidly retreating from the emotional outpouring of her words. He had never been one to withdraw from any conflict, but still he felt oddly weightless for a moment until the feelings dissipated. Soon. She would know soon enough that which she disclaimed, and she would not be so quick to question its driving force nor to judge those who did. He offered her his hand. "Come, damoiselle, sample that which you have never tasted, and if you can still nay-say me, you may return to this room untouched."

So sayest the serpent to Eve, LeClaire thought and her eyes flared in soft accusation. "You play with something holy as carelessly as your men fling dice, absolving themselves by proclaiming it the game of God because the apostles cast lots to select a successor to Judas. But I have no wish to play, my lord, no wish to tempt fate. 'Tis said men can be overcome by their lust. I would not have your sins on my conscience."

Borgia laughed softly at her misplaced concern. "And what of your desire, bratling? What if 'tis you who is overcome?"

" 'Twould never happen, I assure you, for I will not put myself at risk."

"Ah. You run from the challenge?"

"Aye, fast as I can."

Borgia chuckled and took her hand despite her protests and pulled her to her feet. "You have no heart for battle, damoiselle," he said, tugging until she was pressed fully against him. She strained back, wanting, needing, to put distance between them, but he stroked her back as was his way, calming, gentling, destroying her resistance. His words swirled caressingly around her ear. "Methinks that you have glimpsed desire and 'tis yourself that you fear."

LeClaire smiled dismally, feeling her body's heightened agitation and expectation everywhere he touched, the fiery calling of an amoral song. "Do you? Then think so, my lord. I cannot think how to convince you otherwise." *Especially when she could not convince herself.* In tired desperation, her face turned until her cheek rested against his chest, and her arms went about his lean waist.

She held him securely, fiercely, as if by so doing she could protect him—protect herself—from the condemnation he was rushing toward. The rhythm of his life-blood pumped steady against her cheek, comforting in its constancy, but too darkly appealing for a maiden's fears. "I grow most weary, my lord. 'Tis not a seemly discussion for a maid and a man."

"But we will finish it," Borgia said, feeling oddly besieged by her sudden and inexplicable kindness. "At some near time we will see it to its full completion."

He held her tightly for a moment longer, as tightly as she held him, and for once LeClaire did not fear the contact. There was nothing aggressive in his touch, but had any borne witness to his expression he would have seen the painful, unguarded warning there.

Oh, damoiselle, you play the game wrong. I'd have you writhing in passion, not cooing in sweetness. Waste not your tenderness upon one who, in the end, will only disregard it as unimportant.

12

LeClaire's eyes flew open. Dark. A smothering, all-consuming darkness encased her. She struggled to fight her way past the layers of sleep, past the murky gloom of predawn. Something was awry. She could not put a name to the reason for her sudden awakening but knew something was terribly, horribly amiss. Her ears strained to catch some sound, but all was silent throughout the keep.

She crept from her cot and shivered as the cold embraced her. She had remained in her clothing even after Borgia had returned to his room, but it was scant protection beyond the furs. Borgia's warnings about the men had prompted night dreams, no doubt, and that's what had awakened her. But she could not shake the foreboding feeling of doom in the pit of her stomach. It sat there like rancid food, stale and bloated.

Her first inclination was to check on Kyra. She rubbed her arms briskly to ward off the chill and silently padded from her room and down the hall. She found Kyra and Maire both peacefully asleep, but just as she approached Aurel's door she heard a low keening, barely discernible. She paused, alert to some unseen danger, then eased the door open. She was assailed by a rank scent, obscure but odorous, and flung the door wide. She was met by three startled faces, their features abstract in the darkness, but she could make out their great hulking shapes hunched

over what must be her sister stretched out upon the
rushes.

The man nearest LeClaire snarled a vile expletive, and
they all rose and rushed her. A strangled scream erupted
from her as the three advanced, then another scream
and another until she was caught on either side. Bearlike
paws gripped her upper arms to lift her completely off
the floor. She shrieked again, and a meaty fist crashed
against her cheek.

"Leave her!" one of the men growled. "We have had
our fun. She'll bring this ruin down around our heads if
we linger."

LeClaire was struck a blow to the chest that nearly
knocked her breathless, then shoved roughly aside as the
men rushed out. She dropped to her knees, fighting for
air, and crawled to Aurel's side.

Terror—cold, stark and overwhelming—slammed into
her. A small candle burned on a side table and cast feeble
light to reveal Aurel naked and covered in blood. Her
clothes had been torn cruelly from her and lay in an
obscene heap in the scattered rushes. Her long slender
body shook in great jerking spasms, while a rhythmic,
rocking moan canted deep in her throat. Her eyes were
open wide, sightless, as one grown cold in death. Her
upper lip was split and still bleeding, one eye battered
closed, the other still swelling. And she was spread out
upon the rushes, her naked limbs stretched wide and
covered in bruises and blood.

Rage gushed with the bile in LeClaire's throat and she
gagged, then gave an ear-piercing, heart-shattering wail.
She gathered Aurel's mutilated body to her breast and
began rocking to and fro as if she were not too late to
protect her, as if she could take the pain and depravity
unto herself, as if she could make it all come right again.

"Hush, hush," she crooned, gasping with every laborious breath. "Please . . . please," she whimpered, rock-

ing and rocking and rocking, insulating them both with the motion.

Of a sudden the room was bathed in torchlight and LeClaire's ravaged face rose to the doorway. She hurled an anguished cry at Borgia and tried to shield Aurel's naked form. "The light!" she cried, her voice breaking in pain and anguish. "Have you no decency!"

She continued to rock Aurel while trying to hide her from the soldiers accumulating in the hall.

Taking in the situation at a glance, Borgia turned quickly to his personal guards, who had been alerted by the screams. "Roger, stay. Bryson, check on the other two. Leave a guard at each door, and send the rest out to find those who did this."

He entered the room with Roger and shut the door against the prying, morbidly curious eyes. Snatching a fur from Aurel's small bed, he knelt and covered her.

LeClaire's eyes lifted to sear him. "Who?" she rasped out with all the agony of one teetering on the jagged edge of sanity. "Who would do such a thing?"

"She needs care," Borgia said evenly. "I will find whoever did this, but she needs tending first." He nodded to Roger, and Amiens left to find water and linens. Borgia turned back to see LeClaire stroking Aurel's gilded hair in long sweeps, her hand trembling uncontrollably. "We must needs get her to the bed," he said quietly. Aurel jerked, then began flailing her arms about wildly.

"Nay!" LeClaire cried, pressing her sister's battered face to her chest.

Borgia started a protest but paused at the low, inhuman sounds coming from Aurel's throat. It was the first sound of any he'd ever heard her make and it was daunting even to his war-hardened ears. He looked to LeClaire, saw her agony and despair, but knew there were few choices here.

"I will fetch your herb tray. Do you want me to find Hannah or some—"

"Nay," LeClaire gritted out, existing on sheer will-power. "I will tend her myself." She pulled the fur up tighter beneath her sister's chin as if she would shield them both and continued swaying back and forth as Borgia left the room.

He returned with Roger to find LeClaire talking softly to her sister, trying to calm her thrashing. When they entered the room she looked upon both men with undiluted loathing.

"Leave us," she breathed, her voice trembling with fury. "I will tend her alone."

"You will need help," Borgia said reasonably, though his own rage was building at the fact that someone under his protection had been so brutally used in his house.

"Then send for Maire. She should have kin—"

"Nay." The simple word was spoken with sober gentleness and uncompromising authority. "Maire would be hysterical, and I would not have young Kyra see this."

LeClaire looked frantically about her as if searching for answers, excuses, reasons, when there were none at all to be found. Borgia stepped closer, and Aurel began fighting and moaning again. "Please!" LeClaire begged. "She is so afraid; you make her worse!"

" 'Tis not my want to do so," he said quietly, guardedly, and nodded to Roger.

Roger brought the basin of water and strips of linen and placed them on a small table. Borgia stepped forward to place a torch in the nearest wall sconce. Consumed by panic, Aurel began struggling in earnest then. Her eyes dilated with terror, she stared at the men and began writhing and twisting so that LeClaire could not contain her. Borgia crouched low, gave a LeClaire a grim look and forcefully pulled Aurel from her arms, then placed her on the bed. Unrelenting, he pinned Aurel's arms to her sides, while Roger went to her head and held her face still.

"Oh, please!" LeClaire cried, frantic, staring at each of

them in turn. "Have mercy—" Roger's expression was pained, Borgia's implacable, and she turned to her sister. "They are not the ones," she struggled to say calmly. "Please, Aurel, they are come to help." Aurel continued to fight, causing the wound in her lip to tear further and bleed more profusely. Roger gripped her face more securely, his own expression hard, but upon Aurel's pale, defiled skin his warrior's hands were trembling. "Please!" LeClaire begged, near hysteria. "For the love of God, Aurel, please help me!"

Aurel quieted immediately, though her body was stiff and shivering, her eyes wide with panic, her chest heaving and falling in fretful gasps.

Trembling, her own breath rushing in and out, LeClaire dragged the basin of water over and began bathing her sister beneath the furs as best she could and still maintain Aurel's modesty. With every gentle swipe of the cloth, the horrors inflicted on the most docile of humans strangled LeClaire until she feared she could not draw another breath. No part of her sister had been left untouched, no small portion left unbefouled as was evidenced by the bruises and scratches and patches of drying blood.

LeClaire bit the inside of her mouth, tasting the coppery tarnish of her own blood as she tried to hold back the sickness boiling in her stomach. Her world was crumbling, the earth falling away beneath her in huge chunks, but she dipped the cloth into the basin, wrung the pinkened water from it, and continued.

Everything was swelling up within her, her breaths came faster and faster, as if she could not contain them, and the trembling in her hands increased. *Please, please, let me be strong.* She placed a patch of linen on Aurel's lip to slow the blood flow to a trickle, then soothed the cloth over Aurel's neck. When she reached her sister's chest, she stopped and felt the color drain from her face. Her eyes fell closed and her head dropped forward at the unmistakable gouge of teeth marks.

Borgia released one of Aurel's arms to grab LeClaire's when she went pale. He gave her a little shake, knowing she was about to swoon. "Would you have me finish?"

LeClaire's head snapped up to flay him with banked fury. "Nay," she said levelly, every cell, every particle in her so brittle that one more word, one more movement would shatter her like crystal. She took a slow, stabilizing breath and carefully tilted her face back down to her sister and spoke soothingly. "Your lip needs stitching or 'twill leave a hideous scar, mayhaps even fester."

Aurel shook her head, heedless of the burning pain the motion wrought. Roger looked upon the girl's once beautiful face, then at LeClaire in aversion.

"You cannot think to let her make this decision," he said. " 'Twill mar her for life."

Distraught and exhausted to the point of dementia, LeClaire rounded on him. " 'Tis her choice! She cares little for the beauty others find so fascinating. Look where it has gotten her!"

Roger looked to his lord, but Borgia merely shook his head. "Make a poultice to draw it together," he said to LeClaire. And Roger suddenly realized what Borgia had known from the outset. Aurel would have little use for such enticing beauty after this night's work. There would be few men now who would have her for wife.

Unaware of their thoughts, LeClaire finished bathing her sister's inert, abused body with numb, self-protective efficiency. But when the cloth was wrung one last time, the last bandage secure, the last bleak stare exchanged, Aurel began to cry. With a shuddering gasp, her lips trembled and tears began streaming down her cheeks. With a soul-wrenching cry, she turned her face into LeClaire's kirtle and shook with tormenting sobs.

Roger swallowed hard, slid his calloused hands from her head and took a step back. Borgia stood rigidly controlled, his expression cryptic. Like an animal wounded unto death, LeClaire held her sister and stared at the two men, dry-eyed, unable to cry out her own anguish, for it was too deep, too hellish, to be cleansed with tears. Her hand stroked Aurel's head over and over, but not a word did she utter, nor a sound make; nary a single tear fell.

Borgia motioned Roger off to the side and spoke quietly to him, then moved carefully toward LeClaire. When he reached her side, he lifted her hand from Aurel's hair and pulled her away from the bed.

Flung from her daze, LeClaire cried out and struggled to return to her sister, but Borgia wrapped his arms around her to contain her, then gave Roger a brisk nod. Roger went to Aurel's side and began tucking the furs more securely about her, as if solicitous, while in truth he was subtly pinning her to the bed.

Borgia turned his back on the others and clamped his hand over LeClaire's mouth so she would not further upset her sister and half-ushered, half-carried her from the room into the hall.

"Roger will stay with her tonight," he said firmly amid her struggling. A cry from Aurel's chamber caused LeClaire to go still as stone, then fury erupted within her. She clawed at Borgia's hand, bucking and arching to the extreme that he was nearly forced to smother her to subdue her.

"Easy," he whispered as he dragged her to his room. "Be easy," he continued for minutes on end while she fought like a wild thing. On and on the monologue continued as his hands stayed fixed, as she twisted and fought, as Aurel's heart-wrenching cries continued in LeClaire's mind until she herself was sobbing with fear and frustration and anguish.

"Let me go to her!" she cried over and over as he wrestled with her. Her muscles burned from the strain, trembled with her wracking sobs, but she continued to struggle until she had exerted herself to the point of exhaustion.

Spent, she went limp in his arms, shuddering when he eased his grip somewhat. "C . . . can you not s . . . see," she pleaded. "Aurel is so frightened of men. Look what has been done to her! Y . . . you must let me stay with her. Even you cannot be so cruel!"

" 'Tis an atrocity," Borgia said gravely. "But 'twas not done by one of mine. If left to her own now, she will never trust us. Roger will protect her."

"Trust?" LeClaire cried hysterically. "You expect any of us to trust you now? What protection has been shown here?"

The foundations of her world were exploding, sifting away beneath her, and she could not stop it, could not stop the decay and destruction. She felt herself stumbling, groping, clawing for solid ground, for some safe and steady fortress. She clutched Borgia's arms, mindless in her grief, and began shaking him, then pounding at him with all the pent-up despair of the past months, all the horrifying anguish of the present, all the hopelessness of the future.

He stood, silently bearing her assault until she was again completely depleted. She hung, slack and numb in his arms, panting from exertion. She rolled her head back to face him, one lonesome, aching tear held in her thick lashes, as if to release it would mean her total and complete surrender.

"I hate you," she whispered with such an unqualified lack of emotion and absolute calm that Borgia stared back at her coldly. " 'Tis your fault for coming here, for taking what was ours. What was done to her . . . 'tis what you would do to me."

He would not make a useless denial and, without a word, picked her up and walked to his bed. "Stay," he commanded as he laid her down. He went to the bedside table and poured water onto a cloth, then returned.

LeClaire reared up as he approached, but he lightly pushed her back into the covers. "Art injured," he said, and pressed the cool cloth to her cheek.

LeClaire's breath hitched on a sob and she squeezed her eyes shut, as if by holding it all in, it would not be free to destroy her. Her hand rose to push his away, but her cheek throbbed painfully now that attention had been called to it. Her fingers gripped his wrist instead. "Please," she begged. "Please let me return to her. At least let me see to Maire and Kyra."

"They are well guarded." Beyond that he said naught, just removed the cloth to freshen it. His eyes studied her, taking in her gray pallor, the hideous bruise on her cheek and the red welt at the base of her throat. *Damoiselle, what have they done to you?* His fingers went to the neck of her kirtle and she stiffened, but he would not allow her to turn away as he unlaced the blood-splattered garment then pulled her under-shift down partway to see the discoloration on her fair skin. He cursed silently but no less violently; it would be an unsightly purple by morning. He placed the cloth on her chest and she winced, closing her eyes to escape him and what he was doing.

"How did you get these marks?" he asked, and she could hear the icy menace in his voice.

"Let me go to her," she pleaded.

"How?"

"Those men . . . in Aurel's room." Her eyes flew open and her arms hugged her waist, tight, then tighter still, but it was not enough to stop the churning. "They . . . were hunched over her like buzzards, and there was b . . . blood everywhere. She was spread out like . . . like—" The gore burned fiery in her belly, then rose to her throat. She rolled swiftly to her side and moaned in abject misery as she gagged. Borgia pulled the basin near and stood by in stony silence while she heaved and emptied her stomach.

Horrified and humiliated, LeClaire curled into a ball

and turned away as he removed the basin and placed it in the hall, but he returned shortly, pressed her to her back and bathed her face and mouth with the damp cloth. "How many men? Did you see them?"

Please, please! her mind screamed. *I cannot do this.* But he waited, his patience a deadly force that cleaved the silence until it screeched to be filled. A fragile dawn peeked through the window as if to test its welcome, casting his stern countenance in harsh relief.

"T . . . three men. 'Twas dark. I could not see their faces." She clutched his hand with both of hers, and pierced him with her beseeching eyes. "I must needs go to her!"

He only shook his head, merciless in his decision. His fingers traced the bruise on her cheek, then the one on her chest. "Was aught else done to you?" His words were calm, but tinted by the cold promise of revenge.

LeClaire shook her head, fearful of the violence smoldering in his ashen eyes. He untied her rope girdle and pulled it off. Her kirtle followed, leaving her only in her thin undergarment and she began to whine low in her throat, gripping at his hands, her eyes growing frantic.

"Be still," he ordered gently, then unwrapped the bandages from her wrists. The skin was pink in patches but not festered and he tossed the linen aside. He stared down at her for a long silent moment, his thoughts carefully masked. "Your shift is soiled."

She shook her head fractiously, drawing closer and closer to full-blown panic. He could not mean to make her disrobe in his bed, not after all that had been done this night. Borgia eyed her narrowly, understanding and disregarding her qualms. He would make no concessions to her modesty when she lay clothed in her sister's blood. He pulled an embroidered quilt to her chin.

"Remove it now," he said softly, "or 'twill be done for you."

LeClaire clutched the counterpane and lay frozen on

her back, watching him with wary eyes. He crossed the room, and she fought the urge to flee while his back was turned. But she knew there was nowhere to go and removed her shift with bitter, jerking motions. He returned to her side with a chalice, poured wine from a skin and offered it to her.

LeClaire shook her head, but he lifted her and held the cup to her lips until she drank. It was not watered, as she was accustomed, and it tasted odd. She sipped it slowly, fearing its potency, but he held it to her mouth until the last drop was gone.

"Rest," he said, and moved across the room to sit in a chair.

LeClaire gathered the covers close, raised up on her arms and swung her feet over the bed to rise. Dizziness robbed her of momentum and she sat still a moment, waiting for her equilibrium to return. "I cannot stay here," she said, confused. "You cannot think that I will."

"I cannot think otherwise," he said with implacable coolness. "There is no bolt on your door. Until those men are caught you will remain here, just as Aurel will remain with Roger, and Maire and Kyra with the guards now in their rooms."

LeClaire's eyes flared, then searched his a little wildly. "You think this will happen again?"

"I make certain it will not."

"My lord," she entreated, the words a painful moan. Her lids grew heavy, and his face began to waver. She blinked to bring him back into focus, knowing she must argue, must make him see reason. She opened her mouth, but no words came, and her tongue felt swollen and lazy, as did her mind.

Her eyes bleak and resentful, she stared at his fading features. "You have drugged me," she accused thickly as her head slumped to her chest.

Borgia caught her before she toppled from the bed and laid her back down, his features a grim and lethal contrast to the gentleness of his hands. He smoothed the red-gold hair back from her face, and allowed the powder he had put in her wine to do its work.

LeClaire sought wakefulness by degrees. Her head felt heavy, foggy with surreal thoughts and fears to which she could not put a name. Her inclination was to drift back to sleep, but some nagging inner voice kept telling her she must wake. She lifted her head and tried to force her eyes to focus. The haze began to clear and she could make out Borgia standing at the embrasure gazing out over the courtyard. It was strange that he was in her room, but for some reason the situation did not feel as unnatural as it should have. His presence made her feel safe somehow, though she could not determine why.

The cover fell away to expose her bare shoulders and she gasped. She was in his chamber, his bed! The night's horrors slowly began to creep into her sluggish mind, then slammed into her with the blinding stab of a lance. Stark reality revealed its ugly self and she bolted upright.

Borgia turned to face LeClaire as Aurel's name tumbled from her lips in a painful cry. "Sleeping," he said simply.

"I insist that you let me go to her," she said, and made ready to leave the bed. Bare feet and ankles dangled over the side, and LeClaire quickly curled her legs back beneath the covers as a blush spread throughout her body. She turned on Borgia with full-fledged wrath. "I need my clothes!"

He crossed to the bed, pressed her back down and held her there. "Damoiselle, your defiance grows tiresome. It took Roger most of the night to calm your sister. He held her until his arms went numb and talked until his throat was raw. They are both sleeping now, and neither you nor anyone else will be allowed to disturb them."

LeClaire's face reflected her distress. Her cheeks paled, her eyes limpid blue pools of agony. Borgia under-

stood her helpless frustration, but sitting by Aurel's bedside while she slept would do neither of them any good.
He would keep LeClaire away altogether if it were possible, for Aurel looked far worse now in the harsh, uncompromising light of day. Her face was swollen beyond
recognition, blackened by bruises, and it was hard to tell
how much of the disfigurement would fade with time.

Renewed rage had seethed within him when he'd gone
to check on her earlier. He had little use for the emotion
with its tendencies toward disorder and chaos, but he'd
felt it nonetheless. That Roger had felt the same was evident in his tired, furious eyes and choice words. They
would see the criminals brought to justice, but naught
could be done to restore what Aurel had so violently lost.

Borgia heard LeClaire's soft whimper and glanced
down to see his fingers gripping her slender shoulder. He
released her suddenly and soothed the reddened spot
with back of his hand.

Oddly, with a mutual knowing, LeClaire saw that the
demons hounding him were the same ones chasing her.
She had always protected Aurel from whatever meanness ventured her way. There had always been those to
ridicule her sister's affliction but none who would have
done such savagery.

She stared into Borgia's grim features and admitted
silently that it was not one of his men. They were a boisterous lot, often times crude, and several had tried to ply
Aurel with sweet words. But none, nay, not even one
among them would have defiled their lord's house in
such a squalid manner. If not out of regard for Aurel,
then out of respect or fear of Borgia.

Still, she could not find it within herself to find him
blameless. Had he not been so determined to have Ravenwood, no matter the cost to its inhabitants, none of
this would have happened.

She turned her face away from him, her heart so
swelled with burden she thought it might burst. "Oh,

Aurel, why?" she whispered, grinding her fist into the covers. "Why did it have to happen? Why could it have not been another?" She rolled her head back to face Borgia, desolation etched along the delicate planes of face. "Why! She could not even call out! Why not me or Maire? Even Kyra is not so helpless as Aurel!" She pressed the heels of her palms to her eyes, willing herself not to cry, not to disgrace herself so weakly in front of the man who had brought all their misery.

Borgia pulled her hands from her face, and she lashed out at him, striking, flailing her fists, helpless to make things whole again.

Borgia took the blows in good grace, knowing she needed to release her hurt before she buried it so deeply that it poisoned her. But when she was spent, he sat on the edge of the bed and took her wrists. It was with much gravity that his next words were spoken, for he'd had many hours to make a decision that would not rest well with her.

"By last account, the men who raped Aurel have not been found. Sir Guy is missing, and I have sent men to find him, but that still leaves two unaccounted for. You and your sisters will go nowhere unescorted. Not even to the garderobe." LeClaire blushed hotly and Borgia gave her a wry smile. "Bryson is sporting a black eye and bloody scrapes for trying to restrain Maire from going to Aurel's room this morn. She is rightfully upset, but Bryson disobeys my orders under penalty of death. You may caution her if you wish, but know that even if she rebels, my directives will be carried out no matter how it might inconvenience you."

Appalled and incensed and frightened, LeClaire's words burst forth in heated accusation. "You . . . you think we are not safe attending to our personal needs? What man would dare—"

"These men dare all," he said with deadly calm. "They

accosted a woman under my protection. Make no mistake, their life is forfeit, but they must be caught first."

LeClaire quailed at his grim tone. Her lips trembled and she pressed her fist to her mouth as visions of her sister's abused body flooded her mind. Aye, she wanted justice served, but there would be no recompense for Aurel. She had lost all that was dear to a maiden—her chastity and dignity. The men might pay with their lives, but so had Aurel.

"I must needs go to her," LeClaire said, needing to offer what comfort she could, to ease Aurel's pain, though she doubted that anything but time would heal her sister's suffering.

"When she is awake," Borgia said, ready to have done with this discussion. He bracketed her face on each side and forced her to look at him that she not mistake a single word. "Roger will remain with Aurel, Bryson with Maire, and Kyra has been sent under guard to Hannah's house where she will remain for the present." LeClaire stiffened and tried to shrug his hands off, but he stayed firm. "Hannah has a brood of children. 'Tis past time for Kyra to be amongst those her own age and away from adult responsibility."

LeClaire's lips thinned and her teeth clenched. She did not belabor the fact that they needed protection but thought there were other ways to ensure it. "And me?" she grated out, knowing already what her fate would be.

"You will remain here." Borgia noted the understanding in her eyes and the defiance of it.

"Nay, I will not," she said, so deeply furious that the words were hardly above a whisper. "There are other ways—"

"None that I choose," he said with utter finality.

"Why not lock us in the *oubliette!*" LeClaire spat with unbecoming sarcasm. "We have been prisoners since your arrival. Why not make it complete?"

"Were the dungeon in good repair, I might be

tempted," Borgia said derisively. "But, alas, 'tis so ill-suited, the rats have even abandoned it."

LeClaire felt tears burn her eyelids, but she staunchly refused to let them fall. "First slave, now prisoner," she said bitterly. "Do I have no rights here?"

Borgia's firm hands outlined the edges of her sad mouth. "Ah, bratling," he said softly, "a slave hastens to do his lord's bidding. You have never hastened to do mine. I would say you have rights aplenty."

Unrest coursed through her at the darkling glint in his eyes. "I will not share this room," she whispered harshly. "I will not!"

"Aye," he said with unmitigated authority and just the slightest hint of regret for the inevitable death of innocence. "You will, damoiselle. You will."

13

"I'll not!" LeClaire said a bit desperately. She grabbed his wrists and pulled his hands from her face. "Your men and the villagers . . . what will they think? 'Twould humiliate me for them to know."

"They will think what they will," Borgia shrugged. " 'Twill not alter my decision."

"Nay," she said with acrid sweetness. " 'Tis not you they will condemn, nor you who will suffer the embarrassment." Her fist struck her chest. " 'Tis I who will bear the slurs and indignity, I who will be cast in the role of leman to the great Lion."

He could make an explanation to the men, but still there would be those who would assume—already assumed—his interest personal rather than protective. And they would be right. He wanted her here in his bed and would not make empty denials to the contrary. His eyes wandered over her bare shoulders, pale against the vivid burgundy of his quilt, then the undisciplined mass of sunset curls spilling like liquid fire down her back. LeClaire pulled the cover tighter under her chin, her senses alert to the sudden change in his frosty gaze—a gaze as hot as it was chilling.

"I'll not stay here!" she reiterated.

"You would rather risk being molested?" he asked, a hard edge to his voice as his patience for the discussion waxed thin.

"I risk as much staying here," she said sourly, then could have bitten her tongue at his droll, questioning look. Her eyes filled with pain and longing. "I must needs go to Aurel," she whispered. "She must be sorely frightened and hurting. I—"

Borgia's hand reached out and his palm pressed flat against her chest, slicing her words in two. He pushed until she was lying on her back. Steadily he leaned over her, his face drawing nearer and nearer.

"Nay," LeClaire gasped, bolting up against his strong hand. It was solid as a rampart, and as impenetrable. She twisted, causing herself more agony as his hand slid back and forth across her quilt-covered breasts with each twitch of her body. Heat pinkened her cheeks when his mouth drew closer; they flamed red when his lips brushed hers, then darkened to crimson when he suddenly began to chuckle. His breath fanned her lips, fanning the embers of her ire.

"Bratling," he crooned, his fingers trailing along the top edge of the coverlet, "we have played this game before with a key. What is the prize now? One might think you seek more than my protection with such behavior. Perchance, do you endeavor to seduce me?"

"N . . . nay!" she sputtered explosively, her eyes the hazy blue of mid-summer in her confusion. There were no other words expressive enough to vent her outrage, and certainly no explanation for the simmering emotions caused by his hand and lips upon her. It was a lurid, obscene gesture and too bold by half. But he *was* bold, daring any shameless and forbidden thing he chose, and her modesty was helpless against his superiority.

But even more helpless was the way she felt lying flat on her back in his luxurious bed with his hand upon her. It was as if her skin had come alive, tingling with a raw greed she could not appease. She had known the hollow pang of hunger, and this was alarmingly reminiscent of that gnawing ache, that empty clamor that begged to be filled. It was frightful to think that he, in some wretched way, might be capable of satisfying the void, when he was the very one who caused it.

Driven beyond pleas for mercy or compassion, her forbearance strained to the very edge of reason, LeClaire stared at him in reproach. "You, my lord, are a despicable, loathsome creature to take advantage—"

"Damoiselle," he tsked softly, "verily, you must be overwrought. I have no designs on this skinny excuse for a woman's body. I merely sought a diversion. Pray, admit it. You had more to think on than Aurel's tragedy or the men's concerns for the moment."

LeClaire's bottom lip jutted out in pique, and her eyes dropped to her chest. Aye, she was thin, unsightly to one who had spent time among the well-fed, well-gowned ladies of the Norman court. A spark of inferiority, purely feminine in origin, kindled within her, and she had no use for the feel of it. But neither had he a use for touching her as often as he did. She trusted not his insulting words. If she had learned aught, it was that he did nothing without reason, without calculating the risks and rewards, and she was not proof against his diabolical mind. But if she were so lacking, why did he persist in stealing a kiss or a scandalous touch from time to time?

Because he was a knave, a black-hearted, godless scoundrel! She gathered the quilt in one fist and struck at his hand with the other. "Let me rise!"

A knowing glimmer in his eyes, Borgia took a leisurely step back. LeClaire eyed him narrowly as she sat back up, then felt the color drain from her cheeks. Of course she could not rise, not in her present state of undress! Her stubborn chin jutted out farther.

"Leave me," she commanded with false courage. "I must needs clothe myself."

Borgia merely reclined back against the bed's stately post and crossed his arms. "Nay. Were I to leave, you would pounce from this bed like your sweet little backside was afire and disturb your poor sister's rest."

A vulgar, black-hearted, godless scoundrel! LeClaire sighed, there was no help for it. She could not match wits or words with him in her indecent state, could not fight or flee. Her resistance waned in light of the request she needed to make.

"Nay," she pleaded in earnest. "I vow, I will not disturb her. I must needs see for myself that she is well, if there is aught I can do . . ."

"She is not well," Borgia said bluntly, challenging her to refute the veracity of his statement. "She is not well, and you cannot make it so, cannot change what was done to her. 'Twill take some time ere she is strong enough to put her life back together, and you make it harder with your coddling and grieving. She needs not pity now but rest."

LeClaire's obstinate chin quivered, and she turned her face away from him, from his candor. Nay, she could not change things, but there was much she could give in the way of comfort, so much support she could offer Aurel in her hour of need. She must make him see, make him understand—

A commotion shook the hall, and her eyes inadvertently shot back to Borgia's.

"Maire," she breathed.

He nodded gravely and prepared for the storm. Maire burst into the room, her visage ablaze with anger, but tears streaked her face and her teeth were imbedded in her bottom lip to stop its trembling. LeClaire's eyes softened and her heart wept for yet another sister's torment.

A lean, handsome knight followed closely behind her, looking harassed to the point of contemplating murder. "My lord," he offered in greeting, but his tone was clipped, his jaw firm with the grinding of his teeth. He sported a suspicious swelling over one eye, and a deep gouge scored his cheek.

"*My lord,*" Maire mimicked, her chin quavering, though her eyes still blazed with vehemence. She hooked an impudent thumb over her shoulder at Bryson le Fort, one of Borgia's most trusted knights and now newly assigned to her as personal guard. "Sir Imbecile will not let me go to Aurel, nor will he allow me privacy." A tear rolled down her cheek and she angrily swiped it away. "I want this man imprisoned at once, shackled in irons, strung up by his—"

"Sir Bryson guards you by my orders," Borgia said calmly, irrefutably. "He leaves your side under penalty of death."

Maire whirled around to face her jailer. "Call a priest, Sir Knight. I suggest one well versed in the sacrament of extreme unction, for you will soon need last rites!"

Bryson swallowed back the ire foaming in his throat and spitted her with a seething gaze. His hand itched to grab her around the neck, but strangling the little witch was not something that his lord would view as good guardianship. It was the worst assignment of his career, seeing after the little baggage, and he couldn't directly countermand Borgia's orders. But he *would* take a switch to her arse as soon as the opportunity lent itself.

"Well?" Maire said, turning back to Borgia in hauteur to conceal the crushing pain of Aurel's misfortune. "I would like to know, Almighty Master, if you have caught the blackguard?"

"There was more than one," Borgia said levelly. "They have not been caught, and you will have a guard until such time as they are brought before me."

Maire sent a scathing glance in Bryson's direction, then directed her gaze to LeClaire. Her eyes widened in alarm as she absorbed the fact that her sister was in Borgia's bed and her shoulders bare. "You have been despoiled, too?" she cried. "Oh, sister mine! We are set amongst heathen animals!"

Hectic color burned LeClaire's cheeks at Maire's

words with Bryson looking on. The tale would swarm the keep by eventide. She could not bear it, could not abide another ounce of injustice or embarrassment. " 'Tis not as it seems!" she hissed stridently. "I slept here alone. Pray, let us talk of it later."

Maire's rage was barely subdued, but she nodded in deference to the distraught look on her sister's face. Misery filled her eyes and ripped at LeClaire's heart. "Tell me," Maire whispered, painful and childlike in her unfound hope. "Tell me 'tis not as bad as they are saying."

LeClaire's eyes unwittingly went to Borgia, as if seeking aid, then fastened on her sister. "I am sorry, Maire. 'Tis worse, I fear, than any rumor you might have heard."

"Nay," Maire whispered, tossing her head frantically in denial. "Nay," she repeated, then wailed it. *"Nay!* Not Aurel. Not gentle Aurel!" She flung herself at LeClaire, burying her face in her sister's lap as the dam burst. Sobs wracked her slender body as her anguish poured out, and LeClaire squeezed her burning eyes shut as she stroked Maire's silky brown hair in an attempt at comfort—a useless gesture given the horrors inflicted upon their sister.

Maire wept like a child, noisy and choking, unembarrassed. Bryson cleared his throat and shifted, uncomfortable with the sight before him. She was such a hellion, a beautiful insubordinate little rebel who had boldly kicked him when he'd taken liberties. A tigress scratching and biting this morn when she'd discovered him in her room, a termagant when he'd had to tell her about Aurel, a veritable shrew when she'd been forced to let him accompany her to the door of the garderobe.

But she was none of those things now. Naught but a small, broken young woman weeping out her agony for the pain and disgrace of another.

LeClaire continued to stroke her sister's hair, to murmur meaningless words of solace, but the burden of being the oldest, the protector, the mediator, welled up within her until it stretched the strained boundaries of her composure, then weighted down upon her until she felt as if the very air in her lungs was being forced from her body.

She was tired, sickened unto death—mentally, physically and oh, so spiritually—of being the strongest, the one they turned to. Tired of being the one to make things right. She could not do it this time, could not repair what had been done by hard work or sheer will. She could not make things right when they had never been so irreparably wrong.

Ever strong, ever composed, LeClaire dropped her head to the top of her sister's, but she could find no release in bitter tears that would not come.

Few were the times in Borgia's life when he had tolerated a woman's weeping. Nothing bored him more nor moved him less. Maire's, however, were warranted and, he hoped, would effect an inner healing or at least an acceptance of the things that could not be changed. And he understood why LeClaire, so strong and stalwart, did not seek the same cleansing release. She feared she would drown in it. With one last veiled glance at her bent head, he motioned Bryson out of the room, then left the knight standing guard.

Roger was awake when Borgia entered the room; Aurel, blessedly, was not. Borgia felt another spark of fury kindle within him as he looked upon the sleeping girl. By far the most comely woman he had ever seen, she had a luminous radiance as far reaching as the stars, a gentle brilliance as otherworldly as a fantasy. But she was none of that now, naught but a deformed creature of a child's poorest nightmare. He signaled Roger away from the bed that they might speak without disturbing her.

"Did you learn aught?"

"Nay," Roger sighed. "I fear she will not be able to identify them. What do you hear?"

"Guy is gone. We will find him, but that still leaves two." A muscle flexed in Borgia's jaw as his gaze swept over Aurel. "Has she roused at all this morn?"

"From time to time," Roger said tiredly. "She does not stay lucid long. She is so afeared of me, I think she escapes back to the unconscious apurpose."

Borgia frowned. "Is she not easier with you at all then?"

"Aye, some." Roger nodded gravely. "She let me serve her wine an hour past. Small as that seems, I deem it progress."

Borgia nodded, satisfied, and took in the abrasions covering Aurel's mutilated face. It was hideous to the point of revulsive, what had been done to her. There was no explanation for it. Three men could have raped her easily enough without disfiguring her. So, the motive was not base lust but revenge. He suspected Guy, in some twisted way, had tried to avenge his bruised pride. But what of the other two, and why Aurel?

He could only conclude that it was against all the sisters that such had been done, for it struck at the very heart of their love and commitment to one another. Nothing else could have affected them so cruelly. The question now was were the villains done with revenge, or were each of the girls a target for their perverted malevolence?

Borgia's eyes met Roger's, testing, evaluating. "Will she heal, do you think?"

"Compared to what any of us have suffered in battle? Aye." Roger shrugged and sighed. "Aye, her body will heal. But what of her mind? 'Tis my thought that she was not overly stable to begin with, the way she skittered around here afraid of her own shadow. Not that I fault her for that. I have heard Maire say that there were many in the past who sought amusement at Aurel's ex-

pense. It seems that she had that halting speech as a
child, and was so ridiculed for it, she stopped talking
altogether."

Roger glanced at the sleeping girl and lowered his
voice as he continued, "But I have witnessed her hum-
ming to herself when she thought no one was about, and
whispering to her sisters." Borgia cut him a sharp
glance, and Roger shook his head. "Nay, no deception.
LeClaire has not said that Aurel could not speak, just that
she does not. Mayhaps her mind is weak. In truth, I fear
for her sanity now. After this tragedy, she may have to be
locked away ere she does herself harm."

Both men were startled by a loud clank and their eyes
flew to the bed. Aurel stared back at them, fury emanat-
ing like blue-green flame from her swollen, half-shut
eyes. That she had heard their conversation was evident
by the anger on her abused face and the repeated clang
of a chalice as she banged it against the bed's wooden
frame.

Roger looked guiltily at Borgia, then back at Aurel.
Her mind was quite obviously not as damaged as he had
thought if she could show such a pronounced reaction to
his words. He walked quickly to her bedside to make
amends. Gently he bent over her and took one of her thin
pale hands. Aurel snatched it back and rapped him
sharply on the knuckles. Roger straightened abruptly
and sent her a hard look.

"Is there aught I can get for you?" he asked tightly,
wondering where the girl had come up with such spunk.

Aurel nodded, wincing over the pain in her face and
held the chalice up. Roger took the cup, poured wine,
then returned it to her. Aurel gave him a soft, grateful
look, accepted the chalice and promptly flung its contents into his face.

"Damme!" Roger roared, instinctively drawing his
hand back as he jerked upright. Aurel cowered. With a
pained look, he immediately lowered his arm to wipe the

wine from his face. Taking a deep breath, he drew himself up to his considerable height and leaned over her again. There was challenge in his eyes, but no threat. "Anything else?"

Roger paid no attention to the suspicious cough behind him. "Some broth, mayhaps?" he continued. Aurel shook her head warily, but her eyes did not shy from his. "Someone? A person?" Aurel nodded quickly, her eyes pitifully hopeful. Roger seemed to mull it over with great contemplation before he spoke. "Who shall it be? Lord Borgia . . . Hannah . . . Ruth?"

At each name Aurel shook her head. After half a dozen more names, a half dozen more shakes of her head, Aurel began to suspect Roger made them up, for they were so outrageous. Her fist punched the furs and he paused in thought.

"Then who could it be? Mayhaps . . . LeClaire?" She nodded vigorously, her look pleading. "Very well," Roger agreed, all teasing apparently gone from his voice. "But understand this: she too has suffered because of what was done here. Do you promise not to throw wine in her face if I fetch her?"

To his great and stunned surprise, Aurel gave him a soft, watery smile and nodded her head. Roger's breath seemed to quit his body, leaving him light-headed, weak-limbed and thoroughly entranced. Neither noticed Borgia silently leaving the room.

Seeing Aurel had not been as harrowing as LeClaire had imagined. Her sister's distorted face had sent sick tremors through her at first sight, but Aurel had done everything in her power to assure LeClaire that she was coping. It was with untold relief that LeClaire found her tender sister not inconsolable but accepting, nor bent on sacrificing her life as many girls in her situation would have.

But there was a new hardening in Aurel's eyes, a harsh

and bitter reality where innocence had once dwelled among the sweetness and simplicities of youth. There now lurked a shaded silhouette of ravaged pride and a fierce need to cover it. When LeClaire had tears in her eyes, Aurel had not. Dry-eyed in her desolation, the younger sister had patted the elder's hand and silently implored LeClaire to cease.

When the sky darkened outside the keep, there came a summons from Borgia. LeClaire would have gainsaid this command to his chamber, would have tried, at least, to stand firm against his edict, claiming she would stay the night with her sister. But with a bleak and sober stare, then an elegant nod of her graceless face, Aurel sent her sister on her way, turning her joyless but steady eyes to Roger.

LeClaire stared out the window, ignoring the large bed with its mattress of feathers and thick, warm quilt. What comfort she could have found there had this still been her room, what comfort were it not for the man who now laid claim to it, who had ordered her to share it. Borgia de St. Brieuc. The Silver Lion. Mighty conqueror, land-holder, wealthy lord. Thief of a maiden's dreams.

She continued to gaze out the window, and listened intently, beckoning the night to close around her, to shield her, but there was nothing but darkness, no hope, no joy. She could no longer hear the angels sing.

She heard him move behind her—he made no pretense otherwise—then felt his arms go around her waist as he pulled her back against his chest. His chin rested atop her head, so tall was he, so overpowering. Yet, had he been a smaller man, it would have been the same. His strength lay not in size, but in confidence and intelligence.

She could feel the heat of him, wondered on some detached level if even in deepest winter he needed the heavy counterpane that draped his bed. She also felt the solidity of a frame well honed for conquering and taking whatever he desired. His haunting words had proclaimed it, and they now flitted through her mind as his body fitted itself to hers. *I do what I dare in my own demesne.* Aye, he dared much with his strong hands, his firm lips, his bold and compelling words.

His breath warmed the dainty shell of her ear but sent cold tremors down her body. She steeled herself to deny him as she must, but found she had no heart for the battles raging in her life. She was deathly tired of the strife, the turmoil, the confusion. Deathly afraid that she had reached the shredded ends of her tether and there was naught left but a black, bottomless pit beneath her.

He had said she would share this chamber, and no matter how she fought or begged or bargained, his word was law. He never made a decision lightly; never changed his mind once made. There was no recourse at all for her. The light of peace had gone out in her life, and she found the dark a vile and stingy companion. His lips grazed her neck and she shivered, then turned numbly within the circle of his arms.

A commingling of candlelight and moonglow lit the planes of his face, darkening the bronze of his skin, the hollows of his carved cheeks, the slight indention in his firm chin. The jeweled threads of his tunic winked in the muted light, not to be denied their richness even in shadow. Desperate to maintain one last, small piece of herself, LeClaire pressed her palms against his chest.

It was broad, invincible, the perfect rest for a maiden's weary head had he been more than just a nobleman but a man of noble intentions. The muscles beneath the velvet flexed as he tightened his hold on her, and his pulse thumped a steady rhythm against her palms, a forbidden masculine whisper to an unwilling feminine heart.

"This grows tedious," she said, staring listlessly into his winter-gray eyes.

"Aye, I would have done," he replied, his meaning too

clear for a girl who should not have known the subtle implication.

"As would I," she said. "But not in the way you mean."

There was naught he meant to do this night save comfort her. His hand rose to her face, and his fingers flowed through the curls at her hairline, while his thumb stroked her cheek.

LeClaire mistook his intentions and tried to pull back. But as his hands caressed her face, her eyes fluttered closed, denying that his touch moved her, that the warm gentleness of a hand that had brought death could bring life to her pale cheeks. Denying that the vibrations in her body were aught more than the aftermath of a harrowing night and exhausting day.

Her body and will were exhausted by the constant siege of her senses and the battering down of an innocence that had shielded her. He would do what he would, and there was naught she could do with her piddling strength to stay him. There were no more ramparts to be raised, no more barricades left to withstand his assault. No strength in her arms to wield a sword of righteous valor against his impious intentions.

She stared dully into his eyes. His own glittered back at her like silver coins, and they offered so much . . . *so much*. Yet promised nothing at all that she could accept.

His thumb slid across her bottom lip. LeClaire squeezed her eyes shut, blushing painfully at the compelling wrongness of his touch. His calloused hands were rough but so tender against her, rasping out an alluring summons to partake. Her body swelled, blood rushed to the very extremities, and it felt cold and heavy, hot and tingling—life and death only cells apart. Tears burned her lids but there was nowhere for them to fall, no use for their cleansing wash on a body contaminated by weakness and yearning for a man who brought neither love nor morals to his touch.

He wanted her in the meanest way, without even the pretense of love to sway the heart of a foolish maiden. He made no declarations beyond desire, made no concessions for the stain upon her reputation, made no false promises to make his intentions look honorable.

One crystal drop slipped from the tangle of her lashes and made a trackless journey down her cheek, achingly lonesome in its solitary state.

She felt herself being lifted against his hard body but could not open her eyes, could not face her fall from grace nor the man who had brought her to it. She was placed upon the high bed and a sob trembled in her throat but she would not give it leave to further disgrace her. She felt the weight of him beside her and the gentle grip of his fingers on her chin.

"Open your eyes, damoiselle," he commanded, realizing she had finally acquiesced, and on a night when he had no intention of taking her. He wanted her to fight back, to not allow the ruination of another to be the ruin of her as well. "Open your eyes." She shook her head, unable, unwilling to bear witness to her own ruin. "I have brought you to this room for protection, to this bed tonight only for sleep. But had it been otherwise, you need only to bid me cease."

"I have," she cried defensively. "Many times! I have no more strength for refusal."

"No more strength, or no more desire to do so?" His eyes glittered knowingly. "There is a vast difference, bratling. As opposite as yea and nay."

"Then nay!" she said, nearly strangling on the words and her embarrassed anger at mistaking him and thus exposing herself. She felt stripped of honor and dignity, but this time she could place the blame at no one's door but her own. Deep within the most hidden part of herself she was forced to question whether she truly had thought she could not deny him, or whether she truly had not wanted to.

"Nay," she said again, desperately needing to venerate herself in some small way. "Do you ask me a thousand times, then ten thousand will I answer. Nay! I will never come to this bed of my own accord!"

Well done, damoiselle. Wrong, but well done. One charcoal brow lifted over his piercing eyes. "Will you not?" he asked, tenderness underscoring the cool intonation of his words. "It seems to me that you are already here."

14

For the next sennight, LeClaire and her sisters, with the exception of Kyra, stayed abovestairs as they were ordered. The feast had been postponed until William's arrival and would then be held in his honor, but there was little for them to do now. Borgia spent his days as always, training his men and seeing to the affairs at Ravenwood. But underlying his efficient command was the constant and ruthless pursuit of Aurel's attackers, though none but LeClaire recognized the taut determination within him that lingered even at day's end when he would retire.

As Aurel began to heal, she showed them how to work the cloth into simple shifts and tunics. There was little time to make the garments stunning, no golden or silver thread nor intricately woven braid, but the fabric itself was exquisite, of the finest weave and better than any they'd owned.

So fine, in truth, that LeClaire suspected Borgia of supplementing the few bolts of her mother's and uncle's with newer cloth from one of the traveling draymen. She did not question him about it, however, for she did not want to feel grateful to him for anything, however small. It was petty of her and she knew it, but kept her own counsel over the matter. She would not begrudge the others their own small happiness with the garments that were slowly taking shape.

Aurel found an inner, healing peace to accompany her physical restoration in working the delicate linen into long under-shifts with low necks and short sleeves. Often times her eyes would take on a bleak, faraway look and her hands would lie still, the needle and thread forgotten, but there were other times, as well, when a challenge would spark in those haunted sea-green eyes and she would vigorously ply her talents to creating the new kirtles out of silk and velvet, fabrics so much nicer to touch than their common coarse woolen. Some were low-necked, some gathered higher with a drawstring, others laced at the side. All would flow pleasantly over the shifts with their long, tight sleeves.

Maire's joy came from the fact that she would get to wear the fine material, though the rambunctious sister found the chore of stitching quite tedious for her free-flying spirit. She much preferred rummaging through their mother's trunks for the ornaments to complete the gowns.

Of Viking ancestry, their father had been well traveled and generous when he had courted their mother away from the watchful eyes of her guardian. But he had also been a dreamer, reaching higher than his abilities, intelligence and wealth. And in the end he had despised his noble wife and the four daughters she'd given him as naught more than a millstone around his drunken shoulders.

Their mother had saved some of those early treasures, storing them away so he could not sell them, mayhaps as a memento or a cruel reminder of a man who'd not turned out as he'd presented himself. She'd had a fondness for the pretty things that in later life had been denied her, while Maire had a sharp eye for the remarkable skill of the craftsmen and a great respect for the antiquity of the objects.

There was something endearing and enduring to her in the jewelry that had survived generations, some even centuries, to hold their beauty and worth. They were also a testament to the wealth her mother had once known, and Maire would never understand the foolish pride that had kept Alice from returning to her loved ones after she had discovered the true nature of their father.

Orphaned young, Alice was a sweetly pugnacious child and her guardian had loved her well enough in a stern, remote way and provided for her needs as lavishly as if she were his own, until his duty to her was mixed with genuine affection. Out of that duty and concern he had forbidden her to marry the handsome, smooth-tongued Rolf. But, as impetuous as she was giving, Alice had defied him, seeking the romance and adventure Rolf had promised.

Alice had grown old and wasted before her time, her misguided pride keeping her with a drunken, abusive husband. A shell of the once beautiful and vivacious woman she had been, she had only existed later, an emotionally absent parent with naught to leave her daughters but the old stories and the jewels she'd hoarded like a miser.

The treasures were few but varied, indicative of Rolf's wide travels. There were buckles of silver from Fetigny and bronze from Lorraine, an eloquent clasp of Carolingian design with the delicacy of Byzantine technique, a circular brooch from Wittislingen, earrings fashioned after those made popular by the Empress Gisela, and necklaces of stones, goldwork and pearls.

Maire loved each and every piece and had been hard-pressed not to sell them when the sisters were close to starvation. But the sisters had survived, as had the treasures, and now they would finally get to make use of them.

Sewing passed the time well enough for LeClaire, though she would have preferred to be among the villagers. She caught only glimpses of them when they came to pay their tithes by sowing the demesne land or delivering sheaves of corn, cakes of wax or an occasional hen. There were more peddlers now that there was coin for payment at Ravenwood, and they flocked daily into the courtyard like flapping geese, hawking their wares of salt, millstones or the precious metals for tools and weapons.

LeClaire would stare longingly from Borgia's window, wishing she were again a part of the noise and chaos of demesne life, but he had stayed true to his order that they remain abovestairs until sufficient gowns were completed. She had not found it easy to share his room, but easier in some ways than mixing among the soldiers and people again. The thought that she might come in contact with Aurel's attackers made her cringe in cold dread. To think that she might come face to face with one or more of them was bad enough, but worse was the thought that she might be *among* the culprits and not even recognize them. The idea made her feel anxious and craven for not insisting that Borgia allow her belowstairs. But she'd rather feel cowardly and safe than brazen and deflowered.

LeClaire kneaded the small of her back and laid down her sewing. Her fingers ached from plying the needle and she sought a moment of respite. She walked to the window and watched as Kyra tossed a cloth ball with several children of like age in the courtyard below. With a grin of pure mischief, an older boy snatched it from the air and took off running. The other children squealed and gave chase, but Kyra only stood, watching after them as if she had no right to the game.

Two guards stood near, strong and able men whom Borgia had secured as added protection that Kyra might romp freely. They exchanged glances, then one of them prodded her to join the fun. She looked up at her protector and smiled, then shrugged, seemingly at a loss to know what to do.

LeClaire squeezed her eyes shut. She wanted to weep

for her sister, for the childhood that had been stolen from Kyra by a mean-hearted father, servile poverty and her own inadequacies as the eldest. LeClaire had not played as a child, had not run among the heather and bracken, had not fashioned dolls from dried husks or old fabric, nor fenced with stick swords. There had never been affection given to a tame pup or squirrel nor a talking bird perched upon her shoulder. A kitten had once wandered close to their hut, but her father had looked at it askance, called it a witch's familiar, and banished it from the yard.

Nay, there had been no pretty dolls or wooden soldiers, nor games of hiding and chase, but LeClaire could not hold herself blameless. Just because she had not had those things was no excuse for the lack of them in Kyra's life. And it gnawed at her that Borgia, for all his coldness, had known how much Kyra needed them. Le-Claire stood well reproached but she could not help but feel grateful also.

She rested her head against the window's edge, yearning for what had never been, what would never be. It was not like her to grow maudlin over such, but her senses had been stirred by recent months of prosperity. The taste and abundance of well-seasoned food, more leisure time when she accepted it, the scent of beeswax candles . . . a down-filled mattress. She shook her head against the cool stone wall. Such simple and silly things to catch a maiden's fancy, to tempt a saddened heart to feel delight.

The trumpeter announced dinner, and LeClaire watched the hustle and hurry from her lonely post. The knights came from all directions and she knew that all was aflurry belowstairs as the washbowl and aquamanile were brought around for the more esteemed guests while the lesser knights washed at the lavabo. She had never joined Borgia's more formal meals, preferring instead to take food from the common pot when hunger drove her, like the serfs who had no keeper of the hour but worked from daylight to dark with naught more than a water clock that was likely to freeze in winter. The hour meant little when there was work to be done, and daylight left in which to do it.

She turned from the window and resumed her sewing, mentally composing herself for the night ahead. Hannah would soon bring her meal spiced with a bit of gossip, and LeClaire craved the last as much as the first. She wondered how Ruth was faring and must remember to have Hannah make a posset. Was anyone listening to Oswulf's gravelly voice as he made the stories of Gaels and Romans and far-off peoples come alive?

Her hands had gone idle on the cloth, which was just as well, for her last, uneven stitches would have to be reworked. She must needs turn her mind from reminiscing, but it was hard as the faces of the villagers wandered through her mind, not nameless serfs, not defeated Saxons, but her people. Athelstan, Hadrian, Thomas. Had Tobias gotten his fields planted? It was said that young Ceodrid, so close yet so far from being a man, had picked flowers for one of Hannah's daughters.

LeClaire smiled softly, wistfully, at the picture of young Gweneth blushingly accepting the flowers and braiding them for her hair. Thoughts of Hannah brought thoughts of Kyra, and she wondered if her youngest sister would ever have a suitor to bestow sweet gifts upon her as the other sisters had not. Mayhaps if William came quickly, if he believed her claims and found favor with her case, if he restored Ravenwood . . .

LeClaire recalled a ditty about if's and wishes that Tobias was so fond of. Poor Toby, his back scarred from trying to run from the Normans. But even Toby was prospering now. He'd been allotted more land as reward for his good farming and good judgment in crop development and management. The lord of Ravenwood had come upon Toby as he readied his parcel for spring planting, had liked his organization and the fact that Toby did not feel it necessary to run to LeClaire for every decision but trusted his own judgment. There would ever be enmity between them, but that too would fade with time. Both had done as the situation had dictated, one mayhaps with more ruthless calculation and foresight. When Borgia had questioned him, Toby, being no fool, had offered suggestions, and the lord of Ravenwood had seen the value in the simple farmer's logic.

There were others who worked for Tobias now, others whose land had been taken from them because of their fruitlessness or unwillingness to change their ways. There was grumbling and discord among those who thought they'd been wronged, but LeClaire found that their murmurings did not move her as they once would have, for she could also see the value in what Toby had accomplished. He easily paid his tithes and there was now a jingle in his pouch to indulge his wife and children with niceties that had never been possible. Would it have been this way if Borgia had not come?

LeClaire sighed. She liked to think that eventually it would have, but she could not truly know that, could only hope that given time the outcome would have been the same. She looked up as Maire breezed into the chamber, Sir Bryson trailing behind her and looking as he always did, harassed. Aurel also followed, but Roger, walking in behind her, did not appear nearly as inconvenienced as Bryson.

"We have come to bid you good eventide," Maire said without preamble. "Are you in need of aught?"

Aye, my own chamber, LeClaire thought, but she only smiled, heartened to see Maire's irascible nature intact. She nodded to Aurel, glad the bruises were fading, more of her beauty returning daily. There would always be a mark on her lip, but it meant little compared to the inner scars, unseen but always felt, that would never heal. After a short conversation, in which Maire did all the talking, the sisters left to retire. LeClaire bid them farewell, hiding her despondency behind a warm smile.

It was the darkest part of her day, whether night had fallen or was only a dusky promise in the waning sun. Her tray would be removed, the candles lit and the waiting begun. At times heated water was brought in, but her ablutions were done in haste lest Borgia be close behind.

With a wicked smile or sober frown, depending upon his day, he would enter the room they shared. And his handsomeness and virile masculinity would flay a young woman's empty dreams to life. Wanton thoughts often accompanied his presence, no matter how hard LeClaire tried to turn them away. But with increasing and unsettling regularity, her thoughts would turn to the memory of his hands or lips upon her, and her cheeks would blush with only an inkling of the deeper and heavier heat within the very center of her.

She could not abide her restless thoughts and again tossed down her sewing. One gown was complete, and she thought of donning it that she might have some freedom from this room, but still she did not want to go below. She crossed to the door and eased it open, offering a soft word for the guard who stood his post with the stony seriousness of a marble statue. She had become so used to him when Borgia wasn't present that his silence had no effect upon her now. She leaned against the door frame and listened to the sounds below.

The excited squeal of a maid drifted up. Agnes, Le-Claire thought, though she could not see the common room without going to the head of the stairs. The buxom miss must be serving libations, for there were raucous shouts of "Mead . . . Ale . . . More wine!"

Another voice drifted up, one uncommon to LeClaire before the Normans had come. "Whoever wants to hear more must open his purse!" It was a jongleur with a repertory of *chansons de geste* and poetic romances. He struck a melody on his vielle and chanted an interminable tale, inserting from time to time a refrain tune, and the men began to join in.

Their gaiety was boisterous but infectious, and Le-Claire found herself smiling. She did not begrudge them their fun but neither did she wish to be among them, preferring the peace she had known before the Norman invasion, before a man had come and awakened her to unfavorable thoughts and longings of which a maiden should have no concern. A new tune intruded upon her depressing thoughts, and LeClaire's body suddenly went rigid.

> "Beware when Norman corpses lay
> 'Heaped up, the witch-wife's horse's prey.'
> But wait! The Lion charges forth
> To smite the flame-haired witch-wife horse.
> And now he takes the bird to bed
> All pecking done by him, instead."

LeClaire spun back into the chamber and slammed the door, blocking out the ribald laughter, the repeated clanks of chalices and thuds of drinking horns, as they called for more. The jongleur had taken liberties with an ancient saga where ravens, "horses of a witch-wife," were associated with the carnage of battle. He had embellished the old Norse verse and used it to proclaim her defeat at Borgia's hands in poetic and gruesome guise.

Her cheeks burned with humiliation, as if the men below stood before her while the minstrel bellowed out his bawdy tune. She wished she could scream at them to take their evil games elsewhere, but she had no position here, no worth, and none to stand by her if she gave such a command.

Her fists tightened at her sides, but the last victory would be hers. If God were merciful, and she believed Him to be with her whole heart and soul and mind, He would restore her to her rightful place.

The King would come soon, and all her hopes and dreams rested in his sovereign hands. They were not without worth, those hopes, and she had built her future upon them since the Norman invasion. God's grace was sufficient for now, in her conquered state, and she would endure what fate had decreed with as much decorum as she was able. In His infinite wisdom, He had allowed the Duke of Normandy to become King of England, and she believed faithfully, unequivocally, in the deepest most constant part of her, that her restoration lay in that fact.

But she would not sit back meekly, awaiting the future. The saints had been mighty warriors for the faith, not weaklings, and she was still seething when Borgia entered the chamber not an hour later.

She rounded on him with all the virulence of her slighted feelings, her cheeks flushed with anger. "I pray a grand time was had by all."

Borgia eyed her with curiosity as he shut and bolted the door. "Aye, they seemed satisfied when I left them."

"And was the minstrel's song a great source of their fun?" she asked baldly.

Borgia nodded, then smiled slowly as understanding dawned. "You heard his tune."

LeClaire was staggered by the warmth of his smile and the way it seemed to reach deep down into places beyond her animosity. She sought refuge from the unrest in anger. " 'Twas no mere tune! 'Twas a disgrace, and I—"

She clamped her lips together. What would she do? Order the man beaten, hanged? Cruelty would not alter the fact that the song had been sung before all the inhabitants of the keep.

Borgia removed his tunic and worked the laces of his *sherte*. LeClaire's eyes widened at the sight of him in naught but his chausses as he pulled it free. She spun around quickly, rattled to the point of silence. Despite her protests to the contrary, he had undressed every night in her presence, but she had never watched him.

She always scrambled into the bed and pulled the covers high above her head while he went about whatever business men went about before they retired.

Her own nightly ritual included washing, cleaning her teeth with a green hazel twig and woolen cloth and saying her prayers. She had no idea if men did the same and no desire to ask.

But here he was, bold as a shiny new coin, stripping down in front of her. Behind her, in truth, but only because she had turned away.

"Have you no decency?" she cried, then regretted she'd even spoken.

"I have no need of it," he said, and LeClaire started at his nearness. His arms went around her, pulling her back deeply into his chest and hips and thighs, and she was greatly disturbed by the feel of his bare flesh. "Give no thought to the minstrel's words. 'Tis expected of him to mock those in the house that feed him. If you are sorely offended, I'll have him beheaded."

"I *am* offended," LeClaire murmured, feeling sullen and ungracious. Yet a small but undisputed smile tugged at her lips at his outrageous suggestion. "Forsooth, I'd not have you go so far as to relieve the man of his head. Art bloodthirsty, my lord." She twisted slightly in his arms, but he did not release her. Instead, his hands tightened, cradling her against him, and his thumbs began digging softly, circularly, into her ribs.

"Nay!" LeClaire nearly shouted, for she was just at the edge of bursting into giggles, and she could not be so lighthearted when he touched her. "Nay," she said again, more forcefully, for she'd also not be caught as she had a sennight ago. She trusted not his words that she need only bid him cease, but she would test him to the limits on them to ensure her safety. If he were driven beyond whatever piddling morals he held, it would be by his own hand, not her acceptance.

His hands moved to her arms, caressing as they slid up

and down, their long-fingered strength and gentle touch sending unwanted shivers down her spine. She swallowed hard, preparing to rebuke him, but the hands drifted away as he moved back. She rushed to the bed and scurried beneath the covers to remove her kirtle, keeping her face turned while he doffed the rest of his clothing. He would come to the bed naked, she knew, that thought the most unsettling of all. Too many times in the heart of night she'd awakened pressed against that flesh, their arms or legs tangled, feeling so warm and comfortable that she'd been struck with guilt over it. Had it not been for her inactivity of late, she would have been weary unto death with all the sleepless hours she'd endured since sharing his room.

LeClaire felt the dip of the bed, then Borgia's hands upon her again as he turned her toward him. "My lord—"

"Hush, bratling," he whispered, and smoothed her hair back from her face. His hand dropped and he fingered the shift she had refused to remove every night since "her interment" as she called it. "You sleep like a monk," he said. "Are you not afraid of *accidia?*"

"I know not the word," LeClaire mumbled, too close to his powerful body for comfort, too uneasy for rest.

" 'Tis claimed to be the professional disease of the cloistered monk, a spiritual sluggishness that may turn to black boredom, to melancholia." His tone was so serious, LeClaire found herself staring intently into his eyes, until he finished dryly, "They, too, sleep in their habits."

" 'Tis not a habit," she scoffed, but knew it was foolish to indulge his word games when she could not come out the victor. " 'Tis but an undergarment and for the thousandth time I will not remove it."

"Would that you had been here a thousand nights," Borgia crooned, watching her cheeks flush.

"Art a knave," she scolded, "to wish a maiden in your bed."

"Am I?" he asked, dipping his finger beneath the coarse linen, which caused LeClaire to shrink back into the bedding. "You do not know the meaning of the word, bratling. Were I the knave and scoundrel you are so fond of calling me, there would have been much more vigorous and intimate activity in this bed than sleep."

LeClaire's cheeks grew even warmer as did the rest of her body at his awful, mysterious words. She knew so little of what actually happened between a man and woman, and her hunger for knowledge had not stood her in good stead where this subject was concerned. She knew a couple came together naked, but just how they joined seemed sordid and ugly and too frightening for a girl to contemplate. She suspected Maire knew the exact way of things, for she was bold to ask any question, but LeClaire did not have her sister's brazen curiosity, or at least she did not succumb to it.

Still, the mysteries lingered, teasing little pixies on the perimeters of her mind, calling out the haunting refrain that she put her ignorance to rest.

Flustered by her thoughts, LeClaire grabbed Borgia's hand to stay its unacceptable path, but he merely intertwined their fingers and brought her hand to his mouth. His lips caressed, his teeth nibbled the delicate pale skin and his tongue did unmentionable things. And she felt it all so strongly, not on the back of her hand where his mouth made its irreverent journey, but in her insides. Her muscles clenched, then relaxed, only to tighten again with each dip and swirl of his tongue. It was painful and embarrassing, that squeezing low in her belly, along with the hot moisture that seemed to flood her within and without.

Her breath hitched, then fluttered out. The pixies danced, ever closer, their movements growing frenzied as they chanted enticingly to the cadence of her heartbeat.

"My lord," she moaned as his mouth traveled up her

wrist, slowly, steadily, to the bend of her elbow. He pulled the translucent skin into his mouth, sucking briefly, then released her. She pulled her arm back to see a reddish stain upon her skin that tingled and burned as if scorched by a live flame. "You have marked me."

"Aye," he said, his eyes glittering with the same mysterious smile that curved his lips. "I would put my mark elsewhere, as well."

"Nay," LeClaire said, but wondered with a terrible fascination just what he meant . . . and where. Curiosity gnawed at her, relentless, and she wanted to ask the many unseemly questions darting though her mind. Questions of how and why and to what extent.

She could not look at him, lest he somehow see her meddlesome thoughts, and lowered her eyes. A grand mistake. His bare chest was before her, revealed in all its scored strength. The skin was tight but fluid over prominent muscles, marred by small nicks and a thin jagged scar—none of which blemished his masculine beauty. A thatch of charcoal hair fanned out across his chest wall, then tapered off to a narrow column beneath the quilt and ended—

Merciful Father! She knew not where it ended, nor did she want to know! Cheeks afire, her eyes lifted to see him regarding her with a most wicked and amused expression.

"Touch me, bratling," he said. "You want to, no matter how you will deny it." He tugged on her reluctant hand until her palm was pressed flat to his chest. "Touch any and all of me at your leisure. You need have no fear that I will force myself upon you." His voice dropped to that dark, compelling whisper that pulled her insides in so many directions they seemed to tangle into a coiled and hurting heap in the pit of her. "I will do naught that you do not bid me to do."

With a small cry, LeClaire jerked on her hand, but he held it to him, guiding it in an achingly slow and circular motion over the entire length of his upper torso. His skin was sleek and hot beneath her palm, his chest hair curling around her fingertips. His nipples were flat and round, his muscles bunched beneath, stirring her with the differences between male and female.

She had the most wretched and insane urge to press her mouth to his heartbeat, to feel its thunder against her sensitive lips. Her throat went dry, her pulse pounded in her temples and her limbs seemed swamped with languid heat. It was embarrassment, she vowed, that made her feel so warm and weak and will-less.

Her eyes grew wide, fixed upon his, then wider still as he guided her hand lower, circling round and round, over the firm ridges of his belly, the indention of his navel, to the springy mat of hair below. Her breathing grew shallow and strained as LeClaire's eyes drifted closed to hide from the masculine beauty of his body and the dark complement of his bronzed skin against her pale ivory. But a huge knot of fascination still formed within her until finally, in a single and unexcused liberty, her hand flexed and curled, digging into the taut flesh of his abdomen, then spread wide, feeling the downy coils of his hair beneath and between her fingers before she snatched her hand back.

Borgia's own fingers clinched into a tight fist, then forcefully relaxed, and he brought his knuckles to her blushing cheeks. "Art a tempting maid, to be so bold," he teased and watched her color flame higher. "Nay, do not turn away," he said when she attempted to bury her ashamed face in the bedding. His fingers beneath her chin, he tilted her face up and brushed a kiss to her lips, lightly flicking her bottom lip a scant second before releasing her. "I would have you more bold. Have I not said that you need have no fear of me?"

Oh, nay! LeClaire thought a little hysterically. *'Tis only myself that I need fear.*

15

LeClaire smoothed the delicate linen shift, then pulled the exquisite ankle-length kirtle over it. It was simple in its elegance, the pale yellow gown almost stark without braid or embroidery. But because it was the most beautiful thing LeClaire had ever put upon her slender body, she did not notice its lack of ornamentation. She had never been vain, nor covetous of another's good fortune, but for the first time in her life, she wished to view herself in the silvery surface of a pond, or a polished metal hand mirror.

She felt giddy and girlish over a simple kirtle, but she did not mind those feelings so much, for they kept her more pressing worries at bay. In little more than a quarter hour, she was going belowstairs for the evening meal.

She had shared Borgia's chamber for two long, nerve-riddled weeks, an entire fortnight, and still the King had not arrived. The time had been torturous, confusing and something more that she cared not to explore. In a room decorated for war, she had found a peace in nightly conversation and a strength in the rest she had never allowed herself. Each evening Borgia would detail the day's activities for her, and she found his dark humor as arresting as his intelligence. Many nights she found herself laughing softly over some village antic as he retold it, and she began to see a great worth in his open-minded acceptance of the ideas and proposals the villiens put to him when they were brave enough to voice them.

Only the presence of the high warm bed and its disturbing memories could mar the gentle beauty of quiet evenings by the fire. At times when his hands would touch her with tender but obvious restraint, she was stunned that he had held to his word and did not take her, and at others she knew he but waited for her to weaken and null the promise herself. And she wondered which was the stronger power—his word or her honor—which would remain constant?

LeClaire swallowed hard, feeling suddenly flushed. She needed some time below to gain perspective, but going to the common-room meant chancing the unknown nemeses, those faceless fiends who had hurt Aurel.

They would know her, would know they had knocked her to the floor after beating and defiling her sister, would know she could not recognize them—not even if she stood eye to eye with those enemies. The last thought gave her pause, and she rubbed her arms briskly to ward off a chill, though spring was now rushing upon the land as if it must hurry them toward summer. When had Borgia and his men stopped being her enemy?

Her heart did a breathless stutter in her chest. He was her enemy still, yet . . . yet he was not. He was searching for the rapists with relentless precision while he protected her and her sisters from further harm, and he was turning Ravenwood into a prosperous and pleasing village in which to work or visit. For all the turmoil and turbulence in her life, she had equal moments of quiet security when starvation no longer scratched at her door, when frigid winds no longer wept through the cracks in the wall. Meals were tasty and plentiful, as were laughter and song.

Loneliness and desperation had been swept far back into the corners of her mind, caught in the cobwebs of doubt and fear that held firm but were growing more substanceless by day. Only in the evenings, when Borgia came to his chamber, would the gossamer nets grow strong, encircling her in their trap. He had yet to take her by brute force, but night after night he used a different coercion—gentle seduction more frightening and persuasive than his physical strength would ever have been. And she knew at those times he was her enemy still.

A knock on the door startled her, and LeClaire jumped, then tamped down the troubling and confusing thoughts. Maire rushed in, spinning merrily in her own new gown like a sweet-scented gale.

"Sister mine," she said imperiously, then dipped into a graceful curtsy. "How fares your day?"

LeClaire smiled, caught up in Maire's exuberance and startling beauty. Her younger sister's gown was a deep mauve and her cheeks glowed with the same vital hue. "My day fares well; what of yours?"

Maire cast her a deliciously wicked wink and pointed over her shoulder. " 'Tis a most glorious day, save for Sir Imbecile, who will not allow me two steps ere he is tromping upon my heels."

LeClaire glanced at Bryson standing rigid in the doorway, his expression stormy, and felt moved to offer him a smile. Of all the guards, his job was the hardest, she knew, for she had chased after Maire most of her life. Slippery as a fish, her sister had darted in and out of trouble since she could crawl. There was no stopping Maire, no cautioning her, no saving her from herself. But each of the sisters tried, would continue to try, probably until Maire was grown and under the rule of a husband who possessed either a stronger will or sublime patience.

"Would you join us, Sir Bryson?" LeClaire asked in an effort to appear gracious despite her sister's scowl.

"Nay, he is angry. Again!" Maire said with a flippant toss of her dark hair. It shimmied over her shoulders to her hips and swung there like a heavy pelt glinting with sherry highlights. Her eyes flared triumphantly above her impish grin. "I escaped him this morn whilst he attended the garderobe."

LeClaire blushed at the indelicate tattling, then sighed. "Oh, Maire. He but protects you. Can you not see the worth in that?"

Disgruntled that her own sister did not take her side, Maire shrugged and poked her bottom lip out, but there was nary a hint of penance in her eyes. " 'Twas only a small adventure. I merely slipped into Aurel's room for a visit. Moreover, Sir Roger the Ingrate gave me a tongue lashing and brought me back whilst Sir Imbecile was still hitching up his chausses. So where was the harm?"

Explaining anything to Maire was like whispering into the wind and having the words blown back. "No harm in that," LeClaire said. "If 'twas all you truly intended."

"I am neither a fool nor a child," Maire said, and ignoring Bryson's loud snort, continued imperiously, "If I had intended more, I would have done it." In a whirlwind change of mood to chase away the doldrums, she spun around again and flung her arms wide. "What think you of my new gown?"

" 'Tis beautiful," LeClaire said softly. "As are you."

"My thanks," Maire said quickly, satisfied. "But not as beautiful as you, sister mine. You will have every unwelcome knight in the keep stuttering and stammering and choking upon his wine when you go below." A too familiar light suddenly danced in her eyes. "Now *there's* a pretty thought. Mayhaps they'll all choke to death!"

It could not be borne! Maire's irreverence rippled through LeClaire until she pressed her hand to her mouth to stifle a giggle. She gave Sir Bryson an apologetic smile, and tried to perfect a stern look for her sister. Unable to accomplish even a smattering of that, she gave up and spoke warmly.

"Do you join us, Maire? It might do you good to get

out of these rooms for a while." Her smile faded slightly. "Aurel says she will not, of course, but there is no reason for you to stay up here."

Maire's lashes dropped, her impertinent chin lifted, and she sent her guard an austere look. Her tone was petulant but seething with repressed anger. "Sir Imbecile says I may not, as punishment for escaping him. If you ask me, 'tis he who should be punished for being lax in his job."

LeClaire darted a glance at both of them, torn by her loyalty to Maire but knowing there were consequences for all actions. Where her sister's safety was concerned, she heartily endorsed Bryson's guardianship, but where her tender feelings lay . . . well, it was a different matter.

"Can you not forgive her this one mistake?" she asked Bryson.

"Mistake?" he scoffed. Though there was no amusement in his voice, neither was there rancor. " 'Twas no mistake, and well you know it, my lady. I am sorry, I cannot."

Maire shrugged, as if unconcerned, for she would not ruin LeClaire's small chance at freedom with a petty squabble. And, in truth, she would pay Bryson back a hundredfold if it cost her ten years abovestairs. "No matter, sister mine. You shall come back and tell me all, how the men fell over themselves at your beauty, how the jongleur sang of your grace and intelligence . . ."

LeClaire's face paled at the mention of the minstrel, and she heard not the rest of Maire's ridiculous oration. She did not think she could bear up under the shame if he sang another verse implicating her with Borgia in illicit circumstances. But she smiled, for what else was there to do?

"I shall tell you all, Maire," LeClaire promised, "though, no doubt, 'twill be a boring tale." She turned to pick up her rope girdle, but her sister rushed forward to retrieve it.

"You cannot think to wear this," Maire scolded mildly. "Come, we will fetch one much nicer from Mother's chest."

Maire grabbed LeClaire's hand and pulled her into the antechamber. Pushing up the heavy lid of a scarred chest, she rummaged through the layers of old and dusty woolen cloths she had put there when the soldiers were first sighted, wanting to hide her mother's treasures should they mean to sack the keep. She dug deeper, sending rat-eaten woolen and dust flying, until she emerged with a victorious grin. Draped over her arm were two girdles.

"What think you of this one?" Maire asked, her eyes sparkling, her excitement infectious as she held one up for inspection.

LeClaire stared at the crimson silk braided with golden thread and found it quite lovely until she spied the dangling ends decorated with lion-heads stamped out of sheet gold. She'd already been branded as the Silver Lion's; she need not proclaim it in gold. "I think the color will not do," she said evasively.

Maire thought the color perfect but merely shrugged and tossed it back into the trunk. "What of this?"

The other girdle she held aloft was more to LeClaire's liking. Clasped low at the waist with a small buckle of intricately engraved silver, it would let the girdle rest just above her hips while the spun silk of silver-gilt thread would streamer down just below her knees.

"Aye, 'twill be lovely," she said.

Maire beamed and proceeded to fasten the girdle about LeClaire's hips, adjusting and readjusting, until it suited her, while Bryson watched on from the doorway with the look of one plagued by constant boredom.

In truth, he found these female odysseys intriguing, having neither wife nor sister with which to compare the ritual. He'd had his share of feminine companionship, which usually took the form of a quick tumble with a camp follower. The stench and lice that accompanied those brief encounters were a far cry from the simple gaiety and warmth found in these two—a far cry from the innocence.

A base-born knight without the comforts of his own castle, he'd been at Hastings beside his true-born cousin Richard le Fort, who had flung his shield before Duke William while Bryson himself had flung William to the ground at a critical moment in the battle, thereby saving the future King from death. For this Bryson had been granted knighthood.

He did not consider himself a greedy man, but he was ambitious. As a landless knight, Bryson had petitioned William for a Saxon widow who now held her lands only if she wed a Norman. It was not the most desirable alliance, but better than some, for the widow was young, only seven and ten, and she had already been delivered of two sons by her former husband, so she was not barren.

But she was a scared little rabbit when Bryson was in attendance, keeping her eyes lowered, her replies short and toneless. He was beginning to think she could use some of Maire's temper and LeClaire's composure as he watched the young women quibble over the exact placement of the girdle. Maire bent, straightening the folds of her sister's gown, her slender round backside raised in a most provocative angle. Aye, bedding the young widow would not prove such a chore if she were more like the shapely and irascible Maire.

Bryson shifted, a bit uncomfortable with his wayward thoughts. God's bones, he detested Maire with her flippant tongue and cunning ways, and had been kept at Ravenwood only by his oath to guard her. He was the Lion's vassal, but had been given leave to pursue his own ambitions if the King sanctioned the marriage. He had not thought the duties he had volunteered for would extend into weeks and now chafed under the restriction of protecting a girl of five and ten who did not want to be protected and endeavored to thwart him at every possible moment.

"Damoiselles," Bryson said to gain the girls' attention. LeClaire looked up at him with an expectant smile, while Maire cast him a frown, which included sticking out her tongue. Bryson clinched his fists to keep from strangling her, and directed his request to LeClaire. "If you are done, FitzRalph is waiting to escort you below."

LeClaire smiled and nodded, pleased that the young squire would attend her rather than Borgia, though she'd been told she would sup beside Ravenwood's lord. She had wished only to have freedom from her chamber to mingle with the villeins, but the sun was dying when her request had been answered. It was too late in the day to go to the village, but she was invited to share the evening meal. If it was not exactly what she had wanted, it was at least better than another evening spent cooped up in this chamber. She hoped.

As if it were the grandest pleasure in his life, FitzRalph offered his arm to LeClaire. A small smile tugged at her lips for the young squire whose duties extended little beyond fetching and carrying. He was not allowed abovestairs, so never cleaned his lord's room or helped Borgia dress, but he could always be found tagging along behind the Lion during the day's business.

This eve he was nobly presented in his short tunic of twill cloth trimmed with braid made from dyed thread and a woolen cloak gathered at the shoulder with a gold brooch set with colored stones. He could not be much older than Kyra, but he carried himself as if knighthood were imminent and merely awaiting his leisure.

"You look quite grand, Master FitzRalph," LeClaire said. "I knew not that your duties of squire extended also to that of guard. I am more than impressed."

FitzRalph postured and threw his lean shoulders back even farther. " 'Tis my pleasure, my lady."

LeClaire smiled and took his arm. FitzRalph was a far cry from the angry squire she'd been introduced to the second day that Borgia's army had arrived. She suspected he'd wanted to slice her throat for drugging the soldiers, but he'd grown quite pleasant since she'd tended a small wound he'd encountered while cleaning Borgia's armor.

FitzRalph had been tossing the bag full of armor, sand and vinegar and had conked himself on the head. LeClaire had found him hiding in embarrassment trying to tend the small but bloody cut himself. Understanding his need for secrecy that he not be ridiculed by the knights, she'd cleaned and salved the wound, then kept mum about the whole thing. And had gained his undying gratitude since.

The hall was a conglomeration of strange sights, sounds and smells when she descended the stairs. Voices of knights and serving women rose in laughter and teasing over the clatter of tankards and platters, and the delicious aroma of roast and pudding mingled in the heavy air with the more earthy scents of leather and wool. It was at once invigorating and disquieting to LeClaire's spirit—the assortment of unfamiliar faces and foreign accents, the whisper of cool silk and scratchy woolen, coarse language from the same throats bedecked with jewel-encrusted clasps and brooches—the complexities of refined chaos.

Roger de Amiens had just swallowed a healthy drink of wine when LeClaire stepped into the common-room. His tankard hit the table with such force that the soldier beside him jumped.

"Damme, Sir Rog—" Sir Fulk snarled before taking in the sight before him. "Christ's wounds!"

Several other knights and common soldiers turned, and a sudden and uncomfortable silence hit the room.

FitzRalph beamed as if he alone were responsible for the transformation and proudly escorted LeClaire toward Borgia's exalted place at the head table.

With one tremendous shove of his elbow, Sir Fulk sent the soldier on the other side of him crashing off the side of the bench, then rose and offered LeClaire the empty seat. The maligned knight scrambled to his feet, drawing his sword, but Roger intervened by rising and leveling them all with a warning glance.

"Damoiselle LeClaire," he said smoothly, inclining his head, "how radiant you look."

LeClaire blushed, at once pleased and discomposed by the compliment and entirely overwhelmed by all the attention. Her smile was somewhat hesitant. "How fares Aurel? She did not come to my room this eve."

"Nay," he said. "I had business here. A guard is at her door, but she will not allow him entrance to her room nor will she walk the halls with him. I return to her shortly, so mayhaps she will see you ere she retires."

LeClaire nodded, relieved, then turned her attention to the center seat. Borgia sat there in casual elegance, superbly attired in a dark blue velvet tunic girded with a jeweled belt and short-sword. Unlike so many of the noblemen, he disdained the ecclesiastical outer dress of long flowing robes, and wore only a short cape flung negligently over his broad shoulders and fastened with a silver brooch.

One brow lifted, he stared at her, his smile lazy as a hot summer day, as were the gray eyes studying her from tip to toe. There was appreciation in that gaze and more that LeClaire could not determine. It was both stirring and unsettling to her anxious feminine heart to find him so blatantly handsome and yet so subtly dangerous.

He rose when she approached and offered the seat next to him. She had no choice but to accept it, though she could not think how such a gesture would be viewed by the others. Only a wife or elevated guest sat next to the lord, and she could claim neither position. But she took her seat gracefully, while her insides churned and her mind seemed void of any witty or pleasing comment she might offer.

"My lord," she said for lack of anything more profound.

"My lady." Borgia inclined his head, and in full view of the entire hall raised her hand and placed a kiss upon her palm.

LeClaire fought the urge to snatch her hand back, thereby embarrassing herself further. She could not, however, stop the furious blush that rose to her cheeks. She smiled sweetly without once meeting the eyes of anyone near and hissed under her breath, "Knave!"

Borgia brought his mouth within a scant inch of her ear and whispered, "Beware, bratling, that your words do not prove prophetic."

"I am convinced of them already," she replied. "There is no further need of proof."

He laughed lightly and drew back, his eyes roving over her gown. "Art lovely," he said.

He watched her expression warm under the flattery, but knew she would not play the sophisticated amusement by dissembling. There was no coquetry within her, no vanity to be perked by veneration. She put no stock in physical appearance, accepting what nature had given her with little attention beyond cleanliness, and was infinitely more appealing for it. Picking up his wine, he raised it to her, then took a drink.

Flustered by his rare compliment, LeClaire pulled her gaze from his and searched for something to occupy her hands. Having never engaged in such an elaborate meal, she was lost to find no cup at her own place. She eyed him askance, but said naught until he offered her the jeweled chalice.

"I prefer my own," she hedged, uncomfortable not knowing what protocol dictated the affair.

" 'Tis the custom," Borgia replied, and pressed her to accept it by placing it in her hand.

" 'Tis an unhealthy custom, I vow," she said. "When Hadrian's family came down with a complaint a year past, everyone who drank at their table suffered also."

"Mayhaps the wine was tainted," Borgia offered dryly.

LeClaire smiled guiltily at his reference. "Nay, 'twas common wine shared by many families. But only those who passed around the same cup fell sick."

At that she grew silent. She was no physician to make such a statement and her theories had been scoffed at by the villagers on too many occasions for her to try and convince this well-traveled and knowledgeable knight. And there were too many diseases that seemed to move from cottage to cottage, attacking victims without discretion. It was a subject of much concern and consideration for her, but there was no way to find the answers. With naught much more than feelings upon which to base her claims, she thought it best not to speak further of them.

"I have suspected the same things myself," Borgia commented, so startling LeClaire that she gazed up at him with rapt interest.

"Truly, my lord? You have had such an idea?"

"Aye, and I've seen the proof of it."

Her heartbeat quickened in her breast. She felt suddenly as if she'd found a kindred soul, one who would not naysay her thoughts as frivolous nonsense. "You've seen proof?"

"Aye," Borgia said seriously. "Some years past lady Eleanor shared a cup with a neighboring visitor, and they both came down with a stomach ailment." LeClaire nodded intently for him to continue, and Borgia's voice dropped to one of intimate secrecy. "Of course, some say 'twas not the wine, at all, but the kiss they shared after the meal that caused their downfall. FitzWalter was delivered of his stomach ailment in two days' time, but lady Eleanor was not delivered of hers for nine months."

All color drained from LeClaire's cheeks and her heart resumed its normal, impeded beat. "Art worse than a knave!" she whispered, and felt like slapping his handsome face.

"Aye, a knave and a scoundrel," he agreed before his manner became aloof and the usual coldness returned to his expression.

" 'Tis true," she said. "Everything I have called you is true and more."

He leaned close, too close for her to retreat from the intense gaze in eyes that were as cold as ice yet smoldered like charcoal. She turned her face away, and his breath whispered along the sensitive shell of her ear to send little shivers tripping down her limbs. "I await the day you call me lover."

"Oh!" LeClaire cried, blushing. All eyes were upon her then and she snapped her mouth shut, evading their avid glances by lowering her eyes.

Their meal was brought, saving her from further conversation, but she could not forget the looks on the men's faces. They kept their murmurings low, but their eyes were sharp, and she could imagine what they said, what they thought. That she was the Lion's leman, his mistress, to share his bed each night and endure his intimate conversation.

She had no appetite for the sumptuous fare spread before her, the spitted roast so tender it had not been minced or pounded into stew but placed before a carver, nor the fowl dishes of starling and cormorant. Even the pastries of fruit preserved in honey could not tempt her.

As with the wine cup, there was no bowl of her own, and she suspected she was supposed to share Borgia's. But since she would not look at him to learn the way of things, it was likely she would retire hungry and regret her sullenness come midnight.

Borgia plucked a choice morsel from his dish and waved it beneath LeClaire's nose. Her stomach rumbled indelicately, and she darted him a quick glance, wondering what other rules governed these formal dinners.

"Have a taste, damoiselle, ere you waste away to naught but skin upon bones," he commanded softly.

She looked around her furtively to see if the others were watching, if Borgia played some poor game with her. The knights were busy with their own food, taking it with fingers or knives, but there were no women beyond servants in attendance with which to compare an acceptable course of action.

Her stomach rumbled again, and she reached for the food. Borgia drew back and shook his head, then brought it back to her lips. LeClaire sighed and quickly nibbled the tender meat from his fingers, praying it was the correct thing to do and she had not just disgraced herself further with some action reserved for bold women of loose morals. When no one seemed to notice, she swallowed the roasted stag and allowed Borgia a brief glance.

He merely sent her a droll look and chose another piece, which she gobbled just as quickly. He then chose one for himself before offering her a pastry. After several uncomfortable bites, LeClaire sat back and waved him away.

" 'Tis a ridiculous custom," she said. "Mothers train their daughters to feed themselves when they are yet babes, then when they are grown they are fed again? I do not see the value. 'Twould go much faster if I had my own trencher."

"Haste is not of import here," Borgia drawled, as he offered her a piece of fowl. "And not nearly so satisfying as having your lips touch me in a way that can only resemble a kiss."

LeClaire's shoulders stiffened, but she smiled sweetly and put her lips to his fingers, then clamped down with her teeth. After a vicious little bite, she pulled back, fighting the urge to fling the entire contents of his dinner in his face.

"Vixen," he whispered with a lewd grin that was at once tantalizing and threatening. His hand dropped beneath the table and came to rest upon her knee. LeClaire jerked, but he only gave her an innocent, inquiring look and began inching up her kirtle and shift. Her eyes widened and she squirmed, but she could say naught that would not bring all eyes and ears to attention. In no more than a few seconds, Borgia's hand was on her bare knee and inching toward her thigh.

"My lord," she said tightly, flustered to the point of screaming but not wanting anyone to know what was amiss. "I . . . I should like another taste of roast."

"And would you like another taste of me?" he asked.

"Nay, 'twas a mistake, surely—" She clamped her teeth shut as well as her thighs when his fingers crawled even higher, wedging their way between her gripped muscles. "My lord, please . . ."

Heat throbbed in her cheeks and elsewhere, and she could not very well wiggle around without being noticed. Her leg muscles grew taut and quivering, sending pains shooting up her back from the strain. Borgia's head dropped close to hers and she grew more rigid.

"Release my hand, you shameless wench," he whispered silkily. "If you desire my touch so badly as to hold me by force, I'll gladly accommodate you in yon chamber. But even I am not so bold as to do so in front of the men."

LeClaire's eyes fell closed. St. Edward preserve her, she could not tolerate one more second with this unscrupulous demon, could not—

One light, dastardly flick of his long fingers *there*, deep on the inside of her thigh, almost caused her to come out of her seat. Gripping the edge of the table, she forced herself to relaxed her wary muscles, one tentative inch at a time, afraid he would strike again. Borgia removed his hand slowly, sliding it along the inside of her leg until it was finally gone, but the burning and trembling in her lower body continued long after.

The remainder of the meal was a fiasco, the food settling in her stomach like an anvil when she could swallow it past her dry throat. To escape her anger and embarrassment, LeClaire furtively studied the knights, desperately needing to recognize Aurel's attackers, desperately not wanting to. It would not have been so horrid if she had seen them, been able to describe the facial features that had grown grotesque in her mind; then Borgia could hunt them down like the animals they were.

But the not knowing was wearing. Everyone unfamiliar was suspect, every eye that turned her way made her wonder if he knew, remembered . . . gloated.

There was naught to do but push the troubling and useless thoughts aside and study those around her as men not monsters, and try to ignore Borgia's presence so close and commanding beside her. She found the men's camaraderie an odd thing, jovial yet harsh. Their remarks to one another in jest were cutting, the jabs and back-slaps destined to leave marks. They played like they fought, fast and furious, as if even leisure time were something to be chased and conquered, not enjoyed in quiet and restful solitude.

It was too much for her to absorb and assimilate, too many sights, sounds and smells buffeting her from too many directions. She craved peace, those quiet evenings with her sisters when the biggest challenge at day's end was a simple game of chess or draughts with Kyra, when Maire's voice would float softly over the melody of her lute, soothing not humiliating. When Aurel, in her own quiet way, would paint the world in vivid thread or retell legends in pale tincture and bold pigment from her color pot.

LeClaire cut her eyes to Borgia and felt the restive,

unquiet humors stir within her. She wondered what manner of man was he to boldly pursue her one minute and protect her the next. Wondered why he did either. He was a contradiction, too vast in his subtleties, too open in his actions, for her to determine and digest his purpose, his ultimate goal.

He mixed with those around him with the ease of a friend, yet he held himself aloof, detached, on a level few of them saw or understood. They were pawns, all of them save Roger, moving in orchestrated alignment when he directed.

To LeClaire, where the simplicities of life had been tantamount to her needs, wants and desires, his power and adroitness were, at best, disheartening and, at worst, terrifying. Did he play her like a hand puppet or stringed marionette, slyly manipulating portions of her will without her consent or knowledge? She suspected it must be so, for more and more often of late she craved the things he did to her even as she was repelled by them.

Her shoulder brushed his as she rose, and even that simple contact caused the surfaces of her skin to tingle in an odd, disconcerting way. Borgia caught her hand, his thumb soothing the translucent skin at her wrist with a nonchalance that might have been nonthreatening from another. But not from St. Brieuç. He threatened her in ways she'd not known existed in something so simple as a touch. She tugged on her hand, but he held it with firm gentleness, in the same manner his eyes held her—so artful in their deceit—like a cord of silver-threaded silk with the strength of forged steel.

"Do you stay for the entertainment?" he asked.

LeClaire shook her head. She did not dare. "I should like to retire."

"Then seek our bed with all haste, damoiselle," he said with the cordial inflections of a proper host, but his eyes were rapacious as they roamed over her. "I join you soon."

Her backbone straightened at the words spoken for all to hear, and she shot him a furious glance. But the expression in his eyes as he looked back at her was disheartening. For in that one simple look, she glimpsed the lion, hungry but ever so patient, awaiting the kill.

16

LeClaire dragged her pallet from the antechamber into Borgia's room and flung it far from the bed. The possibility that he would not allow her to remain upon it meant naught at this point. She would not chance another night beside him, chance being the brunt of his inequity and end up ridiculed like poor lady Eleanor of the nine-month stomach ailment.

Borgia watched her angry, jerking movements from the doorway in wry amusement. Her gentle curves were outlined in candlelight for only a brief moment as she removed her kirtle and dove beneath the furs. Like a child, she curled into a ball, but he knew well the figure, clothed now in finest linen, was that of a woman.

"Bratling," he drawled, strolling into the room to crouch down beside her, "must you insist upon this when you know it gains you naught but my displeasure?"

LeClaire pulled the cover over her face, and prayed he would depart this life in a most violent manner and be cast into the fiery bowels of hell for eternity before she realized what she was doing. She said a hasty prayer for forgiveness, not feeling one ounce of regret, but also not wanting to lower herself to his base nature.

"Be gone!" she said, the sound muffled beneath the fur.

Borgia snatched the covers from her and tossed them

out of arms' reach. "Have done," he said. "You have made your point, now come to bed."

LeClaire rolled to her back, her eyes brilliant even in shadow. "I am abed! And I shall stay here until the King arrives and delivers me from . . ." Her words dwindled off into a nothingness that roared like thunder in her ears, and her cheeks went pale as parchment. *Merciful Father! What had she done?* Her eyes grew round with fear, for Borgia's suddenly held that intense, calculating look.

"What has William to do with your deliverance?" he asked quietly.

She was not fooled in the least by his casual tone, not when his eyes bore straight into hers like an inlaid silver lance. Her mind scrambled for an answer that would exonerate her, and not be a sinful falsehood.

"He will surely take this chamber when he comes. 'Tis the finest." Her voice held a breathless quality, and her heart crashed against her ribs in waves that rolled sickeningly to her stomach. "You cannot think to make me share your bed, even in some other room, not with William in residence."

Borgia's eyes flickered briefly. *A lie, damoiselle? You do not do it well at all; 'tis beyond you.* And beyond him to dismiss it, but he would get to the heart of her deception later when it was more prudent. "He will have heard of it already," he said flatly. " 'Tis not my custom to share quarters. Some scandalmonger will have carried the tale to him ere he arrives."

LeClaire's eyes flared in shame. Every hideous, unfair and undeserved episode that had brought her to this point in life seemed to converge at once into a hot, expanding ball within her. Without forethought, without even an inkling that she was capable of such, she reared up. Her palm flew out viciously, and she slapped him.

Borgia did not so much as flinch. But his eyes narrowed dangerously upon her, and LeClaire's throbbing hand was trembling when she brought it back down.

"I will not apologize," she said in defiance, but her lips too were trembling and her heart felt as if it were breaking from having done such a common, ignoble thing. It was not his fault that the tale-bearers spewed half-lies to the very person who could save her, and Borgia did protect her, but it was at the expense of her honor and reputation. She fought the tears forming in her eyes, but did not turn away. "Does the whole of England know I have been compromised in my own home?"

Borgia said nothing but his jaw was tense as he picked her up and crossed the room to dump her upon the high bed. He then proceeded to remove his clothing with stiff, precise movements that said his wrath simmered too close, too deadly near the surface of his emotions for him to give it vent.

"I'll not stay here!" LeClaire said, but when his hands went to his chausses, she turned away, unable even in her anger to scramble from the bed and face him clad only in her shift when he stood clad in nothing.

Naked, he took his place beside her and jerked her around to face him. "My home, my keep, my servants," he said with the lethal force that had broken many much stronger than she. "You dare much to think that you do not have to do my bidding. Your very livelihood depends upon your staying in my good graces." His pause was as threatening as his words, and the grip on her upper arms was painful. "Have a care, damoiselle, the livelihood of your sisters also rests in my generous hands."

LeClaire's face blanched, and her eyes probed his for some hint of a cruel jest. "You would not be so unkind," she whispered.

"You underestimate me."

"You . . . you would turn us out? After all this time, after setting guards at our heels to protect us, after clothing us, you would now turn us out?"

"In less than a half-second," he replied coldly, "and without even the smallest regret."

She blinked, but the gesture could not clear the blighted, desolate look from her eyes. "You would not," she whispered, but there was no warm place within her to give emotional assurance to the statement.

He made no agreement or denial, just stared back at her with his unyielding silver-hard gaze. LeClaire blinked once more, staring into his set and powerful face, and despair washed over her with the force of a tidal wave. So, he did string them along like merry marching pieces of wood and cloth, inhuman players in a brutal game of win or lose. When the twine was cut, did they clatter to the stage floor in a crumbled mass of twisted limbs and faded dreams to be swept aside for the next entertainment?

Something essential within her shattered, fragments splintering off in so many diverse directions that she could not collect them, could not pull herself back together. And she did what she had not done solely for herself since she was a child. Her chin quivered, her lashes fluttered and with great austerity she began to cry. Not in dainty little droplets that rolled gracefully down her cheeks, but in great heaving spasms, sniveling bouts of coughing and choking and a veritable flood of tears.

She might have stopped there, but the unexpected release felt so good that she continued in racking sobs, nearly wailing her heart out for herself, her sisters, her loss of Ravenwood, the smearing of her good name and everything else she could think of to rightfully feel sorry for herself.

Borgia's gaze flickered in surprise for a second at her utter loss of control, then he stared at her blandly until the fit passed. When there were but a few sniffles left, he snatched a square of linen from the bedside table and pressed it to her red nose, then folded it and dabbed at her swollen eyes.

"Art done?"

LeClaire nodded, drained and thoroughly ashamed of herself for falling apart under his regard. With a deep sigh, she gathered her composure and scrubbed the tears from her cheeks.

Borgia brushed the red-gold hair back from her temples, his eyes unwavering as they studied her, and his voice was incredibly soft. "I will not turn you out, LeClaire. God's bones, do you not already know this? What are you so afraid of?"

"Art an ignorant man if you do not know," she sniffed, but had no heart for explanation. "I should like to return to my room. Since you have forbidden that, I should like, at least, to sleep upon my own pallet." She sniffed again and brushed away the last straggling tear rolling down her cheek.

Borgia's smile was rueful; it was also brimming with a mixture of old cynicism and exquisite tenderness. "Art the strongest woman I have ever known to be so suddenly given over to self-pity. You could not have been more than six and ten when you inherited this place, yet you salvaged what was left of it and began worthy changes."

"Strong?" she whispered, her eyes wide with disbelief. "You think me strong when I hardly put food upon the table, when my sisters were gowned in poorest cloth, when the peasants' cottages were not fit for lice?" Tears welled up anew at his obvious raillery. "Art most unkind to mock me so when you have brought the people more prosperity than they would have ever known by my hand."

"Silly maiden," he chided. "What did I? I brought a thousand men and more coin than this village has ever seen. 'Tis little acclaim in what can be purchased. Aye, you are as strong and valiant a woman as I have ever known. None has ever dared to stand against me as you have. You are also the most hardheaded. Admit that you are more comfortable here than on that pile of straw."

"Nay, 'tis a miserable bed with you in it," LeClaire murmured, trying mightily not to be warmed by his words.

"That is your fault, damoiselle. 'Twould be most comfortable if you could relax, share it the way 'twas meant to be shared by a man and a woman."

"Aye, shared in marriage," she reproved.

"Do you beg a betrothal?" he asked, and she could hear the wicked teasing in his voice.

"I would as soon marry your horse."

"Ah, bratling, poor Ares could not do for you in this bed what I could." LeClaire blushed furiously, and turned her face away. Borgia's fingers traced the edges of her hairline down to her jaw. His thumb brushed her lips, parting them, then tipped her face back and up to his. "Methinks you do not know what you refuse. Need I tell you the way of things so you are not afraid, tell you what pleasure—"

" 'Tis not for me to know," she said quickly, inexplicably shivery under the calloused pads of his fingers. " 'Tis not . . ." Her words faded with his touch, her lashes fluttered closed as his knuckles slid down her neck, and she fought the urge to tilt her head back, to offer more of what he was taking.

"Then how can you naysay me?" he muttered, watching every expression, every subtle nuance of emotion on her expressive face. In muted shades of apricot her cheeks warmed, and her breathing grew shallow. His hand slid lower to the curve of her breast where her heartbeat struggled to deny the calling of her woman's body. "You should know what you refuse."

" 'Tis not right; I need not know more," she said, but the words were strained, forced past an inquisitive mind that begged such knowledge though her heart stayed constant in the belief that à maiden had no need of improper ideas.

"Nay, damoiselle, there is much more that you need," Borgia said, and pulled her close, fitting softness to strength, molding the delicate lines of her slender frame to one harder and more demanding so perfectly, as if the contrast were needed for balance.

"Then tell me!" she gasped, for even intimate words were much safer than the intimacy of his body pressed to hers when it felt so precise and fitting.

" 'Tis better to show you."

She gave token resistance, though why she even bothered was beyond her. Her reputation was in tatters, the case she would put before the King now tainted by slurs that would shape his opinion of her before he even arrived. What use in keeping herself pure when in the eyes of all she was unclean and unworthy for anything more than being some man's mistress? But she knew she refused him not for what others thought, but for what she thought of herself.

Borgia's lips sought hers, at once gentle and hungry, and any further protest she made was caught and swallowed up in the slow building passion that swirled between them. She was drained from her outburst, her defenses lowered, her resolve left achingly open and vulnerable when it should have been closed to him.

His tongue teased her lips, calling forth shimmering waves of ecstasy to flow through her body like warm, moist currents of air. His hand caressed her back in strong circular motions that grew broader and longer until reaching her hips where he pulled her flush against him. The strength of his body was overwhelmingly pleasurable and frightening, and the forbidden shadows tapped again at her curiosity, growing bolder in their demands with each touch, each fondle, each caress.

His tongue dipped, penetrating the seam of her lips, then touched hers. Light then demanding, he searched the interior of her mouth, and the effect was staggering. Plunged into the hot rivulet of desire, she fought for air, for a way to resurface, but her shift seemed to absorb his heat until it dominated every nerve and pulse point in her body, making her flushed and anxious. She twisted against him, but the friction only fanned her desire and it leaped higher, flamed brighter, until it was an all-consuming fever burning everything in its path.

LeClaire moaned and writhed against him, pleading, denying, and her emotions condensed into a hurting rush of tension that spread throughout her sensitized flesh until it grew too tight, too tender upon her body. She gasped and pulled her head back, but Borgia's mouth dropped to the rapid pulse in her throat, and his hands raced the fire to sear a heated path up her ribs to the sides of her breasts.

He rolled, pressing her to her back as his fingers curled inward and parted the shift, and LeClaire's head jerked back at the sound of fragile new linen ripping, at the sweltering hotness, at the sudden moisture of his mouth in the valley of her breasts.

"Nay, please," she begged, the sound somehow lost beneath the thunder of her heartbeat as his lips traveled a scorching course over her skin. Her hands braced against his solid chest, needing distance between them, and she pushed.

His head lifted and he stared into her eyes as if he could expose her most hidden secrets, then his gaze dropped hot and certain to her breasts. Expert hands spread her ruined shift until her upper torso was completely revealed, and LeClaire's arms buckled to hide herself. But he pulled her wrists away, leaving her so open and exposed to his gaze that she thought she would shrivel up with shame. His hands slowly released her wrists, then his fingers threaded through her own, pinning her to the bed as he braced above her.

"Art so perfect," he whispered in a darkly compelling

voice, then darker still, "Yield." When she shook her head, unable to answer over her splintered breaths, he said softly, "Then know that which you refuse." His head dropped, his lips parted and his tongue darted out to flick once, twice, thrice, on her sensitive nipple. LeClaire cried out and arched high, her fingers digging into his.

"Lie with me," Borgia said, his breath a hot whisper upon the moist peak.

LeClaire only shook her head again, unable to gainsay him, unable to force words past the rushing of her heartbeat as her naked breasts rose and fell in rapid cadence to the blood rushing in her veins. His tongue darted out again, laving, teasing, until LeClaire's nails dug deep furrows in his hands, as if she would claw her way through him.

And he watched her, watched the dewy moisture bead her skin, watched her eyes darken to azure, watched her flesh grow rose-peach with the heat. With consummate awareness, his lips closed around her nipple and he pulled it into his mouth, deeply, tightly, but only once before he released her.

"Lie with me," he whispered again, staring into her eyes, eyes bright with fear and newborn passion.

Her nostrils flared and thinned with every laborious breath, and her breasts continued to heave, tempting, alluring, so appetizing he dropped his head again to inhale her scent, to flick his tongue over the tip of her other virgin breast, then suckle it so briefly that LeClaire's body had hardly risen from its spasm before he was done and staring into her eyes again.

Oh, faithless heart! her mind cried as she felt herself drowning in the swirling gray waters of his eyes. She was wandering, drifting far from all that she knew and trusted, floating upon the dangerous waters of a terrible passion. She had not known temptation would be like this, so deceptively beautiful, like the heart of a flame, all brilliant shades of orange and gold and blue, so compelling that one wanted to get nearer and nearer the warmth. She felt the lure of it to her core, the craving of what was done in love with a man who only desired her in lust. Felt herself slipping and falling down an unredeemable path into the darkness where her body clamored for ease but her soul cried out for freedom.

And she wished for one, tiny, infinitesimal second that he would take her, take the choice and guilt from her by force, that she might be held blameless in the sight of all who would curse her.

The thought struck her with the force of all it hideously implied. The flame, for all its beauty and warmth at a distance, was deadly when it devoured. Her face drained of color, and her limbs went cold, chilled to the bone from such duplicity . . . such honesty.

Borgia watched the passion fade from her face, and covered her body more fully with his, unwilling to relinquish just yet the power he held over her, the desire he had wrung from her. "Join with me," he demanded. His hands tunneled beneath her gown to grasp her narrow hips where he pressed himself against her.

"I cannot," she whispered, shaken and quivering beneath his weight. His hands were like iron bands upon her, his strength so formidable she thought she would smother, and in that moment wished that she would. She had never hungered so, never yearned for something so wrong as his naked body pressed to hers. The fear that she would not escape unscathed this time was much more simple than the greater fear that she would be left with this wanting anguish. "Please, I cannot."

"Aye, you can. You want to. You lie if you say otherwise, for your flesh is yet moist. It awaits me."

She shook her head, tears building in her eyes from embarrassment and confusion and frustration. "Nay, I do not. If my body would betray me, my mind is still fixed."

Borgia's gaze grew shuttered, his jaw inflexible.

"Please . . ." she cried.

"Please what?" he whispered. "You need only ask, and it will be granted. Let me ease your pain."

"Nay," she cried softly. A tear slipped from her lashes to run a jagged course down her cheek. "Can you not see? You would give me more pain than I could bear, for you could not ease the regret that would follow."

Something like remorse flickered briefly in Borgia's eyes, then was snuffed with brutal efficiency. Expertly he had readied her woman's body, and his own male need was a sharp and insistent demand clawing at him, but he could not force her mind to follow. For all his practiced manipulation he'd created a willing body, but he could not change an unwilling mind. And he could not at this impassioned point reconcile himself to that fact.

He dropped his head to her neck, his harsh breathing a faulty reflection of the control he executed over his body, a body poised on the entrance of hers. One thrust, just one, would be the beginning to the end of the indomitable ache in his own loins . . . and mayhaps the end of the ache in hers. He strained forward a mere inch, felt her slick ripeness and more—resistance. Too much resistance for it ever to be easy between them the first time.

He lifted slightly, his arms braced on either side of her. Ash-gray eyes wandered over her pure skin, so fair it shone with the luster of pearls. Her eyes were wide in fear and desire, an open blue sky that he could soar in if he but took the plunge. And his body demanded that he take it now.

He strained forward another inch, heard her gasp and felt her body tighten, felt her inflexible will grow stronger than passion's temptation. His arms trembled from the force of holding himself in check, and he suddenly realized he was too close to the enticement, even for his limitless self-control. He could feel his mastery slipping, could feel the burning irritation, sharp needle-pricks of desire along the surfaces of his skin, could feel the overwhelming urge to thrust himself into her.

He jerked back suddenly, stunned and agitated. Never had he been so driven, so thoroughly consumed by something so inconsequential as the spilling of a virgin's blood.

And he was flooded with awe and amazement at such an obsessive, unreasonable impulse.

The tainted wisdom in his eyes bore into the soft innocence of hers, and he saw the women of his past—nameless faces, faceless names. Peasant and noble, alike. There were many in the early days when the victory of battle would course molten in his blood, untempered and unfettered. He remembered the conquered, their tears and averted faces as they lay passively beneath him in some ravaged keep. Why had they not fought him, told him nay, as this one had?

He knew, of course, had always known, but it had meant little to him. It was his reputation and their defeat. They had feared for their lives, and he had not let them think otherwise, but in undisciplined vigor had taken them without regard for pleasure or smooth words. Had they, too, been this innocent but war weary? *Ah, St. Brieuc, you never even noticed. How disgustingly vainglorious.*

There had been others later. Wealthy daughters, wives or widows, either innocent and ambitious, or merely exotic and uninhibited in their taste for the illicit. Their names and faces were more clear, but the feelings they inspired just as empty, just as meaningless.

Something cracked and shifted inside him; the sickly sweet odors of old machinations permeated the air, musty and stifling, the taste of stale passions dripped from his tongue and the darkness clung to the corridors of his soul like fungus, foul and rotting. LeClaire whimpered and the humors began to recede, overwhelmed by a blinding shaft of unwelcome enlightenment. He saw the stain, the murky filth that cloaked him within, as he looked at LeClaire. He would bring that to her, drown her in its vile depths if he proceeded. Her freshness now carried a weight of reprisal he had never before felt.

Contempt hardened his face, but not for her. It was for himself, for allowing his passions to rage, for the shallowness of those past relationships. And for the all-consuming draw he felt toward this virtuous girl.

He pulled back farther and dropped his eyes to her chest, saw her heart skitter beneath the gentle slope of her breasts, felt his own arms quaver with the strain of holding back. His eyes rose again to hers, probed the fearful crystalline depths, and wondered what would become of this insight.

She shifted fretfully beneath him, sending a surge of renewed desire pulsating through him until whatever benevolent intentions he had entertained were banished beneath the depths of his own self-need.

"Will you lie with me?" he said, wondering if it was the last time he would ask, or merely the last time he would give her a choice—wondered now on some emotionless level if he was capable of either. He knew himself well; there were no delusions on that score. He wanted her, therefore he would have her. But would he continue to seduce her into surrender or be moved to force? The question challenged him, for it was the first time his disciplined patience had been tried, his superior control tested beyond anything he had encountered. And he wondered just how far would it stretch until it snapped.

"Nay, you must know that I cannot." LeClaire swallowed and shook her head, powerless to say more as she stared up at his unrelenting face.

The pure, uncompromising conviction in her gaze castigated him, and a sudden and irrational regret as inflamed as his desire sluiced through him with the furor of a burning torch. *Oh, maiden, the choice is no longer yours. I am most heartily sorry for that.*

He dropped his forehead to her breast. "Say it just once," he breathed, vibration from the sound floating across her flesh until it prickled. "Admit that you want this."

Silence stretched between them, bloated with an urgency and grief that demanded honesty from a stricken heart. "Aye," LeClaire said in a painful whisper, her vision blurred by tears of disillusionment, regret and longing for what could not be, for the fact that she felt such a dishonorable thing at all. Her hands went to his face, as if she would make him see, make him understand. "Aye, but I want what I could never accept."

The crack widened; light poured in until it threatened to blind him, and Borgia rolled to his side and gathered her close, as if he would pull her inside himself, protect her for the briefest moment of infinity from the very thing he would inevitably do to her. His thumb caught a tear as it rolled down her cheek and he pressed it to his mouth, tasting the salt of her shattered soul.

17

"Weep not," he demanded softly. "Your innocence is intact." *But for how long? How long, St. Brieuc, will you let the game continue?*

"Nay," she said, shaking her head. "I do not think I will ever be innocent again." Her voice broke on a sob and she pressed her cheek to his chest and held onto him as if he were the only thing left in a world gone insane. Candlelight played in ghostly shadows upon the walls, a ghoulish reflection of the dark pall upon her soul.

She could not think how she had come to stray so far from all that she believed, how her heart, so weak yet willful, could run toward this stranger. God help her, the feelings he called forth in her could destroy her world, ravish the pledges her stronger mind had once made. As a babe the seeds of faith had been planted within her, at her mother's knee she had learned the value of commitment and its rewards. It was the only thing that had gotten her through the terrible years when her father had grown to care more for strong drink and wandering than his own flesh and blood. How could she now seek out in longing what she knew was wrong, yearn for something that chilled her within and without even as it made her burn?

Oh, Lord, hold me! I'm falling so fast! Deliver me from this churning and fighting inside, for I cannot find Your

place of peace and calm. Pray tell me 'twill pass if I find
the strength to walk away, for I fear I cannot exist like this.

She looked up to regard Borgia, to beg him to release
her, but in his eyes was a strange, tender regret and a
desperate, indefinable look that called to her. Did there
reside in some dark and hidden part of him a place of
conscience that had not been trampled beneath the
weight of war? She chose to believe it was so, for there
was little else to reconcile her. And she needed to believe
that she was safe by his hand. She certainly had not been
safe by her own.

Fretful and confused, her head dropped back to his
broad chest and her hand smoothed over the taut muscles of his back, much as she would stroke the fevered
brow of a child when helpless to give anything more than
comfort. She could not think what she wanted to tell
him, what she needed to convey. Her very life was at
stake, but her body longed to join him in the destruction.

Her breathing hitched on a small moan, and she took a
simple, alternative path. "Pray forgive me for striking
you earlier."

Borgia's chest rose and fell on a deep sigh. "You have
marked me before, bratling. You need not apologize."

The forgiving words from such an uncharitable man
only increased her unhappiness. " 'Twas different this
time. I was angry at others and lashed out at you. 'Twas
not fair."

Borgia threaded his fingers through her hair and let
the silken strands flow around him, as if he could bathe
himself in the soothing colors and emotions of sunset
when the world went still and quiet. But there was little
serenity to be garnered with her body curled into his, her
cheek pressed against his chest like a contented lover's
and her thin shift the only barrier between them. He'd
stormed castle walls with less aggression than he felt
now, wanting to strip it away.

"Little in this life is fair, as you well know," he said.

LeClaire tipped her face up to gaze at him, and her eyes were full of gentle integrity. " 'Tis not true, my lord, and you mustn't think it. There is much that is just and right, though 'tis hard to find it betimes. But one cannot give up the search."

"Ah, you are a philosopher, damoiselle," he said, but the cynicism was tempered. "And what wisdom and enlightenment have you found in a universe that thrives on chaos?"

Her head tilted in thought, so artless, so deeply sincere. "That naught happens without purpose. Though its meaning be unclear, if one but waits upon the answer, all is revealed in time."

She felt the tensing of his muscles, and his voice held a self-mocking edge. "Forsooth, you are spoiled by innocence, your vision clouded by what you would see, not what is. The world is rife with unreason. Tell me then what purpose in what was done to Aurel. What more is there to be revealed than what is already evident? That envy or jealousy, revenge or wickedness are stronger than a maiden's virtue."

"I cannot say," LeClaire answered softly, sadly. "I have no answer for questions without reason. Oft times men get in the midst of God's work, and He is left to make good of a situation gone bad."

"Then what purpose here?" he asked, tipping her face up to his. Though his tone remained serious, there was a hint of wry amusement in his eyes. "What purpose is there in lying unfulfilled beside you night after night?"

The faintest hint of color tinted her cheeks. " 'Tis only by your command that I am here," LeClaire said. "I have not asked for this, nor do I think it right or necessary."

"But by your own words there must be a purpose."

LeClaire smiled, a soft, almost teasing light sparkling in her eyes. "Mayhaps, the Lord is teaching me perseverance, or mayhaps, 'tis just another of those bad situations that He must make right."

"Imp," Borgia accused softly. "And mayhaps I should just take you as is my desire. I could well see the purpose in that."

The blush grew and LeClaire lowered her eyes. How cloyed she had become to lie in a man's bed and banter banalities as if it were commonplace while feeling as if she would wither if he left her. She wished she could absorb his strength and confidence and still remain separate but somehow feared that was not possible. She would not tempt him, but for the life of her she could not halt the words that sifted through her better judgment.

"Why, my lord? Why would you want to join with me? What purpose would that serve save to disgrace us?"

"Why?" Derisive laughter rumbled in his chest, and Borgia tightened his arms around her. "I would show you just why, damoiselle. But I fear the telling of it would shock your pretty ears."

LeClaire dropped her forehead to his chest to hide from his knowing eyes. "I have been shocked more since you arrived here than in the sum total of my life. I would have you tell me anyway ere my curiosity goes begging elsewhere and I shame myself further. You did offer."

"An error on my part," he said. "Can you really mean to convince me that you do not know the way of things? Have you never watched the animals who snap and snarl at each other, but when in season they are compelled by instinct to mate?"

"Certainly not!" she said, affronted.

He could easily picture her turning away, her fair cheeks rosy, her lashes lowered, but then he knew her sharp mind and its constant quest for answers. "Not even once? Just a small peek?"

"Mayhaps once . . . two dogs," LeClaire hedged, then hurried on, "but 'twas so disgusting and awkward that I did not watch long."

"Then why do you want to know now?" Borgia asked. " 'Tis foolish when you would, to my great and painful regret, hold yourself inviolate. Then again . . ." he paused, smiling sardonically, "if I tell you of the unequaled pleasure to be found, it might make you more curious to experience it."

LeClaire's blush deepened to crimson and a forbidden shiver rippled through her at his words. "You shame me, my lord."

"What have you to feel ashamed of?"

"I am ashamed of what I feel when you speak of such," she admitted, then rushed on as if she could outrun the bold words. "And I . . . I would not cause you pain, though you deserve the regret." His palm flew down to lightly smack her bottom and she squealed and squirmed against him, reflooding him with the hot awareness of how tenuous his hold on discipline. "Knave! You would beat me when I only answer you fairly."

"Nay, bratling," he said, his voice strained as he pulled her more deeply into him. "I would but love you."

"Oh, my lord," she gasped sorrowfully, her heart breaking at the sobering thought. "Do you not know? 'Tis not love you seek; 'tis only lust."

"There is a difference in the two?" Borgia said, his voice world-weary with lost memories, the ghost of past experiences. "The animals know naught of love; they but answer nature's call. 'Tis the same with man. Though he would cloak it with pretty words, even make vows before a priest, the fact remains: one is but a nicer word to justify the other."

"Oh, nay!" LeClaire said, truly horrified by such simple logic from a man of keen intelligence. "You cannot believe such."

Her palms went to his shoulders and she wiggled her way up until almost eye to eye with him. Borgia ground his teeth and steeled himself to accept her unconscious companionship when she was normally so uneasy with him. Her hand cupped his cheek, gentle, soothing, comforting, and her eyes searched his for even a hint of mockery. There was naught but a tightness around his mouth and a direct gaze that said he had spoken the words out of honesty as he perceived it.

"My lord," she breathed. "You must never think there is no difference. Love is all manner of things that lust is not. 'Tis kind and giving, not selfish. 'Tis patient and lasting, not self-seeking or self-serving. It believes all, endures all. 'Tis trust, hope and perseverance.

"Lust is but self, my lord, nothing else. Human, fallible, untrustworthy. But love abides. Above all, it *never* fails." Her fingers left his face, and Borgia felt the void as keenly as if it had emptied his soul. "Now, my lord, tell me there is no difference."

He stared at her, chilled to the depths of his black, vacant heart. But it was a safe place, that bottomless core, an easy place to reside without the clutter and conscience of her truths. *Caution, St. Brieuc, she'll soon have you spouting platitudes just to crawl between her thighs.*

His entire body tensed, braced to reject the lulling message of words that were insignificant to his purpose.

"Are you so blind to reality, damoiselle, that you believe such fantasy exists beyond your puerile imagination? A man will take a maid out of desire, or marry her to increase his wealth and position. Love is but a honeyed word to ease a conscience or stroke a vanity."

Stunned and hurt and aching for him, LeClaire gathered Borgia close and held him tight, as if she could infuse comfort and reason. "Oh, my lord, 'tis true I know little of romantic love, but I know what it should be, for I have seen too often what it becomes when corrupt. 'Tis not just a word, nor an emotion reserved only for a man and a woman. What of the feelings a mother has for her babe? A countryman for his homeland?"

"Instinct and loyalty," he said frankly.

Frustrated, LeClaire sighed. "Nay, 'tis that and more. Have you no family? Are there none you have fond memories of, who offered you the warmth and security of love in your youth?''

"Of course," came his softly satirical reply. He grinned ruefully above the crown of her head. *You cannot save me, damoiselle, though I am heartened that you try. But understand that I cannot let this continue, 'twill only be harder for you when my patience is exhausted. I would not have you more disillusioned than you already are.* "I've a large family. Brothers, sisters and parents still alive. But I would not love them in the way I would you, bratling. 'Tis against the most basic laws of nature."

LeClaire gave him a small pinch, smiling despite his words. "My lord, you do not even try to understand."

"I understand that I want you. And I give you fair warning that I will have you."

LeClaire only snuggled deeper within the warm confines of his arms, shielded by a resurgence of her faith at the undeniable fact that moments before she had been utterly helpless in his arms and he had not forced himself upon her. "Nay, my lord, you shall not," she said softly, her eyes shining with perfect assurance. "If you had truly meant to do such a thing, you would have done it. Art a better and more honorable man than you would have me believe."

"Christ's bones, do you tempt me to prove it?" he said, stunned by her sudden trust in him. He splayed his hand across the small of her back and pulled her against him where the evidence of his arousal left naught to the imagination. "Pray, damoiselle, do not inscribe me with virtues I neither have nor want. You will sorely regret it later."

LeClaire blushed but remained steadfast. "Nay, I do not tempt you. Nary should you contemplate evil but should turn your thoughts to goodness."

Borgia nuzzled the top of her head, the clean scent of her hair wafting seductively through his senses. "I think often of how good 'twill be between us when you give up this resistance."

"I will never." LeClaire sighed, then yawned, unconsciously burrowing deeper into his chest. His body enfolded her, his masculine scent surrounded her, and contrarily, his security offered a peaceful comfort that quieted her restless soul. Her body went limp and soft as she melted into him and drifted toward the open arms of Morpheus. "Art a complex man," she murmured on the fringes of sleep. "But you do not know all there is to know, my lord. You do not know about love."

Borgia's jaw tightened. "I know that if you move your hand just one inch lower, you will soon have more love than you bargained for this night."

LeClaire smiled slumberously at his strange words and her hand fidgeted about for his meaning. Springy hairs tickled her fingers and something smooth and hot and incredibly hard brushed her palm. Her entire body jolted awake and her eyes flew to his.

Borgia stared back at her in painful amusement, his control teetering madly on the edge of insanity. "Bratling," he warned through his teeth. "Remove your hand now . . . or not. But beware of the consequences, whatever you decide."

LeClaire snatched both of her hands up and clasped them together against his chest, her eyes wide, her cheeks burning. "My lord," she said, aghast. "I fear I have been played false by rumors! I am not a lackwit, but I confess I believed the horrible tales to some extent. I see now that I've been a fool, for it would not be possible . . . could not be done. You and I . . . it could never happen."

Borgia stared back at her, as acutely amused as he was frustrated. "Damoiselle, I do not know what tales you have been told, but I assure you it could be done . . . and done well."

LeClaire shook her head vigorously. "My lord," she

said, as if heartily sorry for him. "I fear you have been misled also, if you believe such would . . . would *fit*."

Laughter was a poor substitute for the release he truly needed, but he allowed it, albeit soberly, to consume him for a mere second before he dropped his head and kissed the twin spots of color on her cheeks.

"Ah, damoiselle, what a rare jewel you are." His strained laughter dismantled her earnestness, and she tried to bury her face in his chest but he would not allow it. "Nay, look upon me. You have asked for answers; I will give them to you. I fear such innocence is more dangerous than prudent."

More reluctant than curious now in the wake of his humor, LeClaire grudgingly lifted her eyes to his.

" 'Twill fit," he said, "and gloriously so. The body has an amazing capacity to adapt itself to its . . . surroundings." He could see that she wanted not to believe him. It was clearly defined in the half-lowered lashes, the firm set of her mouth. "You have attended birthings; a woman's body must allow for a man ere it can a babe." He watched the delicate flush brighten her cheeks, and on some compassionate level that he had not known mattered, he felt compelled to warn her. "But not the first time. Though I would make it as easy for you as possible, our first time will not be without some pain."

LeClaire's eyes searched for any place to light save his enticing gray gaze. "There will be no first time . . . nor any time," she whispered in stubborn certainty. Her eyes narrowed suddenly in thought. "Why would you want to do aught that causes pain?"

" 'Tis not painful for the man," he said carefully.

LeClaire's eyes flared, then cut into his like daggers. With a tone more typical of Maire, she huffed, "Well, I hardly see the fairness in that!" She fell silent, but Borgia could see the thoughts winding themselves tighter in her inquisitive mind, and knew such would not bode well for him as she asked, "How do you know these things?"

The question was direct, therefore clear. The significance beneath the words, however, was hazy. "What do you mean?"

" 'Tis a simple question, my lord," she said with a hint of agitation. "Art hardheaded, not stupid."

Oh, damoiselle, must I be cautious here? "Men . . . know these things."

"How?"

The stubborn look in her eyes no longer allowed his caution. "By experience, LeClaire. They learn these things through experience."

"Oh!" she said, appalled that he would speak it aloud, though she had suspected it. "You have lain with a woman before." She pushed against his chest as if fearing contamination. "Who is this poor maiden that you seduced, then abandoned?"

Borgia exhaled a deep sigh, deciding that the slaying of innocence was best done quickly, in one swift, clean blow. "Did you think you would be my first? Not one woman, bratling, many women. Too many over the years for me even to remember. You cannot mean to convince me that you do not know of such things."

"Art a fornicator!" she accused, tears glistening in her eyes, though she knew not why the thought hurt her so. She had known before he arrived at Ravenwood that his past was sinful and blackened by unholy deeds, but to think that he'd had carnal knowledge with more women than he could even recall was the shabbiest thing imaginable to her. "Are you not ashamed, my lord?"

Ashamed? Looking into her heart-struck eyes, he almost was. "Nay, bratling," he said very softly. "I hardly remember them, so there is little to shame me."

"Oh, my lord," she sighed, so sad, so downcast. "Art worse off than I thought. At the pace you are going, even hell would spit you out. I must needs pray harder for you, mayhaps even fast and do penance."

"You do that, damoiselle." He smiled as he cuddled

her close and tucked her head beneath his chin. "But the devil will be sorely riled if he loses me."

"Aye," she nodded and snuggled into his chest, content for the first time in his bed. "All the more reason to thwart him, my lord."

Sunlight streamed through the hides in warming rays of muted brilliance. LeClaire sighed in contentment, cocooned in the sleepy haze of awakening. Something tickled her nose, and she burrowed her face more fully into the bedding, staving off the morning's responsibilities for one more small, lazy moment.

Strong arms encircled her, and she squealed as she was rolled to her back. Her startled eyes flew open to see Borgia looming over her, his handsomeness causing a flutter in her feminine heart.

"Damoiselle," he said, smiling languidly as he placed the whisper of a kiss upon her lips.

"My lord," she gulped, thinking him impressive in daylight with his wide shoulders and the sun glinting silvery highlights through his hair. "You have not yet risen."

" 'Tis a matter for some debate," he said derisively, for there were parts of him fully risen. He dropped a kiss to her nose, then traced her profile to her ear. "Do you send me off to meet the day with a token of your goodwill?"

Little thrills raced along her limbs and verily she had to fight to suppress them. Her mood grew serious as guilt fed its way into the channels of her bloodstream, pumping a steady reminder of where she was and the wrongness of it. But still her voice lacked the depth of reprimand she intended. "You need not my goodwill when you are lord here."

" 'Tis for that reason that I demand it," he said. "A kiss, bratling, to sustain me throughout the long, arduous hours of duty."

" 'Tis food you need if you require sustenance," she said, plucky in her defensiveness.

"A table fit for a king could not do for me what one willing kiss from your lips would," he said.

LeClaire's heart picked up a maddening beat with his flirtation. Never in her life had a man cajoled her with pretty words, and though she did not truly harken to them, her mind could not deny that they were ever so pleasant, however ill intended. Flustered, she attempted a stern look. "Words cannot express how wicked you are, my lord, to say such a thing."

"Aye, most wicked," he agreed. "But one must always obey one's lord."

"Nay, one must ever preserve their dignity when you are the lord in question," she said, shaking her head while soft laughter bubbled up inside her. How absurd to feel such gaiety in his arms when she should be appalled. She could only determine that he had caught her unaware, for she had never awakened with him still abed. "The day grows ripe, my lord," she coaxed in an effort to steer his attention to other, less troubling areas. "You had best see to it lest it gets away from you."

"The only thing that escapes me of late, damoiselle, is you."

The mock weariness of his voice sent a reluctant smile to her lips. "And a good thing, too, my lord. I would not abet you in such depraved actions. You've enough marks against you as 'tis."

"Then what is one more?" He grinned and lowered his head.

LeClaire's heart scrambled for a steady beat as his lips touched hers, but there was little more than a quick, hard kiss before he was gone, leaving her gasping and hard-pressed to pull the covers over her eyes in time to block out his magnificent body fully revealed in daylight.

"Come now, bratling," she heard him say in that incorrigible voice that made the blood rush to her cheeks, "you have seen me naked afore. You need not bury yourself like a scared rabbit." With relief she heard the rustle of clothing, then felt the quilt being pulled back from her inflamed face.

"Art evil!" she scolded, unknowingly fetching with her shining blue eyes and pink cheeks. "And I have not looked upon you. I would not do such a thing."

One charcoal brow lifted as he idly laced his tunic. "Why? I do not mind, and I know you for a curious maid. Do you not have even a tiny desire to see a man, to see the difference in the sexes?"

"I have swaddled babes," LeClaire declared. "I know the differences well enough."

Borgia's smile was slow and mocking. "Aye, and you know quite well that the differences are vast, lest you would not have been so stunned yestereve."

"Art cruel to bring up my ignorance," LeClaire said, feeling the heat of embarrassment throughout her entire body now. "I have no wish to speak of the night past."

His silver gaze stroked over her, and his tone grew serious. "Last night exists whether you would deny it or not. Whatever has passed between us, and what is yet to come, cannot be brushed away like dust from an old tunic. 'Tis inevitable, damoiselle. Insanity, mayhaps, but inevitable."

He was gone before she could comment, though what she might have said escaped her. She pounded the bed once, then flopped back down, seething with her inability to handle him better.

Oh, King William, you must arrive soon. Else I know not what is to become of me. She would not admit that the King's visit might not help her at all; it was too terrible to contemplate such a thing.

18

Roger de Amiens stormed into the common-room and slammed his gauntlets down on the trestle table in front of Borgia. "God's teeth, she has done it this time! You'd best come."

Borgia regarded him with a bored lift of his brow, handed the accounts back over to his new steward and nodded for Roger to proceed.

"She has stolen a babe from his father, and she's bringing the child here." Roger shook his head in disgust. "You will rue the day you allowed her freedom again to visit the village. 'Twas a peaceful fortnight we enjoyed ere—"

"Stolen a babe," Borgia interrupted. "Pray rest yourself, Amiens. I fear you've had too much sun."

His words were suspended as his young squire Fitz-Ralph came rushing through the front portal. "My lord, quickly! He's followed her and is about to do her harm!"

Borgia lunged to his feet and was out in the courtyard before the boy could finish his statement. The situation that met him sent a murderous darkening to his eyes.

Her back rigid and her eyes flashing fury, LeClaire was braced for battle as she faced the prior falconer, Alberic. Settled upon her hip was a small child of indeterminate age whose sunken cheeks were streaked with grime and tears. In desperation, he clung to LeClaire with tiny arms and legs, his head buried in her neck.

Teeth bared like a rabid animal, Alberic stood before LeClaire and the child, holding a large stick like a club. His eyes glowed, not with the unstable light of insanity but with pure and deliberate enmity.

"Ye ain't got no rights here, ye sniveling bitch," he snarled in vulgar satisfaction. "Yer no lady now, are ye? Just a slave like all the rest of us, even if ye are trussed up as his whore. Gimme back me boy, an' maybe I'll not bash your highborn skull in."

LeClaire paled under the insults but stayed fixed. Her dealings with Alberic had never been pleasant. She had tolerated his insubordination out of regard for the welfare of his wife, Mary, a downtrodden woman of ill-health who had not survived the winter, and out of deep concern for the child, Giles. But no longer. Alberic had spread his insurgence like leprosy among the villagers, contaminating those of weaker wills with his own polluted ideas, notions not born of a sharp mind or keen intellect but of laziness and greed.

As serenely as if she were talking to a child, she said, "Be off with you, Alberic. You've no more place here with your idle ways and mean heart."

Enraged, Alberic swung the stick with malice, not to strike just yet but to intimidate, to watch her cower before him. He smiled in glee when LeClaire stepped back and stumbled upon a loose pebble. She clutched the child tighter and soothed his back in gentle, trembling strokes.

A crowd gathered, the murmur of voices hushed and anxious as the lord of Ravenwood drew close, his eyes dangerously calm.

"Put down the stick, Alberic," he commanded softly, his hand resting idly upon his sword hilt.

"She's got me boy," Alberic snarled. "Cain't go takin' a man's boy, now can she, m'lord?" His insolent gaze swung back to rake LeClaire. "Git yer own brat, lady, ye know how to do that, eh?"

LeClaire's stomach knotted as the din of voices grew louder with muddled gasps and muted slurs. She knew not for whom the hurtful murmurings were intended but at this moment did not care.

"You cannot have him," she said, so tranquil the voices around her quieted in an effort to catch her words. Her eyes, pleading but steady, found Borgia's. "He is lazy and cruel. He sends the child for food and drink, then beats him for spilling it. The child eats only his leavings, if there are any." Her breathing grew fast and painful at Borgia's cold, unrelenting stare. "He is but a babe of three summers, with no other kin to protect him since his mother died. I'll not give him back, my lord. I cannot."

Borgia glanced only briefly at the child who appeared much younger in his malnourished state, then at Alberic, who stood mere steps away from LeClaire. The knight he had sent to protect her was standing near, sword raised, but LeClaire was between Alberic and the guard.

A gloating look entered Alberic's eyes at Borgia's continued silence. "You see what she does, m'lord?" he sneered. "She thinks she still has the run of the place. Always was above herself, like a bloody queen. Thinks she has the right to take me boy from me 'cause of a little beatin'." His eyes swung back to LeClaire. "Ye ain't so high and mighty now, are ye? Cain't go bossin' us so much these days when yer busy on yer back."

Hot and blinding tears stung LeClaire's eyes, but she faced the man squarely and her voice did not so much as quiver. "I care not what you think of me, Alberic, but you will never have this child again to dole out your meanness upon."

Enraged by her audacity, Alberic roared a vile curse and swung the stick again. It glanced off LeClaire's upper arm in a continuous circular sweep that promised the next blow would hit her face. Lightning quick, Borgia's sword sang through the air and cleaved the stick in two, sending pieces snapping in two directions. Alberic yelped and threw his gaze to the lord of Ravenwood. Only then did he see the icy intent in Borgia's eyes. His face went ghostly white and he choked on his own fear as he was seized by the two guards who had sneaked up behind him.

Borgia's expression never wavered, but his cool voice sliced effortlessly through the tense silence. "A hundred lashes and a sennight in the stocks . . . if he survives it."

Gasps rippled through the crowd at the merciless order, but none dared utter a word. Kicking and screeching demented oaths, Alberic clawed his way out of the guards' hold and stumbled straight for LeClaire.

"We should have taken you!" he snarled like a lunatic. "Should have plowed you that night instead of yer sister!"

LeClaire cried out in horror and had only a split second to turn and shield the child as Borgia's sword arced in a graceful *moulinet* and ran the man through. Someone in the crowd screamed, drowning out the last-breath gurgle in Alberic's throat. LeClaire felt the hard-packed ground hit her knees as she bent double and struggled to hold back the bile in her throat.

From ground level, images swam before her—lilies-of-the-valley swaying in the breeze, their pure white bells nodding in the shaded soil beside the stone-walled entrance, wild columbines standing rigid on their slender stems as if braced to accept the hummingbirds and bees stealing nectar from their red and yellow petals, daisies growing in a profusion of open-eyed splendor. In vivid color and subtle fragrance, they shielded her for the barest moment from a harsher reality, until without warning the images changed to immediate and grotesque remembrance—sunlight striking the blade, the whine of steel cutting the air, red blood, black terror.

Sound rushed in upon her from the crush of villagers,

swirling like discordant, tuneless notes from a rusty lyre. A woman wailed, another wept, a man muttered incoherently, a mother shushed her children and hurried them away from the carnage.

The child in LeClaire's arms whimpered. She pressed his face to her breast, and cooed words of comfort by rote, afraid to rise, afraid of what she would see in any direction—Alberic with his body bloody and lifeless, condemnation of her in the villagers' eyes as his words lived on, dull-eyed pity for Aurel.

She felt a strong hand on her shoulder and wanted to turn herself into the broad, sheltering chest of the man behind her, even as she knew she would be repelled by the hellish, emotionless glint she had seen in his eyes just before he had swung the sword. *Merciful Father! How did a man kill without emotion?*

"Jackal! Wretched, stinking vermin!"

LeClaire's head lifted at the familiar voice and found Maire standing beside her staring at Alberic's bloodsplattered body with eyes full of hatred, satisfaction and pain.

"Come, sister mine," Maire said tenderly, and bent to help LeClaire to her feet.

Clutching the child tighter, LeClaire rose and stared not at her sister but at Borgia. His face was completely closed, every expression guarded. He showed neither triumph nor regret, but she sensed his anger, as powerful and fatal as the sword that had moved in blurred silver in his hand. She sensed also a stygian loathing but knew not to whom it was directed.

The crowd stood silent and watchful as Alberic's body was dragged off by the guards. The worthless man was not much loved by the villagers, and the law demanded he be brought before the folkmoot for justice after confessing he'd had a part in the crime against Aurel, but none of them knew the price for raping a woman, nor to whom that price would have been paid as Aurel had no husband or father. In any case, under their law, Alberic would not have paid with his life. The wergild for the murder of an earl brought three hundred oxen, three times that of an ordinary man, but a slave was worth only a pound.

By condemning Alberic to hell, the Norman was either unbalanced in his sense of justice or he had just placed Aurel's value above anything in their prior reasoning.

The villagers knew not what to make of it all and most fastened their eyes upon the child in LeClaire's arms rather than the lord who stood by in cold, bloodless silence. Young Giles was too frail to beg, so what would become of him? He'd at least had a chance while the father was alive, but there was no chance for survival now unless one of them intervened. Furtive glances passed among them. They were not lacking in compassion for the boy, but none was brave enough to test the lord's mood at this moment.

Finally, the crowd shifted and a path opened as Hannah's daughter, Gweneth, followed by Kyra and her guards, pushed through, but the young girl grew frightfully wary when she reached Borgia. "Ma . . . Ma says . . ." She swallowed, took a deep breath but couldn't speak while standing this near the Silver Lion.

To her young eyes, he was the Devil manifest with silver eyes instead of red. She glanced up quickly at his charcoal hair to see if he had horns but couldn't tell with his height. If she were one bit as bold as her brother, Timothy, she'd ask him to bend down so she could sneak a look. Every horrible rumor she'd ever heard flew through her young mind, and tears suddenly clouded her eyes. Kyra took her friend's hand, squeezed, and posed the question Gweneth was supposed to have asked.

"Hannah says do you want her to come fetch the child? She'll care for him since he has no kin now."

Borgia looked over at LeClaire, who shook her head

numbly. " 'Tis my responsibility," she whispered. "Hannah has enough at her own hearth now."

Borgia nodded and raised his voice for all to hear. "I've long been in need of a page. This lad will do fine."

Gasps echoed through the crowd. They weren't so far removed in their isolation that they didn't know a boy of noble birth usually reached the age of seven before he was fostered out and trained as a personal servant before reaching the rank of knighthood. Giles had neither age nor rank to recommend him, but the lord had spoken. If they knew aught, it was that Borgia de St. Brieuc's word was law.

Kyra nodded, gave LeClaire a soft smile, then dragged a relieved and slightly besotted Gweneth back into the midst of the villagers.

LeClaire gazed up at Borgia in silent wonder, grateful beyond verbal expression for the act of humanity. It was not that she'd thought him incapable of showing such generosity, just that it was so unlike him to bother himself with trivialities of that nature. She wondered at his purpose when he could have commanded any of the villagers to accept care of the babe, and whether willing or just subservient they would have obeyed without question.

Giles, his head tucked in the crook of LeClaire's neck, sucked contentedly on a grimy thumb and stared in childish fascination at Borgia's gilt-threaded tunic. The soothing stroke of gentle fingers down his back lulled the weary child until his eyelids grew heavy, then finally closed in restful security. LeClaire shifted the child to a more comfortable position and struggled with words that needed to be said, words that seemed so inadequate for the supreme gratitude she was feeling.

"My lord—" she began, but Borgia's icy gaze pierced through her with such force that she was stunned by the cold aloofness of it. Her heart became a dead weight in her chest, and her stomach jerked in sickening little spasms with uncertainty. Her hand rose and went to his sleeve in a pleading, consoling gesture.

Borgia glanced briefly at her small hand, then back at her enlarged, questioning eyes. Without a word he turned his back and walked toward the hall. Frozen under his rude dismissal, LeClaire felt rooted to the ground, then rallied under an unreasonable need to have his action explained to her. Gripping the child tightly, she rushed after Borgia, heedless to Roger's hushed warning.

"My lord," she called, but he did not turn to acknowledge her, just continued on into the common-room, then up the stairs. With dogged persistence LeClaire followed him to the bedchamber. "My lord," she said again, soft and pleading. "You must not grieve over Alberic. You but protected an innocent child's life with the taking of another less worthy one."

Borgia rounded on her, his look so contemptuous she clutched the child tighter. "You think I grieve for the life of that worthless mongrel? I have warned you before, damoiselle, do not paint me with virtues I do not have."

"Then why are you so angry?" LeClaire asked, her own ire and confusion rising at his heartless tone.

"'Twas a mistake to kill him at that point, and I do not like mistakes. I needed him alive to get the names of Aurel's other attackers."

"I see," LeClaire said slowly, and feared greatly that she did. "Alberic's life meant naught to you, nor the fact that he was given no chance to atone for his sins. 'Twas merely because you acted hastily that you are angered. Even the defense of the child meant naught."

Borgia's eyes flared, and his sardonic voice sliced through her like a dull blade. "Defense of the child? 'Twas not the child I protected, 'twas you." LeClaire's eyes widened, and he continued with biting sarcasm. "Think you that I would let that cur put his filthy hands upon you? Or that I would even let him entertain the thought of taking you like he did Aurel? His life was forfeit the instant he spit out the confession, but I should have waited until I'd gotten the other names ere sending him to his grave."

The child whimpered, and LeClaire realized she was squeezing him. She relaxed her hold and jostled him lightly to quiet him back to sleep. "You are angry because of a mistake," she said listlessly. "You care not that you spilled his blood, nor that he was coming for the child, nor even that he attacked Aurel. You are angry simply because you made a mistake." She shook her head in bleak disbelief, then gazed up at him, her cheeks colorless but her eyes painfully bright. "Oh, my lord, how I pity you."

He only stared back at her with an insulting lack of concern. But she could suddenly see beneath his rigid posture, his carefully guarded control, to the unstable center of him where incertitude had claimed a small piece of his emotions. He could not abide that, she could see, could not tolerate the fact that he had done something so rash, so chaotically human. And she thought she pitied him even more for thinking it a weakness.

He approached her then, escaping from himself, she thought, one graceful step blending into another until mere inches separated them. His hand cupped her jaw and she would have swatted him away but for the child she held. Eyes, near black in their intensity, stared into hers. "What power you wield over me, bratling, that I would be driven to make such an irreparable error."

"Nothing is irreparable," she said, trembling under his watchful attention.

Her heart thrummed as his hand slid from her face down to her shoulder. His fingers curled in her new gown and he pulled it down to reveal the ugly bruise on her upper arm. Lowering his head, his lips brushed the pale skin above the discoloration for only an instant, then were gone. Heat and mystery flowed through her, slumberously warm, exhilaratingly alive. Her arms began to tremble from the weight of the child, but the tremor in her legs came from another source.

She pulled back to avoid the dangerous, compelling look in his eyes and dropped her forehead to the crown of the child's soft hair and sighed.

"I must see to Giles. He grows heavy." It was such a faulty sounding excuse, even to her own ears, though she did not lie. Borgia ran his palm down her red-gold tresses, then lifted a glossy ringlet to his lips.

"Place him upon your pallet," he said in an appealing whisper. "Then come to my bed." LeClaire shook her head, appalled at the suggestion, as he had known she would be. Borgia smiled and tipped her face up. "How predictable you are, bratling."

LeClaire smiled tentatively in return, heartened to note that his mood had softened somewhat and that he did not seem bent on pressing the issue. "You make it sound like a curse, my lord. I deem it a virtue to be constant in one's convictions."

"Nay," he said, mildly scoffing. "You've more virtue than a man can abide. Is there no convincing you to forget some of these little proprieties? They grow bothersome, damoiselle."

"You consider chastity bothersome, my lord?" she scolded. "I do not find it so at all." Blushing, she looked down at the child and stroked his soft hair back from his face. At the comforting touch, his mouth puckered and made empty little sucking motions until he again found his thumb. "He is a fine lad," LeClaire whispered. "Bright and cheerful ere his mother died."

"Already he is a pest," Borgia said soberly.

LeClaire ignored the jibe and continued to feather her fingers through the child's curls for a time. Her hands were gentle and concerned, but her expression soon turned inward and moody. Finally, her troubled eyes lifted to Borgia's, eyes brimming with confusion from her internal struggle.

"Think you 'tis so wrong of me to be glad that Alberic is gone? I am, you know, and I feel no guilt for it. I am not certain 'tis a good thing to feel no remorse whatsoever." She sighed, burdened by the need to explain, to somehow make it right within herself. "Alberic was ever a thorn in my side. From the time I arrived at Ravenwood, his querulous ways were a hardship, but his wife was a dear woman trapped by her marriage vows and poverty, and I could not see sending them away." She took a deep, troubled breath, lost in her musings. "Many times I tried to reason with him; many nights I prayed for him. All to no avail. Still, a life wasted should be a grievous thing, not a relief."

"Things are not always as they should be," Borgia said. "You should be convinced of that by now."

LeClaire smiled softly. "I am convinced that they will eventually turn out right."

"And I am convinced that you are as hardheaded as yon stone wall if you think anything will change save the fact that you will welcome my attentions soon."

"I am most *un*convinced of that, my lord."

Borgia allowed her an indulgent smile that said she had much to learn, before his expression grew serious. "In any event, you've every right to feel no guilt over his wasted life. Of his own free will, Alberic made his choices. You cannot change a man's nature by wishing or praying him changed, bratling."

"Aye, I know. A man makes his own judgments. Alberic chose to live his life in corrupt ways, but 'tis hard to stomach the fact that his meanness affected so many others." Her gaze dropped and caressed the child as lovingly as her hands did. "But something precious did come of Alberic. I will keep Giles close and care for him until he is truly old enough to train as a page. You will not regret your decision, my lord."

Watching all the affection in the universe flow from LeClaire to a grubby little waif, Borgia wondered if he would not come to regret his decision greatly.

"Never once did I say the little baggage could share our chamber," Borgia said, his expression stern.

Kneeling beside a tub, LeClaire sent him a placating smile over her shoulder, then went back to scrubbing young Giles. The child babbled a string of disjointed nonsense as he splashed the shallow water with flattened palms, wetting the front of LeClaire's bodice more than himself. She scolded him playfully and ran a damp cloth over his face one last time.

"There. Art done, Master Giles." She scooped him up into a swath of soft linen and dried him from head to toe. Looking down at his soiled and tattered clothing, she frowned and glanced back at Borgia. "We must needs find him something more suitable."

"We must needs do naught," Borgia said with dry forbearance. "The hour is late. Cart the little foundling off to Hannah or Agnes. They'll see to him."

Sending him another mollifying smile that said she was staunchly evading the issue, LeClaire carried Giles into the antechamber, sat him in a pool of linen upon the rushes and rummaged through her trunks for something that would fit her purpose. Giles, pink as a new piglet from his warm bath, scrambled up and peered over into the trunk with utmost concentration, unabashed by his nakedness. Hair the color of ripe autumn hung in damp curls to his thin shoulders, promising a cap of deep russet once dry. He pulled his thumb out of his mouth long enough to point at a shiny armlet, then popped it back in again.

"Aye, 'tis pretty," LeClaire said, and handed Giles the jeweled circle, then went back to her search. Giles studied the golden armlet, shook it, then decided it was not such a fancy plaything after all and dropped it back into the trunk.

"Pretty," he said around his wet thumb as his left hand pointed at a girdle.

"Aye," LeClaire agreed and pulled it from the trunk. "And just the thing for a young page." She wrapped him back in the bolt of linen toga-style, then wound the girdle twice around his small waist and fastened the buckle. The gold-stamped lion heads trailed to the floor, and Giles stared down at them with all the appreciation a child of three holds for shiny objects no matter their worth.

"He looks like a Roman lictor with a girdle for his badge of authority instead of a fasces," Borgia commented from the doorway.

"As if I would let him carry a bundle of rods with an ax," LeClaire chided, smiling. She sat back on her heels and admired her handiwork. "Forsooth, young Giles, you do look fine! We must take care that someone does not mistake you for a king's nobleman and whisk you off to court."

Giles merely sucked his thumb and stared at his finery, muttering "pretty" from time to time, while LeClaire closed the trunk. Once done, she turned back and straightened his flowing robes. Dark eyes huge and intense in his young face, he peered at her, then reached out his small hand and touched her cheek. "Pretty, 'Claire," he whispered.

Assessing all the obvious aspects of the situation, Borgia groaned inwardly. If LeClaire's devotion to the child had not already been firmly rooted, it was no doubt engraved in stone now. Her eyes held a Madonna-like glow that softened her features into dreamy adoration. He would never get the child out of their chamber now without appearing the ogre. But then he had ever been a demon in her eyes; what was one more mark against him?

He stepped forward and scooped the child up, settling him upon his arm. "Come, Giles. Let us see if Agnes can find a spot for you below."

Giles cooed in awe at his sudden lofty perch and clung to Borgia's neck while smiling down at LeClaire. He was wholly content with the situation until Borgia took the first step toward the door.

" 'Claire!" he squealed as if he'd been stuck with a needle, then began wiggling ferociously. Borgia gave him a dark look that had sent grown men cringing to their knees. It had no effect whatsoever upon young Giles save to make him yowl all the louder. In ear-splitting decibels that rose an octave with each outcry, the child vented his affront while straining toward LeClaire with outstretched arms.

LeClaire rose quickly to her feet, sent Borgia a fulminating glare, and held her arms out. "There," she soothed, snatching Giles and holding him close. "There now," she continued until the child found his thumb and calmed. She cast Borgia a look of supreme displeasure and marched past him out of the antechamber.

Back in the large room, she settled Giles upon her lap and rocked him as she hummed an ageless tune that had quieted babes for centuries untold.

Borgia waited until the little fiend's eyes were closed and his breathing regular before he spoke. "He cannot sleep in this room."

"Then neither shall I," she whispered placidly without once looking up.

"LeClaire . . ." he warned.

"My lord . . ." she mimicked softly, and Borgia saw before him the fierce instincts that drove mothers to protect their young even at risk to their own lives.

As a soldier he knew when he was beaten, when to retreat and regroup, but as a man he knew only his desire for the woman. The situation dictated caution and cunning, for in banning one he would lose the other, even if he held her by force.

"Damoiselle," he said smoothly, "what do you propose to do with the child?"

A look of feminine satisfaction entered her eyes, and Borgia almost regretted the dissolving bits of innocence that had been both a boon and a burden in the past. LeClaire was growing, changing. In the past, where her courage had run unfettered from her heart's convictions, it was now tempered with life's unalterable realities, and she was learning to use that courage in timely and more effective ways. If her body was yet innocent, her intellect was fast losing the naïveté of that early young champion of Ravenwood.

"I propose that Giles share the bed with me and you take the pallet," LeClaire said.

Borgia's smile was slow and dry as stalks of winter grain. "I think not."

LeClaire's eyes brightened and her quiet laughter tinkled like wind moving through a glazier's shop. "Then, unfair as it sounds, I propose that you take the bed and I share the pallet with Giles."

"Hardly."

"My lord," she said with utmost innocence. "Do you suggest that Giles and I take the bed and you go below?"

"I suggest," he said, controlling the urge to join her winsome play, "that I take the bed, you take the bed, and Giles be sent off to some other keep."

Her smile waned from delightfully charming to mild temperance. "I care for that suggestion not at all," she said. She knew there were few choices open to her and she had best take whatever compromises were available. "I would not submit young Giles to the impropriety of seeing us together." When Borgia merely stared at her, unmoved by her concern, she granted him the only capitulation she would make outside of force. "If I must, I will reluctantly place him upon the pallet and join you in the bed."

Knowing it was the only concession she would allow without all-out warfare, Borgia nodded. LeClaire rose and placed Giles upon the pallet, tucked the furs around him and kissed his fresh-scrubbed cheek. Unashamed, she then knelt to silently say her prayers.

Borgia watched her tender ministrations to the little orphan and thought how like LeClaire to collect strays whether beast or man or entire village. Firelight danced in the gilded locks that hung down her back in vibrant spirals that looked too heavy on her petite frame as she knelt. The nightly ritual was disconcerting for Borgia when he knew so many of her petitions were wasted on him. *You cannot change a man's nature by wishing or praying him changed.* He wanted to repeat the words to her, to snatch her up from the hard floor and order her to cease her useless supplication. But he could not, for it would be like stealing a nun from a convent for no other reason than he did not wish to see her there. And it would do no good. She, in her gentle and stubborn way, would only continue her prayers from the bed.

Borgia found the night long and strained lying next to LeClaire with naught but the uncomfortable memory of her with the child in her arms. She needed a babe at her breast, one of her own body, to suckle and lavish attention upon. Then, mayhaps, she would not be so inclined to mother the people of Ravenwood as if they were errant children too young to be accountable for their actions.

And, mayhaps not. It seemed to be her nature, some innate and established disposition, to coddle and care for others. In any case, it was a moot point. She could not bear a babe without the act that ensured procreation, and she was not yet willing to accept him in that manner, though he sensed she was weakening day by day.

He rolled to his side and lightly placed his hand on her

breast, feeling the gentle rise and fall of her even breathing, the rhythmic patter of her heartbeat. Moonlight washed the fair skin above her shift in translucent ivory. He moved his hand in a soft circle and watched as her lips parted on a small moan, and she unconsciously turned into him, flattening herself against his palm. Borgia felt the stirring, the slow burn and blunt weight of desire fusing into what had become the endless, painful sequence of his nights.

His hand slid around to the small of her back and he pulled her into the hot and aching center of him. Like a nestling, she cuddled there in the peaceful nether world of slumber, unaware and protected from his dark thoughts.

But he knew himself well, knew his strengths and weaknesses, his capacity for restraint. And he knew he could not continue on in this way much longer.

19

LeClaire awoke to vague and restless murmurings within her body, to heat and moisture and tingling in the deep, clandestine parts of herself. Gripped in the uneasy urges that until recently had been so foreign to her, she moaned low in her throat and pressed against the dexterous hand stroking her bare breast—

She jerked back on a gasp as her eyes flared open. "My lord!" Borgia's eyes remained closed as his hand sought added treasure by sliding insidiously down her rib cage. "My lord!" she repeated in a constricted whisper, tugging fretfully on her shift, which was scrunched up about her waist because his arm was beneath it. "I beg you, consider what you are about!"

"I have thought of little else for the past months," he assured her in a tone as lazy as the sly drift of his fingertips. LeClaire swatted at his hands and he rolled to cover her body with his and met, as expected, with resistance.

"My lord, you will crush me!"

" 'Twill be my pleasure," he murmured, and pressed his lips to hers.

" 'Claire!"

Borgia's eyes flew open, then narrowed at the sharp, childish demand. He rolled to his back and cut his darkling glance to the side of the bed. LeClaire bolted up beside him in sleep-tousled confusion and peered around his shoulder. Awareness dawned and her face was transformed by a smile that was no less radiant than daybreak bursting upon the land. In fetching dishabille, she stretched out her hands, and Borgia felt the gouge of tiny knees in his groin and stomach as Giles scampered across him into LeClaire's arms.

"This is intolerable," he ground out. He plucked the child out of LeClaire's embrace and set him back upon the floor. But Giles, having been in a similar situation the night before and come away unscathed, thought it a merry game and squealed with delight as he scrambled back atop the bed and straddled Borgia's chest.

"My 'Claire!" he said, bouncing and rocking with the unencumbered energy of youth. He braced his small hands on the ample expanse of Borgia's chest, while his bottom continued to rise and fall in rollicking unawareness of his peril.

"Infant," Borgia said, regarding Giles with tedious patience. "Have you no manners? You do not ride atop the lord of Ravenwood as if he were some farmer's mule. If you have a care for your continued good health, you will cease this common performance immediately and return to yon pallet."

"My 'Claire!" Giles repeated with a wide smile as he bounced again.

Borgia set his teeth and slanted a glance at LeClaire. "Does the little tyrant speak in nothing more than monosyllabic commands?" At another impertinent jounce, Borgia ordered, "Do something."

"He is but a child," LeClaire consoled, biting back considerable and ill-timed mirth. It would not bode well for her to burst into peals of laughter at the sight of the estimable Silver Lion undone by a babe. " 'Tis good that he is not frightened of you, my lord, especially after Alberic."

" 'Tis a matter of significant deliberation," he returned. He leveled Giles with a look that would doubtless send his men scurrying for cover. "Art a disgrace to the house of St. Brieuc, young runt, with your robe all askew and your lack of comportment. You have no hope of making a proper page lest you learn to conduct yourself in a manner more befitting the office."

Giles's face fell. He stopped his sport and gazed intently at Borgia with eyes a century old in his tired, unsmiling face. His thumb went in his mouth, and his left hand reached to touch the firm line of Borgia's jaw. For endless moments he stayed fixed, neither combating nor retreating. Then, without further preamble, he sighed, lowered his crown of auburn curls and gently laid his cheek on Borgia's chest. "My 'Claire. My Bor'," he murmured around a yawn, and promptly fell asleep.

"Christ's bones." Borgia shuddered under the gradation of domesticity, then lay rigid, an odd tightness in his throat. Unconsciously his hand went to the child's silky curls as his eyes sought LeClaire. "He will never make a proper page. He has no respect for authority."

"He'll come about," LeClaire whispered, her expression soft and possessive at the picture of the fierce and noble lord of Ravenwood beneath the small, helpless waif. *Lord help her, 'twas not so very terrible to look upon him in this light, to watch his strong fingers feather gently through the babe's hair.* And her heart knew what even the man himself would deny. That mayhaps he was not such an evil and awful being after all. "Aye, he'll come about," she repeated softly. "I've no doubt of your ability to make him see reason, my lord."

Borgia smiled wryly. "If I can keep him awake long enough."

A knock on the door sent LeClaire hurrying from the bed and dashing for the antechamber. Borgia did not so much as blink when the door swung open and his guard stepped in, then stopped to stare at him in slack-jawed astonishment.

"Your pardon, my lord . . ." the guard began, but

could not seem to gather his wits over the sight before him.

Borgia cast him an incisive look as he shifted Giles to his shoulder and sat up. The child grumbled his affront at being disturbed, then snuggled back to sleep.

"Out with it, Montaigne. You have not come to bid me good morrow," Borgia said.

Monty opened his mouth, shut it, then opened it again, never once taking his eyes from the sleeping child. "I . . . uh, you . . ." His eyes snapped up to Borgia's as he remembered his mission and he straightened to attention. "My lord! The King approaches."

"Obviously," Borgia drawled. He could hear the clatter and chaos in the courtyard as the trumpeter heralded William's arrival over the dull thunder of hoofbeats and the clang of armor. "I will be down shortly. You are dismissed."

Monty sent one last baffled glance at the child, then nodded stiffly and retreated. LeClaire peeked around the door frame, her eyes bright and shining, her cheeks a picture of high drama. She was gowned in another new kirtle of royal blue that darkened her eyes to gentian.

" 'Tis true?" she asked, a bit breathless at the possibility. " 'Tis King William?"

"So it appears," Borgia said, idly studying her avid expression and the unusually flushed color on her cheeks. *What are you about, bratling? This subterfuge is so unlike you, I fear I must examine it further.* He moved the child from his chest to the bed and flung back the covers to rise.

LeClaire gave a mild squeak and spun around, presenting her slender back to the naked man. He was truly magnificent, however reprehensible his lack of modesty, but she would not dwell upon the glory and embarrassment of that when her moment had come. She must needs collect herself to put the plans she had made into motion. She waited for what seemed an eternity for the familiar rustle of clothing, the metallic cling of a buckle.

"May I turn back?" she asked.

"There was never any need to turn away," he replied.

LeClaire bit back a scolding and waited, impatient and anxious and excited beyond bearing. Merciful Father, the King was here! She would know soon to what extent her hopes and prayers would bear fruit. She would not anticipate that it could be otherwise.

Fully dressed but giving her no indication of it, Borgia watched LeClaire's restless movements. She was fairly dancing with restrained energy over the prospects of the King's visit. He knew she held no pretentious ambitions; it was simply not within her to be so insincere. But something had her shifting from foot to foot, chafing under her self-imposed necessity to keep her back turned while he dressed.

He stole softly across the room and slid his arms around her waist. LeClaire nearly jumped from her skin and tamped down a squeal that would awaken Giles.

"My lord, the King—" His lips nuzzled her neck, while his agile hands played tag with hers to slide up her slender rib cage to her breasts. LeClaire's knees buckled at the fiery spears shooting through her, but her fingers dug into the backs of his hands as if to prove she was made of sterner stuff.

In reality her body was a disloyal infidel with traitorous notions of its own. It wanted nothing more than to fade into him until they merged and it was impossible to tell one from the other. The idea was ludicrous and unthinkable, and LeClaire rallied under the fear that she was growing either lackwit or wanton to have such queer thoughts.

"My lord, the King!"

"Will seek his bed at dark, as will we. 'Twill make my day fly on the wings of the raven to think on it."

It was wholly unacceptable for LeClaire to smile at

such improper words, but the urge to do so was as strong within her as the urge to rail at him. Instead, she stroked his hands as she thought a lover might and turned in the circle of his arms until they stood chest to breast, loin to belly. She gazed up into his eyes, all shining innocence with just a hint of a beguiling smile, and felt his hands tighten on her lower back as he pulled her into him.

"Aye, dark will come swiftly this busy day. The King will seek this bed, and Giles and I will make ours with Aurel or Maire. Where will you place your pallet, my lord?"

"Brat," Borgia chided. "Do not think William will champion you in this useless endeavor. He meddles not in the business of his loyal vassals. You will do well not to be considered a traitor to the crown after that stunt with the wine."

LeClaire only smiled up at him, her heart buoyant with expectation. William was her hope, and that hope would not be dashed until the King himself did it. She would not allow disparaging thoughts and fear of what might be to destroy her good humor.

"I must awaken the others, my lord. There is much to be done."

"LeClaire—" Maire skidded halfway into the room, then stopped to glower at the lord of Ravenwood with his arms around her sister. Her shock would have been comical had it not been accompanied by so much outrage. "Take your hands from her, you Norman—"

"Maire!" LeClaire intruded before her sister passed beyond the boundaries of Borgia's questionable patience. "Be easy, sweeting. 'Tis not as it seems." *'Tis worse if you would know.* But LeClaire did not need Maire's antagonism on this most important day. Her eyes pleaded caution as they looked at her sister. "The King has arrived."

"Aye," Maire said, somewhat mollified by LeClaire's

calm, and she did not mistake the message in her sister's eyes. "I have come to see what must be done."

Borgia allowed his arms to drift from LeClaire, and his eyes were hard as they bore into Maire. "You must needs do naught but stay abovestairs," he said. "William will not tarry here more than a day or so, and I will not have your unruly tongue making war on the King's good graces."

Maire's color faded. She darted a glance at LeClaire, then back at Borgia. "I will do naught," she begged. "I swear it." Her eyes went back to LeClaire, who had gone just as pale. "Sister mine . . ."

LeClaire collected herself and nodded briefly, but her heart was pounding with the duplicity she would have to commit. "All is well, Maire. If we are not needed below, we will busy ourselves here until nightfall. The King will need this room and the antechamber for his squire, so Giles and I must needs impose upon you or Aurel."

Borgia's eyes narrowed at their ill-disguised banter. The two were up to something and they would bear watching, but there was no time for him to ponder the situation at this moment. His fingers cupped LeClaire's chin and tilted her face up. There was warning in his eyes.

"You need do naught below. The servants will see to everything. I require your presence at the evening meal and Aurel and Kyra also. Maire will stay here and care for Giles. I will not have the little beggar tagging along on your skirt tails when I present you to the King."

LeClaire's hands fisted in her kirtle at his command, but she nodded placidly. "Will you send someone for Kyra, so I will not have to make the trip to the village?" She did not want to risk a meeting with the King until the time was opportune. The element of surprise would weigh heavy in her favor if all went as planned. Borgia nodded, and when he had departed the room she grabbed Maire. "Make haste! There is much to be done by evening. We must see that Kyra is suitably attired and convince Aurel that she must also join the meal . . . and," she said with a sense of foreboding that seemed to have marked her days since Borgia's arrival, "we must make some sort of plan to get you below."

"But he has forbidden it," Maire cried, her bravado quailed under the possible repercussions such defiance would evoke.

"You mustn't worry," LeClaire said with more confidence than she felt. "Everything is ruined if you do not make an appearance, Maire. I will take his punishment upon myself if our plan proves futile." Her eyes warmed as she took her sister's face in her hands. "Our time has come and we must see it through. Find your faith, Maire. Truly it will sustain you."

Maire shivered with apprehension of all that could go wrong, then with the windstorm nature of her personality her emotions spun half-circle and she brightened. It had never been said that she was not a chance-taker, and she would not go willy-kneed now that the greatest opportunity of her life lay before her.

"Aye, sister mine," she said, an unholy sparkle in her eyes. "Let us make haste before my guard realizes I've escaped him. No doubt you will have much more trouble convincing Aurel than me."

Had the situation not been so serious, they would have laughed in anticipatory triumph, but the dire uncertainty of their circumstances did not lend itself to such abandon. Instead, they hugged fiercely, offering each other strength and unity to get through the hours ahead.

Maire settled the shiny girdle about LeClaire's hips, then went to her treasure trove in search of the special brooch she had hidden away for this occasion. Aurel stood off to the side, beautifully gowned in a long-sleeved shift of pale ivory linen beneath a kirtle of deep mauve woolen. A silver girdle bound her hips and was fastened with a small replica of the Alfred Jewel, which displayed a figure in cloisonné enamel behind a protective plate of rock crystal.

The original version had been King Alfred the Great's and had adorned the top of his staff, surmounted his manuscript roller, his scepter and a stylus for writing on wax tablets. But none of that mattered to Aurel.

She had never looked more striking . . . or more militant. In her own silent way, she was still protesting the edict that she be presented to the King. Roger, bedecked in his own noble finery, had said he would be proud to escort her below upon his arm, and she had gracefully and promptly refused. He had then stomped and blustered, until he had reduced her to a pool of tears and stormed from the room, mumbling distastefully about women and their fickle temperaments.

LeClaire had then come with the same petition, and Aurel felt as if her safe haven had once again been infiltrated by enemies. She had never been able to deny LeClaire anything, but she had come closer this time than in the sum total of her years.

Maire swirled back into the room, a vision in forest green velvet, her own loins girded in bronze set with amber stones from the Baltic. Her excitement was obvious, but more subtle was the fear evident only in the protection strapped to her girdle. Nielloed silver inlays in Trewhiddle style were set into a fine Anglo-Saxon dagger.

LeClaire smiled softly at her sister, but did not tell Maire that the blade would do her no good if their plan went awry. Though she knew she held no power over Borgia, she would plead Maire's defiance as a result of her own command and hope he proved a fair man in the wrath that would surely follow.

A knock on the door had them all stiffening. LeClaire relaxed first, though her insides churned as if a swarm of hornets had nested in her belly. She took a deep breath and gave the call to enter.

FitzRalph opened the door, then gaped in astonishment. "God's toes!" he sputtered, his eyes racing back and forth among them. At four and ten, his manly inclinations were just beginning to blossom and were jolted into full bloom by the sight before him. He could not decide who was more stunning, LeClaire with her veil of golden-fire hair flowing over her shoulders, Maire with her dark locks as rich as sable or Aurel with her silken mass of sunshine. There was naught for it but to stare at them repeatedly, until LeClaire, hiding a smile, cleared her throat.

"Have you brought Kyra?"

FitzRalph jerked to attention. "Aye," he said, and reached behind him to pull the youngest sister inside.

LeClaire's heart plunged to her toes and her eyes misted over when Kyra stepped shyly into the room. She was gowned in pastel plum linen, her cheeks tinted pink. She was neither child nor adult, but a stirring combination of the two—a young and delicate beauty just on the threshold of womanhood. LeClaire held out her arms, and Kyra rushed into her embrace.

"Art so lovely," LeClaire whispered, fearing for the first time where this night would lead them. Would that she could know beforehand where her plans would take them, before she put them all in danger of being cast out or worse should it all be for naught. But she could not turn back now, did not think the others would allow it even if she changed her mind.

"Well," she said on a deep breath, turning to the others. "It appears all is in readiness."

Maire glanced at FitzRalph. "One moment please."

She walked to LeClaire and held out the brooch that had been their mother's personal favorite. With a gold pin fastened to a shaft of ivory, she attached it to the low neck of LeClaire's gown. Over two centuries old, it had animals interspersed with rosettes and human faces around its border and comprised the personifications of the five senses, with sight in the center. Her fingers trembling slightly from both fear and excitement, she patted the brooch in place, then stepped back.

"Now, all is in readiness," she said.

LeClaire nodded in understanding and faced FitzRalph. "Have you the child?"

"Hannah is bringing Giles as soon as he is fed."

LeClaire smiled sweetly at him and begged a moment alone that they might complete their toilette. FitzRalph blushed to his roots at the various scenes that vague phrase conjured up and was only too willing to retreat to the hall. LeClaire closed the door behind him and signaled her sisters into the antechamber.

"All of you know what you must do?" she asked.

Kyra nodded, only partially privy to the plan. She knew only that if things went wrong she was to seek asylum with Hannah. LeClaire did not think Borgia would hold the child responsible for her own cunning. Aurel stood silent and stubborn, hoping to the last moment to be relieved of the necessity of going below.

It was Maire's duty that was the hardest to carry out. She must see that Hannah stayed with Giles and find some way to get past the guard who would be posted outside her chamber door. She had gone over several options but had not come up with an exact plan. She prayed that in the moment it became necessary to carry it out the answer would be revealed to her.

"I will not fail you!" Maire said fiercely. "Go now, sister mine, meet our King."

LeClaire gave each of them a hug, needing their totality of purpose to strengthen her. "Come, Maire, we will escort you to your room before we go below." That said she went to summon FitzRalph.

When the three young women reached the foot of the stairs all eyes turned their way. A low murmur rumbled through William's entourage at the sight of new and comely faces. Borgia's own men, unaccustomed to seeing the girls so nobly gowned, gawked for only a moment before they rudely elbowed one another aside and pressed forward to offer escort.

LeClaire felt staggered by the approach of so many eager faces and by the avid stares of so many strange ones. Aurel nearly wilted under the attention and cringed back against Kyra, who was too awed by the crowd to move. Borgia stepped forward and the group grudgingly parted to allow him a path. He nodded to FitzRalph and Roger. The squire beamed as he took Kyra's arm, and she shyly accepted him.

Roger offered for Aurel, but she merely gave him her most haughty, dismissive look, fully convinced that he had Borgia's ear and could have prevented this had he been so willing. Roger took her arm anyway and pulled her along, planning retaliation come midnight when the festivities ended and he was once again her guard.

Borgia stood before LeClaire, only his eyes moving as his icy hot gaze traveled over her at his leisure. Her gown molded every delectable inch of her slender frame, and she was bedecked in jewels fit for a queen. He would ask where she had acquired such finery later, but for now he would let her bask in the presence her beauty commanded.

LeClaire wanted to rebuke Borgia for singling her out with his hot, immoral looks, but she only stared back at him with utmost composure. But her pulse did crazy things as she beheld his masculine form in a deep burgundy velvet tunic over fawn woolen hose. His girdle of gold set with rubies rested on the slim musculature of his hips and conjured up fleshly visions no maiden should have in her memory.

LeClaire blushed and snatched her eyes back to his face to find him smiling in that infernal way that suggested he knew exactly what she was thinking.

"My lord," she said graciously to disguise her pique.

"My lady," he returned just as courteously, but there lurked behind his ashen eyes a hint of one whose pleasures had not yet been satisfied but would be soon. He offered his hand and she laid her palm in his, hoping he could not feel her slight tremble. Tamping down her almost overwhelming fear and excitement, she allowed him to escort her to the dais . . . and the King.

William the Bastard, Duke of Normandy and King of England, watched as the young woman approached. She was already an enigma, this woman with whom Borgia de St. Brieuc shared quarters. Save for the short stretch of his ill-fated marriage, the Silver Lion had never openly shared his privacy nor even taken a leman. None doubted that there were women, but Borgia guarded his secrets so well that no proof was ever given, nor required. No woman had ever lost her reputation by St. Brieuc's tongue, though a few had done themselves damage by claiming a liaison with him.

Therefore, the young woman of stunning beauty and demure countenance who approached his royal presence intrigued the King as did her relationship with one of his wealthiest and most trusted vassals.

Having offered his obeisance earlier, Borgia merely nodded to William as he presented LeClaire. She dipped into a graceful curtsy.

"Sire," she said softly, then stood erect to face him.

William eyed her for a moment, his expression a mask of mild interest covering his keen stare. "You rise before you are bidden?"

LeClaire blushed but her eyes did not waver from his. Truly, one would not know she faced the King of England and Duke of Normandy. He was a commanding height, his voice cultured, but his dress, though richly appointed, was only as serviceable as that of a nobleman about to partake of the evening meal. Yet, there was also an air of ruthless authority about him that could not be ignored. "I have never been presented to a King, Sire. I am unaware of the dictates of protocol in such a situation."

William smiled in satisfaction and wondered what else he could glean from such honesty. "Then we will dispense with etiquette for the moment. I admit it grows tedious betimes."

He studied her for a moment longer, and LeClaire stood unflinching under his regard by sheer dint of will and a strength gathered from the multitude of prayers she had been sending heavenward since she had stepped into the room.

"Well, damoiselle," the King said cordially, "I see you do not bear the stricken look of so many of England's conquered women."

LeClaire sensed she was being measured for some reason and knew not how to answer. "Self-preservation, Sire. I do not make a worthy martyr."

William nodded. "Have you resigned yourself then to my reign as so many of your countrymen have not?"

"I offer you my fealty," she said.

"Not an answer, damoiselle. Many have offered as much, then turned rebel."

He was baiting her. LeClaire could feel it but knew not what to make of it. "My father favored you ere his death," she said evasively.

"And you?" the King said with the unrelenting precision that had gained him the crown.

"I did not favor my father." Gasps echoed near, but she would not retreat. She stared straight into the King's eyes and said softly, "But I do favor you, Sire, above all others."

William smiled and again he nodded. "Wise as well as beautiful. I am gratified by your honesty, damoiselle. I deplore deception but am constantly treated to more of it than I can stomach. I trust you will be a loyal subject."

"In every way, Sire," LeClaire said as relief washed through her. "As I trust you will be my loyal King."

If William thought to question such an odd statement, there was no time in light of the small commotion unfolding near his right. A young girl was flying down the stairs, a look of earnest concentration on her face, while a knight chased after her. Shouldering her way through the crowd, she came to a jarring halt just before crashing into his seat and dipped into a low, graceful curtsy.

"Oh, Most Royal and Wonderful"—Borgia lunged forward to grab the little hellion's arm and snatched her to her feet—"Sire!" Maire finished breathlessly and smiled right into the King's face.

William's back had gone rigid and he sat still as stone as he stared intently at the girl. None of his thoughts were written on his face as was necessary for a man of his rank, but his heart quickened with old memories and a whispered, "Alice," crossed his lips before he could collect himself.

"Nay, Sire. I am Maire," she said softly into the hush that had fallen. She glanced anxiously at LeClaire, who nodded for her to proceed, but Borgia's grip on her arm was most painful, an ugly portent of things to come. She looked back to William to see that he was neither smiling nor frowning, and blood began to pound in her temples so that she could not speak further.

"From whence do you hail?" the King asked with calm majestic presence, even as his hand gripped the arm of the dais.

"F . . . from far to the north." Maire swallowed.

"And before that?" he asked more firmly.

Tears clouded Maire's eyes and she looked to her sister for help. LeClaire steeled the nerves that were nearly jumping in her skin. Their moment had come. She smiled nervously and stepped forward.

"From the town of Brionne, Sire," LeClaire said, "near the abbey at Le Bec. Alice was our mother."

Borgia released Maire's arm and shot LeClaire a darkling look. "Well done, bratling," he offered beneath his breath with lethal civility as the pieces began to fall nicely into place. She wasn't a defeated Saxon at all but more, much more. Brionne was part of the king's Norman duchy. And for a goodly portion of William's life, Brionne was where he had been raised.

20

William rose suddenly to his feet and directed his gaze to Borgia. "I wish a private audience with you and these girls."

Borgia inclined his head graciously. "If you will follow me, Sire." His cold eyes cut through LeClaire as she passed, and she prayed with all her heart that her confession would have enough sway with the King to protect her.

Once seated in the master chamber, William had the other sisters presented to him. Each was unique in her own way but with enough similarities for him to see the kinship. There was much of their Nordic father in Aurel with her height and coloring, a bit of him also in Kyra, but too much of their mother in the other two, especially Maire. It was to all of them he posed the question.

"Do you know your mother is descended from Rollo?"

Aurel drifted back into the shadows while Maire and Kyra remained in their place. LeClaire stepped forward to meet the question. "Aye, she was," she answered. "As are you."

William frowned. "You speak in the past. She is dead then. I pray not by the hands of my soldiers."

"Nay, Sire," LeClaire said. "Both my parents have been gone these many years."

"I am sorry," William said sincerely. "Truly, I had hoped your mother was still alive."

LeClaire did not miss the fact that the King did not mention her father in the sentiment. "You knew her well, I imagine. She spoke of you often in her last year."

William graced her with a melancholy smile. "Aye, I knew her well when we were young pups growing up in Gilbert of Brionne's castle."

Maire inched forward, all eager curiosity, enough now to outweigh her trepidation. "Our mother lived in a castle?"

William eyed the young girl wistfully, her likeness so akin to her mother's. "Yea, do you not know of her youth? Of your own estimable ancestry?"

Alice had not spoken much of her childhood, but their father, with his overweening pride, had regaled them often with the stories of their lineage.

"Aye, Sire," Maire said, the King's attentiveness calling forth the imp in her. " 'Tis said that around 911 a pact was made beside a stream between two steep hills at St.-Clair-sur-Epte, on the highroad from Paris to Rouen. Charles the Simple, King of the Franks, met Rollo, leader of one of the Viking armies whose invasions had been pirating France for seventy years. My father said that this was where Norman history began."

"Go on, child." William smiled. "It appears you know the story quite well."

"Well," Maire continued, "Rollo promised to marry Charles's daughter, to do homage to the King and to receive baptism"—she paused and favored him with a saucily raised eyebrow—"which was a good thing, for 'tis said he was a pagan chief." The eyebrow lowered and she continued with the liveliness that was Maire. "In return Rollo would get the vast area of land that would later be known as Upper Normandy. He could keep the land as long as his Vikings kept peace with his lord and helped defend the kingdom." Maire paused to give her audience a whimsical smile.

"This is the part I like best, Sire. Feudal custom was

just emerging then, and it required that when land was given by the King as a fief, the recipient—who in this case is our own ancestor Rollo—should kneel to perform the act of homage, whereby he became the King's man.

" 'Tis said that Rollo was angered to the extreme by the idea of having to kiss the royal foot. But not wanting things to go awry he summoned one of his followers to perform the act. Now, Sire, if one can truly believe what happened next, it seems that Rollo's man seized the King's foot and, amid gales of laughter from the other men, jerked it up to his mouth, laying King Charles flat on his ar—Ouch!" Maire sent LeClaire a fulminating glance at the jab to her ribs, then turned back to William and smiled sweetly.

"Back. Charles was laid flat on his back." She grinned in mischievous triumph. "It appears to me, Sire, that Normans from the first were destined to unseat kings!"

William chuckled at the audacious girl. Maire had her mother's beauty as well as Alice's lively nature. "My sentiments exactly," he said. His voice softened and his expression grew introspective. "Did your mother's life turn out well? I admit, I feared the worst when she took up with your father. The marriage was not sanctioned by her guardian, but Alice was stubborn on that point. She believed Rolf to be a man of honor. I only hope that he was."

LeClaire did not have the heart to tell the King of her mother's wasted life, for it was obvious he had once cared for Alice. Maire, on the other hand, had no compunction about spewing the truth without one grain of caution or compassion.

"Ouch!" she said again at another jab. She rounded on her sister with a bewildered and belligerent frown. "Verily, I shall be black and blue come morn."

The King eyed LeClaire. "You do not wish to discuss it?"

"Suffice to say, Sire, that my mother's life was not everything I could have wished for her. She was the kindest of women, but weak where my father was concerned and no doubt fooled by his elaborate promises. In her defiance, she had chosen her lot in life. I suspect she was too ashamed to return to those loved ones who had opposed the marriage."

"Mayhaps, 'twas just as well," William sighed. "I met your mother when I was quite young. My father had gone on a pilgrimage, from which he never returned, and left me in the care of Gilbert of Brionne. Your mother was a cousin of Gilbert's and lived at the castle. After my father's death a wave of murder and assassination broke over the land. Its first victim was Gilbert. His castle passed into the hands of my cousin, Guy of Burgundy, as did your mother's care. My other protectors and your mother's as well soon fell in their turn.

"I need not tell you 'twas a time of constant escape for me, moving from place to place, trying to outwit my oppressors by hiding in the homes of peasants and woodcutters deep in Norman forests. I did not see your mother again until the siege of Brionne. By this time she had defied her protectors and married your father. Ever loyal to me, she sought to help me escape from the men who would see my demise and, in turn, became a target herself for their malevolence. I was able to help her and your father get away, but it pains me that I did not see to her welfare better."

LeClaire's heart went out to the King, a man of might and strength and even ruthlessness, who could also be tender and regretful. She would not have him grieve over things that could not be changed any more than she wished to grieve over them herself and sought to redirect their conversation.

"'Tis said, Sire, that your Matilda is a remarkable woman, in beauty, character and intelligence."

"She is," he admitted, smiling. "And I have been too long without her comfort. I am eager to return to Normandy. But first I must set things aright here." He looked again at each of the sisters, seeing they bore no outward sign of misuse. "This demesne, it is yours?"

"Was." LeClaire hesitated and dared a quick glance at Borgia. He had said naught since they had retired to the chamber, but she had felt his gaze boring into her back with stabbing force throughout the conversation. His eyes were lazy-lidded now as they stared at her, and she could not interpret the degree of his anger. She forged ahead for she had come too far not to.

"I inherited Ravenwood upon the death of Uncle Robert. 'Twas once a part of the Godwines' holdings until they opposed Edward the Confessor. The King took their lands and awarded them to many of his Norman friends. 'Tis said that this gesture angered many of his noble Saxons and Edward eventually returned much of the land. But Uncle Robert was allowed to keep Ravenwood. It passed into my hands until your men came and took it."

William looked to Borgia. "Did the girls tell you from whence they hail?"

"Nay," Borgia commented casually. "They kept their secret well."

" 'Twas necessary, Sire," LeClaire said defensively. "I could not know what Borgia would do or if you would champion us, if you even remembered our mother."

William waved his hand in dismissal. "Nay, do not make excuses. You were wise to hold your tongue. Had any but St. Brieuc taken your lands, most likely the tale would never have reached me." He slanted an arched look at Borgia. "I trust the girls could have safely confided the knowledge to you?"

"Of course." Borgia nodded, but none knew his thoughts or what he truly would have done when he was a man by reputation and fact that let nothing stand in the way of his goals.

Maire snorted with contempt. "So says he, but there is none to prove it—" Another jab silenced her, but Maire'd had about all she was going to take from LeClaire. "Do you defend him? He makes slaves of us, his men accost us, and no telling what he has done to you in this very room—"

"Cease, I pray you!" LeClaire begged, heartily embarrassed to have her privacy splattered before her like dirty wash water. "We have not suffered overmuch."

William's gaze passed among all of them, then fixed on Borgia. "Have you made slaves of them? Have your men trespassed upon unbroken ground?"

"One has only to see the way they are gowned to know they are not slaves," Borgia said evenly, and only LeClaire detected the hint of warning underlying his tone. "To my knowledge, the men have kept their distance by my orders, though Aurel was brutally attacked. I have dispensed justice upon one of the perpetrators, a Saxon, but the others have not yet been found."

"He speaks the truth?" William asked LeClaire. She nodded stiffly, but Maire would not be silenced.

"He speaks a twisted truth, Sire. We have no rights here but must follow his orders." William only stared at her, finding nothing uncommon in that. Frustrated, Maire continued heatedly, "And ask what he had done with my sister! The great lord took this chamber from her, then forced her to share it."

The King's expression remained steady but ruddy color tinted his cheeks as his eyes sought Borgia's. "'Tis true then, all the rumors? You have made Alice's daughter your leman."

"Nay," Borgia stated with complete calm. He was no fool. No matter that William called him friend, a King had no real friends, he could not afford them. His sovereign power lay only in the loyalty of his armies, just as the favor given his subjects was bought with their fealty and extended only as far as the King's patience and beneficence. "She is here for her own protection."

"And have you done aught that was improper with the child?" William queried.

LeClaire blushed furiously and could meet neither man's eyes. Borgia had done more improper things to her than she had even known existed, but she would not admit it and lay bare her shame before all.

"Must I repeat the question?" William snapped.

"I have not taken her maidenhead," Borgia said coolly.

LeClaire wished greatly at that moment that the floor would open and swallow her up. Her cheeks throbbed with mortification and she could only drop her gaze to the rushes and whisper, "Nay, he has not."

"I see," William said slowly, but could not determine exactly just what he was seeing. "I offer you my regrets, damoiselle LeClaire. It grieves me that you were caught up in this conquest. Had I known these were your lands, I would not have seized them but offered you my protection instead."

He turned to Borgia, the absolute authority of a monarch clearly defined in his expression and tone. "I erred when I awarded you Ravenwood, though you deserve it, and I would not take it back. Is there mayhaps another fiefdom you would accept in its place?"

"I would choose no other," Borgia said. "You know my reasons."

William nodded, naught but diplomacy showing on his face. Borgia de St. Brieuc was too valuable to lose as an ally, too dangerous to have as an enemy. With distinguished tact his eyes went to LeClaire. "What of you, damoiselle? Is there another you would have?"

"Nay, Sire." She stood her ground with wobbly knees and quivering heart. The moment she had awaited in faith and fear had arrived, and she would now know the extent of her blood claim with England's King. "My life, my people, are here. Everything I love and am devoted to is tied up with Ravenwood. I could not in my heart choose another."

William turned his palms up to Borgia and LeClaire in a gesture of reason but his eyes were shrewd. He was in his fortieth year and happily married, unlike the vast majority of his contemporary rulers. Also unlike his brothers, his barons and even his bishops, he maintained no mistresses. Leaving LeClaire and her sisters in this unguarded situation was wholly unacceptable to him, but he knew well the need for caution and discretion.

"I see only one solution then. I would suggest the two of you be joined in marriage and share the rule of Ravenwood. Hence, both of you will achieve your goals."

"Nay!" LeClaire gasped, stunned, and swung her eyes to Borgia. He stared back at her blandly, as if she were solely to blame, and she knew she would get no help from him. She turned her beseeching gaze back to the King. "Sire, please, I have no wish to wed. I am certain lord Borgia does not either."

"On the contrary, bratling," Borgia said languidly. "I am ever willing to meet my King's wishes."

Color singed LeClaire's cheeks as her fear and ire rose. Borgia would prostrate himself before the King to gain William's favor, and she would be left looking the rebellious fool. "Sire," she pleaded, "I too am ever loyal to your desires. I have no wish to gainsay you, 'tis just that I do not want to wed. There must be another way."

"None that will be acceptable to all," William said gently in light of her distress. "Had I known of your existence, there would be no need for such a compromise. But in good faith I foreswore these lands to Borgia. My seneschal, William Fitz-Osbern, is now the Earl of Hereford. Hugh of Grandmesnil, William of Warenne and Hugh of Montfort have been placed in command of garrisons in other conquered shires. To my half-brother, Odo of Bayeux, I have given the command of Dover and the earldom of Kent. There is naught left with which to charge Borgia save Ravenwood, lest he be answerable to another besides myself."

William sighed, touched with concern at LeClaire's forlorn and desperate look. "Damoiselle," he said softly but firmly. "It is nearing three months since my coronation. I have managed to establish a state of tranquillity in this new realm. I can now leave these shores in relative safety and make my way back to Matilda in Normandy. I wish that above all things, but I cannot leave you in this unsettled situation. Have you aught against St. Brieuc that you would turn down such a reasonable and worthy alliance?"

LeClaire's breathing came fast and frantic as panic grew within her. Her face flamed but the rest of her felt chilled to the core. Her lips parted in denial, in protest, in pleading, but no words would come. What could she say, that she did not love Borgia, that he did not love her nor even believe in such? Marriages among the nobility were not based upon emotions that the monarchy would surely view as trivial. One did not deny a King any request, but mayhaps one could bargain.

"Sire, would it be possible to postpone a decision until I have time to mull it over?"

William stiffened under the hint of stubbornness in her soft words. He was a man used to political conflict and debate, but not with women. He found her obstinacy galling as well as humorous, an unlikely and stirring combination in such a young woman. A bit like his own Matilda, in fact. The thought made him smile, but his voice was uncompromising when he spoke.

"I feel it pertinent to resolve this situation ere I take leave of England. You may think on it until the morrow, at which time I will listen to all you have to say on the matter." He rose from his seat and regarded her with strict but fatherly concern. "If you have another solution, I will consider it, LeClaire, but methinks you are being hardheaded about this. There is no finer knight than St.

Brieuc. Any number of young ladies would welcome a betrothal to him. Forsooth, I am bombarded weekly with petitions from fathers who beg just such a contract. He brings strength and wealth to the union and is not an uncomely man. What more could a maiden want?"

What more than strength and wealth and masculine beauty? Merciful Father, only to be cherished as a helpmate not bartered as chattel. Was it really so much to ask? "Only to be my own person," LeClaire whispered painfully. "Just as he wishes for himself. To answer to no one save my God, my conscience, and my King."

If William was stunned by her words, he did not show it. He merely gave her a direct look, then frowned and shook his head regretfully. "You must know that is not possible for a woman. Where have you come by such notions?"

What LeClaire knew of marriage could be summed up in one word: subjugation. By virtue of gender, women had few rights in life, even less in a loveless marriage where their feelings held no sway. Though many went willingly into the arrangement, many others bowed only grudgingly to their father's choices. With neither parent nor protector to oversee her actions, she had thought neither fate could befall her.

"I have been on my own these two years past. I have no need of a husband to rule my actions, to gainsay my decisions. I could have done better by Ravenwood with coin, but we were beginning to prosper—"

"And what then?" William asked, not unkindly but with growing aggravation. "Success breeds greed and contempt. In time you would have had armies beating down your door with war machines to take what you had gained. What would you have done then without the strength of a husband and his men-at-arms, without his position to call upon friends to aid him?"

LeClaire felt hysteria grow within her at each word and knew she was drawing close to full-blown panic. She could feel it, could feel the burning ire invade her limbs until they trembled, the heat of injustice upon her cheeks, the red mist that clouded her vision and reason. And she could not stop it, neither the feelings nor the words that burst from her.

"Can a woman not command her own army? Can she not call upon neighboring friends to come to her assistance? Why must she be shackled to survive?" Borgia stepped up behind her, and LeClaire felt the dig of his fingers in her back, a dire warning to cease her tirade, but she was past heeding his threat or even the rational part of her brain that cautioned her as well. "Why must a woman bear a man's rule?" she continued. "His beatings and lusts, with no consideration offered for her own thoughts or wishes? Why must . . . must . . ."

Merciful Father, she was crying! She had not meant to do so, but all the fear and panic and unfairness had welled up within her until it could not be contained. She dashed the tears from her cheeks with angry swipes, but she could not stop the flow. Maire rushed over and put her arm around LeClaire's waist, her own eyes shimmering with hostility as they stabbed Borgia with a quick glance. Aurel too stepped from the shadows, her chin tilted in silent hauteur, to stand with her sisters. A shy imitation of her older sisters, Kyra followed.

"Blood of Christ," William grimaced as he shot Borgia a disgusted look. "Have they been like this since your arrival, full of lofty, unreasonable ideas and outright defiance?"

Borgia smiled derisively. "Betimes they have been worse."

"And you'll still have the girl?" William asked in mock disbelief.

Borgia only smiled. "You have known these many years past that I have no wish to wed again, but I am ever ready to serve you, Sire."

"Again?" LeClaire's head shot up and her tears stopped instantly. "You have been wed before?"

" 'Tis an obvious assumption, bratling, if I am to be wed again."

LeClaire's eyes flared in pique that he did not want to marry her when he had wanted to bed her often enough. And even though she had no wish to marry him, the idea wounded. But more than that she was astonished to realize she knew naught of his life before Ravenwood.

"What did you do to her?" she asked in an accusatory tone that made no sense at all except in some misguided need for retaliation.

"She died in childbirth," Borgia said evenly.

LeClaire's face fell and guilt sped through her with painful force. "Pray forgive me," she whispered, stricken by her insensitivity. "Truly, I am sorry."

Borgia shook his head dismissively. " 'Tis not a matter for concern, bratling." He paused and gave her a slow, wicked smile that held not a whit of humor. "No doubt she is at rest now. She did not favor me in her bed any more than you do."

LeClaire gasped in embarrassment and her anger returned full force. "Art a knave to bring up such—" She nearly swallowed her tongue when she realized she had forgotten the King's presence. She glanced up to see that he was listening with utmost concentration to everything that was being said. She stared at him for an astonished moment, then closed her eyes and inwardly dissolved in humiliation. She could not even beg forgiveness for her outburst, so ashamed was she. So, she stood with her heart pounding out a dizzying rhythm while the rest of her went limp, awaiting whatever verdict was to be her fate.

William could feel the conflict surrounding the tall warlord and the young woman and remembered his own turbulent beginnings with Matilda. No simpering miss had his wife been but an outspoken woman of vigor and determination. It had taken a greater strength to subdue her, but neither of them had regrets for the outcome. His eyes sought Borgia, then LeClaire.

"There are too many bastards about these days, damoiselle. I would not have Alice's daughters compromised by either man or reputation. I fear you are in danger of both, if this situation is not remedied."

LeClaire's heart raced madly. "I do not care overmuch for my reputation, Sire. 'Tis already in shambles. And I cannot take vows before God that would be a lie." She paused, her breathing fast and harsh, her throat clogged with tears while her eyes glittered with them. "Would you ask it of me? Would you demand that I stand before God and make unholy pledges that would bear no truth?"

William's eyes narrowed upon the obstinate girl whose face shone with righteous commitment . . . so much like her mother. Hadn't Alice defied her protectors to marry Rolf? But the choice had been wrong, and he suspected Alice had regretted it the remainder of her days. He would not allow the daughter to make the same mistake in reversal.

"Methinks you should have been pledged to a convent, damoiselle," the King said. "But since that is not the case, I must do what I see fit." He stood, austere in both dress and demeanor. " 'Twas only for your good that I made the suggestion for you to wed St. Brieuc. 'Tis only for your good and the good of your sisters that I now make it a command."

Color fled LeClaire's face and she felt the world drop out from under her. Only Maire's sudden, tight grip on her waist kept her upon her feet. Borgia's smile was cold as he inclined his head to her, his voice just as chilly with disdain.

"Bear up, bratling. I can think of worse fates."

LeClaire's chin wobbled but she would not give in to the hot, humiliating tears. "Pray name them, my lord, that I might glory in my downfall." The words fell like acid from her tongue, and she despised herself for such plebeian cruelty. A part of her shouted that Borgia deserved the insult, but another softer and much sadder part knew that he too was just a pawn who had no choice in the King's edict.

Despite her resolution to remain steadfast one tear slipped from her lashes and splashed upon her cheek. She squeezed her lids shut to dam the flood that threatened to follow. Taking a shuddering breath, she gathered her composure with grim tenacity and lifted her chin. Her eyes sought the King.

"How . . . how soon?"

"I would at least have a betrothal of you ere I leave for Normandy, but I will think upon it and give you my decision at first light." He turned to Borgia, his look grave but steady. "I would have a word with you in private."

As soon as the sisters had taken leave, William's expression lost its courtesy and turned calculating. "We will speak freely now. Know you that if she will not say the words, no priest will marry you without fear of repercussions from the Pope. What will it take to ensure her compliance?"

Borgia shrugged, as astute as his King but without one ounce of it in his expression. "I know of naught. You see how stubborn she is."

"Aye, a good thrashing might help."

"Nay, 'twill only make her more obstinate."

"Christ's bones!" William snapped. "Is she lackwit as well? You are the best I could offer her. Does she fear men, do you think? Would she rather take the veil?"

"I think she would have gone to an abbey by now if that was her want. 'Tis Ravenwood she desires above all things but without the bonds of matrimony."

"She is unnatural," William said. He paced a moment then stopped, his growing smile laced with cunning and intelligence. "I will take her to Normandy then. Mayhaps she will choose a husband there."

Borgia's face closed over and his voice was politeness itself. Only a friend of long standing would recognize the dark, unbreakable force behind his words. "She cannot survive court life," he said. "The lords will circle her like vultures when they discover the blood that binds you to her. There is no place in all of Normandy where she would be safe, even your own household."

"Think you that I cannot protect her?" the King asked with steel-edged softness. "That she is safer here?"

"She is not easily beguiled by flattery or seduction," Borgia offered with the same hard-rimmed control, "but she is innocent in too many other ways. Spies are easily bought, guards easily bribed to look the other way, as well you know. If she were called to give aid, she would go without hesitation, unknowing that she was putting herself in peril. She would never refuse to help someone she thought in trouble and could be snapped up and ransomed in an instant or bedded by force to secure some scavenger's position at court. In all due respect, Sire, I cannot allow you to take her."

"Can you not?" the King asked nicely. "Then I suggest you do whatever you must to convince her to marry you between this night and the next; you may not get another chance."

Borgia nodded stiffly and the light in his eyes grew cold as dead ash. Conquer and control—rape, pillage and plunder—all had long been a part of his association with William.

LeClaire tucked Giles under the furs of her pallet, then glanced up at Aurel. "Borgia has requested a word with me in Kyra's old room. I shall not be gone long."

Aurel nodded and walked with her to the door. Upon opening it she spied Roger waiting outside like some evil lurker with a grin upon his face and his clothes reeking of ale. She turned her back sharply, and LeClaire slid between the two and moved quickly down the hall to have done with the confrontation awaiting her.

Aurel spun to slam the door in Roger's face, but his arm shot out to block the motion before he bullied his way inside. Catching Aurel below the hips in his muscular arms, he picked her up and twirled around once, unsteadily, then thought better of it and let her slide down him until her toes touched the floor. Aurel pushed against him, her lips tight, but could not detach herself from his powerful hold. She grabbed a fist full of his tunic and shook it, wrinkling her nose at the stale odor.

"Aye, I've had a draft," he blustered, pulling her closer into his body. "But not enough to allow me to forget that you rejected me before all tonight. More was spilled upon my clothing than down my throat, more the pity." He dropped his head to her neck and nuzzled her scented flesh. "Ah, Aurel, you know Borgia ordered you belowstairs, not I. Had I the choice I would keep you locked away so that none could view your beauty but me. I but did my duty as escort; I did not make the demand. And when I would have proudly presented you upon my arm, you turned from me as if I were a leper. My manly pride has been ripped to shreds, bloodied, slain—"

Aurel pulled back and pressed her fingers to his lips. Her eyes were warm and shy as she dropped her head to his chest. Her arms stole around his fit waist and she clung to him. God's own truth, she could not stay angry when she trusted him so completely. He shouted and argued and sometimes reduced her to tears, but he was ever gentle with her person. His frustration and irritation were taken out in words, never with his fists, and always ended in compromise with a care for her feelings.

Roger brushed his lips across the top of her head and wrapped her up in his arms. "I will forgive you, Aurel, for treating me so unfairly if you let me have one small favor."

She smiled and clung tighter, wishing she could make amends in the way he desired, the way he had so often sought since she had healed, but she could not. Her smile faded to painful realization. She was unclean, unfit to share a bed with such a worthy man. She would not sully him with what had gone before, even if she were bold enough to throw her convictions to the wind.

Roger stroked her shining hair in long sweeps, feeling his body burgeon with pent-up desire. He tipped her face up and his lips trailed light kisses along her ear.

"Take me unto you," he whispered. "Do not naysay me again." When she began shaking her head he stilled the motion with his hands. "Nay, no more excuses. Night after night you give me the same faulty reasons. I would kill the others for their transgression if I could, but you know I hold you blameless. I can wait no longer, Aurel. I have been patient awaiting your healing, but I know you well. You will carry this forever if left to yourself. I have not the patience for that." His eyes were hungry and unwavering as they stared into hers. "I am but a simple man, but my desire for you is great, greater than mine own strength. Would you drive me to force you as they did?"

At the sudden fear in her eyes, he kissed her forehead, then her cheek, before he pulled back. "God's blood, Aurel, I would not hurt you or defile you in the way of the others, you must know that by now! I would treat you with care and gentleness, and if I cannot make you forget them, then I would at least chase the memory far back in your mind where it could no longer hurt you."

A tear rolled down Aurel's cheek as she looked into his handsome face. She had never wanted a man, had always been frightened by their leering looks and false declarations. She had grown up with a loathing that had only been compounded by her attack. But she did not loathe Roger. Nay, she wanted him in every way possible for a woman to want a man.

But she was sore afraid. Never one to move quickly or take chances, she had hovered in the shadows of life, aloof and inviolate, as if those darkened perimeters would protect her. But they had not. And now, as she was enfolded in the strength and gentleness of Roger's arms and words, she was more afraid of never knowing him, of never having the chance to wash away the hurt with the healing he offered.

She dropped her eyes bashfully, stepped back and, on legs that trembled, took his hand before her courage failed her, then began leading him toward the bed. She stopped suddenly when she saw Giles sleeping peacefully upon LeClaire's pallet. She lifted her eyes artlessly to Roger and pointed at the child.

Roger de Amiens had never entertained thoughts of strangling children but confessed the idea had a certain appeal at this moment. He groaned and set his teeth. "When does LeClaire return?" When Aurel shrugged, he continued, "Has she gone to Borgia?" At her nod, a sly smile split his face. "She will not be back this night." He swung Aurel up in his arms and carried her the short distance to lay her upon the bed. "We will be quiet as mice, my love, have no fear that Giles will awaken."

He settled himself beside her, reining in long starved passions that he might go slowly for her sake. Aurel shifted against him, feeling awkward and uncertain, willing down the panic that threatened to seize her. Slowly, patiently, Roger soothed her with whispers and kisses and gentle touches, until the promise of what was to come far outweighed the hell that had been.

21

"**Y**ou are his kin." Borgia's face showed only polite interest and a hint of mocking admiration. It was the arctic and unforgiving tone of his voice that caused Le-Claire to flinch.

But she'd known it would come to this. Indeed, had gone so far as to imagine she had prepared herself only to find that she had not. Every emotion she had thought to feel—elation and excitement, joy and anticipation—had congealed in her stomach in stony dread. Everything had gone as planned save for one tiny, horrible, inconceivable fact. William had not restored Ravenwood to her, but had ordered her to wed. Her eyes, brimming with it all, searched Borgia's.

"Art angry with me?"

"Angry?" he inquired, then gave a self-deprecating laugh. "I must commend you for a deception well played. I had not thought 'twas in you to commit such a sinful lie."

LeClaire ignored the mutable shades of irony and more underlying his words. She could not fathom how deep his resentment, so would not try. "I never lied. I merely withheld the full truth," she said. Hands fisted in her skirts, she pleaded quietly, "You must make him see reason. Must make him understand that this is intolerable to us both and we would seek another solution." Her heart trembled in her breast as well as her voice. "You have his favor. He will listen to you."

Borgia's brow arched in ridicule. "Will he? Your mother was not only his kin but like a sister to him; she risked her very life for his sake. I cannot claim as much. I have protected his back in battle, as have a thousand others, but I have not the blood ties that you do. If he will not listen to you, bratling, do not even consider that he will harken to me."

He paused and sent her a truly baffled look, the first she had ever seen on a man whose entire essence seemed to radiate confidence as if it were his birthright. "What did you hope to gain by all this, LeClaire? Did you think, after all the work and coin I have poured into Ravenwood, that William would take it from me and award it to a young woman who could not hope to hold it above a day once my armies pulled out?

"Did you think he would turn a blind eye to the fact that we have shared quarters? Did you really imagine that he would not command us to wed once he discovered your connection to him?" Borgia could see that she had thought none of that in her innocence and single-sighted determination. He shook his head. "Nay, bratling, he will not listen to anything I have to say."

Misery sprang to her eyes and she squeezed them shut a second to block the tears. "He must! 'Twas not my choice to share a chamber with you! 'Twould be a farce and a sacrilege to join us in marriage!"

Borgia tipped her chin up and caressed her pale cheek with his thumb. "Would it? Do you abhor me so much that you would risk a King's wrath to escape the marriage bed?"

LeClaire shrugged his hand off, knowing there was no insecure place within him to worry over such. "You trifle with something that is holy to me!" she accused. "You would make false vows before God, then tumble me like a loose tavern wench with no thought for how wrong 'twould be. With no thought at all for the loss of your dignity or mine own.''

Borgia pushed back the golden-fire hair at her temples, then dipped beneath to catch her at the nape. He pulled her to him until her hands flattened against his chest in resistance. "What know you of tavern wenches?" he laughed in soft sarcasm. "Think you I would take one of them to wife, even did the King order it? More the fool you. But I *will* tumble you beneath me. Not as wench or leman now, but as wife. Your damnable silence has ensured that.''

Uncaring that he was so much a part of the problem when there was nowhere else to turn, LeClaire dropped her head to Borgia's chest and sighed long and low, soul-deep. It was little relief when she wanted to sob and shout and wail at the injustice of having all her plans go awry. Her fingers curled in the velvet of his tunic as tears leaked from her eyes. "Unfair!" she cried, and emphasized it by pounding once on his breastbone.

Borgia caught her fist and brought it to his lips. "Ah, damoiselle, I am most heartily sorry for you. Truly, 'tis the worst of all fates to be wed to such as me. My wealth is only near to that of the King's own treasury, my armies naught but thousands of trained soldiers and the strength of ten times that number in friendships I could call upon in time of trouble. What a wretched life you will lead compared to supporting Ravenwood all on your own.''

LeClaire gave a watery smile against his tunic despite her wretchedness. "You need not scorn me," she muttered. "I have never cared overmuch for those things, even if I do know the luxury of them. I do not speak of economics, my lord, as well you know, but of the spiritual wrongness of making vows that 'twould be a sanctimonious lie." She pushed back to stare up at him. "Can you in good conscience do the same? Can you promise to love and cherish—''

"Mere words to satisfy priests and poets. I will have no trouble repeating them."

LeClaire felt her heart squeeze at the lack of emotion in his voice. "I am sorry," she whispered. "You cannot want this anymore than I do. You have already lost one wife and now must take another against your will. You must be sorely tried."

"Oh, aye." Borgia smiled derisively. "I hold Raven-wood, am given a beautiful and virtuous maiden for wife and stay even more firmly fixed in the King's good graces. I am a man beset by troubles."

"You make it sound a boon."

"To have you beneath me at last? Our bodies joined, your warmth and loveliness mine own? In truth, I call it no curse. 'Tis what I have been seeking since the first."

Hot color bathed her cheeks. "I have not known you for a flatterer," LeClaire chided to cover the embarrass-ment such words called forth. "What you seek in lust you will now promise in love? I have not known you for such a hypocrite either! You call me bratling and mite and skinny runt. I should think you would not want such for your lady wife." He only smiled, that secret, knowing smile that she had never fully understood. "In any case, you should not speak such bold words to me!"

"Ah, you blush," he said, which made her blush all the more. He stroked her cheek and watched the color fade to reflect the pale despair of her heart. "I do not claim to be seeking a wife, though I knew the time would come," he said gravely. "I know also that there are undesirable matches aplenty to be made these days with so many widows and fatherless daughters about to badger the King. I do not regret this alliance so much. I only regret that I must fight you night after night to perform the duties of a husband."

LeClaire dropped her eyes to his chest to escape the full and frightful impact of his words, feeling as bur-dened by his admission as her own troubles. "I am saddened that you must have regrets at all, my lord, as I am saddened that I can think of no way to change the King's mind. 'Tis not as it should be.''

"When is it ever?" he sighed. "Come, damoiselle, ready yourself for bed. You must again speak with William at first light to find out your sentencing."

LeClaire did not fight the smile that graced her lips this time, but her eyes did not shine with it. " 'Tis not a crime to wed you, my lord. Merely a shame.''

Borgia gave a short chuckle and led her to the bed. He had half her laces undone before she roused from her troubled state to realize what he was about. Her hands went up to grab his, and she gave him her most censorious frown.

"I will make my place with Giles this night in Aurel's room. Do not even entertain the pretense that I will stay here with you.''

"No pretense,'' he said, looking suddenly like a predator who had just found its dinner. His fingers untangled themselves from hers and returned to the lacy edge of her shift peeking beneath her kirtle. "Roger shares Aurel's room; he will want no interference . . . Ah, I have shocked you. I did not realize you were unaware, though I should have.''

Her eyes had gone round as a baby owl's and the slow tossing of her head proclaimed she would not believe him. "He but guards her!''

Borgia stared back at her in silence, waiting for her to accept the truth. With a small cry, LeClaire pushed away from him and turned to flee the chamber, but he caught her before she had taken two steps.

"Nay,'' he said, pulling her back into the circle of his arms to restrain her. "He does not force her. Aurel will allow him what she will. 'Tis none of your meddling concern.''

His words brought a flush of indignation to her cheeks, and LeClaire jerked in his arms to free herself. He held her firm and firmer still when her heated words burst forth. "Roger has no right! They are not wed . . . Aurel—"

"Has a mind and will of her own," he said gently, unalterably. "Would you shame her into bending to yours? If she has regrets later, then they are hers to have and there should be none to ridicule her for them." The stubbornness in her eyes lent a sternness to his voice. "You would coddle her until she is naught but a weak and will-less shell. Let her have her mistakes or glories as any other maiden. The fact that she will accept Roger or any man is a testament to her strength and recovery."

"I would but protect her," LeClaire protested.

"Aye, you would protect the world if 'twere possible, LeClaire, but 'tis not." His eyes grew lazy as they traveled over her and his fingers loosened their grip to become a caress. "Methinks 'tis time to protect yourself." He swept her up, then hovered over her as he placed her upon the bed. "Shore up your defenses, damoiselle, if you must. I mean to tear them down one by one and have you this night."

LeClaire's hands shot out and braced against his chest. She thought at first he played with her, his seductive games of past nights that had become increasingly terrifying for how strongly they affected her. But there was something new in his eyes, something hard and determined and laced with regret, something much more frightening than desire. "My lord, the King—"

Borgia silenced her with a kiss and deftly began unlacing her kirtle. LeClaire struggled with all her might, which earned her twice as much time ere she was indecently exposed but naught else. She crossed her arms over her breasts, but her thin shift had ridden up her thighs from their skirmish, and she didn't know which areas to protect most when all of her felt revealed.

"Cease!" she said fiercely. "I vow, I will summon the King!"

Borgia held her kirtle aloft like a victory banner and smiled brittlely as he dropped it to the floor. His fingers went to the tiny ribbon threading the lace of her shift. "And have him or his men see you in this dainty bit of covering? Damoiselle, you have grown quite fearless and brazen."

She longed to smite the strange, hard grin from his face, but she was too busy hiding her personals from his view. He ceased fingering the beribboned neckline and lightly dropped his hand to the pale inside of her exposed thigh. LeClaire squealed and clamped her knees together, then, abandoning all modesty, she gripped his wrist and tugged until she almost tore the skin with her nails.

"My lord, you will cease!" she demanded. "I swear, I will summon William's guards at once."

Borgia lowered himself full-length upon her soft body and pinned her wrists to the bed on either side of her head. "Silly girl," he said coldly, tiredly. "Think you the King will stop what he has commanded?"

LeClaire gasped in disbelief, in denial, but her eyes grew wide and fearful as she stared up into his set face. There was no trace of mockery or deception in his expression or tone, naught but the blatant hideous truth. The full depth of the King's betrayal flooded her, and she thought for a frantic moment that she would be violently ill. "Why?" she whispered, stricken. "Merciful Father, why?"

"He cannot lose me as an ally," Borgia said tonelessly. "But neither can he dismiss his allegiance to your mother. After you left I was given two choices: ensure the fact that you will speak the words before a priest, or allow him to take you back to Normandy where he will keep you until you find someone you wish to wed."

"Take me from Ravenwood?" she gasped. "Oh, nay! He cannot; he must not!"

"He is your King," Borgia said cruelly. "He can do

anything he wishes. Even sanction the taking of your maidenhead."

LeClaire arched up and twisted as if to throw him off, then repeated the action again and again until his crushing weight proved her exertions useless. "I do not believe you," she blazed when she had done naught but tire herself. "I do not believe William is so heartless as to condone such a thing!"

"He did not gain a kingdom by sweetness and compassion," Borgia said. He eased his weight to her side but kept her imprisoned. "Did you really think he was beyond undesirable means to gain whatever he wants? Ah, I see that you did. How innocent of you, LeClaire, how trusting. I will tell you a story then that you might be perfectly assured of just what he is capable.

"In Lille," he began, "a day's ride from the frontiers of Normandy, a young lady dwelt in Count Baldwin's palace. She had Flemish, French, Angevin and Provençal blood in her veins. She descended on her mother's side from Charlemagne and even from the Saxon King Alfred the Great. 'Twas a perfect alliance for the Duke of Normandy but Pope Leo IX formally opposed the marriage, giving as a reason the Church's ban on unions within a certain degree of consanguinity.

"Of course, Matilda is not more closely related than a fifth cousin to William, easy enough for the Pope to grant a dispensation. But he refused for political reasons, the chief one being that Matilda's father was engaged in a dispute with the Emperor, with whom the Pope was then at peace.

"Aside from political opposition, Matilda herself refused William. When the Duke's ambassadors were sent to formally ask for her hand in marriage, she even went so far as to tell them that she would rather be a veiled nun than given to a bastard."

LeClaire's eyes grew round at the woman's cruel remark, but Borgia's next words chased all thoughts of compassion for William away.

"When the Duke of Normandy received that disdainful reply," Borgia continued, "he galloped to Lille in a rage. Not only did he force his way into the palace, and into Matilda's presence, but he clutched her by her long hair, dragged her round the chamber and soundly kicked blow after blow upon her with his spurred boots. He then rejected *her* and left her sobbing and shrieking as he galloped back to Normandy."

LeClaire felt the serious urge to curse her King, but only stiffened. "But they are wed and said to be happy."

"Aye," Borgia agreed. "Unlike some hardheaded women, Matilda profited by the lesson. She was even overheard saying that William must indeed be a proud lord to dare to beat a maid in her father's house and under his eyes."

"I see not the point in this story," LeClaire said stubbornly. "Neither do I believe gossip. 'Tis easy to see that William loves Matilda."

"He must," Borgia drawled. "Against the Pope's wishes, they were betrothed at his frontier castle at Eu, then married by Archbishop Malger at Rouen."

LeClaire went still. Defying a pope was as dangerous as defying a king. More so mayhaps because a sentence of anathema was considered by most believers to be a fate worse than death. "What happened?" she asked.

"They were excommunicated, but it did not last. Later, Nicholas II sat on the Apostle's throne. Lanfranc, the prior from the abbey of Bec, went to the new Pope to plead William's case. The duke was able to purchase the Church's favor with massive gifts of gold, and their marriage was accepted without much difficulty."

"A fine story," LeClaire said cautiously. "But it still does not give you leave to force me to share your bed. The chroniclers describe Matilda as a chaste virgin. I cannot believe the King sanctions your being here."

"Ah, damoiselle, if you quote the rumormongers, then know this: 'tis also said that the beautiful Matilda brought two children from a previous marriage to William's house. No chaste virgin there."

LeClaire clinched her teeth. "I have yet to see the point," she said, while fearing that she saw way too many things. If William took forceful measures, even going so far as to beat his intended, then defy the Pope to gain what he wanted, he would have no hesitancy in allowing Borgia the same leeway. What she did not understand was the reason behind it all. "Why?" she cried. "Why would William authorize such?"

There was a wealth of emotion in the eyes that glittered down at her, yet nothing that LeClaire could name. And Borgia's voice held a quiet finality that was damning. "Because I will not allow you to be taken from here, even by my King," he said. "And I will never allow another man to lie with you."

LeClaire could only stare back at him, aghast and confused. "But why?" she whispered, her lips trembling. "Why would such matter to you? You . . . you bear me no great affection; I should think you would be well rid of me."

Borgia only gave her a small, hard smile. "Forsooth, I bear you more affection than you will allow." LeClaire jerked to free herself from the restraint of his arms and his mocking words, but his hold was constant.

"There are so few ways to lure a reluctant bride before a priest," he continued. "She can be drugged until she must be carried; she can be beaten or starved until she gives in . . . or she can be compromised. At which point there is little reason for her not to speak the vows since, by your own words, she is wed in God's eyes."

"Nay!" LeClaire ground out, angry and hurt and distraught. "How dare you twist my words? You talk of rape whilst I speak of something entirely different."

Borgia's expression closed over and he dropped his

lips to her neck, where he placed light kisses over her smooth skin. " 'Twill not be rape, bratling, I assure you."

LeClaire bucked and squirmed beneath him, finally butting his head with her own so soundly that she saw bright lights dance before her eyes. Borgia reared back and impaled her with a warning stare.

"Cease, damoiselle, ere you knock loose from your stubborn skull what little sense remains. Would you rather the King take you away from here?"

"Nay," she said, caught between tears and fury. "I would rather he took you!"

"Ah." Borgia smiled. "But he did not mention that option."

And he touched her then with hands calloused and strong, like his indomitable will. Every inch of her was stroked and caressed with an expertise that said he had known many women. And that, mayhaps more than all else, kept LeClaire from accepting his physical seduction when her body craved what he was doing, when passion spiraled through her in burning waves that begged no caution.

His hands glided over her so lightly, so fiery, from ankles to temples, their roughness a striking contrast to her smooth flesh, pulling desire to the surfaces of her skin in needy pulses that made her frantic. Despite her increasingly weak struggles, his fingers parted her shift to find her breasts and bared them not only to his touch but to his gaze and his lips.

LeClaire cried out in denial even as her body arched, and she longed to curl into him and give herself up to the wonder of his touch, forgetting kings and sisters and responsibility, to have this single moment in time and be allowed the joy of their hunger instead of the regret. His mouth returned to hers and was insistent that she open for him, and when she finally did, he abandoned her lips, leaving them ravenous for more, to pay homage to her neck, then shoulders. His mouth was strong and demanding as he did all things, and a terrible tremor took her when his lips moved lower to close over the tip of her breast and his tongue stroked her gently. With a gasp, her fingers tunneled through his charcoal hair and she gripped tightly to pull him away, but her motion only increased the suction of his mouth and he devoured her ardently until she was rising to meet him instead of casting him away.

Her flesh absorbed his passion, and her heart cried out emotional surrender for the shelter his protection offered. But when his hand slid beneath her shift to find the moist center of her, her spirit knew that physical fulfillment even with its promise of glory was all there would ever be with a man who had no knowledge of love, and it was not enough.

So for all his experience, and for all that LeClaire was brought breathless and panting to the very edge of completion over the next long, torturous hour, Borgia could not break past her one supreme weapon, and she used it well against him and in some ways against herself.

Above all that she felt, above all that she wanted or needed in the hour that his hands and lips touched her, she knew what he was doing was wrong. And she could not be forced, coerced or seduced into believing otherwise. Even as her flesh wept and burned with the agony and readiness of all he had done, even as her heart pounded out a thunderous rhythm of fear and longing, she would not give in.

Wide-eyed and consumed, hot breaths raging in her chest until it rose and fell in quick jerky spasms, LeClaire managed to break away from his intimate touch. With one last bleak stare at his beautiful face, she ducked her head and curled into a tight ball to ease the alarming ache inside her, then wept as if her heart were broken.

She now knew the full and powerful compulsion of lust, the needy clamor and unrest that shouted at her to turn back and take what he offered, to abandon herself to him against all reason or right. But for all that she hurt in the worst way she had ever known a woman could hurt, she did not equate the feeling with the pure and selfless offering of love. The bright and consuming passions of the two emotions might be so much alike as to be indistinguishable to some, but she had seen love and knew the difference was vast.

She had witnessed mothers at the very gate of death as their bodies, racked with pain, strained to give birth, then the adoration and fierce protectiveness well up on their faces as the child was handed into their arms. She had seen fathers starve as they handed their wife or child their last crust of bread. She had seen battle-scarred soldiers return broken and beaten from fighting to protect their beloved homeland. She had seen the blissful joy upon a young bride's face as she made her wedding vows with nothing to mar the night ahead but nervous anticipation.

And though at this moment she regretted it with all her heart, she would not, could not, give herself to anything less.

His body slick with his own sweat and hers, ripe with unfulfilled passion until ready to burst, Borgia rolled from LeClaire with a soft curse. He lay rigid beside her, one arm flung over his eyes as she scrambled to cover herself. When his breathing slowed, when he had regained control of his voice and his emotions, when everything in him had been shut and locked against her potent lure, he turned back to her, his words brutally harsh in their indifference.

"Go with William then. Godspeed, bratling, as you sail to Normandy."

LeClaire flew from the hall in a panic, searching for Borgia until she found him with the newly established falconer preparing for a day of hawking, the King's favorite sport. Some of the birds were already hooded, awaiting the knights and ladies who would carry them upon their wrists.

Several woman in multicolored jewels adorning silks and linens and woolens stood in a cluster, gaily chatting among themselves or flirting with the knights, as they awaited the day's activity. LeClaire arrived just as Borgia hoisted a dark-haired beauty into her saddle, his hands seeming to linger about her waist as she smiled down at him. LeClaire paused at the twinge of some odd and hurtful emotion that faded as quickly as it had come. She stepped forward, self-conscious and uncomfortable around the strangers.

"My lord," she said to gain Borgia's attention. When his head swung her way, she swallowed at the cold look on his face and said softly, "May I have a word with you?"

The striking woman smiled down at LeClaire from her elevated position, spoke something softly to Borgia, then kicked her mare into a canter to allow them privacy.

Borgia hailed the falconer, gave specific orders, then walked to LeClaire. "Aye, bratling?"

The name suddenly grated on her worse than at any other time since his coming. She could not picture him using some similar sobriquet on the stunning woman who controlled the prancing horse with ease. "'Tis a childish name," she said in pique.

"For a child," he countered.

LeClaire had the terrible urge to fling herself in his arms despite his obvious rejection and bury her face in his solid chest, but of course she could not. No matter that he would certainly think her demented, she would also disgrace herself in front of his peers. Instead, she tangled her fingers in her gown and took a deep, fretful breath.

"Aurel says she and Kyra will not go to Normandy. And Maire has not yet decided. Am I the only one whom the King has given no choice?"

Borgia gazed down at her, then off into the early morning mist, his manner detached. William was irritated with him for not ensuring her compliance the night past, though the King could not in good conscience or politics order Borgia to rape Alice's daughter—not in so many words. His eyes returned to her but were so cold they would have been cruel had they not been so distant.

"You were given a choice," he said.

"I cannot speak the words," she mourned, "anymore than I could do what you wanted last night."

"Then why do you seek me out?"

"Talk to him," she pleaded. "For all you would deny it, I know you have the King's ear." Her hands fisted in her kirtle, and her voice held the same tight grip. "I pray you, go to him. I cannot bear to leave here at all, but especially alone!"

Borgia took a lock of her hair and fingered its silken fire. "I will not intercede for you. Everything in this world is not so firmly dictated as you would believe. Choices are not always made from good or evil, but are oft times the lesser of the worst or the better of the best. Everything is not light or dark, bratling, but subtle shades of dusk and dawn that bleed one into the other until we know not where the right of it begins or the wrong ends."

He curled her hair tightly around his fist, even as his words coiled tightly in her belly causing her to ache with remorse until she wished she'd not come to him. "The sun reaches its zenith only once per day," he continued more forcefully, "just as the blackest part of night remains only a short time. You cannot have one without the other. All else is a continuous transition, striving for balance."

His eyes probed hers, and his voice lowered to a harsh whisper. "But not you, damoiselle, for you there is no middle ground. You wanted what I offered last night, more so than at any other time since our acquaintance.

Still, you would not come to me, could not be swayed even by what you yourself desired."

" 'Twas wrong—"

"Cease," he commanded. "What is wrong or right? Where is the wrong when two people desire each other? I have never played you false and admit I would have preferred to have you as a mistress, would have protected and provided for you well in that position. Yet, when that option was closed to me, I made another choice and was willing to have you as wife. And still you refused. You see only the truth as you know it, and you will not look beyond, will not open your mind to the idea that there might be more.

"Were the people of England wrong to fight for their homeland when William invaded? Then wrong again for swearing allegiance when there was no other compromise available to them? Decisions are made to serve one's best interest. 'Tis never so simple as wrong or right." He released her hair and stepped back. "Nay, I will not intercede for you. Whatever is to be will be done by your own hand. Go to Normandy, damoiselle, and torture some other poor soul until he is made to feel that his manly inclinations are abhorrent and unnatural. I am done with you." He turned away then, his eyes going to the dark-haired beauty awaiting him on the fringes of the group.

LeClaire stood transfixed, empty yet aching as she watched the beautiful young woman hail the lord of Ravenwood with a smile and a wave, watched as Borgia returned the gesture and walked toward her. She turned, blinded by her own tears and ran back to Ravenwood's hall to pack her few belongings.

"So much like her mother," the King of England said as he stepped to Borgia's side, and both watched the flight of a distraught young woman. "Will it be her downfall as well, do you think? Well, no matter, you still have leave to convince her to wed you if that is your desire."

His eyes held a taunting amazement. "In truth, I find it shocking that you have not done so already."

Borgia only stared back at his King with cool regard, naught in his look hinting at either insult or humor. But William felt an uneasy question hover between them. How far could St. Brieuc be pushed before committing treason?

The knights and ladies poured into the hall in high spirits after a successful day of hunting. Wine, ale and mead flowed freely as did the talk of court, politics and other mundane topics of interest only to those who had known each other long. LeClaire sat among them, yet apart, an outsider forced into their midst against her will and want. She had not the words or experience to converse with them and felt keenly the social separation.

Maire, seated near her, was not intimidated in the least as she spoke with vibrant animation to the knight on her right while pointedly ignoring Bryson on her left. Aurel had claimed ill health and been excused, and LeClaire had forbidden Kyra's presence lest the talk turn ribald as she knew it would when wine-soaked tongues grew loose and raunchy with so much imbibing.

Borgia sat next to the woman whom LeClaire had been introduced to as Anne of Mortain. His gaze lifted and collided with LeClaire's, but he only dismissed her silently and turned back to offer the young woman a bite of meat, which she gracefully accepted. LeClaire felt again the odd twinge she had experienced that morn, but she knew not what to make of the feeling. She only knew that she felt wretched and so uncertain about her future that her food sat untouched before her, the grease congealing upon the meat into an unpalatable mess.

The King claimed her attention, and LeClaire turned to him in hurt and mistrust, though naught but grudging interest showed on her face. She could ill afford his anger, but never again would she consign her hopes to him.

"So," William said, "you are off to Normandy with me?"

"If I must," LeClaire said, her noncommittal tone at war with her true resentment.

"Ah, but you will love Brionne," William said, as if he had no inkling that her heart was splintering into small painful fragments at the thought of leaving. " 'Tis but a day's ride from Rouen, my capital, in the heart of the greenest and most fertile region of Normandy and within a short distance of Eureux, of Lisieux, and of the sea at Honfleur. The valley of Risle is a charming place," he continued pleasantly, "as charming and as beautiful as you are."

LeClaire gave him a small smile, one without heart or gratitude, and picked at her food to busy her hands. She darted him a surreptitious glance and said softly, "Might I speak freely?"

"Of course," William said affably, but they both knew one did not speak to a King without impunity. Words must be chosen carefully, cloaked in innuendo, so that the speaker had space to demur if the words were taken wrongly.

"You must know, Sire, that I would rather stay here. In taking me to Normandy . . . does this mean you are taking Ravenwood from me?"

William eyed her askance, fingering the ruby on his chalice. "My reasons are twofold. I return you to your mother's homeland merely so that you may see it. But should you choose a husband from the many worthy souls there, 'twould not be amiss." He turned to her then, a King in his sovereignty, a father in his compassion, a man beset by the trials of both. "I cannot be easy in my duty to your mother if I take Ravenwood from you. But I *will* not take it from Borgia. A girl of your age who has the backing of a King has only two choices: become a nun or become a wife. As a bride goes to her husband's house, I think the choice is fairly clear. Marry Borgia and retain Ravenwood or marry another and share the rule of his demesne."

LeClaire nodded, understanding what she could not accept. "And the others, what of them?"

"I will dower them as well. They may stay under Borgia's protection or come with us."

"But I may not?" LeClaire said with more bitter force than was prudent.

William only smiled and shrugged. "Borgia's interest in you does not lend itself well to the type of guardianship I would demand, LeClaire." He sighed, relenting at the blush upon her cheeks. "Choices are never easy. Had I locked your mother away to prevent her from marrying Rolf, her life might have been easier after she got over her resentment. But then there would not be four beautiful daughters for me to champion. Who is to say what choices are right or wrong? One does what one thinks is best at the time. 'Tis all one can do."

LeClaire hardened her mind and heart against the compelling words so like Borgia's in their content and sentiment. "I suppose you are right, Sire," she said woodenly. "Choices are never easy, but I like to think that mine are made honestly, not because I have been coerced or threatened or played false." She rose quickly lest he take offense and sent her King a pained smile. "If you will excuse me, Sire, I must beg leave of you. I do not feel at all well."

William nodded, realizing LeClaire of Ravenwood was no simple miss but far too intelligent and committed to have played such a sorry game upon. But then he'd had a choice to make and had done so. Only time would tell if it was the right one.

III
THE
RECKONING

Proud midst your ramparts half in ruins
You flaunt your scars of battles long ago,
Witness to blows which struck you to the heart:
Such glorious ruins made you precious in our
sight.

Sidonius Apollinaris

22

Amid hordes of French and Norman knights and men-at-arms, LeClaire stood alone in her private heartache at Pevensey, the port where William had made his landfall six months earlier. The soldiers were festive and anxious, ready to return home with their rewards of private plunder and gifts of gold and silver from the new King of England. Maire, convivial as well with her decision to accompany LeClaire, was full of anticipation and excitement, viewing their leave-taking as a grand adventure.

A gentle breeze stirred LeClaire's cloak, ruffling the fur collar at her throat, a throat unbearably tight from holding back tears and the terrible dread in her belly. She ran her fingers through the fur collar, staring sightlessly at the man who had given her the cloak. Made of a rare snowy white ermine, it was impossible to determine how Borgia had obtained it, more impossible still to ascertain why he had given it to her. Especially when he had not spoken to her more than a few words over the past two days, but had spent his time entertaining the visiting Normans, particularly the Lady Anne.

She pulled the cloak tighter about her as she was helped aboard the ship and shivered at the whip and flap of canvas, the creak and grind of strained ropes that heralded the hoisting of white sails, the ancient sign of victory, to replace the multicolored ones carried in by the invasion fleet.

The English Channel was exceptionally calm for March; it was not the weather that had LeClaire chilled but the look on Borgia's face as she departed England's shores. Craning her neck to look past the crowd of soldiers, her eyes—open and unsheltered and unashamed in her desperation—pleaded with him to do something, to help her, save her from being taken away.

But he merely stood upon the bank in unfeeling and expressionless silence next to Anne of Mortain, with nary a wave nor a word to see her off, no Godspeed for a safe passage nor an entreaty to return. He offered naught in his cold stance save the glitter of his piercing gray eyes— eyes that never once left hers until the ship was too far out for her to see anything but the memory that would remain with her forever.

And there was a curious silence in LeClaire's spirit as he faded from sight, a strange nothingness deep down as if she were not leaving just her inheritance but her whole self behind. The stillness there carried no peace and suddenly frightened her more than anything else in her life had. With a terrible uneasiness she began to fear what she had not been able to face until this moment of separation—that she just might have been wrong or stupid or naïve to reject him. And now there was no turning back.

LeClaire latched onto Maire's arm as they disembarked, stunned by the inhabitants of Rouen. A cry was raised as these normally cold and reserved people crowded into the streets to greet their returning duke with frenzied enthusiasm.

The season of Lent was upon them and might have deterred the men of the Church, but William came bearing splendid gifts of gold and silver ornaments, magnificent vestments and other costly items to reward all the churches in Europe in which prayers had been said for his victory against the English. His lavish endowments brought the monks out of their monasteries and abbeys and the priests from their altars. All to welcome home the Conqueror.

In the weeks and months that followed, the sisters were caught up in the pageantry that surrounded a much-loved and respected monarch. In the duke's absence, Duchess Matilda counseled by Roger of Beaumont had governed wisely, and William found his duchy peaceful and prosperous. There was little time for the sisters to rest or acquaint themselves with this new place before they were ushered along with William and his wife on a triumphal progress through Norman lands.

Everywhere they were greeted with avid curiosity, reserved affection and deep respect. It seemed William's prestige had never been greater, and because of the horrid stories LeClaire had heard about his childhood, of the years he spent hiding in forests and common huts to escape murderers, she felt the people's loyalty to him was long overdue, even if hers was shaded by his duplicity.

And thus began the sisters' days in Normandy, days full of learning the rules that governed life at court so that they not disgrace nor distinguish themselves as what they were—outsiders with noble breeding but common upbringing. They did learn, for both had a quick intellect, but LeClaire could not see how they profited by the lessons. She would never be easy among these people with their cutting wit, deceptive charm and restive clamor for the duke's favor. Emotions ran high and tight as each, even in his leisure, was never at rest. William had come back to them an even more powerful ruler, and they were all the more intent on gaining his respect and indulgence.

Every aspect of Norman life among the privileged was a new and unsettling discovery for LeClaire. She and Maire were without physical duties to perform, and so should have been well rested, but the demand upon their

time and intellect was draining. She would have preferred her energy used up in worthwhile causes rather
than trying to figure out the innuendo underlying so
much of the conversation around her.

She was desperate to be alone at times, nearly frantic
with the need to walk in her own garden and soak up the
solitude of familiar plants and herbs that had been
tended by her own hands. And yet she was equally lonely
for common faces and people who would not judge her
for being more or less than what she was. Her emotions
tilted in nauseating swings that kept her unbalanced and
groping for an even symmetry.

But she began to see Borgia here, in these people he
had grown to manhood with. She might have thought
him conceited at one time, as so many of them were, but
now realized he was not given to vanity or arrogance so
much as it was given to him, as his due—a means of self-
acceptance for the constant way others viewed him. She
did not think such lofty ideals of oneself a good thing, but
wasn't certain he could avoid it after living among them,
wasn't certain they would let him be anything less.

And she began to see how Borgia was so very different
from them all. The practiced courtiers with their smooth
words and petty politics, intrigues and jealousies sickened her as Borgia's straightforward manner never had.
She had feared his power but realized now that though
he could be demanding and ruthless, he was never trivial
or narrow-minded in his decisions or actions. He ruled
with a strong hand but he was ever fair.

The ritual of their days grew stagnant for LeClaire,
though Maire seemed content with it all. Their mornings
began at dawn with mass followed by a light repast. After
the King's business was finished, they were called to dinner and a blessing, then food was carried across an open
court from the kitchen and was never more than
lukewarm. She missed the common pot that hung in Ravenwood's hearth where simple fare was hot and filling

and not so foreign in its content and seasoning. She even missed the simple cups of pewter, wood or horn, rather than the elaborate ones favored by some of the very rich who were more extravagant and exotic in their tastes, as if it were a contest of utmost import to have the newest play-pretty of mounted coconut shells, gourds, ostrich eggs or agates.

As wards of the duke, she and Maire were treated with both overweening courtesy and ill-disguised jealousy, and it was hard for LeClaire to tell from a glance how she would be received in each new place. She would rather commune with the servants who approached from the unoccupied side of the high table and genu-flected with their burdens than the nobility who ate the limitless amounts of gulls, herons, storks or even vul-tures. At times there was even a swan served or a pea-cock, full-feathered with its tail spread, to entice the eye as well as the palate.

The afternoons were a time for hunting, the greatest of noble sports, she was told. The ladies were always in-vited to join and rode astride, so the sisters learned yet another thing expected of them, but LeClaire could hardly enjoy the jaunts through forest and field for fear of coming upon the occasional sight of a poacher muti-lated and left hanging as a warning to others.

She found she had no head for such cruel politics or for the many hours the Duke-King spent in discussion over land grants, marriage contracts and other matters of domestic and military importance, when there was so little consideration given to a simple man just trying to feed his family. She wondered how one with so little could be sentenced to death by those who had so much. The level of unforgiveness among the aristocracy was ap-palling, but she kept her thoughts to herself, not fearing ridicule so much as realizing her objections would do no good. These were learned people who would not under-stand her elementary logic because they chose not to.

And often times she was reminded of Borgia's leniency with the villeins and his generosity.

Court celebrated the Easter feast at Fécamp, in the monastery of the Holy Trinity. LeClaire tried piously to keep her head bowed but was awed by her surroundings. She had somehow expected to feel God's great presence more profoundly in the elaborate churches they visited, but she never found the quiet peace and attainment that had filled her in Ravenwood's simple chapel.

The evening meal found the sisters seated near some of the most powerful men of William's acquaintance. Count Ralph of Nantes, whose daughter was married to King Philip of France, had come to greet the new King of England in Philip's name.

William wore a magnificent gold-embroidered robe for the feast in honor of the Frenchmen. Wine was served in vessels of gold and silver, appropriate for the impressive personages, yet LeClaire could not help but think of the amount of cloth or grain just one of these goblets could purchase for the serfs of Ravenwood.

Her thoughts turned to Aurel and Kyra and her heart beat heavy in her breast as she wondered what they were doing at this moment, if they missed her as she did them, if they were well and happy. She liked to think that they were, even if she could not be.

She linked her hands together tightly in her lap just for the touch, the feel of physical contact that was not threatening or false courtesy. The weeks had left her cold and empty; nothing seemed to fill the void that was growing inside her daily at an alarming rate. Where she had hurt before, there was now a numbness, as if all her nerves had been removed and nothing would ever be painful again because she could not feel, could not react, could only move through the days like the mindless rote of a trained animal.

The meal was drawing to an end when a knight approached her with missive from Ravenwood. A spark of something bright and painful shot through her, and she welcomed the sting, the proof that she was still alive. She stumbled over a greeting for Montaigne, holding back a million questions that he might refresh himself first. She clutched the note to her breast, too many emotions spilling through her for the tranquillity she needed to get through the rest of the meal.

Her attention was demanded by the baron next to her, and by the time she turned back to search for Borgia's knight he was nowhere in sight. She clutched the message tighter, as if to assure herself it too would not escape. It had been delivered with a smile and greeting, so she did not think it bore bad news, but she would wait for privacy before she opened it, for a chance to savor news from home.

The minutes dragged like eons, each one slower than the next. She could not keep her mind on the conversation and disgraced herself several times with inadequate replies to questions she had not heard. Finally, she could not bear up another second and begged William's indulgence. Excusing herself, she raced for the chamber she shared with Maire. Her heart pounding, a slight tremble in her fingers, she tore open the seal and began to read:

Greetings, Bratling,

Tears stung her eyes at the familiar address. Joy mingled with despair and regret, and she had to pause a moment for her vision to clear before she could continue.

'Tis my hope this finds you safely delivered in Normandy. Ravenwood thrives in your absence as it should, but I find there is little challenge in not encountering your meddling ways day after day. As there are none here with your stubbornness, there are none to challenge my authority, save Giles, whom I fear because of your prior lenience will never be put to rights. As testament to my good patience, the child still lives, and you may have no fear for him on that score, but never doubt that he is a trial to me.

I am plagued by the unfinished business you left behind and regret to report that Giles does not understand why you chose to go. He and your sisters miss you sorely, but unlike your gentle kinswomen, Giles is quite verbal about it. We are all enduring the little tyrant to the best of our abilities. If, indeed, "the meek shall inherit the earth," young Giles had best seek his future amongst the stars . . .

LeClaire's eyes misted over again and she could scarcely make out the rest of Borgia's letter detailing the progress of the crops and other minor happenings at Ravenwood. She pressed it to her bosom and smiled softly at his words, fighting the loneliness of being so far removed from all she loved, from all that she was comfortable and peaceful with.

The thought gave her pause, for she could not claim that she had known any peace at all after Borgia's arrival, but in light of her present situation she could more clearly remember that there had been quiet days, days with only her own pensiveness to mar what might have been a secure place had she but seen it.

After their bleak leave-taking, she could not think why Borgia had troubled himself to write her, but suspected there was a bit of revenge in the action, in revealing things she could no longer see or touch or be a part of. But she was not thwarted, for she had missed him as well as the others, missed the nights they spent in conversation discussing Ravenwood's problems and even his mocking smile and dark humor. None of those left behind were ever far from her thoughts and she was far too grateful for any news to worry over Borgia's reasons for writing. By the light of a scented candle she read the letter thrice over, then penned a response back to him and to both sisters who remained. And in the days that followed, she waited anxiously for further word.

On 1 May the court attended the dedication of the basilica of St. Mary at St. Pierre on the Dives. Another letter had reached LeClaire and she chafed at the lack of privacy as she and Maire again found themselves surrounded by prelates and barons for the occasion. They were openly courted now by many of the eligible males who wished to increase their wealth and standing with William and, covertly, by some not so eligible as well who merely wished a diversion.

LeClaire bore it all with little enthusiasm and less patience. The void inside her was growing, a nothingness that spread like a sickness throughout her, insulating her from unwarranted flirtations. Though Maire blossomed under the attention, LeClaire withered with it, finding it all too loud, too colorful and too coarse, even when presented in the most delicate and gracious of terms.

She trusted not their glib words and gallant affectations. There were too many beautiful and urbane women in attendance for her to be singled out so often as the "fairest and most worthy" of their attentions. She would much prefer they speak their minds openly and admit the treasure that lured them was King's gold, instead of likening her hair to flaming sunlight, her skin to ripe peaches and other such balderdash.

"Art lovely, damoiselle."

She remembered the grace and sophistication that was Borgia and his intensity when he had said the words. Aye, he had flattered her, but he had never been superficial or glib with his endearments, even when he teased her, as most of the men in Normandy were.

Their flattery unnerved her, as did the suggestive invitations she never quite caught at first. She had been lured into more hidden alcoves and secluded embrasures than a castle should contain, and was tired to the bone of having to extricate herself from compromising situations. She knew the noblemen found her naïve and gullible, but she preferred that to the stale wisdom that made even the youngest female at court appear old.

As soon as was courteously appropriate, she made her excuses to the dignified baron at her side and returned to her chamber, her spirits both light and weighty at the prospect of more news. She tore open the seal, and Borgia's first words made her smile with more painful joy than she had felt since reaching Normandy.

Hannah says there is not enough food in all of Christendom to keep Giles satisfied. We have sent out extra hunting parties to keep his gluttony at bay, but I fear he will grow to be a giant soon and devour us all . . .

LeClaire hugged the letter to her and sat upon the bed, hearing Borgia's dry, mocking tone as clearly as if he were standing before her, impressive and overwhelming in his masculinity, with just a hint of teasing in his ashen eyes. The memory hurt like a fire in her belly, but it brought a beacon of light back to her impassive heart. She savored it like a honeyed almond just a moment longer before she held the letter back to the candle flame.

Aurel coddles the child unbearably, but I find even the young tyrant is no match for her quiet courage and unbendable will. You should know that Roger has asked for Aurel's hand in marriage, but she has not yet given him an answer. Roger is committed to a foul temper, and I am tempted to demand the girl's acceptance forthwith that we might enjoy a little peace around here. But, alas, I have learned that these sisters of Ravenwood are made of sterner stuff than poor mortal man can endure.

LeClaire's laughter pooled out on a soft sigh as she dropped back upon her pillow. "Oh, Aurel," she whispered. "Art so stubborn to toy with Roger that way. You did not take him unto your bed without first taking him into your heart, so why do you wait?" She rolled to her side and held the letter back to the light to finish it, smiling in spite of the heavy ache in her chest. She had always known she could not keep her sisters by her side forever, but a part of her wished to do just that.

But, nay, each of them in her own time would choose a mate and be taken from her as was natural and right. Still, she found the acceptance of it a difficult thing to contemplate.

The first of July found them at another dedication, the church of St. Mary at Jumieges. Though loneliness was an ever near companion these days, another sadness marred this journey for LeClaire. The archbishop of Rouen, Maurilius, who performed the dedicatory rites, died soon after the ceremony. He was replaced after a time by Bishop John of Avranches, one of the few godly bishops LeClaire had met among William's "pious" *relegusies*, distinguished from the others by his ardor in preaching against the unchastity of his clergy.

LeClaire's eyes met William's during one of the bishop's more heated arguments, but he only returned her stare with a smile and cordial nod. Did he truly not believe that the bishop's words were meant to cover more than just the actions of the clergy? Or did her King just choose not to see it? Whatever his convictions, she could do naught about them. She touched the latest letter in her pocket and waited for the service to be over. She'd had no time to read it yet, but she would. In happiness and despair, in anticipation and growing regret she would read the words from Borgia's hand about the life she had cast aside. And for a time her loneliness would be whisked away.

As those around her talked politics and trivialities during the evening meal, she held tightly to the missive, picturing Borgia's strong hand upon the quill, remembering his strong hands elsewhere as well. She had been touched by others since coming to Normandy, accidentally some would proclaim, ardently apurpose sighed others as they tried to woo her. None of it was proper or right by the ethics of Norman courtship, but she found that men with ambition seemed want to forget rules and manners when it suited them, which left her wary and on guard.

It also made her realize that Borgia's touch had moved her aplenty, even when she had not welcomed it, where the others literally made her ill. There was wonder in the realization and something much deeper—a growing fear that she had thrown everything away by coming here, by not marrying the only man whose touch inspired a desire in her that she had believed wrong. And perhaps it was still wrong without Borgia's commitment of love, but this base lust sought by the others was so much more corrupt.

There had even been an attempt only a sennight past to take her from William's protection by force. A baron of humble means who had been courting her had attempted to spirit her away with cajolery. Failing that, he'd tried a midnight raid upon her room. Whatever his hideous purpose, and what he could possibly hope to gain by such ignoble actions, she wasn't exactly certain, but the attempted kidnapping had been thwarted by Bryson.

LeClaire had grown more careful and mistrustful in the days that followed. At least Borgia had always been open in his nefarious intentions, never trying such sneaky schemes. It was disheartening to realize that evil lurked in many and various places, not just the obvious ones. But she could be easy on one count. The baron was never seen at court again and LeClaire was relieved, thinking he had embarrassed himself sufficiently to stay away.

There were whispers to contradict her theory, though she was never allowed to hear them, and LeClaire passed through her days never realizing just how far reaching Borgia's power was.

She peered askance at Sir James, a handsome and gentle man unlike many of the others at court. He was young and wealthy with impeccable manners. He treated her with courtesy, and she enjoyed his company fully, for they often discussed theology, philosophy and politics at length. She respected his intelligence and found him to be a man of strong personal convictions, but still he stirred nothing within her in a romantic sense any more than the others did.

Her hand tightened on the letter and she rose, made her excuses and hurried to her room. Reaching her chamber, she slammed her door closed and tore open the seal with an impatience that startled her. She took a deep breath to calm herself, then met with plummeting disappointment when she realized the letter was from Aurel. Ashamed and confused, she took another breath to center herself and tried to deflect her oddly swerving emotions by reading the message.

Greetings, dearest sister,

We are all well and happy, save for missing you greatly. Be not distressed, but Oswulf's cottage burned recently. Lord Borgia has moved him into the hall, and I take comfort in the fact that he listens to the old Saxon's stories night after night as you were fond of doing. I have no interest in the military strategy they discuss at length, but Oswulf seems well satisfied with it.

Ruth complained incessantly after your departure until Lord Borgia, in that cold way he has that is most frightening, told her that she had passed her fiftieth year and was recovered from women's ailments, and if she did not realize it then she must be daft, which he felt certain she was not. Ruth nigh collapsed at his tone but must have taken his words to heart, for she has not complained since.

You will be heartened to note that Giles thrives upon all the attention given him. 'Tis a common sight at daybreak now to see the tall lord of Ravenwood strolling about the land with a child at his heels. I must confess that Lord Borgia is ever patient with Giles, and many days we are witness to a most humorous sight at sunset—Giles, quite asleep and content, upon the lord's shoulder as they make their way back to the hall. Though he would not admit it, I think, the lord of Ravenwood seems to care very much for the child. I know Giles cares very much for him.

I visit with Kyra often, and she is much loved by Hannah in your absence. I must tell you that I do fear for your return, for we have been given no word that it may happen soon, if ever. I would be most grateful if you could petition the King on our behalf for an answer and relieve my mind on that account. My candle burns low, so I will leave you now, but I will write again soon. Give my love to Maire and know that you are both missed.

Until then, I remain faithfully yours,
Aurel

LeClaire smiled wistfully as she pictured all the people of Ravenwood, but especially Giles upon Borgia's shoulder, the estimable Silver Lion's strong hands supporting a small child's weight with ease. She remembered other things as well—the gentleness of his hands as he tended to her the night Aurel was attacked. Toby's land grants and the esteem a simple serf had gained. *Oh, my lord, how soft you are betimes for such a fierce warrior.* But she also remembered Alberic's lifeless body and Borgia's expressionless face. There had been no softness in him then, nor forgiveness.

Rolling to her back, she sighed and let her thoughts drift over the decisions she would have to make, for she had realized many weeks past that she could no longer continue on with the way things were now. She had never imagined that William would stay away from England so long, had never considered that she would be so far removed from Ravenwood, that at least a visit from time to time was not possible.

Nearly seven months had elapsed, and there was no hint that they would return soon. Borgia's words of two days before her departure had not faded a whit but grown blindingly clear in her mind. Mayhaps he was right. Things were not so clearly defined as she would have them, for her convictions were graying now, shadows blending one into the other until it was harder to determine the straight road from the rutted shoulder.

She was becoming increasingly aware that perhaps the paths of life were not as many as she had thought, paths of good and evil that branched off in opposite directions, but one path instead—only one rock-strewn and pit-filled lane, never easy to follow but constant beneath her feet. And mayhaps she had been too quick to deny the King's edict, for her heart longed for only one road now—the road that would take her back to Ravenwood . . . and to Borgia.

She sighed and threw an arm over her burning eyes, not wanting to face what she had done. There was little hope in her heart's longing now. Borgia was done with her. He had said it plainly, so cold and remote that she knew he would not relent in his decision, even should she relent in hers. Under the King's influence he might be persuaded to marry her, but did she want him on the very terms she herself had fought against?

Everything else was a hazy conglomeration of doubts and misgivings, but one thing was very clear in her mind. There was no other man she wanted than Borgia, and no other place she wanted to be than Ravenwood. She had been frivolous in throwing away her chance for both, even if it had been the only choice she could make at the time. But hindsight was useless, and she knew if given another chance, if Borgia did relent and agree once again to marry her, she would promise her fidelity and love and keep the vows by an act of her will, until her heart and his could be reconciled. And she would trust God to put the love into a marriage that should have been there from the first.

But how did a man come to understand love when he did not even believe it existed, when he thought it only a word synonymous with instinct and loyalty?

She flipped onto her belly and buried her face in her pillow, crushing the letter beneath her. *Merciful Father, she wanted to go home, and she wanted him!* Almost to the point of accepting Borgia on any terms he would have her. The degree of her desire frightened her, and she could only pray that given the chance to return to him, she would not be selling her soul for it.

Almost nine months marked LeClaire's passage through peaceful Normandy. But things were not so peaceful in England. A revolt against William's regime had broken out. It had been crushed, but fresh rebellions were brewing daily and the King's presence was urgently requested. After so many months spent in loneliness when all around her were gay, so many months feeling like an outsider in the land of her ancestors' birth, so many months appalled at the illicit affairs of court conducted openly and privately, LeClaire finally received the news. William was returning to England!

Her heart beat with the elation of it; color returned to her cheeks and she felt so invigorated she thought she might explode with the ebullience of it. She hustled Maire along with growing impatience to help get the packing done out of fear that William might somehow choose to leave them behind.

On a frigid night in early December, LeClaire's prayers were realized, and shivering under the pale glow of a winter moon, she and Maire sailed from Dieppe toward Winchelsea with William and his retinue.

As their party landed upon England's shores, they were received, if not with the wild enthusiasm of Normandy, at least with dignity. LeClaire, anxious to return immediately to Ravenwood, grabbed Maire's arm and pulled her through the crowd to find William. She needed his consent before his time and energy were consumed by more pressing matters than a homesick girl. It might be weeks before she could gain an audience with him once his English subjects converged upon him with their woes.

She need not have worried as she rushed through the crowded dock to reach William's side. The King was accessible to her, at least in body, but with an impatience poorly cloaked in a thin smile he ignored her request and suggested in a tone that allowed no refusal that she and Maire keep the Christmas feast with him in London at his castle on the banks of the Thames.

LeClaire stopped and let the swarm of people move on past her. They were weeks away from Christmas, a lifetime to wait and see if William would hear another petition from her, much less grant one. Her hand relaxed on Maire's arm and fell limp to her side. She was jostled from behind but paid the pedestrians no heed save to step out of their way lest she be trampled. The wind blew cold off the waters, but she felt not its frigid bite upon her exposed cheeks and hands, not when her insides were already turned to ice.

"Sister mine, come," Maire consoled gently. " 'Tis but a few more weeks. Mayhaps he will reconsider . . . 'tis not so very long!"

But it had already been too long.

* * *

Made of wood and stone and modeled after the old Tower of Rouen, the fortified castle for the King of England was, ironically, a replica of his Norman residence.

LeClaire did not think she could bear it after so many months of absence, did not think she could endure residing here, so close yet so far from Ravenwood. Aurel must surely have accepted Roger's suit by now, Kyra would have matured and, oh, but how Giles would have grown. But she would see none of it, for she could not afford to alienate the King by leaving against his wishes, even if she could find her way back.

Outwardly composed but inwardly frozen, she dressed for the evening's entertainments in a golden velvet kirtle over a shift of thinnest linen. She fastened the mantle Borgia had given her with her mother's brooch, and fought a sharp stab of loneliness, then steeled herself for another night of insubstantial conversation, attempted machinations and the solitary heartache that would accompany her progress among William's followers.

Her steps were light as she descended the sturdy staircase, but her spirits were as downcast and gloomy as a rainy English winter. None of it, however, showed on her face, for she had learned to play the game well in the last nine months, to smile and dissemble and offer an interested countenance to every insipid discussion.

She would tolerate it all as best she was able, then plead fatigue and return to her chamber to pen a letter to Aurel, hoping she and Kyra and Giles would come . . . and that Borgia would bring them. And deep within she prayed that the King would allow her to return to Ravenwood when they made their journey back.

Scented tapers lit the room in muted brilliance as she entered the grand hall. Music flowed from every corner, a nice backdrop for the din of human voices raised in welcome at the King's return. The privileged struggled to gain William's attention without being offensive and everywhere the air hummed with excitement and expectation.

It was not the beauty of the young woman who joined the festivities that captured so much masculine attention, for there were many exquisite females in attendance. But the solitary and inviolate air of mystery surrounding the King's ward challenged a man to delve deeper, to unravel the complexities and objectives of her abstruseness.

They all knew she was favored, as was the dark-haired one, for gossip and speculation were rampant. They all knew she was the King's kin, protected by the blood they shared and his constancy to Matilda. And they all knew she had been lavishly dowered. Many a whisper was exchanged and many an appreciative glance swung her way, but none was more striking, more piercing or more potent than an icy steel gray gaze.

LeClaire felt an intuitive tingle along her spine the instant she entered the room. She paused for only a second, her heart racing in comprehension and anticipation, before she spun around and her eyes collided with the ones she had missed beyond reason.

23

Borgia leaned negligently against the far wall near the entrance, his posture one of relaxed insolence, but his expression was anything but inattentive. His gray eyes beheld LeClaire's with an intensity that would have been alarming had it not been so very welcome to her.

She paused to catch the breaths that had gone skittering away while everything else in her seemed to come alive. And she felt in that moment the full impact of what she had known all along, that she had merely been existing these past months, going through the motions of life while dead to the core inside.

She let herself see for the first time what she had been refusing to see for so long. Ravenwood stood before her in the embodiment of a man, the essence of everything she had dreamed and prayed for in the long years of struggle and poverty—strength, protection, a place to abide without fear or strife. She marveled at the knowledge and was overwhelmed by the emotions that came with it, awakening her to other realizations as well. He was everything she wanted and needed and desired in a man, everything that she could love. And if he could not offer her the same devotion in return, it was enough at this moment that he offered everything else.

She took one small step forward, then another, then another and another, until she was running—unaware, uninhibited and uncaring about how she must appear to the others—straight toward him.

She spared no thought for what her reception might be as she sped across the fragrant rushes, no thought that he might turn his icy stare upon her in rejection, no thought at all for how indecorous she must appear as she leaped the last few steps and flung herself into his arms.

With a slow lift of his imposing brow, Borgia scooped her up in a crushing embrace, then turned and hurried out into the night air away from prying eyes and wagging tongues. His hands found slender purchase beneath her velvet gown and he felt a new and riper maturity against his breastbone.

"My lord," she breathed, eyes shining up into his.

"Bratling," he drawled. "Welcome back."

The name had never sounded so dear. LeClaire could only hide her face in his velvet tunic and grip him harder —so embarrassed, so elated. Her heart felt like wings lifting her higher as her arms clung tighter to his neck, and she inhaled the familiar scent of him as if drowning from the want and felt the familiar warmth flood her cold numb heart.

Every part of her blushed at the outrageous spectacle she must have presented to the people inside, but she cared little for their opinions. Effervescent in her exuberance, she laughed and flung her head back, letting the wind toss her moon-gilded locks where it would, her eyes glittering with the joy of it all.

Borgia smoothed her back in long gentle sweeps before he lowered her slowly to her feet and captured her face in his palms. His eyes probed hers for only a second before his mouth lowered, quickening her heartbeat, and met her lips with a strength and tenderness that she remembered well.

And she opened to him, in longing, in gladness and, for the first time, without restraint. She welcomed him with all the ardor of a smitten young girl, all the eagerness of a woman in first bloom. His tongue penetrated her lips to stroke hers and she blossomed wider, took him into herself as if starved for every touch, every taste. Hungry and ardent she returned his kiss until their breaths were raspy and fast, their bodies flowing one into the other, and there was no way for such passion to be appeased standing in the harsh torchlights of an open courtyard.

Borgia collected himself and gentled the kiss until it was naught but the barest pluck of his lips upon hers, then mere breaths mingling, then eyes meeting a space apart.

"Did you enjoy your travels?" he asked courteously, and LeClaire wanted to trounce him for such a venial question when her entire world had just flown topsy-turvy and her inside was swirling like a fiery tempest.

She took a deep breath to gain her composure, but it was useless when she was so full up with him, with herself, with the moment. Nine months had not changed him. He was still the ultimate stranger—sardonic, unreadable—yet there was a familiarity even in that which was comforting. " 'Twas . . . enlightening," she said huskily.

The corner of his mouth lifted in amused sarcasm. "Not *too* enlightening, I hope."

Merciful Father, it was all too much for her—his face, his form, his mocking cynicism flowing through her like warm honey. The frigid winter night was naught but a nuisance as it closed around her, for it could not penetrate the heat generated by his presence. Feeling flushed and needing to center herself, she summoned the sophistication of the ladies she'd shared acquaintance with for the past nine months and spun away from him. She strolled a few steps and pretended interest in her surroundings.

"My knowledge of worldly matters has increased greatly, I think," she said over her shoulder.

Borgia allowed her game for the moment to enjoy the

sight of her red-gold hair braided back from her face to fall in artful curls to her hips, the coquettish tilt of her smile and the weight that luxury had added to her slender frame. He could see that she had matured in many ways, but there was still an air of innocence about her, a girlish insecurity that suited her much better than the obvious flirtation she must have learned in Normandy. He walked up behind her and rested his hands on her shoulders.

"Such knowledge should be put to the test," he said, so darkly seductive she had to suppress a shiver. "Come, damoiselle, I know of a secluded bower just beyond yon trees where we can indulge in much more amorous play than this lighted courtyard will allow."

"My lord," she scolded, even as she smiled and turned beneath his hands to face him. "You have not changed a whit. Art still a knave."

"Aye," he agreed, grinning in that lazy, hungry way that had so frightened her once but only seemed to entrance her now. "I would taste of this new knowledge you claim."

Rosy color crept onto her cheeks, and LeClaire lowered her lashes from his knowing gaze. "I have not learned so much as that," she murmured. Her eyes lifted back to regard him in all seriousness as she took his hands. They were warm and strong, and she could not deny the comfort of having them linked with hers again, but there were other things as well that she needed at this moment. "Tell me of Aurel and Kyra and Giles. Tell me of everything and everyone at Ravenwood." She paused to blink the sudden mist in her eyes, then squeezed his hands fiercely. "Oh, my lord, I have missed it all so much!"

Borgia's expression drew closed, though a slight smile remained. "How much have you missed it, LeClaire?"

"I . . ." She swallowed the sudden tightness in her throat at his remote look but met his stare fully. "I think a part of me died when I left." She gripped his hands tighter. "I cannot go back. I can't! Oh, pray, don't make me! I have missed it too much!"

"Enough to return under the conditions set down by your King?"

LeClaire's breathing stalled as did her heartbeat; both returned in a thrilling rush. "You . . . you would still have me?" she whispered.

"Foolish girl," he said. " 'Twas not I who defied a King, nor I who could not make the commitment." His eyes grew cool and penetrating as they stared down at her. "But I would not have you back if you come only for the people. I find that I am much too selfish for that."

"I . . ." LeClaire struggled with words that would not come, a way to explain the feelings he would not understand.

"You hesitate overlong," he said flatly. "I should think you would know your mind by now." He bowed and stepped back only to have LeClaire clutch his hand desperately.

"Nay!" she cried. "I will do it. I will make the vows with you." She rushed into his slack arms and pressed herself against his solid length and clung to him as if he might vanish. " 'Tis what I want more than anything; I give you my oath." She tilted her head back and stared solemnly into his eyes. "And if 'tis within my power, my lord, I will teach you love."

Feeling as if the universe had suddenly been emptied when he was looking elsewhere, Borgia sucked a breath between his teeth and fingered the curls streaming down her back. He dropped his chin to the crown of her head as he gazed off into the distance, seeing nothing, feeling nothing but an odd sense of foreboding where there should have been elation. He had gained the victory through unscrupulous but effective means—letters sent strategically far enough apart to titillate but not sate her, just enough news about the people she cared about to make her long for them—and now he would have her as he had desired almost from the first.

Why, then, did he suddenly feel that there would be a terrible price to pay for his manipulation?

William's eyes were shrewd and filled with gloating delight as the two entered the hall. Unless he missed his guess, a betrothal was in the offing and he would see it done with all haste on the morrow. Alice's daughter had not fared well over the past months, as he had suspected. She needed hearth and home much more than the splendor that had been offered her, and he was pleased that he had not been wrong.

His gaze slid across the room until he found Maire flirting with another eager knight. Ah, but this daughter was different. She ripened under the attention paid her, but he must needs choose a worthy mate for her soon else she have naught but disgrace to offer a husband in the marriage bed.

Maire glanced up to see her King staring at her and sent him an impudent wink. Had she known his thoughts, she would have hied herself off to a nunnery. Instead she turned to see LeClaire, her eyes too bright, her expression too content, strolling toward her beside Borgia.

"Oh, sister mine," Maire groaned, slapping her palm to her forehead, "you consort with the very enemy I thought we'd been delivered from." But when LeClaire only gave her a sheepish grin, Maire paled and gasped. "By the robe of Judas, you can't mean you changed your mind! Oh, my dear, idiotic sister! Think, *think* you what this will mean! He'll be my kin!" She cast Borgia a murderously haughty look, rolled her eyes and turned to the knight beside her. "Fetch me refreshment at once, Sir Alwain. I fear I'm about to faint dead away."

* * *

LeClaire's breath purled out in vaporous little clouds in the damp, frigid air. Her palfrey stumbled on the rutted road, and she clutched the reins tighter, but her hands were so numb now she could not feel the leather beneath her fingers. Borgia glanced at her sharply, and she attempted a smile to convince him that she was well, that she could continue the journey on to Ravenwood, but the shiver that accompanied the gesture convinced him otherwise.

He called a halt to the procession and ordered his men to dismount and get a fire going. LeClaire frowned but disregarded trying to change Borgia's mind. There was no use arguing that she was not chilled to the marrow and could continue on when she could not even feel her toes, and there were Maire and the others to consider as well. Her sister's tongue must be frozen behind her teeth for Maire had not complained for the last thirty minutes about being dragged from a nice warm court to freeze to death.

Borgia lifted LeClaire from her horse as the men bustled to make camp and chafed her hands and arms to bring life back to her chilled limbs. As soon as the fire was burning he escorted her over. LeClaire stared at the flames as if she could force them inside her and was grateful for the cup of mulled wine and cold supper soon pressed into her hands. She drank the heated wine quickly, savoring the quick inner warmth that soon transmitted color to her cheeks and extremities. After three cups she felt languorous, a little light-headed and thoroughly content.

" 'Tis delicious," she said demurely, then spoiled it with a small hiccup.

The starry-eyed look on her face warned Borgia that she had partaken quite enough of the mulled wine, but not near enough cheese and bread. He slipped the cup from her fingers and admonished her to retire to their tent.

LeClaire frowned up at him. "But the fire is so warm, my lord. I will freeze if I leave it."

Borgia flashed her a slow smile. "Come, damoiselle. I will warm you."

LeClaire smiled in return, unconsciously seductive with her rosy cheeks and lazy-lidded eyes. "Nay, my lord knave. 'Tis not safe for a virtuous maid to be set afire by you."

Borgia's eyes flared, and LeClaire realized her words had not come out as intended. She wrinkled her nose, perplexed, and tried to sort through the error. "Ah, warmed," she corrected. " 'Tis not safe to be *warmed* by you, my lord."

Borgia sent her an indulgent smile and pulled her cloak securely about her as he pulled her closer. "Is that what I do, bratling?" he whispered seductively. "Do I set you afire?"

"You flatter yourself, my lord," LeClaire attempted to say sternly but ruined the effort with a small giggle when his lips pressed against the side of her neck. "Cease," she whispered, "your men—"

"Art everywhere," Borgia said as he eased back, then led her toward the tent they would share. "You could not be safer this night, LeClaire, but I shall remember to serve you spirits in abundance when we get to Ravenwood."

LeClaire fixed him with a dazed stare that was unaccountably bewitching. "I should share Maire's pallet, I think. The King has not kept us at arms' length these many weeks to have me accosted on the way home."

"You doubt my sincerity?" Borgia asked, but his smile was as wicked as any she'd seen.

"Aye, my lord," she said, grinning. "I doubt it most heartily."

"Nevertheless, I'll not suffer the cold when I need not," he said, and escorted her inside the shelter.

The tent had been hastily erected and served only to

block the wind. There were few luxuries save straw-stuffed bedding covered by a mound of furs. LeClaire crouched down to sit upon the pallet and hugged her knees to her chest to ward off the encroaching chill. Borgia removed his sword, girdle and tunic, then sat beside her.

"Art most unchivalrous," LeClaire chided, even as she snuggled close to him for warmth.

Borgia pulled her down with him in a reclining position and covered them both with the pelts. "Cease harping," he commanded lightly.

"I never harp, my lord. Betimes I might disagree with you, but I never harp—"

Borgia silenced her with a kiss, and LeClaire forgot whatever reprimand she had intended as she dissolved into him. He was warm and solid, a steady fortress against any harm, whether real or imagined, and she could not deny that she had longed for this. For nine lengthy months she had needed his strength and security, and was not willing to give it up now with maidenly protests. She burrowed deeper into him and let all that he represented in her life be only what she needed for this moment.

"Cease," Borgia warned in a tight voice. "You endanger yourself, LeClaire."

She blinked and pulled back, then blushed to see her hands caressing his chest in a most uninhibited way. "Beg pardon," she said meekly, as she drew back and dropped her head to that very chest.

Borgia sighed and tilted her chin up. "You guarded your maidenhead well enough ere you left Ravenwood, do you have no care for it now? If you've a change of heart, tell me forthwith. I've been too long without feminine comfort, and I'm not near noble enough to worry that too much wine is the source of your aggression." He smiled then into her ashamed face. "I'll take you however I can get you, bratling."

LeClaire found that she liked hearing such bold words from him, though it nearly frightened her speechless to consider exactly what he might do if she agreed. She smiled and shook her head. "I beg you consider the priest's words, that a betrothal is not yet a marriage with all its privileges."

"I remember the words," Borgia said. "I just do not see the worth. What difference this night or in a few weeks when the same priest will be dispatched to Ravenwood. The outcome is the same." One finger traveled over her cheek and came to rest at the pulse-point in her neck, and his eyes bore into hers with a darkling challenge. "It will be the same," he said, but she could hear the underlying question in his tone, yet had no need to dissect it, for he soon spoke. "But how much the same? Will you fight me then as now?"

LeClaire merely stared at him, her heartbeat impeded by his directness. For three weeks she had not had to think about such. The King had made certain they were sufficiently chaperoned, so there had been no chance for intimacy. With the wine lulling her into a wonderful, fearless complaisance, she did not want to think of it now. "I will have made vows," she said simply, as if that explained all. "I will honor them." The tip of her finger made a bold pass down his chest. "But I fear you will have to tell me how, else I'll be sore afraid and get it all wrong."

Borgia grabbed her hand and laughed, the sound a bit strained. This new coquettishness was stirring until he looked more closely into her slumberous eyes and realized her words and actions truly were wine-induced.

"Damoiselle, there doesn't seem to be an ounce of fear in you now, more's the pity, especially if you wish to remain intact until the wedding night." He'd take what she innocently offered and gladly, but he'd no desire to hear her cry rogue and scoundrel at him on the morrow for pressing his advantage. Yet he found to his chagrin that he had not a fragment of courage or intent to stop her when her fingers began to draw lazy, curious circles upon his chest.

So, enjoying defeat much more than he had ever enjoyed victory, he lay back with his hands behind his head and his eyes closed to let her explore where she would, neither participating nor retreating under her tempting hands. It was, no doubt, the greatest challenge of his life to lie docile beneath her touch, but he was a man who greatly enjoyed a challenge.

But as her fiendish little fingers dipped beneath his *sherte* and continued to caress him slowly, enticingly, all the way from his neck to his waist, he found himself growing rigid; then when they tunneled through his hair to dip into his navel he grew impatient; and finally when her nails scraped down across his lower abdomen, all the strength he'd gained over a lifetime chose to desert him in a split second.

"Bratling," he warned on an indrawn breath. "I think you go too far." But she went farther still, and his voice caught on a low groan as her hand dropped lower and remained motionless there. His eyes flared open and he realized he hadn't an honorable bone in his body as he turned to his slightly besotted bride to answer her blatant invitation.

And found the temptress at his side curled into him like a child, comfortably and completely asleep. Gingerly he lifted her hand and placed it back upon his chest, then plied a light kiss to her parted lips, thinking the revenge he would enact on the morrow not nearly so sweet as success would have been tonight.

Sunlight beat against the tent but offered no warmth. LeClaire snuggled deeper into the furs and felt the titillating glide of flesh upon flesh. Her eyes flashed open and met Borgia's contented smile.

"When did you remove my gown?" she whispered, appalled to find herself in naught but her thin shift. "And what else did you do?"

Borgia sent her an offended look. "You do not remember? Oh, damoiselle, I thought 'twas your desire for me . . . I would never have . . . The priest comes soon; surely we can be forgiven—"

"Cease," LeClaire grumbled, her head pounding like a thousand church bells tolling at vespers. "You do not care a whit about forgiveness, nor did you do aught or I would know it." Her voice went a little weak. "Surely a maiden would know . . ."

"That she is no longer a maiden?" A brow lifted over his despicable charcoal eyes and his hand reached out to cup her breast. "Sweet, so sweet," he murmured while LeClaire stiffened and attempted to remove his hand. " 'Twas glorious, LeClaire, to have you at last as I had only dreamed—"

"Cease," she said again, breathless this time as her eyes searched his frantically for some hint of mischief. His hand slid down to touch her even more intimately and she choked and pushed against him. "You did naught," she said, more to convince herself.

Borgia chuckled and gathered her close. "Nay, LeClaire. I assure you, had I done more than remove your gown this night past you would know it well this morn."

Plucky with relief, she smiled and said jauntily, "A pity then, my lord. I thought 'twas done and I missed it. I was going to ask you to do it again." But she blushed outrageously then and dropped her head to his chest to spoil her entire attempt at brazenness. She also missed the incredulous look on his face that would have made it all worthwhile.

24

The horses' plodding pace grew tedious for LeClaire, adding to the strain of being near yet so far. She wished to be home now, this very minute, but knew they could not run their mounts into the ground.

"What? Regrets already at leaving court behind?" Borgia asked.

Startled, she looked up quickly and smiled. "Scarcely that," she said. "I was but thinking of other things."

Just now she was thinking that Borgia looked quite fine this morn in his fitted chausses and cerise velvet tunic, a thin sword strapped to his side. He'd left off heavy armor and kept only his broadsword and shield attached to his saddle for traveling. They were separated several lengths from the others, but he had not spoken to her much over the long hours.

But who could blame him, she thought. Her head throbbed dully from the night's excesses, her hair was a tangled mess, her gown wrinkled like a wizened old woman. She must look like the most pitiable street urchin. Surprised that such was even a consideration when she'd never cared overmuch for how she looked to others, she peered at him more closely.

"Have I suddenly grown horns, bratling?"

"I suspect you've had them all along," she teased, then blurted out before she could think better of it or lose courage, even though she might lose face. "Do you think the Lady Anne very beautiful?"

Borgia blinked, then gave her a slow smile. "She is passable, I suppose." *Ah, I see that's got you in a snit, damoiselle. What is it you're after?*

"And just what is your interpretation of 'passable'?" she asked, all the while warning herself to cease baiting him lest she be the one nabbed.

"Well," Borgia said most seriously. "She has not your beauty of face or form, nor your lovely hair, and her eyes are not nearly so blue as yours. They are green in fact, but a very *dull* green. But, alas, I would not be moved to liken her to a mangy dog as you would have me do at this moment."

LeClaire turned from him in a sweet huff of chagrin and humor and set her eyes on the road ahead of her, knowing she had invited and deserved his teasing, however much she had not wanted it. Still, she wondered why the beautiful Anne had remained behind at Ravenwood those many months ago and what had passed between Borgia and the woman when LeClaire left for Normandy. She had heard the rumors linking them before she left England, had heard plenty more abroad. The talebearers gave no consideration to the fact that Anne was married when infidelity was as common as good wine if more discreet.

None of it sat well with LeClaire, gossip never had, and if there was any truth at all to it there was little she could do. She had betrothed herself to Borgia in all honesty and she would not break her vows no matter what she learned when she reached Ravenwood. But still she was apprehensive and wondered if he would answer her truthfully if she asked the questions straight out.

"She is a friend," Borgia said, relenting at her troubled look. "As is her husband, Gavin. They were to sail for Normandy with the King, but Gavin was detained so Anne stayed behind to wait for him." His horse nudged her palfrey, but still LeClaire would not look at him. "My heart takes flight, damoiselle, to think that you are jealous."

LeClaire cut him a penitent glance but could not dredge up a smile. "They are all very . . . free," she said softly. "But I suppose you know that."

"Aye." Borgia reached down to cup her chin and turned her to face him. " 'Tis why I did not want you in Normandy." His smile was as self-deprecating as it was accepting. "There are many things I would do with you, LeClaire, but I would kill any of them for attempting the same."

"My lord," she chided softly, blushing throughout as she fixed her gaze back on the road ahead. "Then you are more jealous than I, for I would only scratch the lady's eyes out, not *murder* her."

Borgia's quick laughter caused the horses to shy and had his men eyeing him with faintly smiling, wholly bemused expressions. Only LeClaire's remained subdued. She fidgeted with the reins a moment, then cast him another glance.

"I suppose, being accustomed to their way of life, you feel the same way they do?"

"About what?" he asked, all guilelessness.

Her eyes shot back to a spot between her horse's ears. "About . . . marriage and fidelity," she began, then rushed on. " 'Tis said that William is faithful to Matilda, but he doesn't seem to demand it amongst his subjects."

"Ah, but then we are not discussing the King's preferences, are we? Nay, I thought not." The sun shone down in warming rays that gilded LeClaire's tangled locks, and her eyes were as blue as a deep pool. Deep and troubled. "What would you have me say, LeClaire? When a warrior is called away from his hearth and absent for long periods of time, he may seek only his pallet at dusk, whilst another seeks a different comfort until he can return home. 'Tis no slight against his lady wife, just the way of things. Will it make a difference whatever I believe?''

LeClaire shrugged, thinking it made a great deal of difference emotionally and none at all factually. The truth was that she would marry him; her hope was that he would not stray. But her fondest wish was that he would never have a desire to do so no matter what his convictions.

"I suppose it does not matter," she said. "But, well, oh! I wish you would be like the one who seeks his cot alone, or I shall be forced to accompany you on every trip away from Ravenwood, and I shan't much like to leave there again after having only just got back.''

For the second time that morning, while his bride blushed profusely, Borgia's deep laughter rang out, and his men were glad of it since they had not heard the like in nine very long months.

The turrets were the first thing LeClaire noticed, for they could be seen from so far away. The flat, crenellated tops rose against the crisp azure sky.

Their party must have been spotted for there was much activity along the battlements, and LeClaire's heart began to race as she realized she was almost home . . . but not home as she had known it, nor even as she had ever pictured it. In that instant she realized her dreams had been soft and simple things, without much foresight or imagination, for what lay before her was a magnificent and noble testament of far-reaching ideas, aggressive architecture and acute planning. Her dreams for Ravenwood had been boundless but her plans had been limited to her impoverished experience. None of her hopes had reached this level of glory and strength, and her pride in it swelled with her unparalleled pleasure.

Her eyes absorbed it all as they drew closer. She and Borgia first, Bryson and Maire next, the others following in a long trail behind. The moat had been completed and there was a stone gatehouse with drawbridge and portcullis. She could hear the trumpeters herald their arrival and then banners were raised at each of the four turrets —a crimson background and silver stitching, but not the lion rampant, or rather not alone.

On one side of Borgia's shield reared the lion—strong, majestic, powerful—but flanking the other side was a raven.

LeClaire gaped, then swallowed and flung her gaze to meet Borgia's. "When did you . . . change it?"

"After you left, after the improvements were complete," he said slowly, his eyes only upon the unfurled banners that proclaimed much more than the fact that he was once again in residence. "I had no doubt that you would be back, you see."

She fell silent, trying to digest it all, wondering if she should be heartened or angered by his confidence. But she had no time to untangle her emotions as they clattered across the drawbridge, then reached the courtyard where a little boy dressed too richly for rugged play crouched in the dirt, lining up wooden soldiers.

Giles glanced up at the noise, then jumped to his feet and began running and shrieking, "Bor! Bor!" As soon as the pair dismounted, the boy flung himself at Borgia's knees, and the warlord caught him under the arms and tossed him high amid delighted squealing, then placed him back upon the ground, for there was one standing beside the lord of Ravenwood who had missed the child more. But, suspicion keen in his eyes, Giles slipped protectively behind Borgia's knees again to peer around at LeClaire.

Borgia put his hand on the child's shoulder and pulled him forward, admonishing gently, "Come, infant. Have you no welcome for the lady of Ravenwood?"

Giles scrambled back behind Borgia's legs, but peeked his head around, his grimy thumb stuck in his mouth. He eyed her narrowly, nine months being a very long time in a four-year-old's life, then suddenly a light dawned in his sharp eyes and he popped his thumb out. " 'Claire!" he squealed on a wide grin, and rushed straight into her waiting arms.

LeClaire scooped him up and buried her face in his auburn curls, smelling the baby-only scents of sunshine and vigorous play. And she could think of no better welcome in all the world than being met by the unfettered exuberance of a young child. Unless it was the refined joy of an older one, she thought, as Kyra came hurrying out of the main hall with Aurel upon her heels.

"LeClaire! Maire!" Kyra shouted, waving and jumping even as she ran forward in a kirtle the color of soft rose that made her look radiant.

Aurel conducted herself with a tad more decorum, not because she wasn't every bit as jubilant as Kyra, but because Roger had her firmly by the arm and was giving a concerned frown at her obviously rounded belly.

LeClaire swallowed and reached out to gather Kyra close, thinking her heart wasn't such a sturdy thing, for it seemed at any second it would burst right out of her breast. Giles complained loudly at being "cwushed" and Borgia took him so that LeClaire could also enfold Aurel in arms quivering too badly with joy to do much more than drape around her sister's shoulder, but tightly. Oh, so tightly.

And then Maire dismounted and they opened the circle for her, and the four of them clustered together and clung, crying softly and clinging fiercely, happier than any of them could ever remember being.

And then there were the others, from forest and field, armory and buttery, storekeepers and stableboys and weavers. They all poured forth from every niche and nook of Ravenwood in joyful welcome. LeClaire was met with a tidal wave of happiness at the remembered faces of Hannah, Tobias, Athelstan and Agnes. Oswulf hobbled out, helped by a young man who proved to be Ceodrid, looking so grown up with nine months' passing to sculpt boyish cheeks and thin frame into a man's. Ruth scolded Hadrian to hurry out of her way, only to find Thomas and Gweneth blocking her path.

LeClaire absorbed it all, like a garden soaking up rain and sunshine, as she hailed a hundred greetings, answered a hundred questions. And though spiritually and emotionally she could have basked forever in the glow of kinship and friendship, her physical limitations soon reached the peak of endurance. Borgia noted the slight droop in her shoulders, her glad eyes growing tired, and he calmly and effectively dispersed the crowd and escorted the travel-weary sisters inside the main hall.

The common-room had changed little; Aurel's artwork still graced the walls, but there were newer furnishings to add elegance to the repaired hall. Though an elaborate meal greeted them, LeClaire took her trencher to the common pot and savored the aroma of simple fare as she ladled out a small portion, for she would not offend Hannah's harder work at the long-tables. Her trenchers side by side she took her meals, one richly seasoned with imported spices, the other a gamekeeper's delight, and thought she would never be a grand lady with her commoner's tastes.

And as Borgia watched a young woman's delight at rabbit stew, her winsome smile and happy chatter, he thought the great courts of England and Normandy had nothing now without the mistress of Ravenwood.

A stream of topics had been discussed, a river of stories told before Giles's head bobbed once, then crumpled over to rest on Borgia's knee. Kyra, her chin propped in her palm, blinked to keep her eyes open, but sleep was moving in fast upon her as well. The hour was much later than any of them were accustomed to and morning would be a greedy taskmaster for the servants who could not lie abed as could the ones keeping them from their pallets.

LeClaire shook Kyra's arm gently to awaken her and admonished her to seek her rest, then was surprised when her sister stumbled sleepily up the stairs without escort instead of going to Hannah's cottage. Her gaze shot to Borgia.

"Aye, Guy was caught," Borgia said soberly. "Posing as English refugees, he and another Norman were trying to obtain sanctuary from King Malcolm III in Scotland. With scores of displaced Saxons flooding in, the King had little use for a Norman with a price on his head, except for the reward, and turned them over to my men. Guy's accomplice confessed with little coercion; Guy tried to escape. My men brought his body back just before you arrived in London, and I did not want to mar your homecoming by dredging up past ills.

"In truth," he whispered, smiling, "I was so taken by your reception of me that I quite forgot all the news I had to impart."

LeClaire gave him a dubious smile, knowing he never forgot a thing, but enjoyed the ease with which she could now accept his teasing and also his effort to distract her from the terrible memory. Agnes came to fetch Giles, and Roger yawned and stretched as he helped Aurel to her feet. LeClaire rose also, needing to speak with her sister in private, but Borgia had also risen and stayed LeClaire when she would have followed.

"The morrow is soon enough," he said kindly though firmly, and LeClaire had the terrible suspicion that Aurel had not yet agreed to marry Roger, even though she so obviously carried his child. Mercifully, Borgia smiled and whispered. "Nay, fear not, damoiselle, they were wed a month past in a small private ceremony as was Aurel's wish. Roger could not convince her otherwise and was too grateful that she had finally agreed to argue about it."

LeClaire felt greatly relieved, though she would have liked to be present. Knowing her sister, she was certain Aurel had wanted no grand celebration, and she had to content herself with the knowledge that things had been done to her sister's liking.

As if nine months had changed nothing, when LeClaire reached Borgia's chamber she looked around for the straw pallet that had been her bed until forced to share his. Borgia laughed dryly, leaned against the stately bed frame and gave her a lazy look.

"Burned. Every inch of it." Sweeping his arm out with a courtly bow, he finished, "Your bower awaits, my lady."

LeClaire smiled and shook her head, thinking him too magnificently made and horribly tempting for one whose heart was too full at this moment to contain any room for denials.

"I think not, my lord knave. I've had no mulled wine to cloud my reasoning and can see clearly that your intentions are evil."

He splayed a hand across his chest, looking so innocent and wounded that she had to fight the urge to laugh, but to unleash any of the emotions within her would leave her open and vulnerable, with no strength at all to resist, and she'd find herself dashing across the rushes into his arms as she'd done in London. There was no chaperone here, and she didn't think herself willful enough to stop him when there was no desire inside her to do so.

Her eyes grew round at the secret admission, and she blushed red as a ripe cherry. Borgia eyed her keenly, smiling with such awareness that she blushed even brighter. He moved from the bed to take the decision from her. His fingers threaded through the hair at her temples and his lips touched hers only once before he pulled back.

"It has been well over a year for me, LeClaire. I have

had no other since the day I came to Ravenwood. I would not ravish you, but I do not think I can wait any longer."

His words stunned and warmed her. But they also revived her maidenly fears and indecision, and she feared she would not go easily to his bed even after they were married, for she was innately shy about such and modest as well, though withholding herself after pledging her love would be every bit as wrong to her as giving herself beforehand.

With a tremulous smile and becoming blush, she gazed up at him and said softly, "But it has been *nineteen* years for me, my lord. Now, tell me who has the more difficult task?"

Three weeks had really not been such a long time to wait for a priest, Borgia thought, not until the priest was detained and the time drawn out like a man stretched upon the torture rack to become three months.

But if the time had been a study in frustrated patience for the lord of Ravenwood, it had been a time of renewal for its returning lady.

As if in a benediction to cover the "lost months," as LeClaire called her time in Normandy, the weather had turned warm early, and spring had burst upon the land with all the healing power of rebirth. The garden was in bloom, its multitude of colors and scents a feast for the senses, a place to play and pray, to refurbish a lonely heart and an uncertain soul. She felt such a sense of completion here, as if portions of her life had come full circle and her dreams and hopes were now meshed with reality. Her sisters and the villagers were happy with the lord of Ravenwood and their way of life. He had supported them through the past nine months with sensible advice and generous endowments, and they had been rewarded with more than just the fruits of their labors and physical prosperity. Not only were they content, the inhabitants of Ravenwood were proud of their accomplishments.

LeClaire felt every inch of their happiness as she twirled like a child in the sunshine, letting the breeze toss her hair and skirts where it would, letting the conflicting thoughts of the priest now seated in the main hall go the way of all conflicting thoughts—far back into a dark corner of her mind where it could not disturb her at this moment. But her troubling thoughts could not be pushed aside and she went still, her rich wedding garments settling about her. By this time tomorrow, she would be Borgia's wife, in name, in body. She was not here to worry over either, but to make her peace over the decision that would lead to both.

She had guarded her heart well since she had met him. It had not been hard early, as frightened as she had been of the dark warlord who had come and taken her birthright. But it had not been wise later, now that she knew what would come to pass. She had wasted so much time in resistance, time that could have been better spent in wooing him toward those emotions she felt so strongly about, emotions he did not believe in. She knew now that she loved him as was right and honorable, but she also wanted to be loved in return as was just.

It was the latter that caused her conflict now, as it had from the King's first suggestion that they marry. In a few hours she would stand beside Borgia and promise all the things a wife promised a husband and hear his pledge in return. But could she take that pledge into her heart, or would it always be merely a contract scribbled on parchment rather than engraved upon the most high?

Mere words for priests and poets. I'll have no trouble repeating them. Something deep within her quickened at the memory and the thought of the physical commitment they would also make to each other, an allegiance far more important to her than his name and land. She wanted their joining to reach far beyond duty and moral obligation. She wanted a communion of mind and spirit as well as body.

LeClaire sighed and cast her gaze upward through the leafy boughs of a hawthorn tree to the limitless universe beyond and listened for the angels' song, the reassurance, the blessing. The sounds of nature greeted her—wind and birds and crawling things—an earthly aria of grand gentleness but not the melody of old.

She closed her eyes to the pleasant things of the earth and sought the greater things of heaven. *Lord, I would never willingly choose the wrong way, but I fear that in this I have been blind and desperate. I desire Borgia's love above all earthly things, a desire You put in my heart, but You must show me the way to his. He has so much to offer that is worthy—strength, gentleness, protection . . .*

She smiled softly, knowing what she had not been willing to admit so many months ago. *All the things I found admirable in the Guardian I also found in him. But you knew that, Lord, didn't you? 'Twas why the Guardian was sent to me with such manly features. But I would have more from Borgia, Lord. I would have his love and constancy; I cannot bear less. Even a man whose past is carved from violence need not spend his future without the most basic and powerful emotion You have created.*

And the chorus began, a love song, softly as the breath of a butterfly at first, then swelling to a euphony that could only have been orchestrated in the highest realms, lifting LeClaire to the place she had searched for, where fear and insecurity were left far behind in a lonely place of insignificance where only mortals of lesser ideals were content to dwell.

She heard Borgia's voice long before she turned to him, not intrusive now but part of what she longed for. She turned and smiled as she bid him welcome, holding out her hand for him to join her in the ethereal concert that filled the garden.

"Do you hear it?" she whispered, hoping against what

she already knew, that the sounds of the spirit could not reach one who believed only in the flesh. "The angels sing for us, my lord, for this day."

He only smiled and lifted his brow in the way that meant he was indulging her. But LeClaire was a woman of great faith and conviction, perhaps now more than at any other time in her life, for suddenly she felt as if her very existence depended upon it. And as she gazed up at him with all she had promised and prayed shining in her bright blue eyes, she knew she would strive until the moment of her death to teach him the music of life.

"I placed your request before the priest," Borgia said, threading his fingers through hers, sensing a fierceness in her as she took his hand. "He says we should hear mass and take the sacraments in the chapel, then we may make our vows here." He brought her hand to his lips and placed a kiss there where her skin had grown soft and pale from her time in Normandy. "But why did you make the request, bratling? Do you think it a sacrilege to pledge yourself to me in God's house?"

His tone was light and teasing, but his eyes were fixed upon some distant unknown point, and the words tore at LeClaire's heart. "Nay, my lord, God is everywhere. He will hear our vows as clearly here as any other place." Her eyes took in all surrounding them, the beauty of living things in plain sight, the promise of it in buds yet dormant.

"From the very beginning there was a garden," she said softly. " 'Twas where He chose to place His first creations. Not in a chapel or monastery or cathedral, those were made by man to satisfy his own vision of grandeur. I would make my vows here where nature thrives and new birth is ever constant." Her eyes looked deeply into his, so deeply he felt somehow naked and ignorant and common in the light of her truth. " 'Tis why I chose it, my lord. There is no more perfect place."

And so it was done. After mass was said in the small

chapel Borgia'd had completely repaired and furnished, they returned to the garden. In a gentle breeze scented by the living things LeClaire had planted for holy days and had chosen to bless the holiest day of all, Borgia and LeClaire exchanged their vows, flanked by villagers and loved ones.

After the last vow was made, the marriage pall removed, the radiant bride held out her bouquet. With an odd twinkle in her eyes, she handed a sample of each to Borgia and explained its significance—the white lily for purity, the red rose for divine love, cherries for the joys of heaven, strawberries for the fruits of righteousness. And, thoroughly surprising a man who was not easily shocked, LeClaire finished by holding out to Borgia a dark red apple.

He cocked one eyebrow and gave her a deeply intimate look. "To represent the fall of man?" he inquired.

She smiled sincerely. "Nay, his redemption."

And with her eyes shining up at him, Borgia thought she just might be.

Suddenly they were surrounded by the cries of "Plenty! Plenty!" and showered with seeds, the symbol of fertility. Laughing and blushing, LeClaire accepted Borgia's hand and the two briskly led the procession back to the hall for the feast and dancing that would include the entire village.

Night fell with a whisper. Only when more tapers had to be lighted did LeClaire realize the time for full commitment was drawing near. Courageous and certain despite her reservations, she did not so much as let her smile waver when some of the older villagers, unaware of tradition, bid them good eventide and made their way home. Too soon for her peace of mind and heart, a full-bellied and sleepy Giles was also carried off to bed.

Borgia took her hand firmly, threading his fingers through hers as if to infuse strength. "The hour grows late," he said. When LeClaire only stared up at him, he clarified. "The feasting will last well into the night, but those who would seek their rest at a decent hour cannot until we retire."

Oh, aye, she should have remembered. Gathering her ebbing bravery for everyone's sake, she smiled brightly. "Well, mayhaps 'tis time then."

She rose from her seat, incontestable in her gaiety, and no one would have guessed that a nest of hornets swarmed in her belly. Except Aurel. The golden-haired sister rose also, offered her husband a gentle smile, then walked the lady of Ravenwood up the stairs to the lord's chamber.

25

In silence she waited.

Anxious and unsteady in naught but the fiery gold drape of her hair and a sheer length of exquisite white silk, LeClaire stood alone, awaiting her husband. The servants were gone, herded off by Aurel's gently reproaching expression at their chatter and giggles. Hardly aware of their slyly speculative exchanges or the protective, compassionate way Aurel had helped her undress and turned back the bedding, LeClaire had chosen to wait nearer the hearth. She was feeling a bit chilled though the room was warm, then alternately warm though a cooling breeze wafted through the windows. The physical incongruence mirrored her emotional state —panicky and excited.

Her heartbeat quickened and her palms grew clammy with doubt and anticipation, much as they had the first time Borgia had come to this room. But her smile was soft and accepting now, as it had not been then, full of hope and joy and her commitment of love.

The door opened, creaking ominously upon its hinges as it had so long ago, but no one rushed in armed and ready to do battle. Instead, Borgia stood silhouetted against the torch-lit hall, dark against light, a stark and severe outline of potent strength even in shadow. Alone he entered the chamber, having banished his men back to their own entertainments, his presence filling Le-

Claire's senses as thoroughly as he filled the rich wedding garments he wore. How well the deep crimson velvet suited him, how magnificent a figure he made girded in jewel-studded silver. The garments bespoke him well, bold and strong and refined, so much like the man. Slowly he slid the bolt, then turned to meet his wife.

Borgia was struck by the sight of her standing small and pale and so fragile in the glow of a low fire. She had been draped, appropriately he thought, in a long flowing length of virginal white cloth, and her knuckles were bloodless from gripping it tightly to her chest.

Veiled from breast to heel, her shape was outlined perfectly, exquisitely, beneath the sheer fabric by the firelight. Time and distance melted away, and he remembered every delicate inch of her, remembered the taste and feel and scent of her as vividly as if there had never been discord between them or the span of nine long months, as if the sum of their time together was contained in only this moment.

Her shoulders were transparent ivory above the silk, her curves softly and sensuously revealed beneath. Her rib cage and waist were tiny enough to span with his hands, yet her breasts and hips sloped out rounder now, healthier. Not more alluring, just more of what he wished for her. Her arms were sleek and athletic, her long legs shapely, and he yearned to have them wrapped around him with the fierce passion he knew her capable of but had never completely experienced.

The raw hunger in him must have been apparent for, seductive and tempting as she stood before him, her eyes held a turmoil of emotion, the confusion and timidity of a thousand unanswered questions. She fidgeted nervously beneath his regard, one foot curling over the other, and her hands gripped the silk tighter.

Borgia's eyes lifted to meet hers, and in the crystalline depths he found many things he had hoped not to see this night. His heart contracted at the fear.

LeClaire shook her head at the unspoken question in his silver eyes and stared at him fully instead of casting her eyes to the rushes as was her inclination. She was not truly afraid, only uncertain of the things she did not know. They had shared this room many times . . . but not in the way they would tonight.

Her eyes lowered for the briefest second, her lashes deep tawny half-moons on her pale cheeks, while the fire spun glittering strands of amber and gold throughout her hair and danced in slow, alluring waves along the silk. She breathed deeply, as she had not since he entered the room, then lifted her eyes back to his handsome face. There were about him many qualities that bespoke majesty, in face and form, in attitude and action. He was a ruler, dictatorial and organized, aggressive and efficient. In his eyes and stance lay a dark hunger tightly leashed, but he could be a gentle man when he chose. And she knew he would choose to be so this night.

Cheeks flushed, she granted him a wonderfully shy but determined smile.

He took a step toward her and watched her eyes grow round, watched her unconsciously take a small step back. He paused to grant her a moment, then moved toward her again, more slowly this time. "I yet see your eyes as you stood aboard William's ship, so much bluer and more beautiful than the water that surrounded you —so much more troubled. I wanted to behead my King for taking you away."

His voice was deep and soothing as he approached, his body so perfectly formed beneath his wedding garments. She was held spellbound with pride and wonder that he had wanted her enough to contemplate treason, that the rest of her life would be shared with him. With obvious determination, she gathered her faulty courage and stood deathly still as he continued to draw closer. Then he too stopped, scant inches from her, and held out his palm.

"You need not be brave, LeClaire, or courageous or stalwart. This is not warfare."

His palm lay open before her, offering, waiting, but she did not take it. Instead she flung herself into his strong arms and burrowed there, like a child seeking shelter, a bride a nesting place. And he wrapped her up in a protective embrace and pushed aside his own needs for the moment in favor of hers. For endless moments they stood thus, she with her insecurities turning her stomach to jelly, he with his passions raging and ebbing like an unstable sea.

He had never known such conflict within himself, save for the time he had almost forced her. He now wished he'd taken her that night, banished her innocence aforehand so that it did not lay before them like an unbreachable rampart. Keeping her firmly encircled he moved toward the bed, then stopped and stepped back a space, his decision hard-won and agonizing but somehow necessary. Taking one of her hands, he loosened her fingers from the grip on his tunic, then took a small, sharp knife from his belt.

LeClaire's eyes widened when she saw the blade, and her cheeks blanched when he lifted it. Before she had time to protest or even question him, he had gripped her index finger and made a slight prick there. Stunned, she gasped but could only stare at him in hurt and confusion as he held her hand over the bedding and squeezed the drops of blood upon the snowy linen sheets. Once done, he lifted her finger to his mouth and kissed the small injury.

"Now," he said softly, staring deep down into her bewildered eyes. "No one can say that the virgin's blood was not spilled this night."

He pulled the revealing silk more securely around her, then lifted her and tucked her into bed, deep under the coverlet where he could not be tempted by the sight of her shapely form silhouetted in firelight. He removed his own clothing slowly, piece by piece, folding each garment meticulously before setting it aside.

LeClaire felt disoriented at his strange behavior but could not seem to take her eyes from him as she always had before, could not turn from the sight of his flared shoulders, muscular chest and the curled hair that tapered down to a narrow waist. His muscles rolled beneath his sun-bronzed skin with each move, his strength visible with each flex, a strength well suited to offer everything a wife needed in a husband.

She wanted to touch him, to feel the physical evidence of attributes that went deeper than skin and bone, to burrow inside him and become a part of everything he was. She was not bold enough to stretch her hand out and follow her inclination, but her eyes devoured every inch of his handsome face to his broad sleek shoulders, then lower to the fitted chausses that rode low on his hips and boldly outlined his masculine form.

Equal portions of delight and trepidation shivered through her when he leaned over and brushed the hair back from her face, then placed a light kiss upon her forehead. Her breathing stalled as she braced herself to accept his presence in the bed, but he only gazed down at her a moment, his gray eyes unfathomable, then moved back a space and said, "Come to me when you are ready, LeClaire. I would not have you fearful in this bed, not this night or any other."

Relief washed through her like a cleansing tide, calming and renewing, until she finally realized the full extent of his words. Her eyes flared suddenly and she bolted up, then flung back the covers and sprang from the bed. She clutched the drape to her like a shield, looking for all the world as if he'd done her some great injustice.

" 'Tis not how it's done!" she said. "Do you mean to shame me, my lord? I am not *that* ignorant."

Borgia's eyes flared also, a mixture of surprise and more. She looked quite formidable and much too tempting in naught but the gossamer web of silk and her shining, indignant anger.

Feeling horribly ill-suited to the task, LeClaire could not think what she should do to convince him; there was naught in their past to prepare her for his caution. She had thought he would guide them in this, had never once conceived of the idea that he would be hesitant when he had always been so aggressive to take whatever he wanted.

Her eyes narrowed suddenly, lazy-lidded and sultry, as she drew from a hidden well within her, one empty of experience but brimming with instinct. Her fingers uncurled in the folds of her covering until it fell loose about her shoulders and dipped low in the back, the silken edge caught only upon the tips of her breasts in front.

"You wanted me well enough, my lord, when 'twas wrong. Do you mean not to have me now when 'tis right?" With more abandon than she ever thought possible, her fingers released the silk completely and it slithered slowly to the floor like a scattered wisp of cloud.

Her arms fell limp to her sides and she stood naked before him in nothing but the red-gold glory of her hair —small, pale, uncertain—but with the blazing conviction that she would be all things to him that a wife should be and would not be denied her own rights also.

Borgia was stunned and somehow humbled by the sight.

His gaze roamed appreciatively over her in amazement and pride as she stood unveiled before him. The firelight paled next to the beauty of her vivid hair as it spilled over her shoulders to her hips, framing a body that was slender and lush with a pure, innate sensuality that could not be imitated or enhanced. Lightning sizzled throughout him and his blood drummed rhythmically with his heavy heartbeat, expanding his desire to a painful and reckless level. Her cheeks flushed but still she made no attempt to cover herself.

"You need not do this," he rasped, "not until you are ready."

"Aye, I must." She was startled to see that this newness in her made him uneasy, as if someone had tipped the platform upon which he stood and he was forced to keep his footing or fall. She felt unbalanced herself but would not retreat from what she knew was right. The two of them had been made one in the eyes of the Church, the eyes of God; there was left only one thing to make it complete in the eyes of each other.

And she could not bear for this uncertainty to lay before them night after night. Her smile was so angelically innocent, it took a moment for him to see the sorcery in it.

"Be not afraid, my lord. I will be gentle with you. If I do aught to offend you, you need only bid me cease."

There was nothing innocent in his returning smile. In truth, it was so wholly wicked, she almost rued her boldness as an impetuous thing, even did it achieve the desired end. His arm lifted and the back of his hand brushed her cheek, then glided down her neck to her breast where he paused to feel the rapid thump of her heartbeat against his knuckles. His smoldering eyes never leaving hers, his other hand rose and his fingers spread wide upon her breastbone, then glided down her torso, soft as a child's wish, stirring as a gale-force wind.

With wonder and adoration he gazed at her, touching her with his eyes as gently as he did with his hands. And with mutual wonder she received both, marveling at the way her body quickened when his gaze swept her, when his fingers slid over her breasts and his thumbs circled the aureoles repeatedly until her insides grew heavy, her breathing shallow and her knees faint.

Her throat grew thick and tight; it was an effort to swallow. Strange new feelings rushed in at her from many directions—exhilarating, frightening, freeing. The pleasure was so intense it robbed her breath for the span of two impeded heartbeats, then rushed back fiery for two more. Her palms rose swiftly to cover his hands and she held him to her tightly for a moment, trying to reclaim her breath, then slid up his arms, marveling at the corded strength there, the contrast of pale skin against bronze. The tips of her fingers came alive, tingling, as she skimmed his sleek, vital flesh. Blood rushed to her extremities, curiously making her feel both weak and strong, and she moved to his powerful chest to tunnel through the mat of hair as if she had never touched him before. And she never had this freely, this aware, without guilt.

He wanted to touch her further also, badly, but checked the impulse to better enjoy her favors as she explored. Her palms flattened on his chest, then her nails raked lightly down to his abdomen, and he checked also the groan rising in his throat so as not to frighten her or cause her to retreat.

Her eyes followed the path her hands made over his wide chest and tight belly just above the thick delineation beneath his chausses until modesty got the better of her and her gaze flew back to his face, though her hands did not. She paused at the sides of his hips, feeling the texture of fine woolen, the slender brawn of fit muscle over bone beneath it, and Borgia fought the urge to take her hands and place them upon him elsewhere as well. A mad rush of desire claimed him, but he steeled himself against it to allow her the leisure of satisfying her curiosity at her own pace, her own discretion.

Her head dropped forward to press a kiss upon his heated skin, so innocent and sincere he was forced to draw a quick breath. "I've wanted to do this forever," she whispered, and the words coursed through him like molten fire both dangerous and compelling. Her mouth played moistly over his taut flesh, her lips and teeth over his flat nipples, and his burden grew tenfold until it became a heavy, unsatisfied ache. Her small hands grew fretful, telling, as they unconsciously fluttered over his sides and belly and thighs without direction, congealing the blood in his throat and lower, straining his resolve to a menacing and unpredictable urgency.

He grabbed her hands and brought them to his lips, conquering the frenzied rhythm of his heartbeat with supreme effort. With poignant gentleness he kissed each of her fingers separately, taking them one by one into his mouth, and did the things he wished to do to the whole of her—suckle and stroke and lightly bite every delicate inch of fragrant skin. Her eyes widened as they stared up at him, artless and unworldly, as she strove to find her way past the difficulty of intimacy. And he struggled with the need to do things quickly, to make it easier for them both, and the added need to let her find her own way beyond innocence and inhibition.

A sigh, sounding so much like desire, escaped her parted lips as she dropped her cheek to his chest and rolled it back and forth as if it comforted her to do so, her breath coming hot and sweet against his skin. She pulled her fingers from his lips, suffering keenly from the short separation, then ran them through his hair to the nape where she held tight and pulled her body into his, needing the complete union of flesh against flesh. Every particle of her that was not pressed to him felt dearth of humanity, lacking every element of life and the vitality necessary to sustain it. And she pressed harder, held tighter, trying awkwardly in her inexperience to merge with him or be absorbed into him.

"Would that I could hide deep inside you," she whimpered. And suddenly there was chaos inside Borgia, as if he himself did not know the way, for in truth he had never traveled it. There had been virgins before, young and eager servant girls who had come of age and were ready to please their handsome lord; his spoiled first wife who had wept and struggled as she thought she should and begrudged him every touch after.

But there had never been LeClaire, sweet and honest and giving, no maiden or mistress to prepare him for the selfless sacrifice of innocence despite the beating of a frightened heart. His hands found her shoulders and caressed her lightly, feeling the small tremors that shivered through her body. Her uncertainty almost managed to take the edge off his hunger, but it was impossible to tamp it down completely.

He bent to retrieve the silk drape from the floor, for her because she was modest, for him because he was too ready to banish that modesty in a rush that would cause her more pain than was necessary. But he could not force himself to cover her again, to hide away the beauty that had taken such courage to reveal. He bunched the fabric in his fist, then rubbed it slowly against her cheek, silk against silk, then her neck and shoulder and finally her rosy breast.

LeClaire struggled to remain standing when he glided the silk across her nipples but her knees threatened to fold beneath her. Her nails bit into his shoulders as she tried to hold herself aloft, but it was nearly impossible as he swirled the cloth back and forth over her sensitive flesh. Her knees trembled suddenly, violently, and her head dropped forward against his bracing chest, crushing the fabric between them. She felt his knotted fists at her midsection as her lips made a quick, clumsy journey over his shoulders and rib cage, wishing his arms would reach out and enfold her. Something desperate was rising within her, and she knew not how to offer him the same profound enjoyment he was giving her. Breathless and determined, she lifted her eyes to his.

"Be at ease, bratling," Borgia whispered at her fearful tenacity. His fist rose, then released the silk, and it floated over her shoulder, caught on the tender tip of her breast for an agonizing second, then fluttered past her thighs to puddle at her feet. Then Borgia's bare hands were upon her, so hot where the silk had been cool, so hard against her soft skin.

His expression grew grave as he looked into her eyes, and she knew the time had come and tried to compose herself, but he only lifted her high against his chest and stood motionless, cradling her in arms strong and secure under her knees and shoulders. She felt the warmth of the fire on her back and buttocks but it was naught compared to the heat his flesh generated against her breasts and thighs. She turned her face into his chest and inhaled his masculine scent, then touched his skin with her tongue because it was not enough just to feel him. She needed his taste as well.

His breath caught on a low groan and his muscles flexed, his hands tightening into steel fists, too aware of the tenuous grip he held on his passions. She tilted her head up to look upon his beautiful face and saw dark hunger there and more, a fierce control that he did not need, not now or ever with her.

Guileless in her spunk, she smiled. "I do not think 'tis done this way either."

With a roguish lift of his brow, he grinned down at her. " 'Tis done many ways. In time I will teach you all of them."

Firelight danced along his bronzed features, making him look both sinister and seductive, godlike and demon. Struck anew by his likeness to the Guardian, LeClaire's palm rose to cup his cheek and she told him things of her past, of a warrior angel sent to guard her who had looked like him.

If Borgia thought her words absurd, he did not show it, just enjoyed the rosy glow of hearth-flame upon her cheeks, the deeper color upon her lips and the warmth of her naked body nestled into his. His desire needed distance he could not endure physically, so he listened intently, restraining his need with a fierce control reflected only in his dark voice. "And what did you think of him?"

"Oh, I thought him wondrous fair," she said, intrepid and positive, though she knew he couldn't possibly believe her. "The most handsome being in all the universe, in fact. He was tall and strong and quite magnificent."

Borgia's brow lifted lazily. "So, you gave your heart to an angel?"

"Nay," she answered, smiling very sadly, very coyly. "You came and took all I owned, and I thought it a terrible betrayal that you had the same face as the one I trusted."

"Ah, I see."

A trill of gentle laughter followed his words, and LeClaire tipped her head back farther over his arm, her coppery curls spilling to the rushes, her succulent breasts straining against his chest and his endurance. "You do not believe a word of this, my lord."

"I cannot." His eyes sparkled like sunlight striking ice. "There is no one here to guard you but me, and I have not one single angelic thought in my head right now."

LeClaire's eyes glittered brilliantly as she looked at him. "But, my lord, what then is a maiden to do?"

"There is naught left to do, damoiselle," he said seriously, "but become a wife."

A tremor raced through her at his darkling tone. "Then show me how," she whispered, the words both steady and thick. "Show me how to be a wife."

"Aye," he whispered back, and his lips took hers, too fierce to be considered gentle, too gentle to be considered anything else.

His tongue penetrated her mouth and slid along the edges of her teeth, slowly, again and again, until she grew restless, needing so much more. She bit down lightly, then pulled him deeper into her mouth where her tongue dueled with his in ravenous delight and the breaths they exchanged grew hotter and faster and sweeter for their frenzy.

Something indefinable coiled taut and achy in her

lower belly. She made a whispered plea as her arms flew around his neck and she curled tightly into him until her bare middle pressed against his firm abdomen. Her breasts throbbed against the steady thunder of his heartbeat and she rubbed against and into him, twisting and turning to ease the agony that only increased with each movement of her body until she felt almost weepy.

He tore his lips from her and buried them in her neck, cinching his arms tighter to still her restive motion and the damage it was doing to his control. He would not take her here, standing inches from the bed, no matter how badly his body demanded it, no matter how ardently she seemed willing. By slow degrees he forced his hands to relax and he began stroking her lightly—her hair, her arms, her back—giving himself time to regain command of his senses.

His teeth nipped her shoulder, and she arched back, allowing him access to more of her. And he wanted so much more that he lowered her along the taut planes of his body, letting her feel his need through the cloth of his chausses to prepare her in some small way for the naked feel of him later. The gesture was pleasurable and intimidating to LeClaire, as exhilarating and dangerous as standing on the edge of a cliff, poised to fall or fly.

His hands, strong and supple, caressed her on places he had touched before, comforting and nonthreatening places, until his tame fondling was not enough to sustain the ardor she needed from him. Her own fingers grew bolder, firmer as they traced over the muscular slopes of his shoulders and upper arms, finding him sleek and smooth, then the firm pectoral ridges of his chest. When her nails raked his flat nipples and lightly scored his abdomen, she heard his breath catch and her eyes flew to his, but he only smiled tender encouragement and continued to caress her more carefully then she did him, but with a brutal restraint that threatened to falter.

It was destined not to last, for their goal could not be

reached by temporal means. His fondling changed slowly, grew more assertive, more far-reaching, and Le-Claire's breath skipped in rhythm to a new heartbeat, an anxious and excited one. His lips took hers again, softly at first, then seemed to abandon all complaisance and devoured her. His tongue swirled with hers, then was gone, and she moaned until he plunged inside again, imitating the eagerness the rest of him felt, filling her mouth and her being with sweet, moist frustration. His kiss was so demanding and consuming, she was lost in the power and beauty of it and never knew when he removed his chausses. She only knew that suddenly there was no material barrier left between them and she could feel him, hot and full, pressed against her, and his hands were now as ravaging as his mouth.

She strained on tiptoe to put her arms around his neck, needing the mind-numbing oblivion of his kiss and the sheltering cover of his embrace. But when her flesh met his entirely a fire started low in her belly, then spread to encompass all of her, and her nervousness and inhibitions dwindled to cinders beneath a need that had lain dormant all her life.

She had only thought she wanted him before, but this new thing was overpowering, enthralling, consuming. And she was glad she had waited until they were wed to feel the full raw power of it, for she never would have been able to deny him if she had known it before.

An earthy moan escaped her throat as she strained into him, needy and restless, her hands moving anxiously over his back and sides, even down to his buttocks where she felt no shame in touching him. His muscles bunched beneath her fingers and she curled her nails into his flesh just as the rest of her body longed to do.

Borgia's hands were everywhere upon her, but more slowly, more controlled, determined the insanity she provoked would not claim him too soon. He caught her beneath the hips and lifted her to better accommodate his height, to better run his lips and tongue and teeth over the silken column of her throat, to feel the pulse in her neck pound out a cadence of desire that equaled or surpassed his own.

Driven by instinct alone, her legs went around his waist as her arms tightened on his neck, and she caught the delicious taste of passion on his lips when he took a quick harsh breath, and she drank from him as if he were a silver chalice brimming with nectar. His hand lifted to slide through her hair and he buried his fingers there as he eased back upon the bed, pulling her atop him. LeClaire gasped but had little need for modesty as he spread her hair around them like a concealing cloak, then caught her face in his hands to sup from her as she had him, in enchantment, in wonder, and with a rising passion that threatened to overwhelm them both.

So giving was she, so rich and sweet a confection, he wanted to consume all of her at once, but would not bloat himself with his urgency. So his hands stroked her slender back and hips as he trailed kisses down her neck to her shoulder and inhaled the scent of her as if it alone was the sustenance he needed to survive. His tongue drew sublime patterns on her fragrant skin, while his fingers traced the line of her spine to the cleft of her buttocks and he dipped low to test her readiness for a moment so brief she might not have noticed it had not every place he touched seemed bathed in fire. Again and again he repeated the excruciating seduction until she grew restless above him, hungry for more than the light touch of his fingers and gentle abrasion of his lips.

With every sweep of his tongue, every nip of his teeth, every tantalizing journey of his hands, her breath grew fast and troubled, her entire body anxious, and she tried to fill the needy emptiness in her with the salty taste of his skin, the feel of his muscular strength beneath her fingers. But nothing was enough to relieve the desperate tension growing tighter within her.

Borgia sensed her sensual panic. It was there in her frantic, searching eyes; in the restive stroke of small hands that didn't quite know where to rest and in the frenzied shifting of her body. "Shhh," he breathed to soothe her, and she gentled slightly at the sound, but her heart was not wont·to follow. It beat against her ribs like wind-swept wings ascending high and fluttery in a storm.

The storm was intensifying inside him as well, and Borgia rolled them to their sides and pulled her flush against him, his hand firm on her lower back, his lips incredibly tender against her neck. He gripped her tightly for fragmented seconds as if he did·not dare do more, and LeClaire could not imagine what he thought he was sheltering her from. What was it that she did not know, that could not be made right if they just let themselves be together as divinely intended? She felt his heart rate escalate as her thigh lifted to cover his and her palm cupped his lean cheek to turn his mouth back to hers, but he pulled away slightly, his serrated breath hot on her sensitized flesh.

"Nay, wait," he warned, struggling to bring control to their love play. Her wounded eyes flayed him and he sighed against her lips. "I but need a moment, LeClaire. I would not give you more pain than you can bear."

"Pain?" she whispered in a raw voice. "How can you think to give me more pain when I am already in such agony?"

Borgia's control shattered like gleaming black crystal, and he rolled her beneath him. "Ah, LeClaire," he groaned, fighting to retain some small bit of sanity. "You cannot know what you are saying. To rush you would—" His words snared in his throat as she arched beneath him, ardent and desperate and unwilling to listen. "There is so much more . . . I can make it easier—"

Again his words were sliced into by her knees spreading and her body arching against his. He was helpless to do anything but answer her. Fighting for mastery of his senses even as he fit himself to her, he cupped her face between his hands, his eyes pleading darkly for time, demanding furiously that there be no regrets.

She only had one as her hands gripped his hips and her body rose to greet his penetrating thrust. She regretted the sharp cry and the look of pain on her face that caused his to grow ashen the moment their bodies met and joined.

"Nay!" she whispered fiercely and clutched him when he would have eased back. "Do not leave me."

Her agonizingly tight body closed around him in searing heat and moisture, and his mouth crashed back to hers, in joy, in defeat, while his body drove deeper and deeper into the sanctuary she offered until he possessed her completely, was possessed by her in turn, and became gripped in a blinding flash of desire that strove to spend itself too unforgivably quick, too irreparably merciless.

His passion-ravaged face was beautiful to behold as she watched him, and she clung to the sight as a buffer against the physical rending. She clenched her teeth to keep from crying out again, for there was nothing in her that did not welcome him. The pain and foreignness of having him inside, stretching and filling her past what it seemed her body could endure, were hers alone to bear and did naught to negate the feeling of right that soothed her initial shock.

But he saw it all, through passion-glazed eyes he saw every small flinch and dull twinge. His jaw clenched and he tensed above her, then forced himself to stop, his full weight covering her like a consecration. He gripped her so tightly she could hardly breathe, but she ignored the painful joining to glory in the triumphant blending of their bodies, the sweetness and joy of having him so totally a part of her.

He lay rigid for a time, his face buried in her neck,

until his breathing steadied and his heartbeat slowed, then drew back to stare at her. His faint, self-condemning smile made her heart tumble low down so swiftly the piercing ache was but a memory.

"Art a witch and temptress," he breathed raggedly. She smiled up at him, blushing, and he kissed the hot color on each cheek, then her lips, before lifting his head, his look troubled. "Art well, LeClaire?"

"Oh, aye," she said, feeling timorous and tearful, but not knowing why. "Art done?"

Done? When his body was screaming for fulfillment? When there was so much more he wanted to do, so much more she deserved than his lust run awry? "Do you want me to be?"

Her eyes were stark and enlarged, her cheeks flushed, and he could see this was too difficult for her. He eased to his side and rolled her to face him, wanting to offer her more than his bestial hunger but also the compassion and gentleness she needed to adapt to his physical possession. He luxuriated in her warmth and tightness, wanting to stay forever a part of her in the way no other man had, but he was too aware that this was new for her. When he withdrew, she cried out in dismay and confusion, and it was all he could do to steal himself against the hurt in her voice.

He retrieved a damp cloth and, to her embarrassment, tenderly bathed away the evidence of her innocence, pressing the cool compress to her while speaking endearments against her lips until her blushing and stammering eased. Abandoning the cloth, he wrapped her in his arms, breast to chest, thigh to thigh, and his mouth made a hot passage from her neck to her shoulder, before returning to plant the sweetest kiss upon her lips.

LeClaire, lost in his concerned eyes, tried to ignore the awful restlessness within her, the unfulfilled yearning she could not understand. She wished he would kiss her as before, move with her and in her, anything but the frightful stillness that seemed stranger now that his body had joined with hers. She dropped her eyes to his chest and whispered, "I am a wife now. Will we get a babe from this, do you think?"

Her innocence was endearing, and he would not shame her. "Sometimes it takes many tries to get a babe."

LeClaire's gaze lifted back to his. "I should like a child," she said, "no matter how many tries it takes."

Borgia's eyes flared like inflamed charcoal and his body responded in kind. His fingers tunneled through the fine hair at her temples and he brought her face so close his whispered words fell across her moist lips. "I wish you had let me ready you more. 'Twould have been better for you."

"I did naught," LeClaire said, affronted. "I submitted like any good wife."

Borgia smiled dryly and tipped her face up to nip her chin. "You submitted too well, damoiselle. I have not known you for such a greedy seductress. You shattered all my restraint and had me randy as a beardless boy."

LeClaire laughed at the silliness of such an idea and tweaked a hair on his chest. "My lord, I fear you've gone daft."

"Aye," he sighed, completely insane wanting her, so savagely ready to ravish her that she must know it as well. His fingers walked down her spine to the small of her back, and she wiggled against him, cleaving his breath and the groan that followed.

"Be still," he urged, but his own hands betrayed him as they began sculpting her body. Shaping and re-shaping, they could not seem to fill themselves with enough of her to satisfy him. They caressed her shoulders and arms, slid down along her sides to her hips, where he massaged slender muscles grown tight with expectation. Not once did she turn away from him or grow sheepish, and her goodness was like a beacon guiding him farther, drawing him closer. He cupped her breasts and stroked her until she grew flushed and anxious, until the tips stood hard and hurting against his palm. His mouth lowered, demanding its share to ease her pain and caused more blissful agony than she knew existed.

Her small, breathless moans were like music, filling him with a sweet hot fervor, each soft pant a supplication for him to partake further. There was a great need in him to go slowly, to make it right for her, to guide and manipulate her in the ways he knew so well but could not seem to conjure.

He found his past experiences were nothing when in her arms, as if he too were callow and untried. He groped for the means to tempt and titillate her body into welcoming him, but she welcomed him already. So he brought nothing of the old and tainted machinations as he readied her, no strategy or artifice as he touched every supple inch of her. He just came to her as she did him, in simplicity and honesty and instinct.

She received him as he did her and caressed him in kind—tender and forceful, gentle and intoxicating. There was almost nothing she would not do, almost no part of him she would not touch or taste or glory in. Her eyes and hands journeyed over him as well, delighting in the feel of his solid strength and the dark intensity of his visage. His breath came fast and harsh when her fingers swept down his belly and she was inspired to travel lower still to the thicket of fine coarse hair beneath. An inkling of shyness remained but she so reveled in the fierce expression on his face as he stared back at her that she went farther still, stroking the tight muscles of his lower abdomen. Her fingers inadvertently brushed against him and he went quiet as death, his body taut and suspended between agony and ecstasy, the concentration so acute on his face that she feared she had erred. Her heart sank and she snatched her hand back.

"Nay, touch me," he said roughly, and returned her

hand to him. "I've wanted this for so long, but 'tis difficult, LeClaire. The pleasure is so sharp when you touch me, I feel much like a madman. I would not endanger you." Then his mouth took hers so she would know the harsh truth of his words, even as his hand urged hers to caress him, and he knew himself demented to encourage her when he was so close to the edge.

Too soon the edge was crumbling away beneath him and he grabbed her curious fingers and pulled them up to kiss each lightly, his breath ragged and quick on the moist tips. Then his mouth found her neck and shoulder, and her own breath grew rapid when she realized what he would do next.

Finally, finally, he eased her to her back, and she went gratefully, opening herself to him. But he lingered at the hollow of her throat building her desire until she thought she would weep, then did cry out as his lips finally found her breast and suckled until she was bending into him for more. He moved between her thighs and she sighed with relief, but he only continued to pay homage to each breast, whispering dark, seductive words over the tips between each hot pull of his lips until she was twisting frantically beneath him.

He gripped her hips firmly, savage and greedy and wanting more. His hand slid down between them, and he watched her eyes widen and her cheeks blush hotly as he sought her copper curls.

"My lord, I do not think—" Then his fingers moved lower still, splicing her words, as his other hand kneaded the contracted muscles of her thighs. "Nay, please," she pleaded, so embarrassed, so breathless.

His eyes bore into hers, molten gray into feverish blue, and he continued to massage the tight muscles of her buttocks and thighs until she relaxed and let him have his way. But his way was a deeply intimate exploration that caused her to tense and rear up when he touched the hot center of her. His fingers flowed over her moist flesh repeatedly until she was alternately melting and arching with each broken moan, gasping out unintelligible pleas for him to end the torment.

Then he was writhing as well, caught up and swept away in her sensual frenzy, grabbing her hips and entering her with a brusque urgency that allowed no caution.

Led by a knowledge as fundamental as breathing, as essential as life itself, she wrapped her legs around his waist and heaved up against him, offering herself fully, demanding he give more of himself in return. His breathing was harsh as he held her tightly, allowing her body time to adjust and expand, but she asked for no succor save his filling presence, this one acute moment in time that she was destined for.

"Go easy," he urged, but she arched again, needing him so, lost forever in the intense look on his face and the breathless sense of exhilaration it gave her. There was a wondrous desire in her to feel his abandon again, to have him move in that alien and familiar way that matched the throbbing of her heartbeat. Her body convulsed around him at the thought, causing his breath to hiss between his teeth. "Ah, Christ, LeClaire . . ."

She answered him in the only way she knew—the self-less giving of love. Whatever benevolent intentions he still possessed drowned in the moist, constricting submission of her body. His deep groan coursed through her, kindling brighter the keen-edged passion, and she contracted her muscles again and pressed against him, holding him as tightly within as he held her without.

His mouth captured hers, slashing across her soft swollen skin, and his words came harsh and grainy against her lips, a warning, a plea. "You need only tell me if I do aught to hurt you."

"You could never," she whispered with such conviction that it plunged him headlong over the edge of whatever residual sanity remained.

Bathed in the light of her offering, Borgia was forced

to give all as he thrust within her, each hidden and unreachable part of himself. Everything he might have held back or reserved faded to nothingness beneath her generosity. The foundation of his control shattered when her cries came unashamed, and he plunged again and again in a timeless rhythm as graceful as a dance, as forceful as the storm consuming them.

And she joined him in the tempest, rising beneath him with each deep penetration until her body awakened fully to the fiery grandeur of their union. Ancient mysteries unfurled, throbbing, and everything within her coalesced and centered on one feverish point, then blossomed and expanded, reaching and straining higher and hotter until her head arched back deep into the bedding, her cries filled the chamber and her inner being shattered like starburst into a million glittering fragments.

She rose against him one last time, calling his name, fusing them so completely they were no longer two but one, one blending with the other, one in purpose and in need, one half made whole.

Borgia felt her ecstasy close around him as his own rushed toward its momentous end, calling forth things he had never known or experienced or even been—a part of his existence hidden and dormant but waiting, waiting for her, for this, for them. And he lost that part of himself as he joined her in the rapturous fury and gained more than he could comprehend in the unbridled blessing of the merging of two souls.

The result was so powerful when their bodies locked in the final conflagration, so mighty and potent and driven, it burned everything from Borgia like a purifying pyre. And he rose from the ashes reborn.

Dawn crept quietly as a kiss into the lord and lady of Ravenwood's bedchamber. Borgia opened his eyes to find LeClaire huddled beside him, her chin on her updrawn knees, the silk drape she'd worn the night before clutched to her chest. Her cheeks shone pink as an over-ripe peach. He eased up beside her and took a lock of her hair, rubbing the silkiness between his fingers, and wondered if she felt as fragile as she looked. He had expected this reaction the night before.

"Regrets?" he asked coolly, his icy control dropping down smoothly to veil any hint of betrayal and need.

She darted a glance at him beneath her lashes, then looked quickly away as her color deepened.

"LeClaire," he began, but she suddenly rounded on him like a playful puppy until he was toppled to his back in a tangle of bedclothes and she sat astride his belly.

She held up her poor, abused finger and waggled it in his face. "You need not have done that," she accused prettily. "What could you have been thinking?"

For a moment, he was taut and unyielding, and she saw the darkling coldness in his eyes. Then he grinned like a lazy cat beneath her, but his tone was serious. "To save you from me."

"What a silly man you are betimes," she chided softly. "Why ever would you think that?"

"You were afraid."

She shrugged guiltily. "I but needed to be shown the way of things. You cannot fault a maiden her insecurities."

"I faulted you nothing, LeClaire. I merely strove to make it easier."

"The great Silver Lion is a coward," she said, then dropped her mouth to his ear to whisper what she would never have been able to say looking him in the eye. "Easier? I wanted it every bit as hard as I got it, my lord."

A great heave beneath her sent her tumbling to her back, and LeClaire giggled outrageously as she scrambled from the bed and dashed into the antechamber, hiding her embarrassed face behind her fingers. Borgia would come after her, she knew, it was one of the things she loved most about him. He had never really let her hide from herself.

The thought drew her to a jarring stop, and Borgia swept her up quickly from behind to keep from plowing into her. He turned her to face him and whatever he thought to say died on his lips at her wide-eyed, bewildered look.

"What did we last night?" she whispered.

Borgia smiled, faintly bemused. "Do you not know? Come, damoiselle, let me refresh your memory—"

But she shook her head, her eyes fierce and direct. "What did we in yon bed? Say it, Borgia."

He inwardly retreated a space from the emotional demands of her words and chose his own very carefully. "You know what we did, bratling. The same thing we are like to do in many more places."

"Say it," she said, unrelenting.

Borgia did not back down this time, just gripped her more tightly, gave her an arched look and said oh, so skillfully, "We made love, LeClaire."

Her heart was in her eyes as she smiled sadly. "One day, my lord, you will say that and mean it."

"I mean it now," he returned, but there was an awful emptiness within him at the words, a dark hollow place devoid of understanding. His lips sought hers to banish the vague, eerie feelings and the doom that seemed to accompany it, and he found comfort in her answering gift.

LeClaire sighed as she gave herself up to his demanding kiss and discovered there were indeed more places than just yon bedstead to share the love in her heart with the passion of his body. There were floors and walls and fireside chairs. But through it all there was only LeClaire seeking what he did not know, and Borgia seeking to fill the void within him with the goodness of her.

She found rapture in his arms; he knew fulfillment in hers. But relief was a fleeting thing, satiation so tempo-

ral, and he sought her again and again to keep the emptiness at bay and the awful sense of foreboding that
followed. Her cries of completion rang out as he filled
her with himself. But it was somehow not enough.

He had wanted her almost from the first and had her
now in more ways than he had dared to hope. Lush and
abandoned, uninhibited and even playful she gave herself to him without reserve or restraint or caution.
Though she blushed with each new thing and teased him
for a depraved knave, she trusted him to teach and guide
her, never growing missish or ashamed.

And as she gave all of herself with a joy unequaled by
any he had ever known, Borgia realized what he had
never understood, what he did not know how to reconcile now. He was an incomplete man.

26

The hall was deathly silent. Servants moved like wraiths to complete their tasks, their footsteps slow, their hearts burdened. Their lady lay wasting abovestairs in the grip of a terrible fever, and there seemed to be naught anyone could do to forestall the inevitable. In the past month a mysterious illness had come upon Le-Claire, striking her down with brutal and debilitating efficiency, and no leech or physician had been able to help.

The lord had sent for them all when his lady had been struck down, from village to nearby township and even to London, he had summoned all who knew anything of the healing arts. The King's own surgeon had been called in, but he too had left like the others, shaking his head in sorrow, at a loss to do more than offer solicitous words that meant naught against LeClaire's increasing pain. She only lingered now, they feared, thin and dissipated and holding onto life by a slim thread of determination.

Agnes heard a chamber door close as she stirred the contents of the common pot in the predawn darkness and cast a jaundiced eye at the stairs. Maire had been hysterical much of the time, raving at them all to do more, Krya spent hours in prayer and Aurel simply continued to tend to her sister with utmost care and dedication. But it was the lord of Ravenwood to whom Agnes cast her bitter thoughts.

He was weathering his wife's decline with a cruel,

dark silence that was more frightening to the people than his ranting would have been. Most times he stayed by his wife's side, but when duty called he went readily and was dangerously efficient in strangling any problem set before him. The servants sensed he resented being approached but at times there was nothing else they could do. And they feared him as they had not since the early days when their lady had been hale and hardy, a strong buffer against his wrath, a consoling peacemaker who soothed them through the transition. They had mourned when she left for Normandy, then rejoiced when she returned to take her rightful place again as their lady. They had not known their joy would be so short-lived.

Hannah tiptoed down the stairs to the great hall and shook her head sadly at Agnes's unasked question. LeClaire's voice as frail as her body, their lady continued to assure them she would be well soon, but none could look upon her now or stare fully into her comforting, optimistic eyes, for fear she would see the hopelessness in their own. Thus, they all went about their duties with heavy hearts, waiting and waiting for the fateful end, their voices already carrying the somberness of a funeral dirge.

Agnes latched onto Hannah's arm and cringed back against the wall as Borgia approached, icy cold in his self-control, whatever emotions he was feeling tightly leashed. Nearly a month had passed since LeClaire's illness, but if he was in agony over his wife's condition, they had seen no evidence of it, no panic or tears or the fits of temper they thought common behavior for a man consumed in grief. Other than calling every healer of any consequence, he had done naught but stay by her bed to show his consideration, and the servants feared, in the dreadfully remote way he had, that soon he would not even do that if it grew too tiresome.

Agnes sent Hannah a pained, resentful look as the lord drew closer, and they both wondered what lay beneath his chest. There was certainly no real heart there that he could be so unconcerned. What would happen to them when their lady, the only one who had ever understood the unpredictable warlord, was gone?

Desperate to escape notice, the two maids slipped back into a darkened alcove and lowered their eyes to the rushes when Borgia passed, his feet striking loudly on the stone passageway that led to the chapel, the only sound to echo in the eerie quietness that had descended upon the hall. They heard the chapel door open then slam shut, rattling the costly stained-glass panes the lord had imported from Rome for the window openings.

"What's he doin' in there?" Agnes whispered, her eyes wide and fearful. They both could hear muted sounds at the end of the long passageway but nothing significant.

"Mayhaps he's gone to pray," Hannah whispered back with more hope than either of them felt. They both knew unless coaxed by LeClaire the lord never went into the chapel he'd had repaired for his wife. Before they had time to gather their wits for further speculation, he was strolling past them again, his eyes as dark and forbidding as the pits of hell.

Glancing furtively at each other, the two servants waited for him to go back up the stairs, then hurried toward the chapel. Oddly fearful, they eased open the door and stepped cautiously inside, then stopped dead still and crossed themselves. The sacrilege that met their bleak stares made them sick with shock. Tears welled up in Hannah's eyes, then rolled down her cheeks. "Oh, saints preserve us, Agnes. He's gone mad."

For LeClaire, Borgia had renovated the chapel to reflect her unique beauty when she went there to say morning prayers. There was naught in the room that was not the finest testament to man's ingenuity and workmanship—altar clothes of the richest silk and linen, chalices of gold and silver studded with expensive jewels, the rare stained glass in the windows carried to Ravenwood at great peril and cost.

But now it was all in shambles. A golden chalice had been hurled through one of the many-hued windows and light shattered the room, striking prisms in discordant bursts of color from the litter of broken glass. The altar had been cruelly overturned, its vestments scattered like rubbish, carved wooden benches shoved aside at random.

The beautiful little chapel had been thoroughly, silently and maniacally destroyed.

Shaking, Hannah bent to pick up an altar cloth, then fell to her knees amid the rubble. "Oh, Agnes, what are we to do?"

Numb with the agony of watching LeClaire's life slowly dwindle away, Borgia stood next to their bed as dawn broke fully over the horizon and light streamed through the windows in luminous glory, bathing the room in the colors of sunrise, the colors of LeClaire.

Trembling, his hand reached out to lift one of her curls, but it lay limp and lifeless against his palm. His fingers closed around it, tight and tighter still, as if he could force luster back into the wasted red-gold locks.

A slender hand covered his. "M . . . M'lord," Aurel pleaded softly.

Borgia cut his eyes to his wife's sister, battling the urge to fling Aurel's solicitous hand off. She could not comfort him. He wished he felt grateful that she tried. With excruciating pain he released the lock of LeClaire's hair and gently slid his hand from beneath Aurel's. "Go to Roger," he whispered. "I'll stay with her this morn."

Aurel nodded and turned to go but paused at the door, struggling to put voice to the words that needed to be said. "M'lord," she began, her tone rusty but firm. "H . . . have you considered—"

"I have considered naught," he returned forcefully to

sever the flow of words he did not want to hear. "Go, please." Aurel nodded and silently left the room.

Borgia eased down on the bed and took LeClaire into his arms, cradling her in his lap. Feverish and suffering, she turned her cheek into his chest and tried to speak, the gesture so weak it severed his heart before she drifted off once again in delirium.

"Shhh," he breathed, hurting so for her he did not think he could bear it, did not think his heart could endure one more second of her suffering without exploding in his chest. She was so frail now, her breath so shallow, he could hardly feel her pulse. The child within her was not well set, the surgeon had said. It had sickened her, made her too weak to fight off the fever.

Borgia knew it had all come full circle now—his manipulation, his selfishness, his greed. He had wanted Ravenwood at any cost and he had been victorious. He had wanted her the same way. This then was the price he would pay?

Price? He had spent a small fortune on the chapel he had just desecrated in his crazed anger, would spend another one to repair it. He had not meant to defile it, had just found himself there in her sanctuary, her retreat —a place she was no longer strong enough to visit. And his dark, grieving fury had erupted, as if by thrashing a place so special to her it would somehow bring her a rescuer or purge his barbarous anger. But his evil had brought no satisfaction, no relief, and no help. Nay, his price would not be material cost but the dark, cold violence in his spirit, an eternal hatred and raging bitterness that he could even now feel consuming him without the light of LeClaire's love to banish it. He would be destroyed. His heart would still beat, his breath would not falter, but his life was forfeit without her.

With shaking hands, he brushed her hair back from her face, then flung his head back and shouted to the heavens in defiance, in desperation. "Come to me!" he demanded, his face ravaged by weeks of vigilance. "Come to me and explain this debacle of human injustice! You are her God; she trusted You! Why have You abandoned her?"

His answer was only the wind as it moaned through the window hides, tormenting him with the sounds of a keep awakening to daylight, the sounds of life. Damning the world for its vitality when his was in decay, Borgia dropped his head to LeClaire's chest and let the agony take him.

"*Ah, I see you have finally come, demanding to be heard,*" came an icily satirical voice from the depths of light at the foot of the bed, "*when you have never been wont to listen.*"

Borgia jerked his head up quickly to face the voice and saw a specterlike vision rise up before him in blinding white raiment with a warrior's strength, a warrior's presence.

But the face was his own.

He neither gasped nor cringed back, though his entire being felt rent by the force of the image. "Who are you?" he asked coldly, steeling everything within him against what he suddenly feared, suddenly knew—that he, with all his strength and power and wealth, was only mortal and now faced the finite conqueror, Death. He swallowed hard, braced and held LeClaire tighter to him as if he could protect her. "Do you come for her?"

The vision only hovered in taunting silence, magnificent and ghostlike before him, omnipotent in his unearthly appearance. Borgia chuckled bitterly at his reflection, ironically not knowing whether he faced demon or angel, damnation or hope. "You cannot have her, do you hear? Go back from whence you came."

"*Ah, but I cannot,*" the image crooned silkily, then added with lethal force. "*Who are you to command me, Borgia of Ravenwood? Who are you to demand aught of me?*"

It took everything in Borgia not to shrivel at the voice; he'd never felt so impotent, so worthless. His eyes wandered quickly around the room, but everything had receded in shadow save for that which hovered before him. "Who are you?" he shot back as if to retain some piece of his authority. Yet, he knew even as he stood his ground for pride's sake that if the Being meant for him to grovel for LeClaire's life he would do it and easily—

"Oh, nay!" the vision laughed softly, cruelly. "Think you that your piddling pleas mean aught to me? Think you that you can beg or barter to stay my hand? What have you that I could possibly want?"

"Take another," Borgia rasped, sick with dread, powerless to appease this cruel likeness. "Take me, but spare her. She does not deserve this."

"You?" the vision inquired softly. "How absurd that you could think yourself worthy to take her place." He paused a moment, his eyes full of compassion but his voice so horribly mocking. "You thought to teach her so much when you arrived here. But you never understood her, never understood what moved her to such devotion or the simple uncomplicated faith that is the essence of her. You wanted her world-wise as you are, as if that is knowledge. You wanted her to taste and feel and see things through your jaded eyes, as if that is understanding. Hers was the song of the angels, but you disdained her for that and would have stripped her of the beauty of her innocence and replaced it with a robe of filth. She brought you love; you gave only your carnal self."

"Nay," Borgia gasped, frantic now at the undeniable truth. "Mayhaps at one time, but not now. I swear it. I do return her love—"

The Guardian looked at the man sadly, and his eyes held centuries of injustice, hatred, bigotry and fear. "You know not the pure, unselfish meaning of the word. If you did, you would let her go." Borgia shook his head and his hand fumbled at the side of the bed for his sword hilt as if he would fight, though he knew in his mind and heart it was useless to battle an illusion. The angel shook his head and said fatally, "Let her go."

"Nay," Borgia rasped lowly, everything in him constricted into a painful knot. "Nay, you cannot ask it of me." Faced with his own self-need, his own self-greed, he could only stare back at his counterpart in loathing and fear, knowing he could never let her go, that he could not spend the rest of his worthless life without her. But he knew not how to stop this reaper from taking her. "Who are you!" he demanded again.

The Guardian nodded his gilded head and spread his arms wide. The beauty of his raiment changed suddenly, gruesomely, to a shimmering, greedy, blood-dripping red. "Behold thyself."

Borgia only stared back, his shoulders stiff with defiance, his entire body held taut against the tremors seizing him. He wanted to howl like a wounded animal, to release his violence until it destroyed the destroyer, but he only managed to rasp out, "Nay, you cannot have her," then screamed with more force, "You cannot ask it of me!" He gripped LeClaire tighter as if to prove his futile words and buried his head in the hollow of her neck.

LeClaire whimpered and Borgia awoke with a start. His head lifted slowly from her chest and he glanced around the room frantically, searching and searching for that which he could not countenance. Disconcerted, he realized the day was well advanced. Shadows were deepening as the sun waned to dusk, and a slight chill pervaded the air. He glanced back down at his wife and his heart stumbled at the transparency of her skin, the lines of pain around her eyes and mouth, the breathing that had grown shallow and more labored.

"Stay with me, LeClaire," he begged, scorched by the emotion he had profaned in the past, so torn by it now he would never again doubt its validity. The awful emptiness she had filled over the past few months, the darkness she had vanquished with the purity of her love was creeping back on him like an insidious curse. "You must fight this, LeClaire, we'll fight this together." He spread her hair around them, an aegis, a shield, his body tensed as if preparing for battle.

She moaned, a painful tearing sound, and it ripped through him until his throat contracted in denial, in defiance, and he held her tighter as if he might keep her by force, feeling the searing agony of the two emotions he had never thought would be his undoing—a fear so profound it was debilitating, a love so complete it was all. His grip tightened and LeClaire whimpered even more horribly with the pain.

Everything in Borgia shattered.

"Do something!" he cried out at the empty room. "I pray You be merciful and ease her suffering!"

But there was naught save the echo of a nightmare to taunt him. *Let her go.*

"I cannot," he choked. "By all that is holy, You cannot ask it of me."

He pulled her into him more gently and rocked her as if he could forestall the moment by sheer determination and the tenderness she had always given him. Turning her wan face to his, he felt what she must have felt so long ago—helpless, insecure and frustrated to the point of insanity—the choices in her life stolen from her with a vengeance until she could do naught but go with the relentless tide or be drowned in its portentous depths. And he remembered the strength with which she had held herself together, when he himself was crumbling now.

"Forgive me," he whispered against her feverish brow. "Forgive me, LeClaire, for never knowing or seeing or understanding the love you held for the people, the love you taught me."

Her lashes fluttered but she did not awaken from the dark abyss that consumed her. "I love you, bratling," he whispered, knowing that he always had, perhaps from the very first, but had been too blind and self-centered to recognize anything so simple, so elemental, so easy. So very, very easy. He shook her lightly, desperate for her to know it as well. "Aye, I do love you."

There was no response, nothing at all but her labored breathing and the unsteady thump of a feeble pulse beneath her dry, hot skin. Borgia pressed her face to his chest and frantically pleaded with Providence to spare her, but LeClaire cried out in delirium with the relentless suffering and it tore at him like a flaming hot sword. For everything he had been able to do in his life, everything he had been able to conquer or accomplish or achieve, he would not be able to do the most important. He would not be able to hold her.

He stared down at her pale face, his heartbeat impeded, and he knew then did he live to see a thousand empty wretched years, he would regret the one selfless act of his life, but he could do nothing else. To live without her would be hell, but to live with her, her body wracked by constant pain would be far worse. The violent hatred, rage and bitterness swelled within him like a black storm, then slowly drained away, leaving behind only the hollow, lonely shell that would be his lifetime purgatory.

"Aye," he whispered brokenly, "if You can ease her pain, I give her unto You. Guard and keep her well." Then his head dropped slowly to hers, and he wept as he had not in his lifetime for a precious life wasted, for the child she would never bear him and for all the empty agonizing years ahead. In complete desolation, he wept for his love.

LeClaire's lashes fluttered open, and she felt a deep abiding peace, a depth of serenity she had never known, though it seemed she must have been striving for it her entire life. She smiled softly and turned her head, but the sight that met her was staggering. Borgia's face lay near hers, for her head was upon his shoulder, but there was naught of the man she knew in the visage before her. His cheeks were gaunt, bearded by two days' stubble, and streaked by dried tracks of moisture. His clothing was stale, wrinkled and turned all askew.

Merciful Father, she had never seen him so unkempt!

"My lord," she said, appalled and frightened as she shook him.

Borgia's eyes flew open, taking in all surrounding him with a quick, frantic glance, then settled upon LeClaire. She pressed a hand to his brow, concerned that he had come down with the fever that had ravaged her, but he gripped her fingers tightly and pressed them to his lips, his eyes stark, then he caressed her face with a mixture of fear and awe. With wonder, his fingers moved over every inch of her face and upper body as if he had never touched her before or might never do so again.

"I love you, LeClaire," he said, his voice raspy with the rapid beat of his heart.

She smiled, bemused and also relieved that he felt cool to her touch, though his eyes still appeared feverish.

"As I love you, my lord. Art well?"

"Aye," he whispered, as if fearful of saying it too loudly. He gripped her forearms and set her back a space to better look at her, his limbs quivering as if he'd run a great distance or fought a great battle. His eyes traveled over every inch, noting the healthy glow on her cheeks, the clarity in her blue eyes, and he pulled her back swiftly within the circle of his arms, afraid to feel the triumph beginning to course hotly through his veins. His gaze went around the room, searching and searching, but there was nothing before him but a shimmering radiance as blinding as the mist in his eyes, as warm as the sudden soft and grateful smile upon his lips.

The chamber was bathed in sunlight; it streamed through the embrasures as if the heavens had poured forth its most brilliant blessing. And with it came the song, so perfect, so clear, a hosanna of the highest magnitude with the simplicity of a breeze through the trees. He had heard it a thousand times, yet he had never really heard it at all.

LeClaire stirred in his arms, and Borgia's gaze shot down to her. "Listen, do you hear it?" he said, the light falling over them like a mantle in rainbow hues.

She smiled at his strange look, then laughed, the sound strong and growing stronger still. "Fear not, my lord, 'tis but the wind."

"Nay," he said, a thousand arias in his heart. "Never think it, LeClaire. 'Tis the angels' song."

Epilogue

Replete, she lay in his arms, feeling the thunder of his heartbeat slow to a gentle thudding. As so often over the past five months, his hand rested on her rounded belly, feeling the miracle of new life stir within her.

"Art so small," he said, his continual concern both a bane and a blessing to her.

"Big enough, I imagine," she said to ease him. "Aurel has been safely delivered of a fine healthy son. I can do no less." She laughed softly, wholly content in his arms. "No doubt there will be scores of babes one day to fill our halls. Maire runs Bryson a merry chase, flirting then evading him, and already your younger vassels look upon Krya with more than doting friendship."

"Let them bear them then," he said seriously. "I care not if you never bore me a child." He had almost lost her once; he would never again take for granted everything she represented in his life, nor the light and love they shared. "Giles is much a son to me; I would gladly leave Ravenwood to him and not endanger you."

"Banish the thought," she chided. "There are many lands you can leave Giles, even Ravenwood if you wish. But I dare say I will give you so many babes you'll have to buy even more land to patrimony them all." At his stricken look she only laughed and snuggled him closer. "Have I not told you time and again that fear is the absence of faith? You must have faith, my lord, for be assured I will *never* give up with you what it takes to produce the many heirs we will beget.''

And so did she seek to prove it.

And so did he believe.

Experience the Passion and the Ecstasy

Heather Graham

☐ 20235-3 Sweet Savage Eden $4.99

☐ 11740-2 Devil's Mistress $4.99

Meagan McKinney

☐ 16412-5 No Choice But
Surrender $4.99

☐ 20301-5 My Wicked
Enchantress $4.99

☐ 20521-2 When Angels Fall $4.99

At your local bookstore or use this handy page for ordering:

DELL READERS SERVICE, DEPT. DFH
2451 S. Wolf Rd., Des Plaines, IL . 60018

Dell

Please send me the above title(s). I am enclosing $_____.
(Please add $2.50 per order to cover shipping and handling.) Send
check or money order—no cash or C.O.D.s please.

Ms./Mrs./Mr._____

Address _____

City/State _____ Zip _____

DFH - 2/92

Prices and availability subject to change without notice. Please allow four to six
weeks for delivery.

From the promise of passion to the peaks of desire...

☐ **Cloudcastle** *by Nan Ryan*
Natalie Vallance swore she'd always protect the land from ruthless strangers like Kane Covington. Then why did his kiss have the power to make her forget everything—except how much she wanted him?

11306-7 $4.50

☐ **No Choice But Surrender** *by Meagan McKinney*
When Avenel Slane made Lady Brienne his captive, she swore she'd never love him. But his burning caress left her powerless with passion and she was left with no choice but to surrender to the fires that burned deep within...

16412-5 $4.99

☐ **Savage Heat** *by Nan Ryan*
He was a proud Sioux chieftain. She was the general's golden-haired daughter. When he took her, he meant to exchange her for the life of her father...until he fell captive to his ravishing prisoner, and bound to a love that could never be.

20337-6 $4.99

☐ **Snowfire** *by Jessica Douglas*
A bold desperate woman...a dark mysterious man. They loved each other in spite of their secrets. But would all their passion fall to ashes when their wild, wicked pasts were finally revealed?

20075-X $3.95

At your local bookstore or use this handy page for ordering:

DELL READERS SERVICE, DEPT. DFH2
2451 S. Wolf Rd., Des Plaines, IL. 60018

Please send me the above title(s). I am enclosing $_____. (Please add $2.50 per order to cover shipping and handling.) Send check or money order—no cash or C.O.D.s please.

Ms./Mrs./Mr._____

Address _____

City/State _____ Zip _____

DFH2-2/92

Prices and availability subject to change without notice. Please allow four to six weeks for delivery.